COLLATERAL DAMAGE

Dan Walmsley

MINERVA PRESS
LONDON
MIAMI RIO DE JANEIRO DELHI

COLLATERAL DAMAGE
Copyright © Dan Walmsley 2001

All Rights Reserved

No part of this book may be reproduced in any form,
by photocopying or by any electronic or mechanical means,
including information storage or retrieval systems,
without permission in writing from both the copyright
owner and the publisher of this book.

ISBN 0 75411 470 8

First Published 2001 by
MINERVA PRESS
315–317 Regent Street
London W1R 7YB

Printed in Great Britain for Minerva Press

COLLATERAL DAMAGE

For my late mother and my dear wife

Part One

Chapter One

The ground felt wet and cold on his back. It soaked through his clothes, penetrating to the very core of his body. He opened his eyes. He was lying on a vast beach, the tide was out. In the background he could hear his mother's voice.

'Guy, will you stop teasing your sisters. Build sandcastles or something and let them play in peace.' Her over-dramatic sigh annoyed him. He pouted. It was dark and he wondered why they had stayed behind after everyone else had gone.

The groan was out of place. He moved his eyes to see where it was coming from, and then his head. The groan was his own, a sound from a separate subconscious hurt that had borrowed his body. It frightened him – a portent of worse to come. Then he started to feel. It was in his back. Slowly. Something was sticking in it and his foot felt hot. He tried to rationalise. Had he been burnt by the sun? He couldn't quite remember. The pain gathered pace. A gentle irritant became a flow and then a torrent. He gasped and fought, opened his eyes wide, looking for less pain. The memories returned along with the pain.

The flash. The noise. The slow motion grind and scream of tearing metal. The cockpit filling with smoke and dust. The near blind panic as he fought the wounded aircraft. The fear – he particularly remembered the fear. It had stuck in his nostrils along with the smell of cordite. It had choked his senses and dulled his brain, made him want to cry out, ignore what was happening. Think other, more pleasant thoughts.

Somehow he had suppressed the urges, and had fought the stricken machine, turning it, inch by inch, towards where he hoped safety would be. Where he stood a chance.

The aircraft had tried to respond. It had wanted to cling on to life just as he did. Together they had managed to stay in the air, but moment by moment the fight was being lost. Kelsall knew the machine was mortally crippled but was reluctant to get out.

Outside it was cold and dark. It was the unknown, peopled by those who would not be kind to him. The aircraft reared and bucked like an untamed stallion intent on its freedom. Any control movements seemed to irritate rather than pacify. He fought on. The struggle, which seemed to endure for a sweating, heaving, mind-numbing eternity, lasted in reality only a few seconds before he felt the shudder and the change of sound. The aircraft told him that it could not go on. He found the ejection seat handle between his thighs and pulled with what remained of his strength.

He passed through a tunnel of sensations: the steel claw of the straps; forces that dragged his very soul to his boots, tumbling, a massive gut-wrenching jolt as the parachute opened, followed by a cold, lonely, slide into a bottomless, dark, empty void. The earth grabbed him. Mother Earth's rough, hoary hands. No gentleness, no motherly comfort. A kind of safety bought at a price – a price paid for in pain and tears.

He drifted in and out of darkness and pain. Images spun and blurred in his brain. His mother's face appearing and disappearing. Smiling. A small smile of rebuke. He had let her down again. A voice – his father's – was somewhere deep in the background. Demanding. Cajoling. Guy wished he would leave. He wanted peace and quiet. He wanted to make his mother laugh and for her, in turn, to make it all right. To kiss him better or whatever she did when he was hurt.

He drifted. A voice, bellowing in his ear, roused him. Peering into the gloom, he could see a large, dim figure bending over him. The ghost of Christmas Past without the humour. An RAF cap badge and a shiny peak, which hid the eyes, were inches away from his face. The mouth, held in a sardonic grin, mocked him. 'Survival, Laddie,' it screeched. 'Rule one, Laddie. Get some fucking protection. Get out of the weather.' Guy shivered, tried to pull his coat around him, but couldn't find the zip. 'The dinghy, Laddie. Pull the fucking dinghy pack towards you. Remember what you were taught.'

The figure danced and spun at the periphery of his vision, mocking and grunting. Kelsall searched for the cord with his right hand, but his shoulder hurt too much. He felt tired. Tireder than he could ever remember. He just wanted to sleep and closed his eyes. For a moment it was quiet, then he heard clicking noises. He tried to shout but only a hollow, empty sound came. Getting his mind to focus was difficult. He remembered the war and the desert, but did not understand how a survival instructor could come to be there.

'Fucking officers.' The voice was back, muttering loud enough for Guy to hear. He moved his other hand. The touch of cold sand and slime made him shiver. After what seemed an eternity, he found the thin nylon line wrapped round his leg. It was difficult to untangle and he started to get hot with the effort.

The figure was no longer there. The clicking had stopped. Guy was both relieved and sorry at the same time. He wanted to rest and be quiet, but not be alone. The infinity of the stars seemed to crush him. As a boy, he had played a game where he pretended to be the only person in the world. He could go where he wanted, do just as he liked with no one to interfere. For a while it was fun, but just as quickly he would feel an unutterable loneliness and have to rush home and find his mother. He would burst into the house as if someone was chasing him and silently bury his head in her skirts, having no explanation for his behaviour.

He tightened his grip on the cord and gave a small tug, feeling the weight of the pack as the slack was taken up.

'That's it, Laddie. What does your mother call you? A fucking sweetheart?' The voice was there again. Guy gave a sigh of relief and made an extra effort to impress. By the time the pack was next to him, he was sweating despite still feeling very cold. He could barely move. He just wanted to lie in the sand.

'Pull the fucking handle, Laddie. It won't bite you.'

The voice was beginning to get on his nerves. Who did this person think he was talking to? He was, after all, a wing commander. He would not be spoken to in that manner. He didn't want it to go away, just wished that it would show a little more respect and appreciate his efforts. It wouldn't stop tutting and the noise was getting louder and more annoying by the minute. He tried to speak, but his tongue seemed to fill his mouth. He found the handle on the pack and pulled. The shock of the effort went right through him. He slipped to the edge of consciousness.

The figure was now calling him a bastard and adding the word 'sir' as though that made it all right. At least it had stopped making that awful noise. That had really begun to grate on Guy's nerves.

'Get in the fucking thing, then. It's no use blowing the thing up if you don't get in the fucking thing.'

Guy was surprised to find an inflated dinghy lying next to him. Slowly and painfully, he moved it until the gap in the canopy was in the right place, then laid his head on the rim. It felt like a pillow. Again he was content to rest there, but the figure who was calling him a bastard wouldn't let it be.

'Go on you fucking wanker, sir. Get in the fucking thing. It's not a woman, so you don't need to be afraid of it.'

Inch by tortured inch, he dragged himself into the dinghy and wrapped the folds of material around him. The security of the dinghy felt like his boyhood bed, a place where nothing could touch him. He felt a wave of near-contentment.

The noise was louder, driving through his body. He wondered how one person, or whatever it was, could make such a sound. Like it had run a great race and was panting inches from his ear, exhaling great lungfuls of air without having the time to breathe in. He just wanted it to stop.

The noise grew, taking on a being of its own. Great wafts of air beat down on him. Sand, blown in the gale, raked at his exposed skin. A light glared in his eyes and everything was subsumed in the vastness of the sound, wind and glare. This was no longer a dream. The great waves of pain which swept through him were witness to that; pain like he had never experienced. They had come for him. But who? It had to be his own side, it just had to be. Part of him didn't care – he could stand no more pain. He thought of death, but to die now would be such a waste, having come this far. It was sorted now; he had it all to look forward to. It couldn't end here in the desert, it just couldn't.

Chapter Two

'Sorry Tom, you'll have to lead. I'm far too busy to get involved in the planning. I'll catch up with you at the briefing.' Kelsall's words cut the silence of the room. They bounced off the high ceiling and the pale green walls before becoming lost in the gentle hum of the computers and the softly spoken 'I fucking told you so's.

Squadron Leader Tom Cookson barely had time to look up from the array of maps in front of him before Kelsall disappeared round the door. Most of the others failed to catch a glimpse, but they all recognised the voice. 'Shit.' Cookson half-whispered the word. He held his arms rigid against the edge of the planning table, head bent forward, hunched between his shoulders, and eyes tightly closed, as though feeling some private agony. 'Shit.' He repeated the word a little louder and then quickly added, in apologetic tones, trying to hide any trace of disloyalty, 'That's the third time he's done that to me in a fortnight.'

He adjusted to the new situation as though he had half-expected it. 'Right, you heard the Boss. I'm going as the leader. You, Ian and Frank,' he glanced at the two men who were working at the adjacent table, 'switch to the number three slot, and you, Hunch and Bertie, can stay at number two. The Boss can fly at number four. He won't like it, but I'm past caring.'

The heads around the flat-topped planning tables nodded in acknowledgement and the subdued mutterings of the crews, as they went about their work, continued as though nothing had changed.

Flight Lieutenant Hunch Jennings, like Cookson, was not surprised. He had just mentioned the wing commander's absence to his navigator. He felt a small surge of elation, having been proved right. He saw a chance to put the boot in.

'I understand the Boss no longer wishes to lead us on this fine day?' he grinned behind his hand and spoke in a stage whisper.

'Hasn't *time* to lead us, Hunch, not, *doesn't want* to lead us,' Flying Officer Bertie Grice caught the mood immediately, his tone that of a mother gently correcting an errant child. 'The Boss is simply a busy man,' he added. 'There's a subtle difference that I'm sure even you can grasp.' Head held low, he glanced through his eyebrows around the room.

'Better prepare some target maps for your man, Robin.'

Hunch directed the comment at the short, balding man on the other side of the table. Granger showed no apparent interest in the remark, but, without looking up, raised two fingers in Jennings's direction.

'Did you see that, Bert? Robin just signalled that he is already preparing two sets. He must have known that the Boss wouldn't be coming to help him. Very perceptive.' Hunch tried to sound surprised.

'We navigators *are* perceptive, Hunch, perceptive and flexible.' Bertie Grice continued to feed the co-ordinates of the route they were planning into the computer.

'Sometimes you talk pure bollocks, Jennings,' Robin Granger ran a hand over his shiny scalp. He sounded annoyed. He had enough to do without preparing extra maps for pilots, even if this one happened to be the Boss. Hunch ignored him and continued addressing no one in particular.

'Flexible, now there's a good word.' He looked thoughtfully towards the ceiling and tapped his bottom lip with a pencil. 'It can mean anything, from bending over backwards or, in the case of Jock MacKensie, bending over forwards.'

Jennings and Grice glanced quickly towards the other side of the room. The remark was meant to carry. The fiery Scot, the target of the jibe, made no response. Hunch could not let it go.

'I hear he's so far up the Boss's arse that he can almost see your boots, Bertie.'

'You cheeky shit, Jennings. Coming from you, with your "yes sirs" and "no sirs" that's particularly rich.'

They both laughed.

'Will you two give it a rest?' Cookson interrupted, weary. He had heard it all before.

'Yes, sir. Of course, sir. Anything to please,' Hunch grinned again at Bertie. He was fond of having the last word, especially when he hit the mark.

MacKensie heard the taunt but chose to ignore it. He thought Jennings likeable but immature. He wondered how long he would have lasted in a Glasgow school. Irony was a costly commodity in those parts, more likely to be met with a fist than witty banter.

'Do you think he's lost it, Jim?' MacKensie kept his voice low. Stamper understood the question, but was reluctant to be involved in such a discussion. The consequences of agreeing seemed dire.

'What do you mean?' he asked. He knew the answer that was coming, but wanted a different one.

'The Boss, do think he's lost his bottle? His nerve?' MacKensie added quickly, in case the first meaning might not be clear enough.

'No,' Stamper sounded hesitant. 'He's far too good a pilot. He's still as good as anyone here, even though he's not as young as he used to be.'

The contrast between the guttural tones of Glasgow and the public school accent of Stamper was marked.

'What's that got to do with it?' MacKensie raised his voice slightly to make the point and then quickly scanned the room, to see if anyone was listening.

'Well, I just don't think so,' Stamper sounded unsure, not wanting it to be true. 'Although, I'll grant you he seems reluctant to lead anymore, for some reason,' he added, the words trailing away, hoping for an end to the conversation.

'I reckon he has,' MacKensie growled and jabbed his pencil towards the map to emphasise the point. 'You just watch, you'll see. He's lost it.'

Stamper slowly shook his head, not convinced, but seeing some truth in his navigator's assertion.

★

Wing Commander Guy Kelsall closed the door softly, as though afraid to disturb the library quiet of the planning room. He seemed to sniff the air like a stag, aware that the hunter was out there, but not knowing the direction. He had seen the expressions on their faces, the small, knowing nods, the curled lips. He wished he had done it differently; marched into the room, maybe, confronted them. Now they thought he was ducking out, not leading the formation because he was afraid, had lost his bottle and gone the way of most senior officers just waiting for the next promotion. He was tempted to go back. Show them he was the boss and could do what he liked with his own squadron. But what would he tell them? He would just end up looking stupid. Stuff them. They could think what they liked. He tossed his head and turned away from the door.

Guy resisted the temptation to pop into the operations room; he was in a hurry. Head down, he rushed through the kitchen and sitting area with their collection of ten chairs and a woefully inadequate cooker and a tiny sink. If a war lasted longer than a week, they would all die of hunger or from fighting to sit down. Across the tiled floor, his steel-tipped heels punctuated the sentences of his imagined grievances. A crew, sitting talking, half rose to their feet, but he passed them without noticing. Turning the corner into the changing room, he almost bumped into someone coming the other way. They went into a silly pavement dance until the incomer had the sense to stand still. Guy, his head tilted back to avoid close contact, grabbed the man by the shoulders and roughly moved him to one side.

'Morning, Boss.' The flight lieutenant grinned stupidly. 'Nice day out.'

Guy had no time for a light conversation. His mood was set by the imagined hostility on the faces of the men in the planning room. 'Are you just coming to work, Kelly?' Guy glanced down at his watch. A faint odour of sweat and unwashed socks reached his nostrils, adding to his irritation.

'Yes, Boss.' Kelly squeezed his eyes half-shut. The half-smile that rarely left Kelsall's face was fixed in place. The mood of the man was difficult to pin down. Kelly was unsure which way the conversation was going.

'What the hell time do you call this to be coming in?' He sounded petulant and the doubt vanished.

'Night flying, Boss. Didn't land till after midnight,' Kelly replied, suddenly serious and a little afraid.

Guy mentally calculated that he was at work two or three hours earlier than required but, in his present frame of mind, could not let it go. 'You need to smarten up your ideas,' he snarled, and rushed passed. Kelly, a bewildered look replacing the grin, raised a hand and opened his mouth to say something in his defence, but found himself staring at a fast-disappearing back.

'What the hell's got into him this morning?' he muttered, before continuing into the building.

Guy hurried through the changing room. The long, open racks festooned with flying clothing seemed to mock him: empty shells of his tormentors. The heavy steel door slammed behind him. Out in the fresh air of an early summer day, he took a deep breath, feeling the relief of being in the open. No matter how he tried, he could not get used to the claustrophobic feel of the great bombproof building. He dreaded being cooped up during the three day exercises which were happening more frequently. It was his secret and would remain so. This was not a place to show weakness. He paused for a minute on the edge of the car park and gazed about, trying to calm himself. He scanned the sky and made a subconscious assessment of the weather, an instinctive act, prompted by years of dealing with the elements. Although he recognised that he had been wrong a few moments earlier, he could not find it in himself to feel sorry.

In the distance he could hear the gentle hum of a generator and then the louder roar of an aircraft engine bursting into life. A crow, startled by the din, took off from a nearby dustbin and flapped noiselessly skyward, a black rag blown in the wind. Guy imagined the airmen rushing to ready the aircraft, the crew in the cockpit, heads bowed as they aligned the aircraft's inertial systems and checked the instrumentation and radios. They would be relaxed, the flight having got underway. He wondered if they had felt the same as he was feeling now: that tight, tense feeling he was getting more and more before he went flying.

Chapter Three

Kelsall allowed the door to slam. It was a signal to his PA and staff in the adjoining office that he was back. In his early days in the job, he had been less assertive and on one occasion had stood for some moments in the connecting doorway, watching them laughing and joking, before they had paid him any attention. He had been angry and frustrated, not knowing how to handle the situation. Instead of bawling them out, he had let it pass. It had rankled with him ever since.

The three people in the office stopped chatting and grinned at each other. They were well aware what was signified by the sound and prepared for a head to pop round the adjoining door. When that did not happen, they relaxed and ceased the pretence that they had been hard at it.

'That you, Boss?' the adjutant shouted. He could not resist stating the obvious. It was a game, one that he hoped annoyed his squadron commander. Flying Officer Jim Freeman was not a career officer. He had signed for a short service commission of eight years, with a self-proclaimed mandate to see the world. So far, after almost five years, he had travelled as far as Norfolk, with only a couple of short detachments in Cyprus and Germany to break the sequence. No matter how he tried, he seemed unable to convince anyone that he should be elsewhere, preferably with a hot sun on his back and a cold drink in his hand. Now, with only three years of his contract to run, he was beginning to give up hope.

'That's right, it's only me, Adj,' the voice was tinged with sarcasm. 'So you can get on with your work for a bit.'

The three grinned again. The ritual had been played out. Jim Freeman did not like or respect his boss. Sure, he had heard all the stories about his abilities in the air. He knew from the chat of the junior aircrew that Kelsall was more than a match for any of them, particularly when it came to strafing with the Tornado's twin cannon. All that counted for very little with Freeman. In a world of files and operation orders, he was far more concerned about the way he was treated and, in his opinion, Guy Kelsall was not the ideal boss. He had never once got past the formal stage. Even in the bar it was 'Adj this' and 'Adj that'. Freeman was unsure whether Kelsall even knew his first name; he had never heard him use it. From the discussions he had had with other people, particularly the NCOs, he knew that his opinion of the boss of 58 Squadron was not unique, he was generally regarded as being a bit of a cold fish.

'Oh, shit, the station commander,' Freeman suddenly leapt to his feet, knocking the cold remains of a cup of coffee over the open file on his desk. 'Oh, fuck.' He tried to squeegee the liquid from the page with the edge of his hand, covering his corporal in a spray.

'Watch it, sir, if you don't mind, I've had my coffee and it was warm.' The corporal hurriedly tried to clean up his uniform. One bollocking from the boss for being scruffy was enough; he did not want another for some time. It had been a reminder of being a kid at school, caught behind a bush with his hand up a girl's dress. He had been degraded, left feeling inwardly unclean as well as physically unclean, when in reality only his trousers needed pressing.

Freeman did his best to clean up the file before straightening his tie and knocking quietly on the adjoining door.

'What is it, Adj?' Guy Kelsall's voice carried the cares of the world. 'It had better be important,' he added with a touch of menace.

On the safe side of the door, Freeman rocked his head from side to side and soundlessly mimicked the last phrase. The little blonde SACW typist quickly covered her mouth to stop herself giggling, while the corporal smiled and nodded, enjoying the moment.

'It is, sir.' The adj pushed open the door a few inches and stuck his head into the gap. His manner suddenly changed to one of solemn deference, someone about to get his ear bent. 'The station commander, sir—'

'What about the station commander, Adj?' Kelsall interrupted before Freeman could finish the sentence. Both men stared, each waiting for the other. 'Go on then, Adj, spit it out. Can't you see I'm up to my neck in it?'

Freeman had a fleeting image of Kelsall, buried from the neck down. Only the 'it' was not paper but something sticky and brown and closely related to a cow's rear end. He had difficulty suppressing a grin.

'He rang, sir.' Freeman sounded as though it was all a distant memory.

'When did he ring? Why didn't you tell me sooner?' Guy wondered why he always had to drag everything out of the man.

'Well, it can't have been very long ago.' Freeman studied his watch looking for a clue. 'Anyway, he said it wasn't very important,' he added.

'I'll be the judge of that, if you don't mind, Adj,' Kelsall snapped. A flush of colour came to his cheeks. 'What did he say it was about?' The instant he spoke, he realised it was a silly question. The station commander was hardly likely to tell an adjutant why he was ringing one of his squadron commanders. 'Thank you, Adj.' He waved towards the door with the back of his hand and picked up a pen.

'JP233, sir,' Freeman blurted, looking at his hand, where he had written the details in biro. It was turning into a sweaty smudge. 'He wanted to talk about JP233.'

'The station commander told *you* that he wanted to talk to me about JP233?' Guy pronounced each syllable carefully. 'On the telephone?' His voice held a note of incredulity which he made no attempt to hide, 'Bloody amazing.'

'What's amazing, sir? That I remembered to give you the message, or that I could remember all the numbers and letters of JP233, or even that the station commander would entrust me with such a vital role in the running of the station?' Freeman almost ran out of breath in the attempt to get it all out.

'Get out, Adj.'

It was delivered without rancour, but with a weariness brought on by many such discussions. Freeman retreated through the door, grinning widely to himself. It was another small victory in a constant battle of finding new ways to irritate the boss.

Guy waited until the door had closed before muttering the word 'shit' quietly to himself. The last thing he had wanted was a long discussion about JP233, with anyone, never mind the station commander. It had turned into one of the banes of his life, and it had only been around for a short time.

'When did the old man say he wanted to see me, Adj?' Guy bellowed towards the door.

'Do you mean the station commander, sir?' The muffled voice contained more than a note of facetiousness. Guy winced slightly, imagining the smug look on the face of his PA.

'Of course I meant the station commander; who else were we talking about?' Guy wished he could fix Freeman with a posting he would not like, but had decided long ago that it would probably meet with approval, no matter where it was. The adjutant's one desire was to get away from Easeham. Leaving him there probably meant more suffering. The only problem was that he, Kelsall, had to suffer as well.

'When you land, sir. I told him you were flying.'

'Then at least you got something right, you bloody moron.' Guy muttered to himself, and then louder, 'Call him back, if you can manage to find his number, and tell his PA I'll be there about fourish.'

Guy felt some satisfaction at having the last word and returned his thoughts to the weapon. He sighed and ran his fingers through his short, wavy hair. Things seemed to be getting away from him a little. First there was the formation and now this weapon. He quietly wondered if it was all getting too much. He fondly remembered the early days. Then he had been convinced he was born to fly. When he first got his hands on the controls of an aircraft, even though it was only a Chipmunk, he loved it. It was all he hoped it would be; a sense of free expression, of control and even power.

He loved the feel of the clothes, the dressing-up to go flying; pure theatre, like stepping into a role. All of it unique, from the white, long-sleeved vest to the old-fashioned long johns; the stiff, one-piece flying suit and the boots which laced up to the middle of the calf. He loved the smell of the cockpit and marvelled at the bulky Mae West which contained such an amazing array of survival aids. When he pulled on the helmet, painted white to reflect the glare of the sun and tailored to fit only him, it gave him a feeling of being as one with the machine.

The training on Chipmunks lasted only a few weeks and the time sailed by. He was one of the first to go solo. There had been no fear then; just a glorious feeling of being alive. Even when the g-force crashed down on his head, so that he could barely lift it, and squashed him into the seat, he felt like laughing and shouting out his joy. Above the trees and the fields, he felt like a master of the world. He was away from the tiresome little people. He was in control.

He had been nervous when he came to fly the Jet Provost and flying training started in earnest. From the moment of his arrival on the airfield where he would spend the next nine months, he noticed a change in atmosphere. Cars seemed to go a little faster on the roads, people appeared to walk with more purpose and, in the background, from the other side of four dark hangers came the almost constant roar of jet engines. Getting out of the car, he found his knees shaky and his mouth dry. He had an urge to turn round and go home, but again found himself in his element. He liked the aircraft and it appeared to like him. At least most of the time, it went the way he wanted to go and, judging by the chat in the crewroom, most of the time sounded quite good.

At the end of basic flying training he was amazed to be awarded the trophies for both best overall performance and aerobatics. He went around for days pinching himself to make sure that he had not died and gone to a place where they played eternal practical jokes. He half-expected some grinning buffoon to pop up from behind a hedge and shout, 'Got you there, you bloody idiot.'

Now, years later, things were not so straightforward. There was more than just the flying to concern him. Having carved a career for himself, he had more to lose and more to worry about. He glanced out of his window; all that lay about him was witness to that. This was his, a fenced-off fortress within the greater defences of the station as a whole. Several hardened aircraft shelters lay scattered about in a haphazard fashion, safeguarding their precious occupants from prying eyes in peacetime and far more destructive weapons in wartime. Their great bulk seemed to grow from the earth, as though giant subterranean beasts were waking from slumber.

Across the car park, he could see engineers scurrying in and out of their own hardened shelter, like worker bees to the hive. Kelsall shook his head in wonderment. Until the advent of Tornado, none of this existed and aircraft were parked in neat rows for all to see and for some, if so minded, to shoot at. Suddenly, as though someone had discovered concrete for the first time, everything became hardened, including attitudes. Guards were posted, carried guns and waved them about in a threatening manner; entry was barred from places which previously had been open house.

Kelsall was comparatively young for a man in his position, already well into his tour as a squadron commander. He was on a roll and his prospects for further promotion were good. It had not always been the case. He had made a slow start but, once he understood how the system worked, he was off and running. He learned early that promotion was not earned, it was acquired. You kept your nose clean, tried to be in the right place at the right time, did the little things well and left the Everest climbing to those who were stupid enough to try. You kept your shoes polished and your opinions to yourself; if you were bold enough to express one, then you had to be more than sure of your ground, and you did so only once. That way, if your boss liked it, then all right; but if he did not, at least you hadn't banged on about it. It was better to do nothing well than something badly.

He was now on his last flying tour before an inevitable series of ground tours, and was determined to make the most of it. After this tour, he would only fly aircraft on a regular basis as a station commander, and that was what he intended to be in the not too distant future. Part of him still wanted to fly, but the rest of him hated the risk both to himself and his career. Consequently, it was becoming more difficult to motivate himself into leading formations. Although he made himself available to lead when the day's flying programme was being written, he often found an excuse to duck out at the last minute. He had yet to admit, even to himself, any motive other than the pressure of work, but the rest of the squadron was beginning to notice.

Chapter Four

A head appearing round the office door, following the briefest of taps, woke Guy from his reverie.

'Possible to have a word, sir?'

'Not now, Brian, if you don't mind. Can it keep? I'm a bit strapped at the moment.' Guy almost had to suppress a chuckle at the sight of Squadron Leader Brian Seagrove's massive ears sticking out from the side of his head.

'Not at all, Boss. I'll come back later.' Seagrove was about to disappear when Guy had second thoughts.

'In fact, just a minute, Brian, come in after all. I want to bounce a couple of ideas off you.'

The big man shambled in. He seemed to have been made at a spare parts factory, where no two things were made to quite the same spec or fitted together properly. His angular frame hung inside his clothes and, after years of stooping under doors, he had adopted the pose of one who could not be bothered to stand upright. Clothes, no matter what he wore, did not look right on him. Even dressed in his best uniform, with his shoes as shiny as the next man's, he looked like he needed a bit of a shake-up. Leaping out of his shoulders was a ruddy, round face, atop of which sat a mop of fair curly hair which defied all reasonable attempts to control it.

The ears sat astride the head like two nosy neighbours peering over a garden fence; they craved attention, not only through their size and protrusion, but also because of their whiteness. It appeared as though the heart had reneged on supplying blood to both the complexion and the ears.

At thirty-seven, he was a year older than Guy, but there the similarities ended. Contrasting with the youthful, almost boyish looks of the more senior in rank, Seagrove was verging on middle age. He considered himself well overdue for promotion and resented Guy's early success.

Seagrove slumped in a chair without waiting to be asked, reached into his pocket, pulled out his pipe and clamped it firmly between his teeth. Guy was just about to tell him not to smoke when, just as quickly, he removed it from his mouth and stuffed it back in his pocket.

'What's the matter, Boss?'

'Nothing is the matter, Brian.' Guy sounded annoyed and wondered for a moment if he was doing the right thing by asking Seagrove for advice. When Guy arrived on 58 Squadron, he had been blessed with two very capable flight commanders. Both, unlike Guy, were experienced in nuclear operations and he had drawn heavily on their expertise. Things had gone smoothly and had given him the opportunity of running the squadron, or at least appearing to, from a remote position. Now both men had moved on. Their replacements were just as able, but each had different backgrounds and Guy was having to take a more hands-on approach. Recently, in one or two areas, his knowledge had been found wanting. Most of all, with the personnel change, he had lost a close friend. They had been able to share a drink in the evening, discuss the events of the day and formulate plans for the next. They had been a team. Guy missed that.

'JP233, what's your opinion of it? Off the record, you understand.' Guy asked. He knew that behind his rather rural appearance, Seagrove had a sharp mind. The trouble was the way he expressed his opinions. They had already had words about pilots from single seat backgrounds not co-operating fully in the operation of the aircraft, and Seagrove, as the senior navigator, had gone so far as to point out Guy's own shortcomings in a fairly blunt manner. It had rankled with him and caused him to be more circumspect in his dealings with the man.

Seagrove looked puzzled for a moment, and instinctively rubbed his hair flat with the palm of his hand.

'My opinion on what precisely? Do I think it will work? Do I think it's a good idea?'

'All of that.' Guy tried to sound indifferent. 'Just give me your opinion.'

'Heap of shit.'

Guy waited, but Seagrove seemed fairly content with his answer.

'That's it then? A heap of shit? The RAF shells out a few million quid on a state-of-the-art airfield denial weapon that can punch twenty-odd bombs into a runway, designed to explode at random, not to mention the hundred and twenty mines that will lie on the surface, hindering the repair process, and you think it's a heap of shit?' He found it impossible to keep the note of incredulity out of his voice.

'Well, put like that, I suppose my statement was a bit of a generality.' Seagrove waved a large, nicotine-stained hand airily round the room. 'But it's all very well for a boffin to come up with an idea. It's another thing completely making it work. Now, if the designer had said to me, here's a weapon that you take to ten miles from an airfield, let it go and it will guide itself down the runway and do all you credit it with, then he would get my vote. Reduce that to five miles,' he continued, warming to his subject, 'and I might still be in favour. Because he requires me to fly it right down the middle of a runway, not deviating from track, not changing speed, at two hundred feet above the bloody ground and in the dark; he certainly does not get my vote.' Seagrove became as close to animation as he ever got. His lips glistened with moisture, and his bony finger rapped the edge of the desk to emphasise the point.

Guy puffed out his cheeks and allowed the breath to escape slowly through pursed lips. 'Well, it's a point of view, I suppose, but it's not going to solve any problems, is it?' he said.

He glanced across at Seagrove, studying his expression. Self-righteousness and defiance were written all over his face. For the second time in a matter of minutes, Guy felt a small prickle of anger. 'We're stuck with it. It's not going to go away. Dismissing it as a load of shit is not an argument that the station commander is going to expect from me in a few hours – now, is it, Brian?' He tried to sound reasonable. 'What he wants to know is not what the problems are, but how we are overcoming them.'

He took another deep breath and slowly exhaled while he considered the tips of his fingers. He gazed over Seagrove's head at a photograph of himself being presented to Her Majesty, the

Queen. It held pride of place among the photos of the aeroplanes he had flown. For a moment, he wondered how they both could hold the same commission.

Guy dragged himself back to the moment and tried desperately to look like a man with a secret. He wondered whether to entrust Seagrove with such a burden. Finally he came to a decision. 'Brian, this conversation we're having is a bit on the quiet. It must go no further than this office; at least, not for the time being. You've probably read in the papers about this joker in the Middle East who is creating something of a stir by laying claim to Kuwait.'

He paused to let the gravity of what he was saying sink in. Seagrove, to his disappointment, showed no change of expression. Guy leaned forward across the desk, lowering his voice to a conspiratorial whisper. 'Well, the powers that be are getting in a bit of a lather. Word has come as far as the station that if he pushes his luck much more, he might have to pay for it.'

Again he paused to let the information sink in and again he was greeted with zero reaction. 'In a word, we might be called on to use JP233 a little sooner than we had bargained for. So now can you see what I'm getting at?' A note of frustration crept into Guy's voice.

Seagrove studied infinity for a few seconds before replying. 'Well, if that's the case, as far as I'm concerned, you can kiss your arse and all the other arses on the squadron goodbye. As I've just said, unless the thing is modified to get it to the target in a more indirect way, then I don't think Saddam Hussein, or anybody else for that matter, need be too worried about his airfields.'

He turned towards Guy and waited for a reply, having thrown the equivalent of a hand grenade into the discussion. Guy found himself staring at the blackened fingertips of his flight commander and wondered, not for the first time, how a man of such forthright opinion could have progressed so far up the chain of command. His lip curled slightly in distaste. 'Right, Brian, thank you for your views; they were really useful.' The irony was either ignored or lost on the man. 'If you come up with any good ideas in the meantime, I'd be grateful to hear them. Now, if you don't mind…'

Seagrove stood quickly, knocking his chair against the wall without noticing. Even before he was out of the room, the pipe was in his mouth and he was vigorously tapping a pocket, searching for his tobacco pouch. The door closed noisily behind him. For a few seconds, Guy was tempted to call him back and tell him to get his act together and not be so bloody cavalier about such important matters, but in his heart he knew the man had a point. Although he had not liked the way Seagrove expressed his opinions, there was not much doubt that delivering the weapon was going to be the critical thing. Unless someone discovered a viable method of saturating the target with aircraft, without them getting in each other's way or, more importantly, being taken out by the fragments from other bombs, a lot of people were going to die.

It was easy to see that the first aircraft might get through the target area, having the advantage of surprise. The same might even apply to the second. It was impossible to imagine that the third or fourth, coming from the same direction and at a similar speed and height, would have a prayer. If they did survive, it would be down to some very incompetent gunners and missile tracking. Somehow, he did not feel it was right to rely on that. Guy groaned. He hoped that he might have heard the last of JP233, at least for some time. He was still smarting from his last encounter with the thing.

Chapter Five

The air marshal had given very short notice of his visit to see the weapon. Guy had assumed that it was just another slightly bored senior officer who needed a day out of his office. Now, with up to date information, he realised the visit carried more serious overtones.

They had gone through all the usual rigmarole. An aircraft taken off flying for the day, cleaned and left in a shelter with all its weapons and external stores laid out neatly in front of it. A crew, dressed in new flying suits and boots, had been assigned to stand by it. In pride of place, in the centre of the display of missiles and fuel tanks, was JP233. It looked for all the world like a long, green, cigar tube; not dissimilar to the fuel tank which occupied the opposite station on the belly of the aircraft. Examples of its contents lay beside it. It was routine.

The squadron received many such visits. Too many for Guy's taste, but one or two provided him with an opportunity to impress someone who might have an important influence on his future. This was one such visit. He was anxious it should go without a hitch. Most visitors were not too familiar with what they were looking at, and explanations rarely required a great depth of knowledge. Guy held to the maxim that bullshit baffles brains. Presentation was the key, and most visitors went away happy by what they had seen rather than what they had heard. With this in mind he had gone to greater lengths than usual to make sure everything was ready for the great man.

Guy was not in the least bit worried as he waited in the otherwise empty car park for the arrival of the staff car. He opened the car door himself when it came to a halt. The air marshal seemed to unfurl from the rear seat, and continued to climb until he towered over Guy. They shook hands and his 'Hello, Guy. Nice to see you again,' delivered in a booming voice, gave no hint that they had only met once before, some years previously.

'Hello, sir.' Guy tried to sound natural as he attempted to return the vice-like grip engulfing his hand. 'Would you like some coffee before we go over to the aircraft shelter?' He had ensured that all parts of the place were in good order and had warned all personnel not directly involved in the visit to be smart and ready for anything.

'Love to, Guy. Have to give it a miss. Short of time. Some other time, eh?' He spoke in a kind of shorthand. 'Like you to meet Ms Quincy. Development. Bowels of the Ministry.' He tapped the side of his nose in a knowing way.

A slim, bespectacled woman in her early thirties, dressed in a smart designer suit, appeared from the rear of the car. In other circumstances Guy might have had more than a passing interest in her. She shook his hand unsmilingly. 'Don't fool with me' was written all over her face. Guy immediately decided to be a little more circumspect in his explanations.

They walked the short distance to the shelter. The air marshal strode out, with Guy and Tom Cookson struggling to keep pace. Quincy made no effort to stay with them, but was content to engage the squadron warrant officer in conversation. By the time they had covered a few yards, Guy was breathless from trying to keep up at the same time as answering questions, which were boomed at him with every stride. He noticed that his answers were often finished off by the questioner before he got to the end of the sentence.

They stopped in front of the display, and the air marshal gave each of the attendant aircrew and groundcrew a cursory nod. He gazed fondly down at the weapons and almost purred with satisfaction. 'What do you think of that lot, Quincy? Cannon, sidewinder, electronic-counter measures, chaff, flares and assorted weapons both nuclear and conventional, and now this.' As he spoke, he gave the large object in front of him an affectionate pat. It responded with a hollow ring. 'The weapon we have been looking for since aeroplanes became part of war. A true airfield-denial weapon,' he added.

Quincy said nothing and Guy, at a loss for words, shot a startled glance at Cookson. The air marshal was fondly caressing a fifteen-hundred-gallon fuel tank in the mistaken belief that it was JP233. He was tempted to leave him in blissful ignorance, but the air marshal invited him to tell him more about its design. The seconds seemed to tick into minutes as he tried to make up his mind what to do. The air marshal cleared his throat irritably:

'Come on, Guy, give us the story on how it works.'

'Sir...' He faltered and tried again. 'Sir, the ...um... basis of JP233 is the two types of weapons that it carries. The first is the runway-cratering bomb.' He reached down and pointed to the slim object shaped like a conventional bomb which lay to one side of the carrier.

'Would it not be better if you first told the air marshal something about the carrier, so he understands the principles of how it works?' Quincy spoke for the first time. The voice was clear and confident.

'Yes, that would be the way to go, Guy.' The air marshal stood to one side, rubbing his hands together expectantly.

'Well, sir,' Guy began again. In his agitation, his hands fluttered aimlessly, trying to find something to latch on to. 'As you can see, the carrier is essentially split into three parts...' He paused, trying to find the words without pointing at the carrier itself. He could see the audience was getting unsettled, and he shot a beseeching look at Cookson. His face remained impassive. 'The outer shell breaks into two pieces as the weapon is fired.' He spoke quickly and moved away from the carrier, hoping no more needed to be said.

'Show me, Guy. You could have told me this much over the phone.' The air marshal was not to be fobbed off.

'Right, sir.' He swallowed hard and moved towards the carrier. 'This is it, sir. You see the join here, well this is the—'

'Hang on a minute, Guy.' There was more than a hint of irritation in the voice. 'It seems that for the last few minutes, I have been labouring under the impression that the thing you are pointing at was a fuel tank, and that thing over there was what we had come to see.'

'Well, you just made a simple mistake, sir. It's easy to do. They both look very similar,' he added in a weak voice.

'It's not that I made a mistake that worries me, Wing Commander, it's the possibility that you were going to let me go away without putting me right.' He glared down at Guy.

'No... no, I was going to tell you.' He sounded unconvincing.

'Right then, let's get on, shall we?' The tall man folded his arms across his chest and glared, his lips compressed tightly together.

'As I was saying, we have twenty-four cratering bombs in the—'

'Twenty-six.' They all looked at Quincy. 'Twenty-six,' she repeated, without the slightest doubt. Guy looked at Cookson and he nodded imperceptibly.

'Twenty-six, I meant to say, sir. I'm sorry. Anyway, these are ejected along the length of the runway. They are designed to penetrate into the runway, leaving only a small hole. The trick is that they detonate at random over the next twenty-four hours and create a subterranean hole which is very difficult and time consuming to repair.'

Having received no more interruptions, Guy was beginning to get his confidence back. He turned to the other part of the weapon and picked up an object not much bigger than a large tin of dog food. The sides appeared to have been peeled back to the halfway point, giving it the look of a half-eaten banana. 'This little baby is the *pièce de résistance*,' he continued. 'It simply sits on the surface, having been ejected at the same time as the cratering bombs, and the minute someone or something touches it – bang! – off it goes and plays havoc with the cleaning-up operation.'

Guy seemed pleased with himself and the air marshal quietly nodded his own satisfaction. 'How many of those bomblets are there, Guy?' he asked after a few seconds.

'One hundred and eighteen, sir,' Guy replied without hesitation.

'One twenty.' Again, they all turned to look at Quincy, who stood impassively at the rear, with her arms folded. 'There are one hundred and twenty of the things.' There was now a hint of exasperation in her voice.

'Well, Guy, thank you for going to all the trouble of giving us this little briefing. One way or another, it's been most illuminating, and I'm sure we've both learned something.' The tone of his voice was scathing. Without more ado, the air marshal turned on his heel and, with the dreaded Quincy in tow, strode towards his car. Guy and the others did not move until the car was well clear of the site.

'Have you not got some work to be getting on with?' Guy's tone was menacing.

Returning to his office after the presentation, Guy gave the adjutant the run-around for most of the morning. He had to take it out on someone. The feedback from the briefing had not been long in coming. The station commander phoned within an hour, stressing that the squadron must start practising with JP233 immediately. He emphasised that if there were any gaps in their knowledge of the weapon and how it might best be deployed, then they had better be ironed out. Without spelling it out in words of one syllable, he left Guy in no doubt that his visitor had been unimpressed.

Guy blamed the woman, Quincy, or whatever her name was. He wanted to strike her. Cause her some physical hurt for all that she had done. How he hated her.

One way or another, women seemed to have been the bane of his life. This woman had marred his standing with the air marshal, and it was not the first time that this sort of thing had happened. There was the incident with the girl all those years ago, that had almost cost him his career and been a source of worry ever since. Hardly a day went by without the fear that it would return to haunt him. Most of those who knew about it would have left the RAF by now, and would not harm him. But one person, who knew the whole story, was still out there. Somewhere. He had tried to bring him down then, he could strike again.

Chapter Six

Women had played a major role in Kelsall's life. From the time of his earliest memories, with three older sisters in the house, he had been swamped and submerged by them. They filled the house; fussing, bossing, teasing. His friends, when young, were intimidated; later this turned to flirting. He stopped taking them home and largely kept his own company. There had been advantages. He played the system and ducked the household chores. Cries from his sisters of 'Why can't Guy do the washing-up or make his own bed?' usually got the reply, 'Oh, he's a boy, he'll do it wrong, it'll be as quick if you do it in the first place.' They pouted and complained, but he got away with it.

Early life had held no terrors for him. He was the product of a Middle England well-being. He had a good brain, when he chose to use it or when the subject interested him, but his school reports were littered with 'could do better's and 'has potential but does not try's. He treated sports in a similar way. The object was not to play the game but to get his face on the team photograph. He slithered through school and life like a snake through grass, leaving his surroundings totally undisturbed.

Guy's father, a doctor, had hoped that he would follow him into the medical profession. Guy had different ideas. Compassion was not one of his stronger suits and the sight of blood, particularly other people's, did not elicit the urge to stem the flow, but rather an instinct to look the other way. He had different plans, that dated from his first air show, where he had seen, smelt and heard his future in the form of Hunters, Canberras and Vulcan bombers.

Afterwards his room had taken on a different look. The early decorations of childhood, largely chosen by his mother, were hurriedly removed and replaced by anything to do with aircraft. Spitfires, Hurricanes, World War One stringbags, modern fighters and bombers, they all had a place. He drew them, built models and collected books until there was barely enough space left for the bed. What drove his mother mad when dusting and cleaning was a godsend at Christmas, when all that was required to satisfy him was something to do with aeroplanes. Aunts and uncles loved him for it.

As soon as he was able, Guy applied to join the Royal Air Force. For the first time in his life, he pulled out all the stops and made sure he looked and sounded right. He sailed through the aptitude tests and the medical. The RAF liked what they saw. The selection board had only one reservation – his lack of authority in a leadership role. His ideas were sound, even astute, but when it came to expressing them and getting a reaction, he lacked presence. He seemed too easily swayed by the initiatives of others, if forcefully put. 'Still,' the wing commander in charge of the selection board reasoned, 'he's very young. Given time and opportunity, he'll do all right.' He was in.

Despite growing up surrounded by girls, Guy knew very little about them. He knew they giggled, blushed and feigned coyness, and went into silly fits of swooning and crying at the mention of certain boys' names. But he had no idea what really made them tick, nor did he care. That began to change in his teenage years. He watched them more and more; invented reasons for bursting into their rooms when they might be undressed. Their complaints had prompted his father to give him a man-to-man chat about the facts of life; most of which he already knew.

His father had emphasised the importance of respecting the opposite sex and the man's role in caring for the women in his life. He had related what he was saying to the knights of old, and compared them to modern-day fighter pilots. It had all sounded so prissy and old-fashioned that Guy had found it difficult not to burst out laughing. He had assured his father that he was sorry, but did absolutely nothing to change his ways, except that he was more careful how he went about his peeping. From his early teenage years, he liked two things in life: aeroplanes and girls.

Despite this interest, Guy had few girlfriends before joining the RAF. Most of these came from sisterly hints that so and so 'liked' him. Every time he plucked up the courage to ask one of them out, his face seemed to erupt into a mass of pimples. He also had to endure the knowing half-smiles and nudges, certain that anything he did would be reported.

These dates provided him with very little in the way of experience or a lasting relationship. A cuddle in the back seat of a car; a few bouts of slap and tickle in the precarious surroundings of the girl's front room, her parents never far away. It was invariably more slap than anything else, and although Guy often suspected that the girl would have liked to have gone further, they never did. Then along came Helen. Nothing in life had prepared him for Helen.

He was in the middle of his flying training on the Gnat. Life was all he hoped it would be – the life of a young fighter pilot. He had only to walk down the street to wonder why everyone else did not want to be one. He felt like tapping all the young men on the shoulder and asking if they realised what they were missing. He was baffled how anyone could sit in an office, day after day, when there were jobs like his, and, what was more, he was getting paid to do it.

From dawn, when he was awakened by a small, wizened Welshman serving an umber-coloured, sickly sweet liquid which he said was tea, until he tumbled into bed at night, Guy was in heaven. Someone cooked for him, made his bed and tidied his room, while he spent the day either flying or learning about it. In the evenings, he was able to enjoy a beer with like-minded colleagues. And the Gnat. He especially loved the Gnat.

It was as different to the Jet Provost as a racehorse was to a hobby horse. It was quick, very light to the touch and more than a little feisty. Its acceleration and incredible rate of roll could leave the pilot breathless in surprise. It was a pilot's aircraft. It soared and dived and cavorted through the air like a pedigree, but, like most pedigrees, it had its unpredictable side. A harsh control input at slow speeds could easily put it into a spin and, as some had found to their cost, once in a spin it was very reluctant to come out of it. Its quirky ways, when pushed beyond its safe limits, had already claimed several lives, but, for those who could cope, it was a pleasure to fly.

Guy could cope. He watched the faces and listened to the stories, and knew that he was carrying on where he had left off. In the crewroom, he started to emerge from the crowd. His advice was sought. For the first time in his life, he was truly in his element. He watched for the tell-tale signs of those who were struggling. The way crews walked in from the aircraft said it all. If the instructor walked ahead, it had been a bad trip. If they walked together, laughing and joking, it had been good. He was in the latter group, but some of his colleagues were definitely not. One failed to get clearance to go solo, and was out. Another scraped through that hurdle, but failed the halfway progress check, and he was out. The rest, in their varying ways, plodded on. Then there was a collective relief when the last to take the test came through the door smiling.

'We'll have a bloody party.' Staines was always the first to see an opportunity for having a good time.

'Where will you get any women in a godforsaken place like this?' Guy was just as quick to see the down side of things, which was probably why they had become such friends.

'I don't know. We'll ring the hospital and invite some nurses over. Anyway, plenty of people have girlfriends at home. They could invite them up. Should be good fun.'

Guy shrugged. He made some tentative inquiries, to see if any of his old girlfriends were interested, but the journey seemed to put them off. He was quite prepared to have a few beers and watch the proceedings.

By the time Guy entered the room, the party was already in full swing. He could not believe that Staines had found so many people; the place was packed. He took his usual position, on the edge of the crowd, enjoying what he could hear of the conversations around him. As usual, his input was small, but his mates were used to that. Then she seemed to appear from nowhere. She stood squarely in front of him, a hand on hip, and smiled. He looked down at her and returned the infectious grin. The face was attractive; not strikingly pretty and certainly not ugly. It had an openness. He had a fleeting thought that his mother might describe it as brazen, but his mother was a hundred miles away and not the wrong side of four pints of beer. Nevertheless, he took a quick, subconscious glance around the room, just to make sure. He looked at her again and liked what he saw: the round face, the large eyes and the surrounding mass of short, blonde curls.

'You're not saying much, are you?' Her eyes twinkled, and the voice, along with the pose, was provocative. For a couple of seconds, he had difficulty thinking of something to say and was suddenly aware that everyone would be watching. A second quick glance around the immediate circle showed that no one was in the slightest bit interested, particularly as a couple of the girl's companions had joined the group. She waited, neither smile nor stance changing.

'Well, er...' he finally croaked, 'I'm just enjoying the scene, really.' It sounded so banal that he could have kicked himself.

'Would you like to dance, then?' she asked, to his surprise. 'You could enjoy the scene from there.' She grabbed his hand and, before he could reply, steered him towards the dance floor.

Guy was accustomed to dancing, having often been railroaded by his sisters into taking part, as they experimented with the styles and steps of the latest fads. He had a good natural rhythm and, once he overcame his natural diffidence, they danced well together. No conversation was required, or even possible, above the din, and they were only able to exchange furtive glances and embarrassed smiles. Guy began to relax.

They danced several quick ones, until a slow one by Simon and Garfunkel started. Guy turned to leave the floor. She grabbed his arm.

'Let's dance to this. It's one of my favourites,' she said.

He smiled, and before he realised, she had snuggled up close, her head just barely up to his shoulder. They swayed and moved easily despite the difference in height. Guy was only too aware of how well she fitted into his arms, and the effect it was having on him.

'What's your name?' he suddenly asked. His voice came out as a rasp of sound dried up by the heat and excitement.

'Helen,' she murmured dreamily. 'What's yours?'

'Guy,' he replied and the conversation ended before it had begun.

They learned the barest facts about each other. She was twenty-one, came from the north of England, and had been to college for two years. He was obviously RAF, a student pilot and from the Midlands. She had two brothers, and he had three sisters. He wanted to fly fast jets and she wanted to travel.

Then she produced a rabbit from the hat. 'Where's your room?' she asked. He felt the colour coming to his cheeks.

'Well, it's in the mess.' He felt stupid stating the obvious.

'I know that, silly, but *where* in the mess? I'd like to see it.' In the dim light he could see the same expression on her face, half-challenging, half-mocking, that he had seen when they first met.

'You're not really supposed to.' He kept his voice low, partly from embarrassment and partly from a fear of being overheard. 'We aren't allowed to take girls there.'

The stupidity and the inanity of the rule hit him instantly. He felt about ten years old and irritated at such petty bureaucracy.

'I know that,' she laughed. 'But if you tell me where it is, then I'll meet you there. No one need ever know.'

She lowered her voice and eyelashes together in a conspiratorial manner, and her mouth puckered slightly.

God! thought Guy, and his mouth, which in the previous seconds had regained some small amount of moisture, instantly lost it again. His head and loins fought a pitched battle somewhere in the region of his stomach, and it churned loudly.

'Rules,' said his head.

'Sex,' said his loins. Sex won by a country mile, as it had done for centuries.

'It's the top floor, west wing, number 322. I'll go ahead and unlock the door, if you like?'

The words tumbled out as thought they were in a race to get to the end of the sentence. He stood looking at her for a few moments and then hurriedly glanced around the room. He was half-convinced that it was some sort of set-up and that the minute he made a move the room would erupt into howls of laughter. But no one was taking the slightest notice. He looked again at her face, not quite believing the situation. He was, after all, the man, supposed to make the running and, so far in this particular contest, he was not even at the starting blocks.

'Well, get on with it then,' she almost ordered, in a voice which suggested that these opportunities did not come too often, and this one was not on hold for an indefinite period.

'Right,' he stuck his finger in the air and nodded. 'Yes, right then.' He tried to sound a bit more businesslike, failed to achieve it, shook his head a little, and turned towards the door.

Halfway across the room, he felt a hand roughly grab his arm and was dragged a couple of yards before regaining his balance.

'Where the bloody hell have you been? You randy little bastard. I saw you cuddling up to that little blonde piece, you sly sod.'

Staines thrust his face close to Guy's and breathed beery fumes over him. It was obvious from his rocking motion what he had been doing while Guy had been dancing.

'You're not going to bed already.' It was not a question, more an order, and Guy felt irritated. 'I'll get you a beer.'

Guy gently placed his hands on his friend's arms to steady him and glanced towards the girl. She was watching, and he made a futile shrug in her direction.

'Ian,' he reassured his friend. 'I'm not going to bed, merely to the bog for a pee, and if you keep me hanging around much longer, I'll do it all over your shoes.'

He spoke as if talking to a disobedient child, emphasising each word. It seemed to strike a chord and Staines blinked rapidly before muttering, 'All right, then.'

Guy made sure that Staines was in a vertical position before releasing his hold and turning towards the door. He rushed to his room, taking furtive glances behind him to make sure he was not being followed, unlocked the door in a flurry of fingers and thumbs, made a final check up and down the corridor, then burst in. He was hot and flushed and felt as though he had come through a crowded place with a notice saying 'On a promise' pinned to his back.

Well, half a promise, he mused, or it might not even be a promise at all, just his imagination, or just some silly girl who was genuinely curious about where he lived and what it looked like.

'Surely not,' he muttered to himself 'What would she want to see this place for?'

He rushed around throwing items of clothing, which had been left lying around, into drawers. His thoughts were racing. How should he approach it?

'Clean your teeth.' He almost shouted with relief, as if it were the answer to one of life's eternal mysteries. He rushed towards the sink, tripped over a discarded shoe and collided with the corner of the armchair, giving himself dead leg. He staggered towards the sink as though his life depended on it and squeezed the toothpaste too hard. The paste fell over each side of the brush, and he hurriedly piled it all together with his finger before stuffing it in his mouth. The beer and the paste mingled into a foul taste, which he quickly spat into the sink. A long strand of mucus extended from his lips to the basin. He brushed it away irritably and it attached itself defiantly to his hand. He was reminded of being at the dentist's, and idly wondered for a moment why that always happened.

He looked at his watch; it was now fifteen minutes since he had left the party. 'She's not coming.' The thought hit him with a jolt. 'She's changed her bloody mind.' His disappointment was far greater than he could have thought possible. He slumped on the edge of the bed and stared between his feet at the patterned carpet. He considered going back to the bar, but rejected the idea because he would only look stupid if she were still around.

He decided on bed, and was just about to get undressed when he heard the faintest tap on the door. He flung it open and almost dragged her into the room – partly out of fear that she might be seen and partly from relief that she had arrived.

'Steady on, big boy. All in good time,' she laughed.

He released her hand, muttered 'Sorry,' and stepped away from her.

'So this is where you pilots live?' she said.

Chapter Seven

She strolled around, examining the room's meagre contents. He stood in the centre of the floor, circling on the spot, wondering what to do next. 'What's this?' she asked, bending over the chest of drawers, examining a small photograph.

He leaned over her shoulder. As their sides touched, she straightened and half-turned, her face raised towards him. They were extremely close, and Guy had little option but to put his arms around her. They kissed – a soft, gentle kiss on the lips, as though between brother and sister.

'Mmm,' she whispered, 'got anymore where that came from?'

The remark annoyed him. It sounded like a line from a second-rate Hollywood movie. She did not wait for an answer, but took his hand and led him towards the bed. They sat on the edge, and Guy hesitantly placed his arm around her shoulder. They kissed again, this time with the first hint of passion. Then, for the first time that evening, Guy took the initiative, and gently laid her back onto the bed.

She sensed his awkwardness and, as if by magic, he found that any buttons or catches which might have caused him difficulty were already undone by the time he got to them. With the last piece of clothing gone, they both quickly and shyly slipped under the bedcovers. Guy felt a small pang of regret that he had not seen more of her body. They made love in a slow, easy way and managed to climax together. For Guy the act was both a release and a disappointment. He felt he had been a bit of a novice, but when he looked across at her, she smiled in a satisfied way and it improved his confidence. He stretched. The single bed, which had seemed more than big enough a few moments before, was suddenly cramped.

'Sorry,' he muttered, as his knee made contact with her leg. She smiled at him again but made no reply. The overhead light glared in his eyes. He turned, to get it out of his field of view and again their bodies touched. The bed felt hot.

He was beginning to worry about getting the girl out of the mess, but she seemed in no hurry. The thought occurred to him that she might want to stay the night, and he began to rehearse scenarios for getting rid of her. He stole another glance at her. She was lying flat on her back, her eyes closed and the little half-smile played on her lips. 'Don't go to sleep,' his mind screamed, but it came out as a guttural croak. She opened her eyes slightly and looked towards him.

'Sorry,' he said. 'I thought you were going to sleep.'

Her smile turned to a full-blown grin.

'Why, you're a dark horse. Are you set to go again already?' she asked.

She eased herself up onto an elbow and half-turned to face him. As she did so, the cover slipped, and Guy caught an alluring glimpse of her breast before she covered it. Momentarily he was aroused.

'It was your first time, wasn't it?' She looked him boldly in the eye, and he turned away, colour rushing to his cheeks.

'Well, not exactly,' he mumbled.

'What do you mean, not exactly? It's not an exact science, I'll grant you, but it has fairly rigid dividing lines between when you do it and when you don't. I think you'd agree? I mean when you're up in your little aeroplane, you're either up or down; there's no in between, is there?'

She patted his arm in a patronising manner, pleased at her own analogy. He was frantically searching his mind for a glib reply but none came. All he really wanted to do was tell her to leave, but for some strange reason his father's lecture on treatment of the opposite sex came into his mind. He glanced at her again, and she was propped up on both elbows, looking round the room. This time, when the covers slipped down, she made no attempt to hide her breasts. He had a sudden urge to cup one in his hand, and was contemplating how to go about it.

'What's that lot over there?' she suddenly asked.

'What lot?' He followed her gaze to a pile of clothes, which were draped untidily over a chair.

'Oh, it's just some flying clothing. I left work in a hurry. Didn't have time to change,' he explained. 'It's my immersion suit and some other stuff, it keeps the water out if you have to eject into the sea.' He made it sound as though it was an everyday occurrence.

'Let's have a look.'

She was out of bed in a shot, and her bare bottom shimmied beautifully as she rushed towards the chair. His thoughts of a few minutes ago disappeared as he stared, bewitched, at the vision in front of him. Previously, totally naked women had only appeared to him from the glossy pages of magazines, but those images did not come close to what was he was seeing now. Naked, she looked even better than he had imagined. Dressed, she looked a little on the heavy side, but now, although not slim, she was in perfect proportion, from shoulder to waist and down to the two perfectly rounded forms of her buttocks. Her back gleamed and danced in the changing shadows. Guy sat up in bed to get a better view, careful to pull the covers up to his waist. He could only catch tantalising glimpses of her breasts, which bobbed up and down as she picked up items from the chair. He peered from side to side to get a better look.

She picked up the vest and gave it a cursory look before disdainfully tossing it away. Next, she held the long johns and giggled when she realised what they were. 'Does your mummy not want you to catch cold when you go flying?' Her voice was heavy with sarcasm.

He was about to tell her they were to stop his legs being chafed by the G-pants, when they joined the vest on the floor. She threw them with a sweeping motion which gave him his first view of her front. The picture was lost as quickly as it had appeared, only to be replaced by an even more beguiling sight, as she bent over to pick something from the floor. Life in a rural grammar school had not even begun to prepare him for such a vision. He fought hard to control himself.

Just when he thought life could not get any better, it did. She now held up the G-pants and turned towards him.

'What on earth are these?' she asked, holding the dark-green garment, a note of incredulity in her voice. The pants resembled a pair of cowboy chaps with inch-wide straps across the back. In her curiosity, she had lost any remaining inhibitions, and he had lost his power of speech.

'G, er...' he swallowed hard and tried again. 'G-pants,' he managed to blurt out, and with a further swallow was able to add, 'They're to stop pilots blacking out under high G loads.'

It occurred to him that she probably did not have a clue what he was talking about, but his mental resources for further explanation were limited. He was wholly absorbed by the vision before him. This was definitely not the lifeless form of a girl in a glossy photograph; it moved and danced, wobbled and bounced. The changing shadows with each movement brought changes of shape and interest. He was totally sold on it and wanted it to go on – in fact, given a choice, he would have passed up on visiting the hereinafter and stayed where he was for eternity.

'How does it work?' she asked. 'How do you put them on?'

He moved to help her, but a sharp pain, as his erect penis snagged on the bed covers, told him that he was in no shape to go rushing about the room.

'You step into it.' The words came surprisingly easily, as his mouth was now salivating so much that he was suddenly at the point of drowning. 'What they are...' His voice was falsetto, and he cleared his throat and tried again, this time achieving a more resonant tone. 'They're inflatable trousers with lots of little tubes running through the front of them, and, when you experience g-force air is pumped into them under pressure, and it stops blood pooling in the lower body.'

It was the longest speech he had made all evening, and she gave him a look of surprise tinged with a little scepticism.

'That's right,' he encouraged. 'Take hold of the large flat piece at the top, and step through the loops.'

She followed his instructions and wiggled beautifully as she pulled the thing upwards, giggling when the cold material touched her abdomen. It created a slight shiver that set her body in motion.

'Now, pull the straps tight at the back,' he instructed.

He was bouncing up and down on the bed in his excitement and, as she followed his instructions, little folds of flesh bulged alluringly between the straps.

'The zips next. Yes, those on the outside of your legs.' He had to hold himself in check to stop himself shouting as she searched for them. 'Good... good,' he encouraged, thoroughly enjoying the way her breasts swung from side to side as she moved. 'Wrap the material round your legs... yes, yes, like that; now connect the two sides together with the zip.'

It took her several minutes of huffing and puffing to fasten both legs of the G-pants in place. For him, it was several minutes of undiluted pleasure. Until that moment, he had no idea how a relatively simple structure like a breast could take on a life of its own. One second it was flat to the body, as she straightened and pulled the hair from her eyes; the next, it was hanging, pendulous and pear shaped. He definitely wanted one for Christmas. By the time he had finished pondering on the problem, the pants were in place.

She stood up straight, legs apart, brushed a stray curl behind her ear, and grinned at him. Her face was red from effort, and wore a look of triumph. Now the design of the garment gave him a whole new focal point. Beneath the broad band of material which covered her lower abdomen, the mass of curly hair gave lie to any doubts he might have had about the naturalness of her hair colour. He was mesmerised, and it took all his former training in good manners not to stare. Her attention was drawn to the tube which was hanging from the side. She grabbed it, and gave it a little shake, as if holding a snake.

'What's this for?' she asked.

'Come here and I'll show you,' he answered.

His manner suggested less than good intention behind the invitation. She backed away a couple of paces.

'No, it's okay, really. I won't hurt you. Just come over here and I'll show you what happens in the aircraft – honestly.' He tried to sound sincere.

Reluctantly, she edged towards him, wary that he might make a grab for her. As she came within range, he put the tube to his lips and blew into it with as much force as he could muster. The air circulating through the pants caught her completely by surprise as she felt them inflate and gently squeeze her legs and abdomen. The look on her face changed to one of pleasure and she laughed. It was a pleasant little infectious chuckle, and Guy joined in.

'Go on, do it again,' she pleaded, childlike. This time, knowing what to expect, she savoured the experience with a little grin on her lips.

Then, suddenly aware of his closeness, she pulled away and at the same time noticed his uniform hat on the chest of drawers. She walked stiff-legged towards it, picked it up and gave the badge a brief examination before unceremoniously plonking it on her head. The brim almost covered her eyes, and she tilted her head back, to peer at him. He was left with a picture of a pert little nose, a mischievous grin and a spray of blonde curls cascading beneath the hatband. With the grin fixed in place, she grabbed the end of the hose nearest her body and started to twirl it. With toes turned outwards she set off round the room, imitating a Charlie Chaplin walk.

In all his magical career, the maestro never came close to achieving the effect that a simple student, dressed only in a pair of G-pants and an RAF officer's hat, achieved in those few seconds. Guy totally lost all inhibitions as he clapped and cheered his personal cabaret. He was at a total loss where to look next; the bouncing breasts, the cute little rolls of flesh that protruded between the straps or the alluring triangle, which tantalisingly darted in and out of the shadows.

As suddenly as she had started, she stopped and turned her attention to the last piece of clothing on the chair – the immersion suit.

'Cor, this is heavy,' she grunted as she attempted to pick it up. With books and charts stuffed in all the various pockets, and the double-thickness skin, the suit weighed several pounds. She struggled to get it into a position where she could make some sense of it. 'You people must be weird or something,' she muttered. 'Have you lot got a department somewhere that designs kinky clothing?'

'It's quite simple, really,' he answered. 'Just hold the bottom part of the zip in both hands, let the back part fall and then step into the legs.'

He made another attempt to go and help, but realised that he was still not in a fit condition to do so.

After a couple of false starts, she sat on the edge of the chair and with some difficulty managed to get both feet in place. He was instantly pleased he had stayed put, because the view from where he was sitting was far better. She struggled to her feet, lost balance and wobbled forward, before halting her unsteadiness by clutching the end of the bed. Not for the first time that evening, Guy had the urge to grab a handful of breast, but resisted, knowing that the floor show was still not over. She pushed herself upright, steadied herself and then began the task of dragging the mammoth garment upwards. Eventually, after much grunting and heaving, she had the thing held at chest height.

'What now?' she puffed.

'You've got it cracked now,' he encouraged. 'Just put your arms in the sleeves and push your hands through the elastic wrist-seals.'

She wrestled and grunted and again her breasts danced to a tune of their own. He was trying to decide which of them was his favourite. 'What now?' She interrupted his reverie.

Her head was being pushed forward by the zip, and she was peering at him from under her eyebrows, her arms held parallel to the floor. A religious image with tits flashed into his mind, and he shook his head slightly to dispel the unseemly thought. 'Reach behind you and pull the zip over your head,' he instructed, 'and then push your head through the rubber seal, as you did with the arms.'

The breasts flattened to her chest as she reached up behind her head and then pinged back into place as she heaved the suit over her head.

'Help, I'm stuck.' Her muffled voice came from inside the suit, and her head bulged in the neck seal.

'Just push your head upwards,' he shouted, and then, for the first time, became aware of where he was and lowered his voice. 'Go on, push,' he repeated, more quietly.

The top of a blonde head slowly began to appear through the gap. Hair, eyebrows and ears were dragged downwards by the friction of the rubber and, as each in turn was released from captivity, it bounced back into place with a life of its own. Finally, the rest of the face appeared with a rush. She stared at him in wonderment.

'You're kidding. *You have got to be kidding.*' She emphasised each word. 'You can't possibly go flying in this stuff. I can hardly move a muscle.'

'You haven't finished yet. You've got to close the zip and then you would have to wear a Mae West. Anyway, you don't need one of those,' he added as an afterthought. 'You've got your own.' He smiled at his own joke.

'Is that it then?' The suit billowed around her, and she seemed to have shrunk from the effort. 'How does the zip work, then?' she asked.

'Just reach up to your left shoulder with your right hand, find the toggle and pull it. It's a bit stiff, you'll have to give it a good tug,' he added, trying to be helpful and get it over with.

She followed his instructions, and, as she strained, the zip finally began to move. Slowly the two halves of the suit came together. With a final grunt, she finished, gave a self-congratulatory nod and, for the first time, realised how uncomfortable she was with the cold material next to her naked skin. She gave a little involuntary shudder. Next, she tried moving and walked round the room like a climber in the last leg of an assault on Everest before suddenly flopping back in the chair exhausted. One of the straps on the G-pants nipped her behind as she landed and she gave a little squeal.

'I know now why you wear long johns.' She gave the offended area a rub. 'I bet you're particularly careful where you store your private parts when you go flying, aren't you?' She added with a wicked grin.

He grinned, inwardly wincing at the thought of something tender being trapped in the G-pants as they inflated under a pressure of six G. It seemed particularly pertinent in his present condition. She struggled to her feet, needing the support of the chair, and wobbled once more round the room like a deflated

Michelin man before coming to a stop at the end of the bed. She looked at him and, for the first time, it seemed to dawn on her the effect she was having on him.

Again the small smile appeared on her lips, and slowly, very slowly, she reached down to her left hip and began to pull the zip upwards. Her eyes never left his face, while his darted from hers to the ever-widening gap about her waist and chest. Agonisingly slowly, she raised the upper part of the suit to her chin and, with as much dignity as she could muster, pulled it over her head. One by one, she retrieved her arms and then, bare to the waist, began to lower the thing to the floor, needing a slight wiggle to get it going, but now accentuating the movement for his benefit. She tried to kick the suit away, almost losing her balance as it refused to budge. Instead she stepped daintily to one side before reaching behind to loosen the straps of the pants.

'Leave them. Leave them on.' His tone was somewhere between a plea and an order.

Her eyes widened, both in surprise and recognition of the idea. She paused, and then moved towards the bed. As she came within arm's length, he grabbed her arm and pulled her towards him.

They made love on top of the covers, hurriedly and passionately. It was a flurry of arms and legs, each intent on their own satisfaction, but such was their arousal and selfish pursuit of their own pleasure that the climax was mutually satisfying.

Afterwards, they were again suddenly aware of their nakedness, and crept shyly under the covers, partly from a sense of modesty and partly in need of warmth. They said nothing, reflecting on the events of the last few minutes. He, for his part, marvelled at the sights and pleasures that he had just witnessed, and she at the extent of her own boldness. Each, in their different ways, was incredulous at what had happened. They made love once more. It was more a winding-down of passion than a resurgence of it – a natural end to the evening.

Guy, his passion spent, was now back where he had been an hour before, faced with the difficult conundrum of how to get rid of his illegal guest without her being seen. It occurred to him that he knew nothing about her. He was not even sure of her name. It was hardly appropriate, after the shared intimacies of the last few hours, to ask. He did not even know if he wanted to see her again.

Then she did it once more, answering his thoughts.

'Must go,' she chirruped, as if leaving the vicar's tea party.

She dressed quickly, and as demurely as she could in the circumstances, with her back to him. He, despite what had just taken place and sensing her need for privacy, looked at the ceiling. Then, before he could make up his mind whether he would like to see her again, she leaned over, gave him a sisterly peck on the cheek and was at the door. Guy was going to say something about not being seen when she again read his thoughts. She opened the door carefully – gave a quick listen, popped her head out, glanced in each direction and was gone. No 'goodbye', no 'see you' – nothing. He lay there, and a tumult of emotions crashed down on him – elation, relief, guilt and finally tiredness. He slept.

Chapter Eight

Over the next few days, Guy's mind was in turmoil. His Monday flight was the worst he could remember. The instructor, having taken control after the speed dropped dangerously low on finals, had threatened to kick his arse, or worse, if he did not pull his finger out. He mooned about the place, passing friends in corridors without acknowledging them, missing meals and generally acting like a lovesick fool. He knew he was not in love, but his mind hummed with a barrage of questions. Did he want to see her again? Without doubt, part of him did. Did he find her attractive enough? Was she even his type? But, most of all was what they had done together normal? Did all girls behave in that way? If he asked Staines about it he would get no help, but simply sarcasm and ridicule.

'I had this girl in my room the other night, Ian, and after we'd had it away, she jumped out of bed stark-bollock naked, and made a big thing of trying on my flying clothing, including the immersion suit. Then we did it a couple more times before she went home, and I haven't heard of her since. Now, is that normal?'

'Absolutely, Guy,' Staines would reply, wearing a grin like a banana. 'Nothing odd about that. Why, only the other day, I had a girl in my room and we did it on a buggy. Now, I admit that's verging on the kinky, but there's nothing abnormal about your situation.'

He wondered about his sisters. Did they behave like that? He somehow could not get his mind round the image of his mother shouting to the girls as they were going out of the door. 'Have you got your G-pants with you, darlings? You don't want to be caught short.'

'Well, Mum, I've got mine but Louise is going to try a buggy tonight.'

'Oh darling, a buggy, are you sure? It sounds a bit risqué to me.'

'Mummy,' Celia takes a deep breath, 'don't be so old-fashioned. It's perfectly normal these days.'

His mother chuckles good-naturedly and says, 'I don't know, you young things these days. If we did it on a bicycle when I was a girl, we would have been accused of being common, and now you're going to give a buggy a try. What next, eh?' She would return to the kitchen wiping her hands on her apron, muttering, 'Well, do be careful, that's all.'

Guy eventually decided he would have to sort it out on his own. By the end of the following week, it was not just a case of did he want to see her, but a matter of when. He was desperate. He rang both the hospital and the nurses' accommodation, but drew a blank. He tried the local college – nothing. He even stood and watched the nurses changing shifts, in the hope of seeing her, but still had no luck. After two weeks of trying, he gave up. She had disappeared from the face of the earth.

Although the memory of the evening stayed with him, Guy quickly realised that once his efforts to find her had drawn a blank, he needed to pull himself together and get on with his flying. Things were hotting up on the course. People were beginning to talk about the future. Now, it was not just a simple case of getting a posting to fast jets, it was which particular fast jet.

In the last few years, the RAF had virtually re-equipped. Gone were the old Canberras and V-Bombers of his boyhood. They had all been replaced by a different breed of machine. A faster, sleeker, more dangerous-looking beast was in service, one that would bite back given half a chance, and that was what Guy wanted. In particular, he wanted the Harrier. It intrigued and beguiled him. It was the pick of the bunch. To be considered good enough to fly one he had to be among the best on the course. He also knew that he had blotted his copybook with his performance after the night with Helen.

He set about making amends. Others, he knew, were keen to fly the Harrier. One or two had pushed him close for the prizes during basic training; a further slip would probably blow his chances. He was not found wanting. When the list of postings appeared, his name was at the top and right next to it was the single word 'Harrier'.

With that particular worry out of the way, his mind began to wander back to that evening. Helen occupied his thoughts more and more. Her face had blurred with time, but the other memories were, if anything, enhanced, as he went over them time and again. Not only did he want to see Helen again, he needed to see her again. But how? Then it suddenly dawned on him. Somehow, Staines had got her there in the first place, maybe he could do it again. With as much indifference as he could muster, he tried to introduce the subject.

'Why don't we have another party, Ian?' They were standing in the bar watching the interminable autumn rain pound on the window.

'A party? You want a party? You don't like parties.' Staines put a hand on his friend's forehead to see if he had a temperature.

'I like parties. Whatever gave you the idea that I didn't?' Guy tried to sound enthusiastic, while at the same time pushing the hand away.

'Oh, just everything. Like, you're always the last to arrive and the first to leave. Like the fact that you've never mentioned having one before. I could go on.'

'Well the pressure's off now. Maybe I just feel like a good time.' What he really wanted to say would have caused Staines to drop his pint.

'We could, I suppose.' Staines spoke slowly and the words came as a relief to Guy. 'The last one wasn't bad was it? Not that I can remember too much about it, for some reason.'

'You were pissed, that might have had something to do with your memory loss.' Guy smiled, he was getting his way.

'Pissed? Me? You must be joking. Drink with the best of them. No, I must have been feeling the strain of the course. Some of us have to do a bit of work to get by, unlike others I could mention.' Staines prodded Guy in the chest. 'Anyway, a party doesn't sound like a bad idea. I'll give it some thought.' Guy wanted to tell him to invite the same girls, but kept it to himself.

When the evening of the party arrived, Guy found himself unexpectedly nervous. What if she was there and did not want to see him? His edginess refused to leave, and he was slow and somewhat reluctant to get ready. He was halfway through his preparations when Staines burst into his room. From his demeanour it was obvious that he had already started drinking and the fumes quickly spread through the air. 'Come on, you slow sod. The thing will be over before you've scraped the bumfluff off your chin.'

'Don't you ever knock when you come into someone else's room, you loudmouthed lout?' Guy was a little irked, but after a glance at the grinning face it was hard to retain any anger. One regret of the evening was that Staines had been posted to Buccaneers, having, for some reason beyond Guy's imagination, expressed a desire to fly with a navigator. After the weapons course which would follow, they would go their own separate ways.

'Stop being such a ponce and move your arse, will you? None of the birds down there is going to give you a second glance, particularly if you walk in with me. So it's no use going to any great lengths over a lost cause.' He picked up Guy's jacket and threw it towards him. Guy was tempted to ask him if Helen had been seen, but did not suppose Staines would remember her.

They walked into a party already in full swing. As they entered, the noise and heat hit them. The similarity to the previous party was inescapable. He let Staines go in first and tentatively glanced round to see if she was there. He moved towards the bar, and still there was no sign of her. Having ordered a couple of pints, he rejoined Staines, who was already back in the swing of things. Further glances, from behind the security of his pint pot, revealed nothing. She was not to be seen. Part of him was relieved. He began to relax. By the time he had downed a couple of beers, his foot was tapping to the music which was blaring from across the room. No one seemed to mind. It was the end of the worst part of the training, and those who had survived were at last beginning to feel some confidence that they might make it all the way into a squadron. It did not enter their thoughts that one of those present would be dead within the next two years, and two more would later be killed in flying accidents. On this night, they were all invincible. Guy was so infused with this feeling that he even asked his boss's wife to dance and, once he had recovered from his own audacity, was surprised how well she performed. Until now, he had only seen her from a distance and in his mind had equated her with his mother. Now, close up, he realised that she was much nearer to his own age and she was certainly at home on a dance floor. After a couple of dances, he was covered in sweat while she still looked as fresh as when they had started. When the music ended, she gave him a sweet little smile and gently squeezed his hand.

'I enjoyed that.' She was slightly breathless. 'You dance well. Where did you learn?'

'Sisters,' he shrugged. 'Would you like another one?' He tried to sound indifferent but was quietly hoping that she would, although he hadn't a clue where it would lead. She gave him another smile and glanced over her shoulder.

'Better not, all the other girls will be getting envious. Me keeping you all to myself.'

Guy sensed he was being turned down in the nicest possible way. He escorted her back to the bar and turned to find his drink.

'You salacious little sod.' Staines was instantly at his elbow.

'Salacious, sal–ac–ious.' Guy pronounced each syllable. 'You've been using a dictionary again, so you can sit up at table and eat with the adults, and it's got stuck up your arse, hasn't it?'

Staines ignored him. 'Not content with bonking the hell out of little blonde bits, you're now trying it on with the boss's wife. Is there no end to your debauchery?'

Guy wheeled round, surprised; not because Staines had noticed him dancing, because he made it his business not to miss a thing, but because of his reference to Helen. 'What the hell do you know about that?' he asked, even more colour coming to his already ruddy cheeks.

'Oh, I have my methods.' Staines knowingly tapped the side of his nose with his forefinger and tilted his head to one side.

'Come on, you bastard, tell me.' Guy made a grab at his friend, who, in deftly avoiding the lunge, knocked a glass to the floor.

Staines was quickly on the other side of the room. The sound of breaking glass went unnoticed, and Guy moved the broken bits to one side with his foot. Raising his eyes from the floor, he noticed a leg which was elegantly crossed over another. The girl was sitting quietly on a bar stool, and Guy realised that the flying glass might have hit her.

'I'm dreadfully sorry,' he shouted. 'I didn't see you sitting there. We didn't hit you, did we?'

She shook her head and smiled at him without speaking.

'Look, let me buy you a drink, to make some amends?' He leaned towards her to make himself heard, and the delicate aroma of her perfume contrasted sharply with the smoke-filled atmosphere. Again, she simply shook her head without attempting to reply. Although on another occasion Guy might have found the manner of her refusal offensive, he found none now; she made it seem so natural.

'Would you like to dance, then?' He held a hand towards her and was a little surprised when she effortlessly slid down from the stool and took it.

She was only a couple of inches shorter than him and, as she straightened, she flicked a long strand of blonde hair over her shoulder. He led her across the room and caught the grinning face of Staines watching them through the crowd. Guy frowned and mouthed a phrase which left Staines in no doubt that he was to keep his distance. Staines feigned a look of shock at the suggestion and turned away. Guy wondered how he knew about his evening with Helen and why he had not mentioned it until now.

Guy and the girl faced each other on the dance floor, gently swaying to the over-loud beat of the music. He stole glances at her, liked what he saw. She was slim and wore a simple cotton frock, which came to just above her knee. Her make-up was light and the only jewellery was a simple pearl necklace. The effect was pure and uncomplicated. The face held an aura of quiet calm, as though nothing in life would bother her. She danced easily, head tilted back, arms by her sides, while her hands danced to a tune of their own. Her shoulders moved with an easy grace and her hips, slightly thrust forward, kept time with the music. She was lightly tanned.

'Have you been on your holidays?' It was the only thing that Guy could think of, and he had to lean close to make himself heard.

'No.' It was the first time she had spoken and, if that was all she was going to say, he was in for a hard time. They danced on. She made no effort to leave, and he was in no rush to go either. Both seemed content in their own worlds, neither embarrassed by the inability to hold a conversation.

Eventually, he took her hand and led her back towards the bar. The party was beginning to thin out. Guy, looking at his watch for the first time, was surprised how late it was. Most of the instructors and their wives had gone, drawn away by the need to relieve babysitters. An air of relative calm had returned to the place. Guy shook his head to clear the noise and glanced sideways at the girl. He was still holding her hand and she seemed happy to let him. Her forehead was damp from sweat and a few tresses of hair were stuck to the skin.

'Would you like that drink now?' he bellowed, before realising that there was no need.

'Lovely, I'm really thirsty.' She brushed the sticking strands of hair from her face and shook the rest down her back. 'Orange juice, please.'

'Nothing stronger?' he tempted. She smiled in a knowing way, leaving no doubt that she knew what she wanted.

He returned a few moments later with two pints of orange juice. She gave him a quizzical look.

'You said you were thirsty.' He grinned.

They chatted quietly, once away from the music. He found her easy to talk to, although not very forthcoming about herself. All he got was that she was a student, and he missed hearing what her subject was. She was more interested in his life, and was full of questions about the Gnat and flying training. It was something he was only too pleased to talk about; the time passed quickly. When Guy next turned to look, the room was almost deserted. A couple in the far corner were deep in conversation, their heads pressed close together, and a few couples were still on the dance floor, arms wrapped tightly about each other.

'Like to go for a walk?' he asked.

'Where to? It's a bit chilly outside.' She gave an involuntary shake of her shoulders, as though she were suddenly in a draught.

'Well, we could go to… er… my room.' He blurted out the last two words as though not really wanting her to hear them, eyebrows raised in expectation.

'No, definitely not. I've been told all about you RAF types and I'm not going there.' He sensed that further discussion on the subject would be futile, but was not going to let the honour of the service go undefended.

'What do you mean, RAF types? We're as honourable as the day is long. No harm would have come to you.' He tried to sound sincere, but could see from her smile that he was wasting his time. He grinned back. 'Well, okay, we'll not risk going to my room, but how about taking a wander round the place, stretch our legs?'

She still looked doubtful, but he was emboldened by the beer and felt relaxed with this girl.

'Oh, come on, nothing's going to hurt you. We'll just have a wander and I'll show you the sights.' he insisted.

'The sights?' she asked, suddenly interested. 'You have sights to see, as well?'

'Oh, yes.' He sensed the interest and warmed to the task of persuading her. 'We have rolls of honour, original paintings and, wait for it…' he gave an imitation of a drum roll, 'a snooker table that Joe Davies once scored ninety-seven on while beating Fred Smith in the RAF finals.'

'Who is Joe Davies?' she asked, 'and who is Fred Smith?'

'You mean to tell me you've never heard of the great Fred Smith?' He looked at her in mock wonderment.

'No, I have not. Who is he?' she asked. Again she flicked the hair from her face with her hand, having let it fall forward across her face. He realised it was one of her little mannerisms.

'Neither have I,' he teased.

She grinned and playfully pushed him. 'Come on, I can see I'll get no peace until you show me round your precious mess.'

Chapter Nine

They crossed the room, hand in hand, stepping around an upturned bar stool and discarded, half-empty glasses. The place was suddenly a mess, cigarette ends and bottles crowded the window ledges and one of the curtains had been partly dragged off its rail. A picture was hanging at an angle, making it look as though the bowl of fruit and copper jug depicted in it might fall out. The couple in the corner had finished talking and where locked together in a passionate embrace. The girl's dress had ridden up her thigh and she was trying to pull it down without interrupting the kiss. Guy felt slightly embarrassed at this public show of affection and turned away, but the girl seemed untroubled.

'I don't know your name?' he asked suddenly.

'Samantha.' She sounded embarrassed. 'It's the old story; my father was convinced I was going to be a boy and he hadn't come up with any suitable girl's names by the time I arrived. What's yours?' Guy told her. She nodded to herself, letting the name roll around her mind. They relaxed into easy conversation as they wandered along the passageway towards the reception area.

'What are these?' she asked.

She stopped and looked at the boards which lined each side of the corridor. Each was about three feet high, the wood stained dark mahogany and bearing a list of names in inch-high gold letters; alongside each name was a date.

'Oh, those are the rolls of honour I was telling you about.' He let go of her hand and stood with both his arms stretched to one side, as a theatrical compere might when introducing the next act. 'Very grand, don't you think?' he asked.

'Are all these poor people dead? There are such a lot of them.' Her voice trailed away at the end of the sentence.

'No... no, silly.' He took her hand again. 'Quite the opposite. These are the names of people who have won prizes or trophies during their flying training on the Gnat.' He tried to keep a mocking tone from his voice, realising that the idea of all those people being dead had upset her.

'Oh.' She sounded relieved. 'Is your name up there then?' she added more brightly.

'Well, not exactly,' he answered.

'What do you mean, not exactly? It's either up there or it's not. There doesn't seem to be an in-between.'

To emphasise her point, she stepped close to the wall and peered hard at the edge of the board. Guy had an immediate sense of *déja-vu*, only he was in no doubt when and where the previous conversation had taken place. Although the subject was entirely different, both girls had used the same mocking tone. He groaned inwardly.

'What I mean is,' he paused and tried to sound patient, as though he were talking to a particularly difficult child, 'my name is not up there, yet.' He laid emphasis on the final word.

'Oh, you intend to win a prize, do you, Mr Cocksure?' she teased, poking his upper arm with her finger.

'No, not that either.' He grinned sheepishly and squirmed away. 'I've already won two of the trophies. It's just that they haven't got round to putting my name up... so there,' he added in a childish way, and in turn poked her upper arm. At least, that was his intention, but, through a combination of her quick movement and his poor aim, dulled by beer, his finger landed fair and square on her left breast.

'Oops, sorry,' he giggled rather stupidly.

She ignored him, pretending that nothing had happened, released his hand, and marched up and down the boards, demanding to know which would bear his name.

'That one,' he pointed, 'and that one, over there.' He swivelled round to find the second board and staggered slightly, realising, that for all his exertions on the dance floor, he was still a little drunk. She moved towards the first board and stood looking up at it.

'The Wragg Trophy,' she read aloud, 'presented to the student producing the best overall performance in the air.'

He moved behind her and encircled her waist with his arms. She did not resist, but turned within his arms and planted a soft kiss on his lips. He was aroused.

'Aren't you the clever one, then?' she asked looking into his eyes. She gave him a second, more lingering kiss but, before he could tighten his embrace, pushed him gently away.

'Come on then, show me the rest of these fabulous sights,' she challenged.

Slowly they wandered down the corridor, hand in hand. They went past the reception area and into the foyer. Guy noticed that the front door had been closed and locked for the night. The place seemed suddenly deserted, apart from the faint strains of music coming from behind them. She glanced around the foyer.

'Is this one of your original paintings?' she asked.

She was facing the only one showing an aircraft. It was a night scene, with World War Two aircraft being loaded with bombs and fuel for their next missions. In the scene, it was raining and men seemed to be scurrying everywhere, heads bent against the elements. For such a difficult scenario, the artist had captured the atmosphere perfectly. The girl gave an involuntary shudder, as if feeling the strength of the wind and rain.

'Well, it's not my painting,' he said 'but it is original. Painted by a chap called David Shepherd, a few years ago.' He tried to sound knowledgeable.

'I know him,' she replied, 'at least I know of him. Doesn't he paint animals though?'

'He does now, but when he was trying to make his name he painted quite a lot of military things. Lots of messes have his work. I like it,' he added, almost to himself.

'Oh, so do I,' she enthused, not to be outdone. 'I particularly like the way he gets the reflections in the puddles. I get a distinct feeling that I would rather be in here than out there on that dreadful night.' She gave another little shiver and snuggled up to him.

'Is that the end of the sight-seeing tour, then?' Her tone was a little mocking.

'Just one more to go, remember. The fabulous snooker table.'

'Ah, that. Well, I'm not that fussed about seeing an old snooker table. "Seen one and you've seen 'em all," is my motto.' She tossed her head in a dismissive manner. 'Green top, brown sides with holes in them, very little more to be said.'

'Ha! That's what you think? Well, you couldn't be more wrong, Miss Smartypants, because this one's not like that at all. Oh, dear me no.' He let the moment of drama build. 'Brown sides with holes, I'll grant you, but certainly not a green top – nothing so common. *This* one has got a burgundy top, and that's something to tell your grandchildren about, is it not?'

'I'm not really bothered.' She shook her head, unimpressed by his sales talk.

'Come on, it'll only take a minute, and it's really something you shouldn't miss.'

She allowed him to steer her across the foyer towards the corridor on the opposite side. When he opened the door, the room was in darkness. Guy stuck his head in and whispered loudly, 'Is anyone in there?' There was no reply. 'Come on, no one's here.'

He gently pulled her into the room and fumbled around for a light switch. After a few seconds, he found it and the table was bathed in the glow of its overhead lights. The rest of the large room was still in semi-darkness, and she could see in the gloom ancient brown leather armchairs lining the walls. He gently guided her towards the table.

'See, I told you, burgundy – looks good, doesn't it?' He sounded proud of himself.

She stepped forward, slowly reached out and touched the cloth, almost as though she were afraid of hurting it. She dragged her outstretched fingers across the surface, and each finger left its own trail in the cloth. Guy watched her face in the half-light. It held the delight of a child making ripples on a still surface of a pond. He reached across and pulled her towards him. She did not resist.

He kissed her and she responded, her lips parting slightly. He felt aroused again and held her closely to him. Again, she did not resist, but put her arms about his neck and responded with equal ardour. She enjoyed the close contact and moved fully into his embrace. She felt him shift slightly and, with the movement, was turned so that the snooker table was at her back. The kisses increased in passion and their bodies moved against each other in mutual enjoyment.

Slowly, hesitantly at first, his hand moved down her back, across the top of her buttocks and then rested for some moments on her hip, seemingly unsure of its own direction or intention. Then it moved up her side, pausing again just below her armpit, before uncertainly cupping her breast. She moved a little, as though straining away from the hand, and whispered, 'No,' not as a rebuke, but rather as a request. Guy complied, and felt her relax again. They kissed for a few minutes more, before he tried the same manoeuvre again, only this time there was no resistance. The movement was not away but towards, and he could feel the hardness of her nipple through the material of her dress. He knew that she, too, was aroused.

Now, the mystery was becoming unravelled. Girls, as his father had suggested, were not icons to be revered, treasured and guarded. They were living, breathing, responsive and sexy beings. They liked the same things he did. They wanted sex as he did. What he had experienced with Helen, a few weeks ago, was not an oddity or a one-off, it was just a normal woman responding and even initiating the sexual act in a normal way, unreserved and uninhibited. They were, if not hunters, then at least more than willing prey. No, his father, with his Victorian outlook and values, had been wrong – this was modern woman. What he wanted, she wanted. What he initiated, she would respond to. He felt a sense of power, an awakening, as though he had found the answer to one of the mysteries of the ages. She was like his aircraft – if he pulled the right levers and hit the right switches, it would respond kindly – do what he wanted, go where he wanted to go.

She felt the muscles on his shoulders tighten. He snorted down his nostrils, like a bull in a field might when issuing a warning not to come too close. The hand covering her breast tightened and the other, in the small of her back, increased its pressure. The table was no longer a support but a barrier against movement. It began to hurt her.

Guy's hand was now inside her dress. It went under her bra and roughly levered it over her breast. She wanted to gasp and tell him to stop, but his mouth covered hers; not in a gentle way of shared kisses, but it was hard, open and smothering. She could feel his teeth against her lips. She tried to move her head backwards, to relieve the pressure, but the edge of the table hurt her even more. She groaned deep in her throat.

He heard the groan and took it to be a moan of pleasure. He felt the thrust of her hips as she struggled against him and read it as passion. In a burst of supreme confidence and lust, he moved his hand from her breast and, in one movement, raised the hem of her skirt to her waist and trapped the material between their bodies. His hand returned to her crotch. He felt her dampness.

He knew it. He *knew* it – she was as keen as he was. Her arousal was just the same as his. He rubbed her some more and felt the twist of her hips respond to his touch. It was time for him. He reached for his trouser front and fumbled for the zip. He couldn't find it and, for the first time, moved his mouth from hers to look down. She screamed.

'Shut up, you bloody fool. Someone will hear us,' he growled.

For a moment he was confused; it had not sounded like a cry of passion. He wrestled with her for some moments, trying to clamp his hand over her mouth. She wrenched her head away and screamed again.

'What the hell is the matter with—' Before he could finish the sentence the room was bathed in the full glare of the overhead lights.

'What the hell is going on?' The voice was stern and full of rebuke.

Guy squinted over his shoulder and adjusted his eyes to the sudden brightness. As they came into focus, he could see a young man in full dress uniform. Quickly realising it was the station orderly officer, Guy was just about to tell him to clear off and mind his own business, when the girl pushed him to one side.

'Thank God,' she groaned.

Her skirt fell into place and she hurriedly pulled the top of her dress together. Sobbing, she rushed past the newcomer into the corridor.

'What the bloody hell is going on, Kelsall?' he repeated. The tones were less measured now, the anger was coming through.

'Nothing.' Guy tried to smile, looked briefly at the man and then turned his eyes to the floor. He fumbled with the front of his trousers, to make sure they were done up.

'She was just getting a little excited that's all. Nothing for you to worry about. Just finish your rounds and I'll go after her and make sure she's found her way out of the mess.' Guy was beginning to sound more sure of himself. 'Nothing to worry about,' he repeated, 'as you can see, nothing happened.'

He opened his hands in front of him in a gesture of peace and innocence, as if to say, 'Look, not a mark on them.'

'You disgust me, Kelsall!' The words were spat out. 'Even if she doesn't, I'll be reporting this, so you'd better get your story straight,' he added, 'you can be damn sure I will.' With that, the newcomer turned on his heel and rushed out of the door.

Guy reached behind him and felt for the support of the snooker table. He felt confused and a little sick. His mind was reeling. What the hell was going on? One minute, he was locked in a passionate embrace, and the next second, he was being accused of rape or something. It didn't add up.

He shook his head, to clear it, and tried to go over the last few minutes in his mind. He was close to tears. Great waves of varying emotions swept over him. First anger, then shame, then a feeling of being persecuted and, finally, one of fear. Fear for his reputation, but mostly a fear of what might happen to his career. He almost stumbled out of the room and quickly made his way back to his own, hoping and praying that he would not meet anyone he knew. Once he made the security of his familiar space, he threw himself on the bed and, for the first time in many years, wept like a child.

Chapter Ten

The orderly officer was not enjoying the evening. The place had been packed full of revellers and, wearing his best uniform, he had stood out like a sore thumb. Wherever he went, he got more than his fair share of ribbing. People had gone out of their way to offer him drinks, knowing he had to remain sober. Once, when he entered the bar, a young woman, who was slightly drunk, had draped her arms around his neck and, to everyone's amusement, loudly declared how much she loved handsome young men in RAF uniforms, and invited him to run away with her. He had blushed, which only increased the enjoyment of the audience. It had taken several embarrassing minutes before he was able to extricate himself. He had given the place a wide berth for the next few hours.

Then, he had been called to the NAAFI, to help sort out some trouble. By the time he arrived, the duty sergeant had already sorted it out and the place was quiet, but he had thought it prudent to close the bar. He could see from the faces of the more sober element, that he was spoiling their fun for the sins of the few, but once the decision had been made he had been obliged to see it through. And now this.

He had been making the final check of the night. The doors had been locked and, although it was possible to leave the building, no one could get in without a key. His other duties complete, he was on his way to bed, with the sincere hope that he might be left in peace. He heard the first scream as he passed the door of the snooker room. At first, he thought it was someone fooling about, although it startled him. The door to the room was ajar and he entered without being heard. In the light from the snooker table he could see only one figure, who appeared to be bending over. Then, as his eyes had adjusted to the light, he had seen the woman. The one with his back to him appeared to be searching for something, and he heard him harshly order the woman to be quiet. She screamed again, leaving him in no doubt that it was a genuine cry for help.

He reached for the switch and, as the light came on, the girl struggled free. He could see that her dress had been pulled up to her waist, and he caught a glimpse of her breast as she hurriedly tried to cover herself. She rushed past him, sobbing as she bolted through the door. The man turned and he recognised Guy Kelsall, one of the men on the senior course. The look on Kelsall's face had confirmed all his worst fears. The sly half-smirk, suggesting they were all men together, had angered him more than he could have thought possible. It had taken all his resolve not strike out. Quickly, he thought of the girl. Was she hurt? Did she need help? He merely stayed long enough to warn Kelsall that he would be reported, before he went rushing after her.

By the time he reached the corridor, he was just able to catch a glimpse of her as she disappeared round a corner at the far end. He raced after her and, in his haste, almost knocked over a couple of late party-goers. He heard a muttered, 'Watch it, mate,' and shouted an apology as he hurried on. When he rounded the corner, there was no sign of her. For a moment, he thought he had lost her. Then, from a darkened doorway a few yards in front of him, he heard a muffled sob. She was standing with her head bent, hands covering her mouth. Her shoulders shook as she fought to control herself. The orderly officer stopped and then slowly walked towards her, trying not to frighten her. When she saw him she started like a frightened fawn.

'It's okay,' he whispered. 'I'm not going to hurt you. I just thought you might need some help, that's all.'

He wanted to put his arms round her shoulders, but in the circumstances thought better of it.

'He seemed so nice, I trusted him.' She blurted out the words and then lapsed into a fit of crying.

If he had any doubts about taking the matter further, they were dispelled by the sight in front him. Her shoulders heaved in great waves of distress and she wiped the tears and her nose with the back of her hand. He reached in his pocket for a handkerchief and offered a silent prayer that it was clean. His mother had spent half his life lecturing him about carrying dirty hankies. Now, in the circumstances, he suspected the girl would have been pleased with a piece of sacking. She took it, wiped her eyes and gave her nose a hearty blow, then held it towards him.

'No, it's all right, you can keep it.' He tried to sound as though he were being chivalrous and not just refusing it because it had been used. She said nothing, wiped her eyes and gave her nose a second mighty blow.

'You're feeling better now?' he asked.

She nodded, gave another great sniff and nodded again.

'Are you hurt?' he added.

'No, I'm all right really, just a bit shaky, that's all. I'm probably being a bit silly; over-reacting.' She raised her eyebrows, glanced up at him and gave him a brave little smile. 'He frightened me. It was so sudden. I might have sent the wrong signals, I don't know. It's just that one minute everything seemed all right and the next... well, he seemed to change.'

She gave another sob and the orderly officer was afraid she was going to start crying again, but she shook her head defiantly and sniffed. 'He had no right to grab me like that.' She was angry now. 'I'm sorry for being such a nuisance. You must have other things to do without having to fuss over me.' She gave another blow into his handkerchief and shook her head, as if to clear it.

'Are you sure you're all right?' he asked again. She nodded. 'I'm sorry, but I'm going to have to ask you a couple of questions, if you don't mind. If you feel up to it, of course – there's no rush, but I just need to know who you are and where you live. I'm going to have to make some sort of report about this, that's all.'

'No, I'd rather you didn't. I don't want to make a fuss. Can't we just forget about it?' Her anger had quickly turned to nervousness. 'You see, I'm staying with my sister, here in the mess. She's OC Accounts, or something like that, and she'd be furious if I were to cause any trouble.'

'Look,' he tried to sound sure of himself, 'it will all be kept in-house, I promise, but people need to know these things. It might not stop there, might it?'

She nodded quietly to herself as though trying to assess him. She had already put too much trust in one of his colleagues for one night, then she came to a decision.

'All right, I'll go along with you, but please be discreet. I really don't want this all over the place.'

She told him who she was and how she had come to be invited by her sister for the weekend. There was the party, and they intended to spend some time shopping. She recounted the evening as far as she could remember and told how they came to be in the snooker room. As she recalled the final moments there she gave another involuntary sob, and the young man put his hand on her shoulder in a brotherly gesture. She did not pull away as he thought she might, but seemed to take reassurance from it.

'Come on,' he said, 'I'll take you to your room.'

'I'm not sure I can remember where it is,' she giggled.

Chapter Eleven

By nine o'clock the following morning, the orderly officer felt he had already done a day's work. After seeing the girl safely to her room, he returned to his own and thankfully had not been called out again. He woke from a fitful sleep, thick-headed and tired. The bedcovers were scattered all over the place and the sheet beneath him was wet with his sweat. His head spun. Thoughts about what he had seen would not go away. They just rolled around in his mind, teasing and tormenting. Perhaps the girl had been right and he should forget about it. He wanted to pretend nothing had happened, but it was impossible. What he had seen was a crime, no matter where it was committed or by whom. If he did nothing and it happened to someone else, he would be partly responsible. He could not let that happen. But knowing he was dealing with a fellow officer made it the most difficult thing he had ever done, no matter how much he was disgusted by what he had seen.

Although fully awake at seven o'clock, he gave Kelsall's boss a reasonable time to get out of bed before calling him. Squadron Leader Barry Clark was not pleased, even though he was awake. He was certainly not on duty and was nursing a hangover from the party. He tried his best to dissuade the caller by telling him to contact the station duty officer, which was the right channel for such matters, but the young man had insisted that they meet in person.

'It better be good,' Clark growled, and was assured that it was.

'Give me time to finish dressing then come round to the house. You know where I live.' He slammed the phone down.

The doorbell rang before he finished tying his shoelaces. The dog barked, and he heard one of his children shout, 'Someone at the door, Mummy.'

Clark looked across at the three inches of dark unruly hair which protruded from the bedcovers and muttered, 'No point telling Mummy, she'll be the last person to answer the door for at least an hour.'

He had a small sense of loss at what might have happened if they had been allowed to lie in and waken together. He even thought about the possibility of creeping back to bed after seeing his caller, but knew that the kids would be up and about by then, demanding to be fed. 'This had better be bloody important,' he muttered again. He opened the front door and was greeted by a pale-faced young man in full dress uniform who stood rigidly to attention and saluted. The paying of such a compliment to a half-dressed, unshaven senior officer seemed a little incongruous to Clark. He let it pass without comment; it was the way of things.

'Come in, what's your name?' Clark asked, but before the man could answer, he ushered him into the house. The orderly officer entered nervously, pressing his back to the wall, creating maximum space between their bodies. Clark, sensing that he was unsure whether to remove his hat or not, gave him the lead.

'Take your hat off, come in here.'

He led the way to the lounge and apologised for the dog which was avidly sniffing the newcomer's shoe.

'Sit down,' he sounded brusque and tried to lighten his tone. 'Ignore him,' he pointed at the dog, 'he'll get bored in a minute and don't pat him,' he added as the OO bent towards the animal, 'Hairs on your uniform, they're all over the bloody place,' he added softly, looking round.

They sat at opposite ends of the room and a moment of heavy silence passed.

'Well? You haven't come here to fiddle with your hat.' Clark sounded testy again.

'Sorry, sir. No,' he muttered.

He placed the hat on the side of the chair, and his hands fluttered aimlessly in the air looking for something to do. The dog suddenly turned its attention away from his shoe and made a dart towards the hat. The OO was just in time to grab it and switch it to the other side of the chair, before a wet snout half-lunged over the arm. The OO heard the soft sound of teeth coming together and recoiled into the chair. Clark half rose and waved the dog away, giving what he thought passed for a smile of encouragement.

'Sir,' the OO swallowed hard. 'Last night, at the end of the party, about one o'clock, I came across a couple in the snooker room and it looked like...' he paused trying to find the right words. 'They were... well, I think she was about to be raped.' The sentence rushed out and seemed to fill the room with sound, like a train emerging from a tunnel. Clark shook his head slightly as though trying to adjust to the volume.

'Rape? You said rape? In the mess? In the snooker room? Last night?' He stopped himself. He was beginning to sound stupid.

'Yes sir, I think so.'

'You only think so? It's the sort of thing that you ought to be bloody sure about when making an accusation like that.' Clark's voice was raised to a shout. The strength of the response made the OO jump.

'Well, I am sure, sir.'

He sounded anything but sure. Retrieving his hat from the edge of the chair, he started to pick at a loose thread. The dog returned with something in its mouth and stood inches from the stranger's leg, wagging its tail and demanding attention.

'I heard a scream and then another. I switched on the light, and she came rushing past me. Her dress was undone, and she was very frightened. After I recognised who she was with, I went after her and tried to comfort her. She was very upset.' His voice trailed away.

Clark let the images settle in his brain. A small child, in yellow pyjamas clutching an old blanket, rushed into the room complaining of hunger. Clark put his arms round her, assuring her that he would be along in a minute. The child stuck a thumb in her mouth and glared at the newcomer. The OO smiled at her, but it only had the effect of deepening the frown on her forehead. They both watched her slowly edge towards the door, trailing the blanket. Clark waited until she had left the room before asking.

'You didn't switch the light on and then hear the screams? It wasn't you who disturbed them and just embarrassed her?'

'No, sir. Definitely not. I'm certain I heard the screams first, and then I switched on the light.' Clark took some assurance from the positive tone.

'Who was the man?'

'Kelsall, sir. He's on your squadron. That's why I came to you first.'

'Kelsall? You're sure it was Kelsall? He wouldn't say boo to a goose.'

Clark half-rose from the chair and then sat back heavily. He rubbed his temple, his hangover was suddenly much worse.

'One more time,' he said. 'You're absolutely sure of your facts? If I'm to take this to the CI and we find out you've been sleepwalking or something, your feet won't touch the ground,' he threatened.

'Honest, sir. I'm certain, absolutely certain.' The voice held a note of fear. He was beginning to wish he had kept his mouth shut.

'Right then,' Clark stood and groaned quietly as the loss of blood from his head caused further suffering. 'You go round to Kelsall's room and tell him not to leave the station until I say he can. Better still, tell him to stay in his room, unless he's dying of starvation. Okay... thanks, you did the right thing coming to see me. It must have taken a bit of effort. Oh, by the way, you'd better hang about as well in case we need you, and keep your mouth shut, okay? Not a word to anyone.'

*

Guy Kelsall had also slept badly. A glance at the clock showed that he had been in bed an hour. The room was in darkness and it took him some moments before he could assemble what was going on in his brain. He remembered crying, but must then have slept or passed out. His mouth felt like he had chewed a piece of coal and he instinctively reached for the glass of water. It was not there. Visions seemed to leap from the empty place on the bedside locker: screams, dreadful accusing looks, snarled threats. What was it all about? He went over the sequence of events until his head hurt. She had been willing enough. He had not done anything she had not wanted. But the screams and the look – they told a different story. His emotions see-sawed. They went from hurt to fear to shame and then back again but, as the night had worn slowly on, these were replaced by feelings of injustice and then anger. He tried to reason that nothing would come of it. The OO was one of the boys. When he had calmed down and talked to the girl, she would explain her over-reaction. That would be the end of it. He got to the point where he could think no more, and fell into a fitful sleep.

He woke to a knock on the door, suddenly realising that he had slept in his clothes. He licked the palm of his hand and made an effort to smooth down his hair, trying to appear as though he had just dressed. The knock on the door sounded again, urgent, challenging. Kelsall rushed to it. The sight of the orderly officer rekindled all the fears of the night and he fought to control them, feverishly hoping the visitor would say it had all been a dreadful misunderstanding. The look on his face told a different story.

'From Squadron Leader Clark, you're to stay in your room except for meals until he says otherwise.' The young pilot officer gave him a withering look, and without waiting for a reply, turned and walked down the corridor.

★

The chief instructor, Wing Commander Tim Legg, like Clark was also not pleased to be called on a day off. He listened as Barry Clark told him as much as he could over the phone. Clark was one of his better squadron commanders and his judgement could be trusted. If he said it was important and could not wait then that was the probability.

'Okay, Barry, just give me a few minutes to get some things sorted out, and I'll see you in my office in about half an hour.'

His wife was standing in the doorway watching him, a look of resignation etched on her face. 'I know. I know,' Legg held his hands in the air. 'I promised to take the kids to the swimming pool. I'm as disappointed as they will be,' he lied, 'but that was Barry Clark. He said it was important and you know he's not given to exaggeration. He says one of the students got up to something in the mess last night after the party, and if we don't sort it out straightaway it might get out of all proportion.'

The explanation roused little understanding or sympathy. Without replying, she silently turned and walked towards the kitchen, the slant of her shoulders telling him all he needed to know. She was not happy with their current tour. It was in the wrong part of the country, miles from family and friends, and absorbed too much of his time. The promises that it would get better as he became more familiar with the job had not been fulfilled. If anything, the pace had increased. He shrugged. There was nothing he could do. If she did not like it she would have to lump it. Whatever she thought, it put the bread on the table and gave them an enviable standard of living. Still, if someone was found to be out of order they would live to regret it.

★

Barry Clark wasted no time. Once he discovered the girl was staying in the mess as a guest of her sister, he set off to find the room. He did not want either of them raising a fuss before talking to them. The CI had stressed the importance of keeping a sense of proportion. Rumour and counter-rumour would only hide the facts. It was possible the orderly officer had made some sort of mistake, or just interrupted a lover's tiff. He did not really believe that, but he was trying to stay open-minded.

He made a couple of telephone calls, discovering that Flying Officer Jenny Glover was the OC Accounts Flight and had only been on the station three months. Clark recalled meeting her in the bar one evening after work. She was a tall, statuesque woman who carried herself well, but, he recalled thinking, after their brief conversation, that she was not the sort of woman to whom he was usually attracted. She had an air of total independence. A determination, in what was essentially a man's world, to hold her own.

The room was on the top floor, facing the open sea. It was one of the finest views of any RAF mess in the world. Across the sweep of the airfield, the sea carved its way between Anglesey and the distant Lleyn peninsular. Between frequent rain showers and squalls, the far mountains of Snowdonia emerged, etched dark against the sky, guarding the mainland coast. Seagulls screamed and swooped at window level, while on the nearby rocky outcrops gannets and cormorants rested and dried their feathers. But Clark could remember the downside from his own student days. When the wind blew, which was often, it was like travelling steerage in a tramp steamer. Drainpipes rattled, the roof seemed to lift with every gust and the wind played tunes through every gap and cranny. It had been so bad one night that sleep had been impossible and he had cried off flying the next day.

He tapped lightly on the door and it was instantly swung open as though he were expected.

'Come in.' No 'please'; no 'sir'. He was definitely expected. The woman holding the door was tall and slim. Her blonde hair was straight and almost to her waist. She wore a plain white T-shirt and jeans, which accentuated her figure. Her feet were shoeless. Clark took a moment before reconciling her with the rather formal figure he had met as OC Accounts.

'I'm Barry Clark. I think we've met before in the bar?' He held out his hand towards her but was ignored.

'I know,' she snapped. She was not going to make it easy for him.

He looked around the room, surprised how a woman's touch could transform a drab room. Soft, womanly influences were everywhere. A peach bedspread had replaced the issue striped one. A rug, which toned with the bedspread, lay on the floor and the curtains had certainly not come from a military source. Scenic pictures replaced the almost compulsory aeroplane prints. He was about to compliment her taste when he noticed another person sitting in the half-shadow by the window. He nodded towards her, and heard Jenny say, 'My younger sister, Samantha.' Her tone was protective.

He reached across, and again offered his hand. This time it was silently taken and he muttered, 'How do you do'.

Close up, he could see that her eyes were red-rimmed from crying, and she looked as though she had not slept for some time. He suspected that Jenny would be in charge of the proceedings and turned back towards her. He thought of sitting down to minimise the sense of formality and looked around for somewhere, but saw nothing apart from the edge of the bed. He discarded that as being too familiar in the circumstances, and moved his position to face both women.

'Jenny,' he kept his tone quiet and gestured towards the floor with the palms of his hands, 'I've had a visit from the orderly officer, and he mentioned some trouble in the mess last night. He said it involved your sister and one of my students.' He raised a hand to indicate that he wanted to finish what he was saying before she spoke. 'Before I go and talk to the CI in a few minutes, I want to try and find out what happened from all points of view.'

She faced him, one hand on her hip in a gesture of defiance. Her expression spoke her loathing.

'At this stage we are not trying to apportion blame, just get to the bottom of the situation,' he added, less assertively.

Jenny crossed the room, and sat on the arm of her sister's chair. She took her hand, held it to her breast and slowly rubbed the back of it. Then she raised her eyes and looked straight at him. 'My sister is staying as my guest for the weekend. This morning, I went to her room in the east wing because we were going shopping. I found her still in bed. She was crying.' She paused and continued rubbing her sister's arm in slow, protective movements. 'At first she wouldn't tell me what was wrong. She said, she didn't want to make any trouble, but eventually I got her to tell me what had happened. Your *student*,' she spat the word, 'is at best guilty of indecent assault and at worst of attempted rape.' The girl in the chair started to weep softly and the elder sister stroked her hair before adding, 'Sort that one out.'

The odd thought occurred to Barry Clark that at no time since entering the room had any deference been paid to him as a senior officer. Jenny Glover had not once called him 'sir'. He was, he realised, being branded as a male. He was not expected to react positively to a situation like this, other than to pay lip service. The two girls, particularly the elder, did not expect justice or sympathy. He would have to tread very carefully, or the whole thing could go very wrong.

A moment passed and the girl's crying subsided. He turned his attention to her. 'Samantha, I'm very sorry this had to happen and spoil your visit. Are you hurt at all?'

She shook her head, wiped her eyes and blew her nose. 'No, I'm all right really.' She let her hair fall forwards, then grabbed a handful and carelessly flung it back across her head. 'I just had a bit of a shock that's all. We were getting on so well. We had a few dances and a couple of drinks. Not too many,' she added quickly, 'We were dancing mostly. Then we went for a walk around the mess. He showed me the trophy boards and some paintings. He seemed so nice, and we were getting on so well together.'

She stopped, blew her nose again, and Clark waited quietly until she was ready to continue. The silence held for some moments so he gently asked, 'How did you come to be in the snooker room?'

'He said I should see the burgundy cover as it was a rare thing.'

'The burgundy cover?' Clark sounded a little incredulous.

'Yes,' she said and shrugged, 'it sounds silly now, but I think it was a bit of a joke, really. They're normally green, aren't they?' She added, as though explaining things.

He waited a few moments before prompting, 'And then what?'

'We started kissing.'

'You let him kiss you?' he asked. She glanced up quickly, a look of doubt and suspicion in her eyes. He was angry with himself for interrupting. 'Sorry, go on, please.'

'Yes, that was all right. I was enjoying it even, but he tried to go a little further. I said "no" and he stopped.' She twisted the handkerchief in her hands and looked at the floor. 'Then he moved his hand onto my...' she paused, searching for the right word, 'onto my bosom.' It sounded so old-fashioned that Clark almost smiled. 'I thought that if I didn't let it go any further than that, it would be all right, and he'd stopped before when I'd asked him. But suddenly, he changed. He started holding me really tight. He had his mouth all over mine, and I could hardly breathe. Then his hand pulled my dress up and he grabbed me.'

She sobbed loudly at the memory and her sister cradled her head and whispered, 'There, there.'

'Then, his mouth moved, and I screamed. He sounded so angry with me that I thought he might hit me. He tried to put his hand over my mouth, but I was so frightened that I screamed again. Then the lights came on, and a man in uniform was standing there.

Clark nodded, and quietly congratulated himself on his interview technique. She had corroborated the orderly officer's version about the lights without being prompted.

'I'm going to have to go and talk to the student now, to get his version of events.' Clark gave Samantha a little tight-lipped smile. He admired the way she had told the story. He had deliberately omitted mentioning any names and, from the expression of the elder sister, he could see that it had not gone unnoticed. He quietly went towards the door. The two sisters, huddled in the armchair, hardly noticed him leave.

*

Clark found Kelsall's room, and the tap on the door was immediately answered. Again, he had been expected. Since the orderly officer's visit, Kelsall had pulled himself together. He had shaved, dressed and brushed his hair, but looked very pale and was fighting an urge to be sick.

'Sir, hello.' He tried to sound surprised at seeing his boss. 'What can I do for you? Come in.'

He held the door wide, almost disappearing behind it. Clark had a momentary desire to hit the young man, but controlled himself and tried to sound businesslike. 'Morning, Guy.' He kept his own tone matter-of-fact.

He glanced again round the room. The contrast with the place he had just left was marked. This was definitely a male preserve. It was spotlessly tidy, another give-away that he had been expected. He knew from experience that on a Saturday morning, after a party, there would not be a tidy room in the mess. He marched to the centre of the room, leaving Kelsall standing by the door. 'I've been told by the orderly officer that there was a bit of trouble in the mess last night.' Clark paused for a moment to let the message sink in. He saw Kelsall stiffen slightly. 'I think he's already been to see you?'

Kelsall merely nodded, and Clark was surprised how young he looked. He had known the man for nearly six months, and yet realised that he hardly knew him at all. He had even flown with him a couple of times, and remembered that once he had overcome his nervousness at flying with the boss, he had put in a pretty good performance. But outside that experience there was nothing about him that he could recall, except being totally surprised when he had asked his wife to dance a few hours ago.

Clark pretended to look hard at the aeroplane prints for some time before he suddenly turned to face Kelsall. Their eyes met for the briefest of moments, before the younger man looked away. In those fleeting moments his eyes seemed to say it all. They were shifty and wary and frightened at the same time. 'What's your side of the story?' The directness of the question made Kelsall jump slightly. It threw him off-balance mentally. All his carefully rehearsed answers went out of the window.

'It wasn't like you think at all. She was as keen as I was. It wasn't supposed to be like that. We were having a nice time. I thought we liked each other.' He sounded even younger than he looked; a little boy explaining to his mother why he had got mud all over his clean suit. 'We were kissing and... well, it was going a bit further, but not much, and then she screamed, right in my ear. I thought she had seen a ghost or something, and then she screamed again, pushed me away, and rushed out of the room. When I turned round, the orderly officer was standing there.'

He paused, almost out of breath, and Clark remained silent, watching.

'That was it, honestly, sir. I meant her no harm.'

He held his hands towards the older man as though in supplication and Clark noticed that the door was still open.

'So you behaved like a perfect gentleman?' Clark sneered. He did not wait for an answer. He saw a rush of blood to Kelsall's cheeks, before marching straight out of the open door and back the way he had come without looking back. He heard the door close softly behind him, and thought he heard a sob, but was not sure. He reached the landing, and lent heavily against the banister. 'Bloody hell,' he groaned.

His mind whirled. He was in the jury room. All the evidence had been gathered and heard; now what would he recommend to the judge? He was fairly convinced no one was lying, but was also convinced a wrong had been perpetrated. But what degree of wrong, he was not sure. His first reaction was that Kelsall, having had too much to drink, had just misinterpreted the signals and over-stepped the mark. What he had just heard from Kelsall seemed to bear that out, and even Samantha's own description of events suggested she had not exactly discouraged him. But even allowing for that, his actions had been reprehensible, and could in no way be condoned. How far would it have gone if the orderly officer had not arrived on the scene when he did? In a court of law, the situation would be anything but clear-cut. The more he thought about it, the more he was sure that formal action would not be appropriate or advisable. To drag it through a court martial would be degrading for the girl, an embarrassment to the service, and would probably achieve nothing in the end. He shook his head, again whispering, 'Bloody hell.' Now, he would have to go back and explain it to the girls, but before that the CI was waiting.

The drive from the mess to the CI's office took five minutes. The place seemed strange without the hustle, bustle and constant noise of aircraft in the background. The office was on the first floor, and enjoyed a panoramic view of the airfield. As Clark knew to his cost, the CI was not always bent over paperwork, but used his vantage point to keep close tabs on what was going on outside his window. His latest fad was aeroplanes taxiing too fast, and complaints had come to Clark about both students and instructors alike. In fact, the instructors had turned out to be the worst offenders.

The knock on the office door was greeted with a deep-voiced 'Come in'. The CI was sitting at his desk surrounded by paperwork as though it were any other day. 'Thought while I was here, I might as well catch up a bit.' He waved his hand expansively across the desk.

'Sorry, sir, I hope I haven't kept you waiting too long. It took longer to talk to everybody than I thought.'

'Not a problem, Barry, sit down.' The South African accent had almost disappeared during the twenty years since he arrived from his native country to join the RAF, but the word Barry was pronounced Birry.

Clark sat down and took a moment to gaze round the room. He liked this office. It was light, airy and tastefully decorated. Apart from a few tankards and one aircraft painting, it could have been the office of any city executive.

'So, what's the problem?' Legg clasped his large hands together and leaned forward across the desk. A smile was on his lips, but the eyes remained passive. 'Sorry, would you like a coffee or tea?' he suddenly asked, as though forgetting his role as a good host.

'No thanks, sir. I would just as soon get on with it, if you don't mind.' Clark knew the CI's reputation for working all hours, and his long-suffering wife was not averse to crying on his own wife's shoulder. He did not want to be complicit in keeping him any longer than necessary.

It took him several minutes to relate the story of the previous evening. Legg listened without interruption. When Clark finished all he said was, 'What do you recommend, Barry?'

'Well, sir I don't think we should take it any further than these four walls. I know the sisters want to drag Kelsall to the cleaners, well one of them does certainly, but I don't think it will serve anybody's interest, particularly the girl's. It would also kill Kelsall's career stone-dead.'

'I don't give a shit about Kelsall's career.' Legg brought his fist down hard on the desktop. 'If he is guilty then I would personally kick his arse from here to next Christmas. But I take your point that there is some doubt about his intentions,' he added, lowering his voice. He gazed out of the window for some moments. The clouds were skimming the tops of Holyhead mountain and dark clouds were gathering behind. It was probably going to rain. 'Right, I'll see him here this morning. He won't know what has hit him until he's forty miles down the road, and he'll be that far by lunch time. I'll give him the mother and father of a bollocking, and then kick him off the station. He can pick up the pieces at his next stopping point.'

He rubbed his hands together as if he were relishing the prospect. Clark almost felt sorry for Kelsall; the CI held an awesome reputation for not pulling punches.

'Thanks for your time, Barry, you've done a good job. I'd be grateful if you could just do a couple more things before you go home. Get Kelsall to get his backside here at once, and call on the Glover girls and try to explain what we are doing and why. I'm sorry about that one, it won't be easy, but as you've seen them already, it might be better if you see it through.'

Chapter Twelve

Nothing had changed in the room. The younger sister was still sitting in the armchair, and looked like she had been crying again. The look of hostility in the eyes of Jenny Glover had not lessened and, as Clark explained what they had decided the best course of action would be, her cheeks reddened in a glow of anger and her fists knotted into white claws.

'The cover-up, eh?' she sneered. 'All boys together. Come and say a few words to the girls, apologise and it will be all right.' The elder sister spat the words.

The force of her outburst shocked Clark. He was momentarily at a loss for words and it took some moments before he regained his composure. When he did, he felt angry. Anger at the assumption that he could be party to a cover-up. He glared hard at the sister, fighting to control himself. He was opening his mouth in protest when Samantha spoke: 'I don't want it to go any further.' They both turned and looked at her, startled. They had been so intent on their own opinions that they had almost forgotten she was in the room. 'I don't want it to go any further,' she repeated. 'I'm not hurt and it will only drag things out if we have to go over it all time after time.'

She burst into tears and her shoulders heaved as she tried to suppress the sobs. Her sister rushed to her side and put her arms round her shoulders. 'It'll be all right, I promise.'

As Jenny spoke she glared up at Clark and then turned her attention back to her sister. He looked down at them, wanting to touch them, to make them aware of his concern and sympathy – one was riddled with self-doubt and guilt, the other smarting in self-righteous indignation. He let out a long sigh, and realised the complexity of the problem, longing for a black or white solution. The answer, as always, lay somewhere between the two.

The next time Jenny looked up from comforting her sister, the expression had changed. Gone was the animosity of moments before, replaced by a look of a childlike pleading. A tear welled in the corner of her eye and slowly trickled down her cheek. She made no effort to wipe it away. Her expression almost implored him to take this ugly thing away. He understood, but felt powerless.

'Okay, sir.' It was the first time she had shown any deference to his rank. 'We'll go along with you. Not because we want to or agree with you, but simply because we have to. That's the way it has been for centuries, and I don't suppose it will change. But it doesn't make it right. It just isn't right.' She covered her face with her hands and sobbed uncontrollably.

'No, Jenny. I'm afraid you're right. It's not right and I'm afraid I can't make it so, much as I would like to.' Clark felt a surge of despair well up inside himself. He took a last look around the room. In its simple decoration he saw so much pride and hope, the simple ambition of a young girl for whom the future was bright and a place existed for her in it. Now this. He hoped and prayed that it could be put in the past and left there, but he had his doubts. As he left the room, both sisters were crying in each other's arms.

*

Guy rushed around the room like a headless chicken. He was not sure what to wear. It had been clear from Squadron Leader Clark's second visit, a few moments before, that he was not being summoned for tea and biscuits. What to wear suddenly became important. If he wore his number one uniform, he would be admitting that he was expecting a bollocking or worse, and so might be suggesting guilt. It was Saturday and he should be in civilian clothes, but to pitch up like that might upset the CI even more. He settled on his working uniform, and was glad he had gone to the trouble of changing out of his flying suit at work. Working dress would also allow him to wear a hat. If it was going to be a severe bollocking, then hats were a major part of it. A 'Stand up, hats on' bollocking was considered degrees more severe than the sit-down 'Now you've been a bit of a naughty lad' sort.

Once dressed, he felt sick again and wished he had eaten some breakfast. He still was not sure he deserved any sort of censure. The more he thought about it the more he started to feel badly done-by. He could not shake off the feeling of impending doom. He felt threatened: he was worried for his career and knew from hearsay that this CI did not take prisoners. A student on an earlier course had been caught in bed with another student's wife, and he had been off the station in minutes and out of the RAF in days.

For the second time in less than twelve hours, he swept through the corridors of the mess hoping not to be seen. He made it to the car park, praying that his car would start. It had rained during the night, and his car was notoriously difficult to start if it even sniffed moisture. The starter wound over, slowly at first, and then the engine kicked into life. He breathed again. The thought of getting Staines to run him across to the CI's office gave him a cold sweat.

'A bollocking, Guy? You, getting a bollocking, Guy? From the CI himself Guy? For trying to shag a maiden in the snooker room, Guy?'

During the short drive, his life passed before him. He asked himself, and failed to answer, more 'what if' questions than he could cope with, and his head began to spin. The doors into the building, which would normally have been locked on a Saturday morning, all opened for him. It was like a movie where the hero enters a series of dark, mysterious corridors and is led inexorably to his fate. Except that this was no movie, and he was certainly no hero. The 'come in' that greeted his tap on the door was quiet and measured. It was the sound that the fly heard from the spider in the nursery rhyme; it was the endearing call of Granny Wolf to Little Red Riding Hood. His blood ran cold. Any residue of anger at the injustice of his situation dissipated in a flash. He was frightened, his knees went weak and his stomach felt leaden.

He entered quietly, hoping not to waken the menace within. He made a quick survey of the room, the window, the desk and the figure seated behind it, bowed over writing. He crossed to the desk with as much military bearing as his legs would allow, came to a passable halt and saluted the picture hanging behind the bent figure.

Hell was suddenly inches from his face. The figure behind the desk seemed to leap at him, and his world was filled with a bare-toothed, bulging-eyed aggressor. He felt small droplets of spit hit his face and his natural instinct was to retreat, but he held his ground. The voice when it came was controlled, threatening and dangerous. 'You are a disgrace to the uniform you wear, to your family and to yourself. I do not wish to see you on this station, or anywhere near me ever again.'

Each word was delivered in a slow, deliberate cadence, full of disgust and loathing. Guy's eyes were blinking rapidly; keeping time with every syllable. He had never been so frightened in his life. He could not have spoken even if invited to do so. He fought to control his bowels and his tears at the same time. Slowly the enormity of what he had done hit him. He wanted to show remorse, to apologise, give assurances that it would never happen again, but the face in front of him intimidated him so greatly that it hindered his breathing.

'You will pack your things and be off this station within the next two hours. Any administrative requirements that need tidying up will be done for you.' The face moved imperceptibly closer and screamed the single word: '*Out!*'

A fist crashed on the desk in emphasis, and Guy felt the hot breath of the man. He was blinking very rapidly to hold back the tears and a single one escaped and trickled slowly down his cheek. It was a final humiliation. He needed to find energy, which he did not think he possessed, to salute, turn and walk out of the place to safety. Only when he reached the sanctuary of the outer office did he allow his emotions free rein and, for the second time in a matter of hours, he cried like a baby.

*

The next two weeks passed in a turmoil of emotion and uncertainty. Guy did not even know if he was still in the RAF. Each day he scrutinised the post for the dreaded letter that would tell him it was over. His family, who simply thought that he was on leave between courses, watched his erratic behaviour with alarm. He ate little, kept mainly to his room and was largely monosyllabic in conversation. Any attempts to find out what was troubling him were greeted with snarling replies that everything was fine. His father put it down to the stress of flying training, and assured the rest of the family that he would be all right if they left him to come out of it in his own time.

At the end of the allotted leave period, it took all of his courage to pack his things, get in his car and make the journey to Devon. During the drive, he rehearsed what he would say to his parents when he returned unexpectedly the next day. When he checked in at the guardroom and found that his name was on the list of those expected on the next course, his joy and relief were such that he wanted to kiss the corporal who was leaning through the hatchway giving him instructions on how to get to the officers' mess. The fact that it took the man three attempts to get through to the new student prompted him to tell his mates later, 'If that thick bastard gets through the course I'll show my bare arse in Tiverton marketplace at high noon.' Had he followed up on his threat, the people of that good Devonshire town would have been in for a shock.

Chapter Thirteen

Wing Commander Kelsall pushed back the chair, and ran his fingers through his hair. Apart from aimlessly moving paper around, he had not really achieved anything. Despite sharing his information with Seagrove, he was no nearer to solving the problems of JP233. He looked round his office. A feeling of pride swept through him. It was the manifestation of his achievements – the pictures on the walls, the small models on the window sills and the tankards all represented phases of his life. He had flown Harriers, Jaguars, Hunters and Gnats and now Tornado, a pedigree that anyone would be proud of. The squadron pilots, he knew, referred to this office as the Boss's 'I love me room'; not that he cared, it gave him pleasure and a lot of satisfaction.

From his earliest days in the RAF, he had wanted this job. During officer-training, they had been taken on a visit to a Lightning squadron and had been collectively introduced to the squadron commander. Guy had been totally in awe of him; such poise and panache, confidence, self-assurance, even handsome. Guy had the feeling that there was nothing this man could not achieve. He loved the way his pilots referred to him as 'the Boss'. Guy wanted that. He wanted to fly aeroplanes, and he wanted to do it as the Boss.

Now, he was there; he was 'the Boss' and was proud of himself. He had worked hard, ridden his luck and taken his chances. He had neither trodden on people to get there, nor allowed anyone to stand in his way. It was his own doing. Although, over the years, he had grown in confidence, the rank and the increased responsibility were not the panacea that he had hoped for. The job was lonely, and he found decision-making hard. He was willing to put up with it, knowing it was not for ever.

This would be his last flying tour. If he could complete it with a reasonable reputation and the good will of the station commander, he would be set. He still enjoyed the flying once he got going, and flying the Tornado with a navigator for the first time was a pleasure. The problem was the risks it placed on his career. Now he was not only under threat from his own errors, but also those of others. It was like walking on eggshells. His office was where the buck stopped and, unless he was in a position to dissociate himself from those errors, he was in the firing line. Leading formations could cause him problems. The leader carried the can. The trouble was, the more he ducked out of it the easier it got and, he suspected, the more noticeable. Still, if that was the case then so be it. He had come so close to losing his career once. That memory was still fresh in his mind, it drove him.

Guy had been surprised by his own ambition. Apart from wanting to fly and then realising that he wanted to be a squadron commander, he had never been unduly bothered by the call of high rank for its own sake. But it had grown on him. He had found great pleasure and pride with each promotion, but also surprise that he should have been thought good enough. Then, as familiarity with the job set in, he began looking towards the next one and asking himself, Why not? Was he not as good as that person, or even better than that one? Could he not do the job more effectively than his current boss? It would occur to him that he could, and he would begin working towards the next rank. Now he was looking at a job as a station commander. He liked the idea of being the man at the top of if not the biggest tree, the local one at least. He enjoyed being called 'sir' by all ranks up to and including squadron leaders. As a station commander he would add wing commanders to the list.

Tours of duty followed a similar pattern. First, a gradual awareness of the new rank, and pleasure in the privileges it brought. He would be relaxed, fulfilled and challenged. Gradually it would change, and he would find himself looking upwards and onwards. Measuring himself against his superiors officers. It would begin to dawn on him that he was capable of doing their jobs as well, if not better, than them. At this point Guy would begin to tighten up. He would become protective of his achievements and more careful about how his performance was being viewed by those who could influence his future. He would wish his time away, yearn for the day when another annual report would go into his personnel file with all the right ticks in the right places. He was at that point now in his present tour. It had gone well so far, only now, unlike previous tours, there were far more people who could put a spanner in the works.

Guy looked at his watch. He had better make a move, the briefing would be starting shortly, and he wanted a word with Tom Cookson before it started. 'Have you rung the station commander yet, Adj?' he bellowed. He heard the muffled reply and grunted, 'Enough sense to find the number then?' to himself before shuffling a bunch of papers into a drawer and locking it. 'Going flying now, Adj. Try not to burn the place down while I'm gone.'

'Righto, sir,' reached his ears but the, 'You stupid sod,' was intended for closer company.

Guy had decided, in the last half hour, to get Cookson to change the plan for today's attack. He knew he was being unfair in leaving it so late, but that was too bad.

Cookson was beginning to bother him. He could not quite put his finger on why, but something in their relationship was not quite right.

Squadron Leader Tom Cookson had a very similar background to his own. Slightly younger by a year or so, they had been in the training system at the same time, albeit on different courses, so they had not known each other. When he arrived on the squadron, Guy had welcomed him as a kindred spirit, hoping that they could form a working relationship similar to the one he had enjoyed with his predecessor. The early signs had been good and, through their shared experiences on Jaguars, they had initially got on well together.

Cookson hailed from the north of England. His accent had almost disappeared over the years, but occasionally the flat vowels of his native Lancashire came to the surface, particularly when he had drunk too much. Quite the opposite to Seagrove, he was attractive to women and looked the archetypal officer and fighter pilot, carrying himself with an easy grace. Good at sports, he had excelled at golf in his younger days, when career and a lack of family had permitted, playing to a handicap of four. Now it had risen to eight and, although he did not play as much as would have liked, he was still fiercely competitive.

Cookson's other strong attribute was an unflappable nature. In the air, he remained calm and confident in all circumstances, and it was often a great assurance to the less experienced crews to know he was around. He took his flying extremely seriously. Tough in the air and tough in the briefing room, he had seen too many people killed in flying accidents to do otherwise. He was intolerant of both his own mistakes, which he admitted freely on the rare occasions when they occurred, and those of others, particularly if the perpetrator was foolish enough to try and hide them. Then they would be fixed with a cold blue eye, and left in no doubt that neither the mistake in the air nor the cover-up would be acceptable.

Guy Kelsall soon realised that his hoped-for alliance between himself and Tom Cookson was not going to happen. While the flight commander was never less than helpful, and always deferential to the requirements of his boss, he was rarely less than formal. Apart from the few occasions when they let their hair down in the mess, Guy was unable to get close to him.

Further evidence that the hoped-for alliance was not going to happen followed a pairs formation bombing exercise. Guy had flown as number two to Cookson's lead. After a standard battle turn, Guy had failed to materialise in the correct position. The matter in itself was almost insignificant, and was not particularly dangerous, but it would have meant a loss of mutual cover if fighters had been around. In the debrief, Guy had tried to excuse himself by laying the blame on his navigator for being a bit off track. Cookson had looked him directly in the eye and told him to 'sharpen up'. Guy had been stung by the rebuke, and had been about to ask his subordinate who the hell he thought he was talking to, when the look on Cookson's face told him that an argument would be futile. Since that time, Guy had been wary of the younger man.

Another thing about Tom Cookson began to worry Guy. Occasionally the way Cookson looked at him made him wonder, a certain glance which suggested that Cookson had the edge, and was not overawed by him. Guy knew that the younger man, although interested in his RAF career, did not consider it the be-all and end-all of his world. If the RAF was not prepared to accept him as he was, then all right. He could just as easily take himself off to the airlines, and try his hand there. Perhaps that was all it was. The man was just self-assured in the knowledge that he could do just as well elsewhere, and was unafraid of the annual report which Guy was obliged to write. This air of independence began to irritate him.

The irritation was slowly turning to something deeper; a sense of mistrust, nervousness, even dislike. Guy told himself that it was irrational and unfounded, but it made no difference. He wanted Cookson off his squadron. But how? The man was good at his job. He was popular with his peers and subordinates alike and, for all Guy knew, might have friends in high places. He decided to wait for something to turn up.

As Guy entered the planning room, the quiet calm, which he had left an hour ago, had been replaced by a noisy buzz. The crews, having completed their planning, were standing around chatting, each man, in his own way, dealing with the mounting excitement and pressure of the coming trip. Although it was only a training sortie, they all knew the dangers. That was the least of it. No one wanted to be the one to make a mistake. They were on view, highly trained professionals ready to go about their business, each man the audience of the others, prepared to applaud the good bits but ready to come down hard on any mistake, particularly if it brought danger. The next few hours would be as intricate as any West End production. The parts were clearly defined and rehearsed, each player knowing that the curtain was about to rise. Although no one would be shooting at them, the scenario would be acted out as if that was the case. They were coping with the moments in their own way, some quietly going over the route again, others loudly swapping stories.

The noise subsided slightly as Guy made his appearance, but quickly returned to the original level. He was greeted by Granger, clutching a set of maps, which he held towards Guy. 'Your maps, sir. I've drawn them exactly as you like them,' he said, with a heavy emphasis on the word 'I've', to let Guy know that he was not in the habit of drawing pilots' maps. Guy recognised, but ignored the intended jibe. Granger was not his usual navigator.

'That's most kind and considerate of you, Robin,' his tone condescending in reply. 'I suppose you've picked crappy IPs?' Guy asked with a cursory look at the maps.

'They're okay.' The round face cracked into a cheeky grin. 'I didn't want to make it too easy for you, after all, wing commander is only one rank away from walking on water, isn't it?'

Robin Granger was an experienced Tornado navigator, who was well into his second tour on the aircraft. He had flown his first on a German squadron, and had come to Guy highly recommended. To Guy he was one of the problem people. Not because he failed in his duties; in fact it was quite the reverse, he was good at his job. The problem lay in his being totally average. His appearance was average; his performance in his secondary duties was average; in all he was a very forgettable person. It was only when it came to flying with him or, more importantly, writing his annual report, that Guy remembered he was on the squadron. Guy had no trouble writing reports on the good ones and even relished filling a page of career-damning prose on the bad ones, but when it came to the Grangers of this world he struggled.

'Want to go over the target runs before the briefing, sir?'

'Quickly then, Robin. I want to have a word with Tom Cookson before we go flying.'

They went to a far corner of the room, and Guy laid each of the maps in the correct order. He could immediately see that Robin Granger had done a beautiful job preparing them. The initial points had all been highlighted in oblong boxes drawn at right angles to the line of attack, and the heading for the attack was written in bold print at the side of the box. The line to the target was subdivided into timing marks – one for each ten seconds of the run – and on the other side, distances to go to the target. The target itself was set in the middle of a triangle, the base of which was again drawn at right angles to the line of attack. From the apex of the triangle a line and an arrow indicated the escape route. None of the three runs was more than twelve miles from the IP, and each IP was a large unique feature which would be relatively easy to acquire visually and to overfly.

Guy nodded appreciatively and muttered, 'Not bad, not too bad at all. Almost up to my standard,' he added with a slight grin.

'We are here to serve,' Granger replied in acknowledgement of the veiled praise. He mockingly tugged at one of the few strands of hair that remained above his forehead, and bowed slightly.

'If I were you, I would be careful not to tug too hard on that lot. There's not much left to be obsequious with,' Guy said.

Granger only smiled, the mouth moving but the eyes not seeing the humour. Guy was pleased to have had the last word; crewroom banter was not one of his strong suits. Now he was beginning to relax, and was looking forward to the trip.

'Right, Robin. Thanks for a good piece of planning. I must dash and find Tom. I'll catch you up in the briefing. Any idea where he is?'

'Last seen in the ops room, sir. Putting the last touches to his briefing slides.'

'I'll see you in a minute then.' Guy touched the navigator gently on the shoulder and turned away.

Chapter Fourteen

Tom Cookson faced the two large boards which covered the entire width of the operations room. One, which belonged to the engineers, showed the serviceability of the aircraft, their weapon loads, and where they were situated on the site. The other, the preserve of the aircrew, indicated which crews were matched with which particular aircraft, and the order in which they would fly throughout the day. Each was constantly updated by a sergeant, who sat in front of numerous communications systems linking him to other parts of the squadron and to the main station operations room. Like the rest of the building, all the systems were hardened and protected, their linking cables buried deep under the ground. Only a lucky strike would be capable of destroying them.

'Don't tell me we've got a spare aircraft as well, Sarge?' The mock surprise in Cookson's voice was not lost on Sergeant Carter.

'Indeed you do, sir.' His tone mirrored that of his superior. 'None other than Fox Charlie in HAS 12. It's not exactly ready yet, but I have it on the best authority that it will be more than serviceable by the time you've finished your briefing. Don't I, Sergeant Jones?' He raised his voice, shouting in the direction of his colleague at the adjacent consul.

'You do indeed, Sergeant Carter. I have the personal assurance of the squadron warrant officer himself that Fox Charlie will be ready on time,' Jones grinned.

'There you are then, sir. The warrant officer's personal guarantee. Solid as the Bank of England, that,' Carter said.

'Once you have both stopped sounding like a pair of maiden aunts at a vicar's tea party, I'll take it as read then.' Cookson continued to write on the briefing slides without looking up.

The two sergeants grinned at each other, and waved daintily as Cookson added the information to the acetate sheet from which he would brief the crews.

'There you are, Tom. Can I have a quick word, please?' All three men turned as the wing commander walked into the room.

'Sure, Boss, no trouble. I've just finished the slides, so we've got a few minutes before the brief.'

Guy took Cookson by the elbow and steered him to a corner of the room. 'I'm sorry this is coming a bit late in the day, Tom, now that all the planning is complete. I should have mentioned it earlier, but things are happening. I'll explain more about that later. I've already spoken to Brian, but I'll have to ask you to change your plan a little and simulate using JP233 on one of today's targets.'

'Done, Boss. Not a problem.' Cookson shrugged slightly, and pointed airily at the slides.

There it was again, Guy thought. That air about Cookson that so annoyed him. It was as though the man was in his head, and he did not like it.

'I don't mean a mix of weapons. I mean a complete attack using nothing but JP233,' Guy emphasised.

'No sweat, Boss. As I've said, that's what we've planned. I've just been checking the modification state of the aircraft, and all of them, the spare included, have the mod; so we'll be able to do it.'

'All four?' Guy had some difficulty hiding his surprise. 'How are you going to get all four over the target, and not have them stretched out for miles? You've thought about cross-cover, I suppose?' He was beginning to sound like a spoilt brat who was sulking because he wanted a toy, but then discarded it the moment he got it.

'Well, Jack Frost and I have had our heads together on this for a few days now, and we reckon we might have come up with a way of getting the aircraft through the target quickly while sacrificing only a minimum of cover.'

The way Cookson looked at him left Guy wondering, for the umpteenth time, where he had seen it before. Their paths had crossed somewhere, Guy knew, but for the life of him could not remember where.

'Let's go into briefing, sir. Hopefully, it will all become clear.'

Cookson turned and left the room, and Guy was momentarily lost in his thoughts. 'Briefing in two minutes, you lot,' Cookson shouted.

The sound of Cookson's voice in the next room brought Guy back to the present, and he followed them through to the briefing area.

The room erupted in noise as the crews grabbed their belongings and shambled towards the briefing room. A tall bar stool crashed to the floor as Grice missed his footing and his G-pants tangled up in it.

'If you need a lift down, you've only to ask. Now that your mummy isn't here, I'm more than willing to give you a hand,' Jennings gloated.

'Hunch,' Bertie tried to sound patient, 'If you were the last fucking person on earth, I wouldn't have your hands near me, even if I were covered in ants and needed a scratch. It's bad enough flying with you, without having to touch you.' As he regained his balance, he aimed a kick at his pilot's heels, who in turn stumbled against one of the desks. Hunch was just about to retaliate, when the voice of Squadron Leader Jack Frost stopped him in his tracks.

'Stop behaving like a couple of overgrown schoolboys, and get yourselves into the briefing, before I set about you myself.'

The look on the face of Jack Frost was enough to convince anyone that when he threatened it was worth paying attention. A tough, truculent Yorkshireman, half his thirty-six years had been spent in the RAF but, unlike Cookson, his accent remained unchanged. Of medium height, he had a very powerful build, more suited to the rigours of manual work than the delicate tasks of finding radar fixes, but in this he was among the best. The trouble was finding a suitable pilot to pair him with. He tended to dominate the cockpit, intimidating some of the younger pilots. The solution had been to pair him with Cookson. While it was not ideal to have two squadron executives in the same aircraft, the partnership worked very well.

The briefing room resounded to the clattering and banging of steel leg restraints on steel chair legs, chair legs scraping on bare concrete, and muted thuds and giggled apologies. Like the rest of the building it was small; even with only five crews it was tight for space. When the whole squadron assembled it was a meat market. In the moments it took them to settle, Cookson stood quietly at the front, facing his audience, a frown of concentration on his brow. The lights were out and the room was dimly illuminated from the shafts of light coming through the pane of glass set into the door, and from the slide projector. Guy watched him from a position halfway down the narrow room. He knew that look. Had seen it time and time again in his mind's eye. It had almost burnt a hole into his soul. But where? In which lifetime? Then it came to him. The half-light, the frown and the unblinking eyes. The orderly officer. That night so many years before in the snooker room. It had to be. The orderly officer – the one who had reported him over that silly matter with the girl. The one who had come so close to costing him his career.

Guy's mind was in turmoil. A cold steel hand seemed to grab at his guts. He felt physical pain. His breath came in short, sharp bursts and he had difficulty remaining in the room. He fought the urge to run. Slowly, he calmed himself and tried to think. If Cookson and the orderly officer were one and the same person, why had he kept it to himself? Surely, he could not have resisted letting him know. Perhaps he had forgotten, or simply been told to keep his mouth shut. Perhaps even more sinister reasons lay behind it, and he was waiting for the moment, but for what? Perhaps he was simply wrong, and Cookson was not the same person at all.

Chapter Fifteen

'Sir,' Cookson frowned and raised his voice slightly. 'Wing Commander Kelsall?'

Guy realised that he was being spoken to. 'Sorry, Tom. What did you just say?' He shook his head slightly as though coming out of a trance. 'I was far away, I've got a lot on my mind at the moment,' he added weakly by way of explanation. He felt as though he had been hit by a sledgehammer. The shock of his discovery had left him stunned.

'The slides, sir. Have you copied the details down and then we can move on?' Tom Cookson tried to keep the exasperation from his voice, but in his opinion you left other work behind when you went flying. The mix was too dangerous.

Guy had not written a thing; he tried to pull himself together. If he had been leading and the same thing had happened, he might well have thrown the offender off the flight. He busily started to note the aircraft numbers, who would be flying them and their location into the pad on his knee. It was only when he got to the fourth flight that he realised he was flying in that slot. Another wave of irritation swept over him. Cookson had done it to humiliate him. The number four position was invariably occupied by the least experienced crew. It had no responsibilities, other than to stay in position and keep a good lookout. As the most vulnerable aircraft in the formation, it would be first choice for any aggressor. He was tempted to tell Cookson that he would not fly there, but that would make him look childish. Everyone in the room was watching him and he quickly finished writing and again muttered, 'Sorry Tom.'

'Moving on then,' Cookson whipped the slide off the projector and quickly replaced it with another. He stood to one side and allowed the crews time to note the information down before going over the contents. 'We'll take off in two close pairs, separated by twenty seconds. Keep close formation until clear of the local area, and then widen out into battle. Jack will cover the route in a minute, and I'll come back to the targets after that.' He replaced the slide with another. 'Tanker details. It's a VC 10 today, and it will be in area four at 12.30 Zulu, at twenty thousand feet. Once we leave the low-level area and begin to climb, close up the formation a bit, and then the radar unit won't get in a twist because we're spread all over the sky.' He spoke quickly, expecting each man to instinctively know what was coming. 'Standard join on the port side, take your fuel to full, and then clear to the starboard and wait until everyone else has finished. Bounce, you try and get in there first, and then, when you see that we're nearly finished, you can leave and take up a position for your next attack. Any questions?'

'Sir, what if Hunch takes all afternoon on the tanker like he did last time?' The remark was greeted with a few guffaws, and Bertie Grice had to move quickly to avoid being thumped by his pilot.

'I suspect, Bertie, that if you keep your mouth shut, and let Hunch get on with it, you might just make it home for tea.' It was Hunch's turn to grin. 'However,' Cookson added, 'if you don't get your fuel, you come home and – I don't want to add any pressure – you buy a round of drinks in the bar this evening. Jack.'

Frost got to his feet, and swung a board out from the wall on which he had hung a half-million scale map of Northern England and Scotland. The entire route was drawn on it. Apart from the Boss, everyone was familiar with it. Only the navigators carried copies. It enabled pilots to concentrate on flying the aircraft, but more importantly stopped some of them cutting the navigator out of the loop. The Tornado provided them with a moving map display which gave a similar picture and, with a careful commentary from the back seat, they were more than able to follow the progress of the flight.

'This is a long sortie,' Frost paused to let the remark register, 'so all those with small bladders had better make sure that they have a pee before they walk to the aircraft.'

'Yeah, yeah. Thank you for that, sir.'

The speaker had not been allowed to forget the occasion when he had been unable to plug himself into the 'pee tube' in time, and had emerged from the aircraft with a large damp patch on the front of his flying suit. Even then he might have got away with it, but one of the ground crew had drawn attention to his plight by bellowing that it must have been raining hard as the Tornado was usually fairly waterproof. Now he would just have to put up with the jibes until someone else came along with a bigger gaff. Frost waited for the laughter to subside before he continued. 'Out of here at low level; up the Trent and into God's country.'

'I didn't know we were going to Sussex, Bertie? You told me we were going to Yorkshire.'

'Shut up, Jennings.' Frost's mouth formed into what for him passed as a smile. 'As I was saying, across the Cleveland Hills, and coast out north of Whitby. Once we get north of the Humber, it's clear for the bounce to attack so keep your eyes open.'

He continued going over the route, highlighting points to be avoided, danger areas occupied by the army, and places where nuisance from noise would be injurious, such as hospitals and old people's homes. No minor detail was left out. 'Watch out for power lines here,' a heavy finger jabbed at the map, 'and whatever you do, don't go over this farm. I've just had the RAF police in again investigating a complaint that another of his cows aborted because we flew too close. I think he must be lonely up that hill, and complains so that he can have a bit of company.'

The weak joke was answered with an equally weak response. Guy shuffled uneasily in his seat at the light-hearted way in which one of his executives was treating such a serious matter. By the time he had finished, Guy was forced to nod his approval. Despite the flippant manner in which Frost occasionally went about his business, he was a first-class operator, and the plan proved it. It gave no nuisance to anyone on the ground, avoided all towns and built-up areas, and the runs into the targets appeared to be well thought out.

'Thanks, Jack,' Cookson returned to the front. 'We've got three targets today, and a live run on Tain range. We'll simulate conventional thousand-pounders for two of the targets and the run at Tain, but on the third we'll all simulate dropping JP233.'

The remark was greeted with a low whistle from the back of the room and someone muttered 'punchy'. Cookson ignored the remark. He placed the maps of the first two attacks side by side and pointed at the first.

'Standard runs to the IPs and splits, as you've all drawn on your maps. Everyone happy about that? Next target, we'll go for loft attacks from all four aircraft, then we can keep the separation to a minimum.'

He described the pull-up point for all the aircraft, which was two miles short of the target. The four lines on the map started from wide positions and converged towards the triangle that marked the aiming point. 'First two aircraft recover to the right, and the second two to the left, then each pair go for a reverse turn and we'll all be back together again three or four miles past the target. Don't forget to make sure you have got a package before you start the pull-up.'

He looked hard at Jennings and Grice, who on the attack two days previously, had passed through three thousand feet on the pull-up before they realised that they had made the wrong selections. Not only had the simulated weapon refused to release from the aircraft, but in holding the climb longer in the forlorn hope that it would, they had made themselves very vulnerable to enemy missile fire.

'Point taken, sir,' one of them muttered and Cookson nodded.

'For the third target, as I just said, we'll all simulate carrying JP233. Jack and I have been doing a bit of thinking about how to get the aircraft through the target in under three hours, and we think we might have come up with a new slant.'

'They've been thinking, Hunch. I told you they could.' The remark, meant for Jennings's ears only, escaped into the sudden silence.

'Thank you, Grice, for your confidence. We'll discuss it in my office later. Now, if we could have no more stupid schoolboy interruptions, I'll get on.' Cookson sounded annoyed.

The run into the third target was slightly longer than the others and, like them, resembled a plan drawing of the entrance to Clapham Junction, with lines coming from all sides and converging at the centre before diverging. Each aircraft had a different IP, and the lines bent out away from the target on both sides before turning back towards it. To Guy, at first glance, it looked very similar to the first two attacks. It should have looked very different. The lines should have all been running the same way down the centre of the runway, not as they were drawn. Just what was Cookson playing at now? He was about to remark on the fact when Cookson interrupted his thoughts.

'The more discerning among you will notice that we are not all running down the centre of the runway.' Cookson sounded almost smug. 'In fact,' he continued, 'only the first aircraft is doing that; taking advantage of surprise to get the maximum damage done. The next three aircraft will all cut across the runway. The first at the threshold, the second in the middle and the third at other end. The spacing can be reduced to about fifteen seconds, and that's only necessary so we don't get in each other's way. We can be through the target and out the other side before they make up their minds which of us they're going to shoot at.'

He stood back and glanced at the board behind him as though admiring his handiwork.

'It would appear to me that there's a slight problem,' Guy sounded hesitant. 'If you cut across the runway you run a risk, because of the spread of the cratering devices, that none of them will actually fall on the hardened surface.' He felt a small surge of pleasure that he had put his finger on what was an obvious weakness in the plan.

'Well, you would be correct, sir, if the angles were at ninety degrees to the runway. We've done some calculations, spoken to the manufacturers and they've agreed that if we keep the angle to the runway at less than forty-five degrees then at least three of the bombs, and possibly more, will hit. If the intervals we hit along the runway are accurate, we could close the thing for just as long as by doing it the other way, and increase our survival rate a quantum amount.'

'That gets my vote,' the Scottish tones of Ian MacKensie came from the rear of the room.

'Any other points?' Cookson asked.

'I've got one, sir.'

'What is it, Bertie?' Cookson failed to hide the irritation in his voice.

Jennings and Grice were one of the more junior crews on the squadron, and had the talent to become good operators, but they were immature at times.

'Well, sir, I think you should angle the first attack also.'

'Go on, Bertie fill me in,' Cookson tried to sound tolerant.

'Well,' Grice sounded less confident than moments before. 'It seems to me that it would be difficult to get the aircraft right down the centre of a runway anyway, never mind keeping it there because the margins for error are so small. If you angled off a little bit there would be more room for mistakes, and very little loss of effect. As you pointed out, if only half the runway is damaged, a determined operator would have few problems operating from the other half.'

'That's a good point, Bertie. I'll bear that in mind when we plan in future, and as it's early days in JP233's development, anyone else who has an input, don't keep it to yourselves.'

Cookson was genuinely pleased that Grice was beginning to think things through, and decided he would go easy on him later. The thought occurred to him that both Grice and Jennings might benefit from a crew change. Neither would like it, but that was not the point. Both would probably prosper in more mature company.

'Right, any more points before we move on?' The room remained silent. 'Okay, Jim and Ian, you can leave and plot your attacks, and the rest of us will just go over our own tactics.'

The bounce crew made their way to the door.

'Don't forget we're going to the north and not the other way.'

The remark was silently answered by MacKensie holding two fingers up behind his back.

Guy was lost in thought again. The plan had knocked him for six. It was so simple and yet, like all things truly simple, it was brilliant. Why had he not thought of it? And it had come just in time for the station commander's meeting. Even if the results were not as good as he expected them to be, he would have something to report. He woke from his reverie just in time to hear Cookson putting the final touches to his briefing. This bit was routine and although Guy missed what was said he was confident that he would hold his end up.

'Keep good position,' Cookson was saying, 'fly fifteen hundred metres across the formation and no more than a mile and a half between pairs. Keep a good lookout. Remember, Hunch, you're covering my tail, so if Stamper and MacKensie get a shot at me, I'll hold you personally responsible.'

'Not a chance, sir. They might as well stay at home,' Hunch grinned.

'You mean like last time, Jennings, when you let the bounce shoot my ass off.' Flight Lieutenant Tony Langstaff prodded Jennings in the back to emphasise the point.

'I had a touch of the flu that day. I should have been in my bed, but I bravely pressed on, knowing that I was needed.'

'You would have been more use in your bed playing with your teddy bear.'

'Or whatever,' someone at the back added.

The place was plunged into semi-darkness as Cookson switched off the projector. He stood for a moment and looked at each of them in turn and once more Guy had an uneasy feeling that he was right about where they had met previously.

'Right, let's go and do it. Grab the rest of your kit, or whatever you have to do, and the out-briefing will be in five minutes.'

The room erupted into noise, signalling the end of the briefing.

'Ian, a quick word please,' Kelsall kept his voice low, as though imparting a state secret.

'Yes, Boss.' Squadron Leader Ian Ord turned towards Guy. He was a big man with a chubby face which should have lent itself to smiling, but rarely did. Instead, over the years that Guy had known him, it was becoming more hangdog. His cheeks were losing their firmness and beginning to sag. By the time he reached old age, he would resemble a bloodhound. In other respects he resembled a sea lion, slow and clumsy on the ground, but once in his environment another being. If Ord had been able to show the excellence he was able to produce in the air in his other duties, he would already be a rank higher. Instead he would probably struggle to make one more promotion.

'The bounce will be looking for me in particular today, Ian, as I'm at number four, so keep an extra good lookout, okay?'

'Sure, Boss, not a problem.' To those who did not know the man, his slow, measured tones would not have inspired confidence, but Guy knew better. If he had to rely for his life on anyone, this would be the man. 'The same thing occurred to me,' he added.

'Good man,' Guy patted his upper arm and turned away. In all the conversations they had attempted in the past, none had lasted longer than a few sentences and had been mostly about flying. Now he was wise enough not to hang about to labour the point.

Chapter Sixteen

In the far corner of the planning room, Stamper and MacKensie had their heads together, putting the last touches to their attacks on the formation. Their role was to simulate an enemy fighter. They were new to the job, only recently having been considered good enough. Both were into their second tours on the aircraft and, as well as becoming bounce-qualified, they had been made four-ship leaders. They took their role very seriously, enjoying the responsibility, but to a casual onlooker their relationship appeared anything but responsible. They were one of the least likely-matched crews on the squadron.

Stamper had found his way into the RAF by way of public school and two years at university, where he had failed to meet the second year standards. He liked to attribute his failure to an overwhelming desire to fly aeroplanes, but in reality it was more to do with his overactive social life, and a dislike of his chosen subject. He had picked theology, because at the time he had felt some calling towards the Church. Within weeks of starting the course, he had not only lost his virginity, to a well-balanced reader of English Literature, but had also lost any urge towards a future saving souls.

The Church's loss was the RAF's gain, and they welcomed this tall, handsome, well-spoken young man as one of their own. He had not exactly sailed through the training, but had done enough to keep his head above water and convince his mentors that he was competent to fly the Air Force's latest attack aircraft. He had not lost his urge for the good life either, and continued to pursue an active interest in the opposite sex. He had learned from previous mistakes, though, and was now more careful not to allow one pursuit to interfere with the other.

By contrast, Ian MacKensie had done it the hard way. Raised in a less than salubrious part of Glasgow where most of his contemporaries expected no more from life than a job in the shipyards, he had harboured different ambitions. At school, although clever enough not to show it, he worked hard without appearing to be a swot. The teachers had recognised his talent and willingness to work. Without holding him up as a shining example of what could be achieved, thus earning MacKensie at best a life of verbal abuse and at worst some thumps round the head, they had quietly nurtured his talents. By the time the exam results were out, and he came away with some of the best the school had ever seen, it was too late for his less able contemporaries to take revenge. He transferred schools and continued his higher studies. He found the atmosphere more conducive to working, but now encountered a prejudice, not against his mental abilities, but against his background. On completing the course, again with impressive results, he decided that Glasgow was no longer the place for him.

The RAF was not top of his list of attractive future employers. He had little idea of what he wanted, and only wandered into the recruitment office out of curiosity. Once inside, two things had changed his mind: a large picture of a Tornado with two young men wearing strange suits standing in front of it, and the offer of a free railway ticket and three nights' accommodation close to London while he attended the selection centre.

On arriving, his first impressions had not been favourable. He found himself surrounded by what he considered southern, upper-crust layabouts who would probably not know a day's work if it hit them. During the first evening, as he watched from the edge of the crowd, he realised that they were not so different. Certainly they sounded different, and had different backgrounds, but he recognised that underneath they all wanted the same thing – a job with reasonable prospects, which was not too boring and had the possibility of a little adventure. Underneath, they were all scared stiff they would miss out.

He did not change his opinions completely, but he did go to the first interviews with a more open mind. He was surprised that his accent and long hair received no comment. The interviewers genuinely seemed interested in him as a person. They wanted to know how he had done at school, what his views of society and political beliefs were, and why he wanted to join the RAF. They appeared unaffected when he told them that he was a socialist, and that he didn't really know if he wanted to join the Air Force. He was quite surprised and pleased to get an invitation to go back the next morning. It rather screwed up his plans to spend the day looking around the English capital, but he would still have a day before he had to go home.

He found the aptitude tests easy, and actually began to enjoy himself. The leadership tests were absorbing, and he found to his amazement that he was often the one who came up with a solution. By the end of the afternoon, he was the first person others turned to for help. When asked on the third day what he thought about becoming a navigator he was so surprised that he blurted, 'It's never crossed my mind.'

'Go away and think about it then,' said the tall wing commander, 'and by the time we've made up our minds whether we want you, you might have made up your mind whether you want us.'

He returned to Glasgow without setting foot in London, his mind in a whirl. What only a few weeks previously had not even occurred to him now seemed a possibility, however remote. But they wouldn't have him. He was simply not their type. Not with his background and upbringing. Why, they even had some difficulty understanding what he said. He dismissed the idea as fantasy, and yet could not banish it completely. As the days lengthened into weeks, the hope began to fade. He even gave up checking the post, what there was of it. Apart from bills, most of them reminders, and junk mail, nothing came through the letter box.

Then it came. A long pale blue envelope addressed to him. He grabbed it before anyone saw it, stuffed it in his pocket and immediately left the house. He walked the streets for three hours before he took it out of his pocket. He checked the name on the envelope again, and even then could not bring himself to open it. It was another hour before he did, and by then he had never wanted anything in his life more than for the letter to say 'Come and join us'.

★

'Look, if we come in high from this direction, we'll have the advantage of the sun.' Stamper leaned over MacKensie's shoulder and scowled at the map.

'That's exactly the cowardly, sneaky way I would expect an Englishman to make an attack.' MacKensie chewed the end of his pencil as he thought about the suggestion. 'And that's why it looks like a perfectly reasonable idea to me. We'll also have the advantage of this hill once we get to low level.' He pointed the end of the pencil at the map. 'And,' he added, 'if you make a complete codswallop of the angles and we get into deep shit, we can always make our exit through the valley there.' Again he prodded the map with his pencil and a small shard of wood dropped onto the surface, which he brushed away irritably.

'Me? Make a codswallop, as you so quaintly put it, of the angles? It's more likely that, with your well-known deficiencies as a navigator, we will probably never find the bloody formation in the first place!' Stamper's voice rose in mock indignation.

They planned three more intercept points, and worked out the fuel reserves before they would have to leave low level to go up to the tanker. 'If we've got spare fuel we could get a quick in-and-out job just here.' MacKensie stabbed at the map again.

'From what I've heard, and the source as always is impeccable, that sounds a very fair summation of your sex life: a quick in-and-out job.'

'We Scots are known for our endurance and staying power, I'll have you know,' he said, neatly folding the map, stowing it in his bag and consigning the much-injured pencil to a slot on his sleeve, 'that allowing the wind to swirl round your bollocks when wearing a kilt gives you that little bit extra.' He balled his fist and punched towards the ceiling.

'All you Scots do is talk a load of bollocks,' Stamper replied.

'You have to have the last word, don't you? Have I ever told you, it's one of the least endearing features about you and your nation as a whole? This habit of always wanting the last bloody word.' He turned on his heel and marched out of the room with Stamper in tow. To anyone who did not know them it would have appeared incongruous that two such men could enclose themselves in a tiny cockpit and successfully fly a modern fighter, but in reality they were the best of friends. This quickly became apparent if anyone tried to intervene in one of their interminable arguments.

They left the briefing room first, to get ahead of the main formation and set up their air patrol. MacKensie trailed the taller man as they walked to their aircraft. He wished he had taken the transport, but had been persuaded by Stamper that the walk would do him good. The aircraft was parked in one of the furthest shelters, and the weight of his equipment was beginning to make itself felt. He muttered, not for the first time, that he ought to do something about getting fit, but knew that the next time it became a choice between a pint in one hand and a fag in the other, or wrestling with an iron bar in the gym, the pint and the fag would win.

'Come on, you tardy little bastard. We won't get airborne before dark if you don't get a move on.' Stamper, something of a keep-fit fanatic, was striding away hardly out of breath.

'"Bastard" I can live with, "little" I can just about take,' MacKensie gasped between the words, 'but the last person who called me "tardy" is now flying Shackletons in Cornwall, because it is the only seat they could get his swollen arse into after I had finished kicking it.'

They passed the first of the shelters. The great reinforced doors had been opened a few feet, and inside they could see signs of activity as the ground crew prepared the aircraft. The same routine was being enacted in all six shelters. To the crew of three men, a corporal and two technicians, it was their aircraft until it left the shelter, and they cosseted it like a baby. Both Stamper and MacKensie were too young to remember a time before the great hardened sites had come into existence, and they merely took it all for granted, but it was testament to the fact that Great Britain was no longer an island. Wars might still be fought on distant fields, but now enemy aircraft could easily bring the fight to the homelands. These overgrown, brown Nissan huts were the last line of defence; capable of withstanding all but a direct hit. Stamper had often wondered why they had been stained brown and then set in a sea of regulation length green grass, which left them obvious from the air.

'Come on, you slow sod, catch up. At this rate the war will be over before we even get to the aircraft.' MacKensie had fallen behind again and was beginning to fight for breath.

'My mother was right, I should have got a proper job instead of acting as a nanny to an overgrown control freak.'

'I doubt you even had a mother. You were probably spawned under some flat northern rock, and reared by toadstools or something.'

*

The main group of the formation finished the final briefing. They noted the latest weather synopsis and state of the diversions airfields in case anything went wrong, and moved through the changing room and into the open air. A change was beginning to take place. The group camaraderie of the briefing had gone, and been replaced by a quieter, more serious air. The pairing of the crews became obvious as they walked through the car park towards their aircraft. Grice and Jennings were in one of the nearest shelters, but were nevertheless in a hurry. Conscious of their inexperience, they wanted maximum time to set up the aircraft, and to be in some sort of relaxed frame of mind before the first check-in call came over the radio. They had flown together for the best part of a year, and were the best of friends both in and out of the cockpit.

They had first met at the Tornado Conversion Unit. .Both were on their first tours of duty although Jennings had joined up more than a year before his navigator. The extra time reflected the increased time needed to get through pilot training. Consequently, he had recently been promoted to flight lieutenant and would not allow Flying Officer Grice to forget this fact.

Their first meeting had not been an instant success. Albert hated his name. His primary school teacher, a tall Olive Oil type character, with a long skinny frame and bulging eyes, had formed his earliest memories of it by pronouncing it in high falsetto tones with great emphasis on the last syllable. The playground, in the early days, had often rung to the sounds of other children mimicking her tone as they laughed and pointed at him. It might well have been his undoing had Albert had not been made of sterner stuff. He was nobody's laughing stock. Tall for his age and good at sports, he quickly showed he could look after himself. He quietly waited for one of the bigger boys to pick on him, and with a ruthless couple of punches to his face had sent his tormentor in search of the teacher to tell what had happened. Albert received a slap from the cane, but it proved worthwhile as suddenly no one seemed keen to make fun of his name any more. It was in a similar way that Jennings got off to a bad start when they had found they were crewed up together.

'What's your name, son?' Jennings had asked. Grice had looked at the man, who, if he stretched his imagination, might be all of two months older than he was.

'Albert Grice.' He shifted uncomfortably in his chair.

'Albert Grice?' The other man repeated. 'Al... *bert*!'

He stretched the last syllable to breaking point and Albert's fist screwed into a ball between his knees.

'Al... *bert*,' he repeated but with less emphasis on the 'bert'. 'Can't say I've ever come across an Albert before. Where on earth did you get it from?'

Jennings was never to know how close he came to being clocked, but at that moment a burst of laughter came from the other side of the room. It had a momentary settling effect on Grice.

'My father was very keen on reading about World War One heroes, and he named me after Albert Ball, VC.'

'Well, I can't call you Albert. You don't look anything like a hero to me, and besides, it might bring bad luck.'

Albert thought that if this pompous fool did not shut up the bad luck was about ten seconds away, and all of it would be coming towards him.

'I'll call you Bertie. That sounds much better, don't you think?'

Albert clenched and unclenched his fist. It did sound better. He did not like the way it had come about, but had to admit that it did have a better ring to it.

'What's your name anyway?' Bertie asked.

'Hunch Jennings.'

It was Albert's turn to snort. 'Hunch, you say? You're called Hunch? Now, how the hell does anyone come across a name like Hunch?'

'It's a long story, Bertie. I'll tell you sometime.'

'I've got loads of time, son.' Albert laid heavy emphasis on the word 'son', but it drew no response whatsoever.

'It happened one night at school.'

'What the hell were you doing at school, at night?' Bertie interrupted.

'Boarding school.' Hunch looked at his newly acquired navigator as though he had grown two heads. 'If you're going to keep interrupting, it's going to be an even longer story. As I was saying, the school clock on the main tower was beginning to get on our nerves, with its constant chiming – someone had to do something about it.' He paused as though that constituted an adequate explanation.

'So, because the clock was chiming you got called Hunch. Well, that seems more than logical to me.' Bertie was beginning to wish that he were somewhere else. Maybe it was true what they said about pilots at Nav School: that they should all be locked up until they turned thirty. It certainly seemed to apply to this particular specimen.

'No, no, no.' Hunch was getting exasperated. 'I volunteered to climb up the outside of the tower to stuff my jacket into the hands of the clock so that it would stop chiming.' Again he paused as though enough had been said on the subject.

'So, you're climbing up the outside of the clock tower, at night, with a jacket in one hand to stuff between the hands of the clock, and the Archangel Gabriel appears to you as if in a dream and says, 'Henceforth ye shall be known as Hunch, and all men shall know of your deeds.'

'Are you taking the piss out of me, by any chance?' It was Hunch's turn to be a little miffed.

'Me? Take the piss out of a pilot and a night clock-tower climber? Not at all, I have far too much respect for the breed. It's just that, despite my better judgement, I have this burning desire to know what happened next.'

Hunch looked at Bertie and a slow grin spread over his face. 'You know, Bertie, I have the strangest feeling that you and I are going to get on just fine together. What happened next was that it went unearthly quiet below, and when I looked down, instead of the three mates that I had left standing on the ground in the moonlight, there were four, and one of them was a little fatter than the rest and bore a striking resemblance to the headmaster. When he spoke, I could instantly tell from his voice that he was not tuned in to the funny side of the venture, especially as his first words were that I should stop going upwards and climb through one of the porticoes into the upper bell tower. That turned out to be thoroughly bad advice, because unlike your supposition, old Bertie, I did not have my jacket in my hand. It was stuffed up my shirt at the back, and when I tried to get in through the opening I got stuck. To cut this story down to any sort of size, it took three hours and the local fire brigade, watched by the entire school, to get me out. The rest, as they say, is history.'

It was Bertie's turn to grin. The more time he spent with Hunch, the more he liked him. He was a character who seemed to have the knack of doing all the right things for the wrong reasons. He had gone to university because his father had wanted him to join the family business; read aeronautical engineering because it was as far removed as possible from the manufacturing industry, and had joined the university air squadron because a particularly attractive young woman, whom he was trying to chat up, had joined. All this had conspired to give him an interest in aircraft that he never knew existed. By the time he graduated with a borderline second-class degree, a hint of a beer belly and more hours flying than any other cadet, he was marked as a social, likeable individual with a fair amount of aptitude for flying. The instructors on the squadron had no hesitation in recommending him for further training. One other thing helped him to stand out within the environs he was keen to join – he was black.

*

Ian Ord and Frank Langstaff arrived at HAS 8, and Ord immediately went into the small cabin, which acted as the engineers' crewroom and dormitory in times of war or exercises, to sign for the aircraft. Langstaff made his way straight to the aircraft, which straddled the centre line of the small hangar and dominated all about it. He had never quite lost his first feelings upon coming close to the aircraft. Its dark brooding colours and aerodynamic ugliness, seemed to dare him not to come too close. He knew it was inanimate, but the message always seemed clear: get in if you like, fly me if you really want to, but don't be surprised if I bite. Langstaff shook his head in wonderment at the beast, took a deep breath and climbed the steps to the cockpit.

The great one-piece canopy was already raised on its single hinge and, after checking that the safety pins were in place on the ejection seat, he climbed in and sat down. Once settled into the high-sided rear cockpit, he lost his nervousness and became quickly engrossed in setting the inertial navigation system into alignment with the precise co-ordinates of the aircraft's latitude and longitude. In the air, he would update it from time to time using the radar, and retain the accuracy of the weapons' delivery systems. Only then could they operate totally independently with no reference to external navigation aids. The thief in the night.

He was well into his prestart routine by the time Ord climbed into the cockpit. The engineer, who had helped him fasten his safety harness, moved forward to help the pilot, and through the whirring of gyros and the thickness of his helmet, he could hear them chatting without knowing what they were saying.

With the ground crew gone and the steps taken from the side, Langstaff felt a small surge of isolation until he heard the familiar puff of breath as Ord activated his voice-operated microphone on his face mask.

'You okay, Frank, any problems?'

'No, Ian, I'm nearly there. The alignment has got about another couple of minutes to run, and then we'll be ready.'

They had agreed that no rank existed in the cockpit.

'Right, I'm there as well. Everything seems okay this end. What did you think about that little briefing by Tom Cookson? I was watching the Boss's eyebrows and they nearly shot through the roof when Tom came up with that attack profile.'

'It seemed a reasonable idea to me.' Langstaff was purposefully low-key. He knew Ord's last ground tour had involved weapons procurement. One of his projects had been JP233, and he had made clear his dislike for the thing. In fact, he had quietly worked hard to get it scrapped, or turned into a stand-off weapon before being told to wind his neck in and accept it.

'Best bloody idea I've heard so far about the sodding thing. Anything that gets us quickly through a target that's likely to be defended up to the hilt gets my vote. I only hope the Boss doesn't get jealous because it wasn't his idea, and puts the kibosh on the thing.'

'That's it then, the nav is in align. I'm ready to go.'

Langstaff whipped the oxygen mask from his face and took a lungful of fresh air. Again it was a time for waiting, keeping the chat to a minimum in order not to miss the check-in calls. The airmen took their positions on the ground: one to monitor the engine start and the others to open the great doors. In wartime, they would be left closed, but the smell and fumes from the engines made it desirable not to follow the practice in peacetime. As the doors slowly rumbled back, the light of summer replaced the gloom. Both men were ready to get on with it, but the waiting continued. It was a part of the job, and each individual coped with it in his own way. Once out of sight of the others, some brought small books from their pockets, while others dragged dog-eared copies of old crosswords from under their perspex knee-pads, and were still as mystified about the answers as they had been previously.

*

In HAS 6, Guy Kelsall and Robin Granger finished their checks and were ready to go when the crew chief came on the intercom.

'Sir, I've got an indication down here that the flight data recorder has packed up.'

'Can't you do anything about it, Chief?' Guy gave a great inward groan and tapped his fingers on the side of the combing.

'The corporal's gone to see if we've got a spare, and whether we can get it here in time, but I can't do any more here.'

'Haven't you got a circuit-breaker you can pull and reset?'

Guy could feel himself getting hot. His frustration stemmed from the fact that the unserviceability would not affect the operation of the flight one jot, but a rule barred the aircraft from taking off without it. If the stupid man had kept his mouth shut, ignorance would have been bliss.

'I've tried that, sir, and it's no good. Just a minute.'

He moved the earpiece from the side of his head and bent towards a second man who had come from the hut.

'He says stores have got one, sir, but it will take about half an hour to get it here, and about the same to fit it.'

'What do you think, Chief? We could go without it.'

'I don't make the rules, sir.'

It came almost as a taunt; the unspoken implication that if you break the rules, how do you expect us to keep them? Guy removed the mask from his face, laid his head back against the rest and closed his eyes. He wanted to shout, scream and swear, but instead wearily put the mask back to his face and quietly said, 'Let's get the spare, Robin, before someone else nicks it.'

Chapter Seventeen

'Trent, check in.'
'Trent one.'
'Two.'
'Three.'

Silence. Cookson waited a few seconds before he spoke again. 'Trent four, check in.' Again he allowed a few seconds to pass.

'Ops, have you heard from Trent four?'

'No, Trent lead. I think he's gone for the spare, but I'm not sure.'

Cookson looked at his watch and made a mental calculation of how long he could wait. In the rear cockpit Jack Frost read his thoughts.

'Can't wait more than two minutes, Tom, or we miss the tanker bracket and the TOT at Tain. Things are tight enough as it is.'

'I know, Jack. Anyone else I would just leave, but I particularly wanted the Boss to be on this one to see the attack. You don't think he's pulling another one to get out of going, do you? No.' He immediately answered his own question. 'He wouldn't do that, would he? Trent four, check in.'

He tried again. This time the radio came to life. 'Trent lead from four.' The voice was a little short of breath. 'We've just got to the spare. We'll be ready to taxi in about eight minutes.'

'Can't wait that long, four; you'll have to catch up. Trent, check in.' He went through the routine again to make sure that the others were still with him. 'Easeham Tower, Trent formation request taxi.'

'Trent formation, taxi for runway two three. Use the northern taxi track, the QFE is 1014.'

The noise of the four aircraft filled the air as they simultaneously nosed their way out of the shelters into the sunshine. Guy cursed as one of the four passed the open doors of his HAS. He had arrived at the spare aircraft out of breath and very hot, having run the hundred yards between the two buildings, only to find the corporal still in the process of signing for the latest repair work. 'I thought the aircraft was supposed to be ready?' His voice rose to a shout.

'It is, sir. I've just got to sign the job sheet and we're there. It won't take more than a couple of seconds.' The corporal did not look up from writing.

'I was told the bloody thing was ready some time ago. What the bloody hell have you been doing in the meantime? Farting about, I suppose.'

Guy was red faced, and the tantrum caused the corporal to lose his way among the documents. He paused and airily waved his pen above the page.

'What is it now, Corporal?'

'I don't suppose you know the date, sir? It's gone out of my head,' he added weakly.

'It's the bloody thirteenth, and if you don't get on with it, it will turn out to be very unlucky for you.'

The man bent over the forms, quickly scribbled his signature, and wordlessly passed the book to Guy for him to sign. He kept his face low over the desk; he was close to tears with hurt, anger and frustration. The whole thing had taken less than a minute, but to both men, for different reasons, it felt like an hour. Guy felt momentarily sorry for his attitude to the young man, but he said nothing and rushed out to the aircraft, slamming the door behind him.

'And fuck you too, sir,' the corporal hissed through clenched teeth.

Guy pulled his helmet over his ears just in time to hear the leader call him to check in. He was now very hot and bothered, and was beginning to wish he had found some more work to do in his office. If the next few minutes did not go well, he would pack it in. A bead of sweat trickled down between his eyebrows, and he moved his hand to brush it away, forgetting that he had lowered his clear visor. His hand hit the perspex, and he cursed again. 'Right, settle down,' he muttered to himself, 'this is no way to go flying.' He closed his eyes and tried to get the tension out of his system.

'You all right, sir?'

He opened his eyes. The airman who was helping him strap in was leaning over looking at him. 'Yes, yes.' His voiced sounded tired. 'I'm just trying to cool down a bit, that's all. You've got the pins out?'

The airman waved the pins in his face, stowed them, and scurried down the ladder.

'Right, Robin. After that little shemozzle, let's see if we can pick up the pieces.'

In the rear cockpit Robin sounded almost indifferent. 'The kit is almost in align, Boss, and I've worked out that if we go at medium altitude straight up the Vale of York, we can cut out a lot of the wiggly bits, and catch them up just to the north of the Cleveland hills with very little lost.'

Guy actually smiled at the description of part of the route as 'wiggly bits'.

'Okay, call me when the kit is ready.'

'It's there right now.'

Guy could see the map display between his legs suddenly shift position. 'Chief, are you on-line and ready to start engines?'

The corporal on the ground fumbled with his switch as he replied. '…to start,' was the only thing that Guy heard.

'Say that again,' Guy shrilled.

Both the corporal and navigator assumed he was talking to them and answered at the same time. Both replies were equally unreadable. 'Shut up.'

The remark was addressed to the nav, but again both men assumed he was talking to them. A silence followed. 'Chief, if you don't get your act together in the next couple of seconds, you'll be washing up in the airmen's mess for a month.' The tone was menacing, Guy had already lost the little composure he had regained.

'I'm sorry, sir, I said you were clear to start.'

The engines roared into life together as Guy pressed both starters at the same time. The place filled with noise and fumes as half the vapours failed to find their way to the ventilation system at the rear.

'You're clear to disconnect, Chief.'

Almost before the luckless corporal could take the communication lead from the side of the aircraft the great bulk moved forward, and he had to scurry to take his position by the door. Even then, he had to duck as a wing tip swept over his head.

The aircraft reached the main taxi track as the first aircraft of the formation took off. Even through the thick canopy and the padding of his helmet, Guy could hear and feel the roar and power of the engines. Again, luck was not in his favour. The fresh, south-westerly wind meant they would have to taxi the whole length of the airfield before take-off. He was too busy with his own checks and calculations to notice that the shape of the formation had changed. The leader had gone alone, and the other two were following as a pair to cover his rear. The change had been mentioned in the main briefing, but Guy had missed it. Suddenly he found himself heading too quickly into a corner, and hit the brakes hard causing Robin to strain against his harness.

'Steady up, Boss. At this rate we'll be a smoking hole before we get to the others. I've already said that we can make up the time.'

Guy's first reaction was to ask who the hell he thought he was talking to, but good sense and training had taught him that the man was right. He should not take so much anger and aggression into the air.

'You're right, Robin. Sorry, I was a bit hot under the collar.'

He took three deep breaths, which were strong enough to activate the intercom. To Granger, it sounded as though he were blowing up a balloon.

They lined up on the runway and were given immediate clearance for take-off. Guy held the brakes on and gently moved the throttles to the forward stop. Within a circle of a hundred yards, all life was suspended as the noise took over. Then he shifted the throttles through the detent, engaged the afterburners and released the brakes.

Both felt the surge of power hit them as the plane leapt forward. The ground, which for a second seemed to move only at a snail's pace, was in moments a blur to the side and then with a lurch they were airborne. The noise and frenetic pace seemed to leave them. Like a penguin jumping from rock to sea, the aircraft was in its rightful environment.

'Clear the danger areas in the Wash, and then steer three-four-zero. If we keep at five thousand feet, we'll be well clear of all the active airfields, but under the airway; that way we shouldn't have to talk to anyone.' Granger sounded relaxed and sure of himself.

'What speed do you want, Robin?' Guy also relaxed. It seemed to be the same every time these days. A great deal of trouble to get in the air, but once there, his troubles seemed to slip away. He made a mental note to try and remember that in future; it might help his motivation.

'About four-forty knots should do it; no need to go flat out and waste fuel.'

Guy looked around him. His head, through years of training and habit, never stopped moving. The day was almost perfect, with patches of puffy cumulus covering half the sky with their base at about four thousand feet, and only small amounts of cirrus well above that. The visibility was excellent. They passed to the west of the Wash, and he could see from the number of sandbanks that the tide was out. The tiny black dots of the seals, as they basked in the sunshine, were just visible. The brightness hurt his eyes, and he reluctantly pulled the second visor down. Once they got to low level, he would put it up again to increase the range of vision. They levelled, and all movement seemed to stop. It was quiet, peaceful and in complete contrast to the aggravation of a few minutes before. The air conditioning had lowered his temperature and only the cold wetness of his vest was a reminder of his anger and frustration.

'Nice day, Robin.'

'Lovely day, Boss.'

They lapsed again into silence. Granger fiddled with his radar in between looking out, and Guy almost subconsciously gave the controls little corrections to keep it on heading and height. No matter how much he adjusted the trim, the aircraft held steady for only a couple of minutes.

'I think I'll give Linton a call, just to tell them we're passing through their overhead. They might well have some poor student in the forced landing pattern, and he won't be looking out.'

'Yes, it's probably worth it, Boss,' Robin agreed.

Guy set the frequency on his radio. He would normally have left it for the nav, but he had spare capacity.

'I'll give them a call then,' he said.

Chapter Eighteen

Stamper and MacKensie sat at ten thousand feet over the North York Moors, flying a race track pattern. The main formation would pass beneath them in two minutes. The trick was to swoop down on them suddenly, and that required an early sighting. If they dropped too soon, they would get in front, but if they left it too late it would become a long, drawn-out tail-chase, with the advantage going to the formation. Although they knew exactly the position and timing of the group, the weather conditions were not in their favour. The dark upper surfaces of the Tornado blended beautifully with the dark brown moorland, as they moved in and out of the shadows. Both men were becoming increasingly fidgety as the stared at the ground.

'Keep the bloody bank on, you English prat.'

Stamper had levelled the wings slightly and the tops of the engine intakes seemed to grow from the sides of the aircraft, obscuring MacKensie's view.

'Stop whingeing and get looking.'

'Thirty seconds.' MacKensie suddenly sounded very business-like. Stamper pulled the aircraft tightly through the last few degrees of the turn, and they both felt the increased level of G-force.

'There.' It came almost as a shout from the front seat. 'Just crossing that small lake.'

'That'll be number one or two; look for the pair behind,' MacKensie answered.

Stamper held the throttles against the stops and the nose of the aircraft dropped as he started to descend, even before he had seen his quarry. The speed increased rapidly. Two-fifty knots... three hundred... and the aircraft juddered slightly as the wings were moved into the forty-five degree swept position. Four hundred, and the aircraft's controls became firmer in his hand.

'I've got it.' MacKensie's voice was quiet and devoid of any of the excitement he was feeling. This was Saturday night in a Glasgow pub. Keep it in; keep it low-key; show no emotions. 'Your three o'clock.'

'Got it.'

Stamper caught the mood and the aircraft levelled momentarily, and again they felt the G as he turned it hard to the south. The intended victim was lost for a few seconds as it passed beneath and then, as it appeared on the northern side, Stamper reversed the turn.

'Okay, I've got the second one of the pair. That makes three, but the other one must be well up with the leader and out of the way.'

The nose of the aircraft dipped to an angle of forty-five degrees and the speed nudged five hundred knots. Stamper's front windshield was entirely filled with a view of the ground. With the sun behind them, they had all the advantage. It had the ingredients of a good attack.

★

'Trent four, Linton Approach, you're clear through my overhead at five thousand feet, and clear to go low level to the north of the zone. The only traffic I have is medium altitude to the west. I think they must have all gone to lunch, except me.'

'Okay for some, eh? Thanks, Linton. Going low-level this time.'

Guy released the button of the transmit switch on the control column, and the frequency went quiet. He gently eased the nose of the aircraft down and, although the speed increased a little, he ignored it.

'Just ease back on the speed, Boss, or we are going to be ahead of the team.' Granger was quick to spot the increase. 'We've got about five minutes before we should see them, and they should be in our one o'clock.'

Guy pulled the levers back and jinked slightly to avoid a small cloud. As they dropped through three thousand feet, the world opened up. The last of the cloud was above them, and the visibility superb. Now Guy was in his element. The cares of half an hour ago were forgotten, and all the old feelings returned. Careers could go to hell – this was why he had joined.

The ground appeared to wake from its slumbers as they descended. Houses and farms seemed to shout their individuality. Trees emerged from hedgerows to stand proudly erect, and the distant horizon lost its flatness as hills and valleys created themselves before his eyes. At two thousand feet it all began to move. Slowly at first, and then more quickly as it got the idea until, at two-fifty feet, it was whirling past the cockpit with the gaiety of a May Day parade. Now the adrenaline was beginning to flow. Even the aircraft seemed to catch the mood and responded instantly to the smallest input from the pilot, climbing the side of a hill with the breathless fitness of an athlete, only to drop down the other side with the sureness of an Olympic skier.

'Get your eyes peeled, Boss. We're getting pretty close. Odd we haven't heard them?' Robin mused, half to himself 'The bounce must not have made his first attack.'

★

'Buster.'

The three pilots in the formation reacted instantly, simultaneously slamming their throttles forward to give maximum dry power, while the navigators craned their necks to spot the aggressor.

'Trent three, Bogie at four o'clock high, range two miles.'

Six pairs of eyes swivelled to Ord's precise call. He had not seen the bounce; just caught the flash of sunlight on its wings, but it was coming from precisely the direction he would have chosen had the roles been reversed.

'Not bad,' he muttered and knew that his call must have irritated Stamper and MacKensie.

They would have wanted to be closer before being spotted. Time was now on his side. He had at least a few seconds spare, and that time would give them vital speed. He worked out the angles. Just a couple more seconds and the bounce would get his sights locked on him. He could hear the sound of the radar in his headset.

'Two, three counter starboard,' Ord barked the order.

The rear pair banked hard, and the G-force rose to four-and-a-half on an unseen gauge, but no one noticed. They turned towards the bounce, and now the choice belonged to Stamper. He could follow Ord and get his kill, but with the knowledge that Jennings and Grice were making him the meat in the sandwich, or he could switch his attention to them. He chose Ord.

Ord and Langstaff were beginning to lose sight of the bounce, as he came hard into their six o'clock. They were now relying on the younger crew to make the calls, and it was getting very tight.

'Come on, come on,' Ord muttered impatiently.

'Bounce, switching to me, reverse the turn.' Jennings sounded anything but calm.

Ord rolled the aircraft through one hundred and twenty degrees of bank. Despite having done it a hundred times before, and in the certain knowledge that the other aircraft was unarmed, he felt a wave of relief. Now, if everyone played his part properly, the single aircraft, even though he had some advantage of position, should not be allowed to get a shot off.

Ord and Langstaff now craned their necks in the other direction. They were breathing like weightlifters, in short, gasping spurts. Ord's arms were beginning to get heavy. Then he saw his number two exactly where he expected him to be. Two fine sprays of dirty vapour streamed from the engines, straining at maximum thrust. He knew that on the ground the opinions of those watching would range from anger at the disturbance to wonder and admiration at the sight. As the Americans put it so succinctly, it was the sound of freedom. Low to his left, a small flock of sheep scurried a few yards in search of cover, and then halted as though needing a rethink. Ord took his eyes from the ground, and with a final wrench of his chubby neck, peered from the corners of his eyes at the gap between the two aircraft. The bounce was high, and rolling hard towards the number two.

'Have him visual, two,' he said to reassure his wingman and disconcert the attacker. 'Keep the turn going.'

He was tempted to go straight for the bounce, but was experienced enough to know that once the pair lost their mutual cover, they reduced their chances. It was also making an assumption that there was only one attacker. While that was true of this attack, the object was to practise for what might one day turn out to be a real situation with a real enemy and real weapons.

The bounce committed to the wingman. Ord could see the smoke from the engines cease and knew that he had engaged his afterburners.

'He's going for it in a hurry, Frank,' he grunted to Langstaff. 'The burners have just come in.'

'Getting a bit desperate, eh?' Langstaff allowed himself a small smirk. He was nervous in these situations, although it would have taken wild horses to drag it out of him. He thanked the gods nightly that he was crewed with Ord.

The bounce, to Ord's surprise, did not use the afterburners to give him extra speed, but to give him a better turn. He must have been close to the aircraft's limits as he seemed to turn away from the number three, and almost present his tail to him.

'What the bloody hell is he playing at?' Langstaff said. 'It's almost as though he were inviting you to have a go at him.'

'Looks like it.' Ord had no sooner got the remark out when the bounce came to an area of sky where the cloud cleared. The aeroplane seemed to rear upwards for a moment, and the bank was reversed. In the next few seconds, it was over the top of Ord, canopy to canopy. He caught a quick glimpse of the airbrakes extending, and then the wings swept forward to twenty-five degrees.

'The bastard's switching to us,' he said to Langstaff and then transmitted, 'Trent, keep the turn going, he's switching back to me.'

The calmness had gone from his voice. The feint had been brilliant and unexpected. In dragging off all his speed and quickly reducing his radius of turn, the bounce would, in the next thirty seconds, be right on his tail. But the attacker had put all his eggs in the one basket, because thirty seconds to a minute was all he had at the slower speed. After that, he was wide open to a counter-attack.

Ord now knew that he could not keep station with his wingman. The bounce had achieved part of his goal. If he reversed his turn he would fly straight across the front of the attacker and do his job for him. He needed to decrease his own radius of turn, and for that he needed afterburner. But afterburners were to heat-seeking missiles what blonde, busty girls were to sugar daddies. He held his hand firmly on the throttles, but resisted pushing through the detent, and tried to work out the new angles. The bounce was coming to his six o'clock, but would need a few more seconds to get inside the turn and get some lead on him. Was it possible for the number two to get across the gap between them in that time? Ord doubted it, but it was his best bet if he kept the turn going. He took a quick glance to the front to clear his flight path and then craned his suffering neck again to peer over his shoulder. He could see that Langstaff was doing the same thing.

Neither man saw the other aircraft. They felt it. Like the kiss of a wraith, sinister and frightening. Then all hell broke loose. As the aircraft caught the slipstream, it rolled violently onto its back and skewed, until the occupants felt it was travelling sideways. The great slab of the tail corrected it, but before Ord could get any sort of response from the controls, the nose pitched towards the ground. For what seemed a lifetime, he stared at the coarse moorland which filled the entire windscreen. He felt the controls respond and the temptation to roll the aircraft and pull at the same time was almost overwhelming, but he knew that that would only drag him into the ground. With all the courage he could muster, he held the aircraft in its descent towards the ground, released any back pressure, and spot-rolled the machine. Only when he was the right way up did he pull. He pulled like he had never done before. Six G, seven G – the limits were meaningless figures; all that mattered was that the aircraft responded, and slowly it did. But the deadly race between sky and ground was still on. Mother Earth, who nurtured and cared for her people, was now the enemy, and she wanted them. Both men screamed, silent, formless screams. The G-forces which pressed down on them were of no consequence, they were not felt. But the aircraft was filled with the life-force. It too wanted to survive and slowly, agonisingly slowly, it turned its face to the sky and survival.

'Jesus Christ! What the fucking hell was that?' Langstaff's voice came half-shout, half-sob.

Ord was too frozen on the controls to respond. He relaxed the back pressure and allowed the aircraft its moment of triumph as it soared towards the heavens. It could go on for ever for all he cared. He was still not sure that he had not died and was making a celestial ascent. Only the thumping of his heart told him that he was alive, and he wanted to shout for joy, but there was work to be done.

'Mayday, mayday. Trent three, we've had an airmiss. Knock it off, knock it off.'

'Bounce out.'

'Trent three from lead, are you okay?' The calls all seemed to come at once.

'Affirmative, lead, we're okay, but I've got more lights on in the cockpit than I can count. I'm heading for Leeming.'

'Three, from lead, do you need an escort?'

Ord was now in control of both the aircraft and his emotions. 'No thanks, most of them are just resets. I'll sort it out and, if they all reset, I might even continue back to base.'

'Right. Trent check-in.'

'Trent two.'

There was a short pause. 'Trent four, on frequency.'

'Trent four, confirm you're on frequency?' Cookson sounded surprised.

'Trent four, that is affirmative, we are on frequency.'

'Four from lead, do you know about the airmiss?' Again a pause.

'Er… lead from four, that might have been us; we got a bit close to someone, but no harm done.'

Ord and Langstaff heard the exchange. It was all they could do not to interject. 'Keep it, Frank. We'll have our say on the ground,' Ord spoke through clenched teeth.

Chapter Nineteen

Guy saw an aircraft almost immediately after Granger made his thirty-seconds-to-go call. He was quite proud of himself; the old lookout was still as good as ever. He watched it for a moment. It might just have been another stray Tornado in the area. It stayed high in his one o'clock, and appeared to be manoeuvring hard. Then it occurred to him that it was probably the bounce setting himself up.

'Trent formation, from Trent four.' There was no reply, and he tried again.

'Trent four, this is Linton approach. You're still on my frequency.' The call was weak, but clear.

'Shit, Robin, I thought I told you to take the radio and change freq.'

'No, sir, you've got the radio, and you never said a word.'

'Look, don't argue. Just change the bloody thing, and make the call.'

Guy sounded tetchy. He was watching the other aircraft and it was, through a series of twisting manoeuvres, holding position in his one o'clock. Suddenly, it turned hard across his nose, and started to grow very rapidly as the distance between them decreased. Then the second aircraft appeared. He could not believe what he was seeing. It was as though it had come out of the ground, belly up to him. There was not even time to warn his crewman. He just pulled and closed his eyes. A small whimper escaped his lips but was not strong enough to activate the microphone. Guy heard Robin quietly swear as the G forced him down. 'Sorry, Robin, there was another one. I didn't have time to call it.'

'Well, there's the second one below us now,' Granger called as they crossed Jennings and Grice by a hundred feet. They continued to the north. Guy was sorely tempted to continue in that direction and pretend they had been nowhere near the place. He knew he would never get away with it.

'Cookson must have changed the shape of the formation and pushed number two to the back,' he added weakly, trying to seek some explanation.

'He said he would,' Granger answered.

Guy's response was a grunt; his feelings towards his navigator were changing rapidly. He simply could not believe what was happening; did not want to believe it was happening. He wanted to run and hide. He wanted to be given the opportunity to relive the last few seconds, and he would lie, cheat, anything, to avoid being responsible for the happenings of the last minute. It could happen to anyone, he reasoned, risks of the job. Other people made mistakes all the time. He didn't. Not Guy Kelsall. Not in the air, anyway. It had never happened before. Sure, he made mistakes, everyone did, but he had always managed to hide them, and his reputation had stayed intact. Now that was gone in a matter of moments. He would be banded with some of the others on the squadron; the makeweights, the cannon fodder. The subject of the quotation in the squadron line-book: 'Flying in formation with him is like taking a naughty puppy for a walk'. No, he could not stand that. He would not have it. Granger would pay for this one.

'Jesus Christ; *Jesus Christ.*' Guy sounded on the verge of hysteria. 'It's your fault. If you'd changed the bloody radio over at the right time, none of this would have happened.'

'But you could have done it as well.' Granger's voice was full of anguish and hurt. 'It's not all my fault.'

'Shut up, just don't say another word.'

*

Stamper was feeling quite pleased with himself. He had been spotted sooner than he expected, but as it was Ord who had seen him first, it came as no surprise. He had hoped than Jennings would have been the nearest man. They were doing a fair job though. The formation was turning and thinking, and that was what he was supposed to achieve.

The situation was quickly developing into a stalemate, but then, on the counter, the sky in front of him had opened up and given him more room for manoeuvre in the vertical plane. He was aware that what he was going to do could be construed as aerobatics, but the chance was too good to miss. They could argue the case on the ground. He also knew that if he washed his speed off he would only get one chance. He could just imagine the look on Ord's face as he swept over the top. He was tempted to shout 'Got you, you bastard,' but knew he was dealing with the best, and the old dog might still have a trick or two up his sleeve. Once they had crossed sides, he was surprised that Ord did not call for a reverse turn, but merely tightened his turn. It gave Stamper a new problem. Instead of a relatively leisurely close-in for the kill, he would only have about half a minute before Jennings again became a factor in the fight. Suddenly, from nowhere, Jennings seemed to be there. Straight between the two aircraft, and from an unexpected side. 'How the hell did he do that?' Stamper asked, but before MacKensie could answer the calls came over the air.

'Let's get the hell out of here, Jim.'

*

Cookson reorganised his formation. He was tempted to ask what had happened, but this was not the place. It was sufficient that everyone was still in one piece. It would keep until the debrief.

'Trent two, you become Trent three. Number four, you become two.'

The call hit Guy like a further slap in the face. Cookson was making one of the junior pilots on the squadron a pairs-leader over him.

'Bounce, you stay out until after the first target, and let everyone settle down again. Trent, acknowledge.'

'Trent two.'

'Three.'

'Bounce.'

*

Jennings and Grice could hardly contain their emotions.

'Did you see it, Bertie? Did you see how bloody close they came? A whisker, I swear it was a bloody whisker!'

'I missed it, Hunch. But I saw how close three came to hitting the ground. I'll bet Ord and Langstaff'll have no need for laxatives over the next few days, that's for sure. He missed that heather by feet; in fact, when he cleans out the intakes, he can probably go down to Covent Garden and sell the stuff at sixpence a bunch. We could sell tickets for this debrief.'

'Yeah, that's for sure. The Boss against Cookson; a bit like a heavyweight championship.'

Despite the chat and the fact that the bounce would not reattack for several minutes, their heads were going like metronomes, from side to side. The experience had only served to remind them that they were in a dangerous business.

'Bloody close, though.' Hunch could not get it out of his mind.

'Shut up, Hunch, and get on with the job. The target is coming up in a few minutes, so get it sorted in your head what you're looking for.'

'You're right, Bertie, but shit, was it ever close?'

'I feel sorry for poor old Robin Granger. The Boss will find some way of pinning the blame on him.' Bertie was grunting as he tried to talk while moving his head.

'No, why should he? The jet looked like it was right in front of them; that's the Boss's area of lookout.'

'I'll just bet you, that's all. I've flown with him, and he doesn't *make* mistakes; at least he doesn't admit to them. Anyway, get your head down; we're coming in to the first target.'

They passed through the first target, and felt that the film would show it to be a good attack. The buried water tanks, which were simulating a camouflaged headquarters, went straight down the middle of Hunch's bomb-fall line, and he allowed himself a small triumphant 'yes' as the automatic release took place. They came hard off the target to their right and craned over their shoulders until the other aircraft came into sight and then, with a further hard jink in the opposite direction, they were in good battle formation.

Concentration was poor over the next few minutes. The bounce made two attacks in quick succession, and claimed a kill on both of them. It was not his intention to make both the intercepts on Jennings and Grice, but that was the way it turned out; the fact that neither Guy nor Granger picked him up when it was their call did nothing to improve the already-strained atmosphere in their cockpit. Guy was pleased to get through the second target without further humiliation.

All the members of the formation were beginning to settle down. Drills had to be carried out, and the simple matter of coping with the routine of fuel checks and position updates brought some order to the operation. They swept to the east of Newcastle and the weather in the southern part of Scotland, if possible, improved, with the air as clear as wine. The ground seemed to shine with newness after recent rain. The hills were all umbers and ochres, and the rivers glinted as the sun caught their reflection. The sky changed colour from cerulean at the horizon to a deep cobalt above their heads. It was a place to stop and admire; to breathe in the air, and cast all worldly woes to one side. Guy did not see any of it. His mind was on the bounce. Where would he come from if he were flying the aircraft? How would he go about it? He went through the last three attacks again to see if there were any patterns being followed by Stamper and MacKensie.

They had come in high twice and once from low-level. All the attacks had been from the rear, and Guy had a feeling that Stamper, flushed with his success, would want to try something more adventurous. The hills were becoming more mountainous and an aircraft could easily hide among them. Guy was still watching over his shoulders but, more and more, he felt that the aggressor would come from somewhere in the front quadrants. Then he saw it. No more than a fleeting glance between the ridges before it disappeared, but it was enough. He kept silent, not wishing to alert Stamper, but made the slightest of turns away from his partner, widening the gap between them. The bounce would have to show himself in the next few seconds and when he did, it would be time enough to alert the number three.

'You're getting a bit wide, Boss. We'll lose cross-cover if you widen any more.' Granger sounded anything but confident about his assertion.

'I know, Robin, but you'll see why in about three seconds.' Guy just had time to get his reply in before he heard the call.

'Buster.' The call came from Grice.

The bounce was directly in front of Guy, but was too close for a straight shot. Stamper was a little shocked that the aircraft were not quite where he expected them to be. He reacted by climbing slightly to leave room between himself and the nearest one. It cost him a few precious knots of his speed and, in taking time to make up his mind which to attack, lost some of his positional advantage. The two aircraft, apart from increasing power, had yet to react, and the bounce went high between them, waggled gently, as thought still in doubt about which to take on, and then committed to the number three. Guy smiled to himself; he was looking for his first kill of the day.

'Counter starboard.' Guy's call was crisp and businesslike.

The other aircraft cranked on the bank as it turned towards him and the sun glinted momentarily off its canopy. The bounce followed, expecting Guy to keep his heading for a short time and then follow his wingman to keep the parallel formation. Guy had other priorities. He wanted Stamper in his sights, and nothing else. No matter if there was a second aircraft; no matter if he were losing cross-cover. All that mattered was his pride. He paused for a second until the tail of the bounce aircraft was abeam him and then pulled for the vertical.

'What are you doing, sir? We'll lose cross-cover.' The catch in Granger' s voice relayed his feelings.

Guy did not reply. At two thousand feet, he rolled the aircraft on its back and gently pulled the nose down to the horizon. He had it just right. The bounce was now in his two o'clock, and turning straight back across his nose after Jennings and Grice. They were lambs to the slaughter if Guy got the next thirty seconds right.

He cranked the wings to the forward position as the speed decreased through two-fifty knots, and pulled hard towards the bounce. His radius of turn was now far smaller than the faster aircraft, but if he did not get into position quickly and correctly, he would not get a second chance. So far so good, he was manoeuvring inside the circle of the other and cutting the distance between them. The bounce appeared in the top of his windscreen and seemed to stay there. 'Come on, come on,' Guy muttered between gritted teeth.

He wanted to use his afterburner, but he was already close to minimum fuel for completing the rest of the low-level and getting to the tanker. Slowly the aircraft started to slide down the window. Guy engaged the missile system and the tracking cross appeared in his head-up display. With his thumb working the wheel on the control column, he quickly moved the mark until it was lying over the aircraft and waited for the radar tracking from the missile head to make a lock-on. Again, it seemed to take an age, and Guy had the urge to yell at it, but, at the peak of his frustration, it locked and the tell-tale distance circle appeared around his quarry.

'Fox two,' he called in jubilation.

The film would confirm his kill. His mood lightened.

'That's the way to treat these young upstarts, eh, Robin? They think they're the only kids on the block.'

Granger did not reply; he just wanted to be on the ground and out of the aeroplane.

Chapter Twenty

The formation pulled out of low-level to the south of Berwick, and immediately the change of atmosphere engulfed them. Gone was the frenetic pace of flying at two hundred and fifty feet with the ground rushing by them. There was a peace. Even the noise in the cockpit seemed lower, and for the first time the crews took the opportunity to take a leisurely look around and marvel at the sights. Hunch took off his face mask and dragged a hand across his mouth, luxuriating in breathing fresh air for the first time in an age. With the first lungful his features contorted in apparent agony, and he quickly clamped his mask over his face. 'You've farted in here, haven't you? You dirty bastard.' His voice was shrill with indignation and disgust.

'It was only a little one, honestly.' Bertie sounded anything but contrite. 'Anyway, with your flying, I would be justified in shitting myself. Besides, I thought it would give you something to talk about. Take your mind off the tanking by providing you with comfortable, home-like surroundings.'

'They might be comfortable, home-like surroundings for you, my son, but some of us live in homes where the sounds are those of fluttering angels' wings, and the scents are the incense of the gods.'

'You call wallowing in the sounds of heavy metal and last night's extra-hot curry angels' wings and incense? I've been in your room when it would be unwise to let a fully trained decontamination team in without giving them twenty-four hours' notice.'

'Look, just shut up, Bertie. I'm trying to get myself in the mood for the delicate operation ahead. I feel a good one coming on, and I don't need unpleasant odours clouding the issue.'

Tanking was one of the few operational pursuits left entirely to the pilot. Some navigators tried to help by giving verbal guidance, but in the end it was down to the skill of the pilot.

Bertie had tried it all with Hunch. He had talked. He had shut up. He had talked about something completely different and one time had been in the middle of a joke as they had come up behind the tanker, but it had all been of little use. Hunch seemed to freeze once he got into position. He was not the smoothest pilot at the best of times, but mention the word tanker and he became downright ragged.

They continued up to eighteen thousand feet. The tanker would be at twenty. Cookson had checked them in on the fighter control frequency, where the tanker would be listening.

'He's forty miles on your nose in a right-hand racetrack. He has a couple of chicks with him, but they'll be gone in a couple of minutes, so you should have him all to yourselves for the next twenty minutes.' The ground controller sounded bored as he stared into his radar tube.

Hunch heard Cookson acknowledge the call, and gave a small sigh of relief. He found it difficult enough doing the job when he was being watched by those he knew, but if there were members of a strange squadron there looking over his shoulder, it was far more intimidating. Debriefs following refuelling exercises seemed to be full of people trying to find the best simile for his performance.

'It was like watching an elephant shagging a camel in a cupboard,' or 'like a sword fighter with a melon stuck up his arse,' had been two of the most recent. Hunch invariably grinned and thought of a suitable reply, but it was beginning to get on his nerves.

'Don't look at the basket,' he heard Bertie say. 'Look at the marks under the wing of the tanker and fly in formation with them, but most of all *relax*. I'll get tense enough for both of us. A joke, Hunch, honest, just a little joke in very poor taste,' he added quickly.

Nothing would have given Bertie greater pleasure than to watch his friend enter smoothly and pick up his fuel. It was pure frustration to sit helplessly in the back, and not be able to do a thing to help, while Hunch parried and thrust, lurched and shied. Bertie often thought that if he had closed his eyes and just taken a wild stab, he might have done better. Now, he tried to divorce himself from the operation, even to the point of removing his mask and grinning at anyone who was watching with his shoulders and hands raised as if to say, 'Nothing to do with me, mate'. He knew it was tantamount to an act of disloyalty, but sometimes he could not help himself.

Hunch was beginning to think that his inability reflected somehow on his manhood. The act was so overtly sexual that the comparison was valid. Simply put, a large phallic object needed to be inserted into a gently receptive basket before the juices of life, in this case aviation fuel, could flow. He had tried all forms of persuasion from gentle coaxing to the nearest equivalent to rape, but with little success. The basket seemed to sense his overeagerness, and despite an early response to his advances, turned its face away at the last minute. He felt it was undoubtedly female in its behaviour. It was outwardly shy and skittish. It issued a come-on and yet played hard to get. Unacceptable advances were treated to a stinging rebuke as the basket flung itself loudly against the side of the cockpit. If, on the other hand, the approach was the right one, it would be accepted with the softness of a kiss. Hunch had only experienced that once. It had happened almost by accident when he had still been concentrating on the line-up and Bertie had whispered, 'Go for it, Hunch'. The feeling had stayed with him and wanting it to return was almost a drug.

The problem had even crept into his sex life. 'Why did you do that?' he had found it necessary to ask after making love to his current girlfriend.

'Why did I do what?' She dreamily stretched across the bed and tickled the underside of his chin with a long index finger.

'Put it in for me?'

'Put what in for you?' A frown crossed her brow and she propped herself up on one elbow and stared at him, oblivious of her nakedness.

'You know... it. When we did *it*, you put it in for me.' He glanced absently towards the end of the bed.

She followed the direction of his eyes and a look of understanding crossed her face.

'You want to know why I helped you to put your... er... thingy,' she searched for the right words but failed to come up with a better term, and indicated the general area of his crotch with a small shake of her head, 'in... er... that is to say, while we were making love?'

'In a word, yes.' He could feel his cheeks becoming warm.

'Have you been eating jelly babies again and they've gone to your head? What on earth do you want to know something like that for? Is it not sufficient to know that somehow or other it gets done?' Her tone was becoming a little aggressive. 'I always do it for you. That's the way it is.' She flung her head hard against the pillow and rolled away from him onto her side. Her entire body language suggested that he let the matter rest. He surveyed the delicious curve from waist to knee and had an urge to run his hand along its length, but his mind was totally occupied with other things.

'You don't think I'm capable of doing it on my own, do you?' he suddenly blurted.

'It's not a question of whether or not I think you're capable of doing it on your own.' Her voice held a dangerously menacing tone, as though she were speaking through clenched teeth. 'I thought it was a joint operation and the question of demarcation had never arisen. If you feel that you want someone who just lies there and lets you get on with it then you had better find somebody else to do it with.' She moved over to face him and two small dots of red highlighted her otherwise pale cheeks. She pulled the covers round herself and sat erect on the bed, staring hard at him. Again, the signals were unmistakable and Hunch knew he should have left it there but could not.

'No, no, it's not that.' Rule one: when in a hole, stop digging, occurred to him but the advice went adrift. 'It's just that, well, I've been having a bit of trouble with my tanking lately; you know not being able to make a smooth entry and all that and I just wondered if...' He didn't get to finish the sentence. A naked body flashed before his eyes, a bundle of clothing clutched to its chest, and rushed into the bathroom.

'If you think I'm going to stay around here and listen to you prattle on about who should do what during the act of love-making, and then be compared to a Victor tanker then you've got another think coming.' Her sentences came in short pants as she hurriedly wrestled on her clothing. She reappeared, stuffing nylons into her handbag and was through the door without a backward glance.

'Listen, love, I wasn't comparing you to a—'

By the time Hunch had followed her to the door, it was pointless; she was no longer even in the corridor.

★

The four aircraft had moved closer together, enabling Cookson to manoeuvre more easily onto the tanker. 'Trent, tanker at twenty miles in your twelve o'clock. Do you need any more assistance?' The voice sounded keen to go for a cup of tea.

'No thanks, Border. We can take it from here. You're happy with that, aren't you, Jack?' Cookson added, talking only to Frost.

'Yes, I've had him on radar for the last ten miles now, with a good point. You probably need to come about five degrees to the right to get a good angle on him.' Frost as always sounded confident. 'You should be able to see him in a couple of seconds in your half past eleven.'

'I've got him. Spot on, Jack.' Cookson kept the line he was flying until the dot on the horizon started to move slowly into the ten o'clock position. Then he turned towards it. At first it looked as though he had gone too soon and that the formation would finish in front of the tanker. He held it steady in the centre of the windscreen and slowly, as the larger aircraft grew in size, its aspect, relative to them, altered until they were a thousand yards behind and closing the gap quickly.

'Trent, you're clear to join on the port.' The tanker captain's voice broke the silence. It was the only call of the well-rehearsed scenario. Cookson expertly converted the remainder of his excess speed to height as he climbed through the thousand feet of safe height that separated the two units.

The VC10 continued to grow as they closed the gap. Its sand-coloured camouflage glowed golden in the afternoon sunshine. The sight never failed to impress Hunch. The great, long, sleek aircraft, with the four engines stuck up under its tail almost as an afterthought, seemed to hang motionless in the sky. The only movement was the gentle rocking of the two Tornados between him and the tanker. It was a sight to die for, and yet he could feel himself tightening up as he looked at it. Slowly, the two baskets attached to their hoses snaked out from their wing pods and swayed in the slipstream. At least he would not have to wrestle with the main fuselage hose, which had the extra problem of being difficult to line up on.

'Clear on.' The tanker pilot's voice sounded remote and disinterested.

Cookson and Stamper in turn dropped a few feet, and then moved across behind the tanker, carefully avoiding its slipstream. They each settled behind a basket and waited, Cookson on the starboard side and Stamper on the port, then both moved slowly forward. Hunch watched, mesmerised. He was hardly breathing. Part of him wanted them to make a pig's ear of the thing, and part wished he could make it look so easy. They both got to within a few yards and again paused, as though they were talking to the basket, telling it they would be gentle and not hurt it – just keep still and it would be okay. Cookson moved first. It looked for a moment as though he was going to drive the nose of the aircraft right into the basket. As the gap closed to a couple of yards, the basket felt the bow wave of the aircraft and dutifully moved down the starboard side of the jet and, as if drawn by a magnet, directly onto the probe. Hunch allowed himself to breathe.

'That's the way to do it; that's the way to do it.' Bertie's voice was a mimic of Mr Punch.

Now Stamper moved forward. The routine appeared exactly the same. Pause, forward a little, wait for the basket to move and then in. This time the basket was dancing to a different tune and as the probe came into contact it snagged on the rim and the two locked together. The basket moved through almost ninety degrees before Stamper was able to stop his forward motion and back off. The probe and basket disengaged themselves and the basket, released from its captivity, shook itself in the airflow like a wet dog emerging from a river.

'You can do that, Hunch. You're as good as he is.' Again Bertie, in his own nervousness, could not resist the jibe.

'Get stuffed, Grice. If navigators had to do this, every basket in Her Majesty's Air Force would look like lace curtains in a haunted house.'

Stamper reorganised himself and gently moved forward. The basket and probe again appeared to eye each other up and the Tornado waggled slightly before the two came together.

'Fuel flows.' The faceless voice in the tanker acknowledged that two good contacts had been made. The two Tornados lay beneath the VC10 like contented pups beneath their mother. The world lapsed into silence again.

'Just remember, Hunch. Don't look at the basket, formate on the wing markings, and it'll be all right. Even Stamper didn't get it the first time, so there is no rush.' Bertie sounded like a mother talking to her child on the first day of school.

'You're right, Bertie. Formate on the lines and relax.'

'I am relaxed, Hunch.'

'Not you, you fool, me.'

'Trent one and two, you've had your quota, clear to disconnect.' The aircraft slid backwards, dragging the hose with them. At the full extent of the reel, the probes disengaged, and again the baskets shook violently before the airflow calmed them. As Cookson and Stamper moved to the starboard side the controller said, 'Three and four, clear behind.'

Hunch hit the switch, and the probe grew out off the side of the aircraft. He felt it drag in the slipstream, and the aircraft yawed slightly in response. The whole thing felt heavier and more difficult to fly until he pressed his left foot on the rudders to correct the drag and then trimmed. 'Relax.' Bertie could hear Hunch talking to himself.

They moved down, stabilised and then crossed beneath the rear of the VC10. It seemed to grow, and for a moment filled the whole sky before they emerged on the other side. The basket sat directly in front of them, gently rocking from side to side. Hunch could have sworn it was grinning at him. He frowned and banished the image from his mind. 'Inanimate, fucking object,' he grunted with a hint of disdain.

'What was that, Hunch?'

'Nothing, Bert, just talking to the basket.'

'Addressing an equal then?'

Hunch chose to ignore the remark. He glanced along the underside of the VC10's wing and found the guidance marks, adjusted his position and waited. The lights on the top of the basket housing changed from red to green. It was the signal to proceed.

'Clear to engage.' The remark was superfluous. In the corner of his left eye, Hunch could already see his boss moving forward. In what seemed only a few seconds he was in and the controller announced, 'Fuel flows on the port.'

It was a little extra pressure that Hunch could have done without. 'Right, here goes,' he muttered. Hunch moved the aircraft a fraction to the left and climbed a few feet. The basket hovered a couple of yards in front of the aircraft's nose. No matter how hard he tried to ignore it and fly on the tanker's guidelines, it was there. He pushed the throttles forward and the gap between them closed, slowly at first, and then more rapidly as the engines began to overcome the inertia. The basket moved in copy-book fashion: slightly sideways on the bow wave and then upwards. Hunch caught the sight of it heading dutifully towards the basket and his heart gave a small leap of joy. What he failed to notice was the rate the two were coming together. With a mighty click they were joined. A bullseye, a hole in one, a triumph.

'A bit quick, Hunch,' he heard Bertie exclaim from the rear.

Hunch pulled his left hand back a fraction in response to Bertie's call and grinned under his mask in acknowledgement of his triumph. That would show the bastards. He glanced quickly at the basket firmly ensconced on the probe before turning back to look at the wing of the tanker. To his horror the windscreen was rapidly filling with the basket pod. He had nowhere to go but to follow the hose as it was pushed into its housing. His hand pulled back on the throttles until there was no further movement to be had. But still he pulled, and still the aircraft moved towards the pod. When the relative movement stopped, he was six feet from its rear, with the airbrakes out, and his feet hurting from pressing on the ground brakes. If they had been on the runway, rubber would have been scattered to the four winds. His eyes were saucers, and he almost felt on first-name terms with the rivets that surrounded the pod. The underside of the tanker had lost its romantic golden glow of a few minutes previously, and was now oil-streaked and slightly battered. For a brief, endless moment, it was his world. The sun had set, and he had visions of being sucked into the black hole.

On the starboard side, four unseen mouths, which had started to grin at the sight of Hunch closing too rapidly, were fixed in mirthless grimaces. Inside the tanker the controller crossed himself and mouthed a silent prayer. Only Kelsall sat in relative ignorance of the charade, quietly congratulating himself on his own tanking prowess.

Slowly, achingly slowly, the two machines began to separate. Hunch allowed himself a small gasp of air which rattled around his throat. He would live, the tanker crew would live, their children would have fathers for another day. The sun reappeared in the sky.

The gap opened. Ten feet, twenty feet and his left hand started to push forward on the throttle. Thirty feet, and although they were still travelling over the ground at a speed of three hundred miles an hour, they appeared to be going backwards; downhill like a kid on a very slippy slide. Forty feet, and the hose could not hold them, and snapped away from the probe. They careered over the cliff in stomach-leaving, sphincter-clenching freefall. Hunch wanted to put his arms outwards to break his fall, and Bertie held stupidly onto the window struts. By the time Hunch's brain had told him there was a better way to do it, and the engines had had time to wind up, they were forty feet below the tanker. It took several seconds for the sinking feeling to stop and a few more before Bertie found his voice. 'Well, Hunch. With the obvious small error excepted, that was spot on, now go and do it again.'

'Not too bad was it, Bert? I think I've made a significant step forward there. Not to mention a very significant step back. Do you think that I've got time for a bloody good cry before I have another go?' Hunch was breathless.

It took Hunch ten minutes to get his fuel. During that ten minutes the world turned in slow motion as he closed the gap, stabilised and moved again towards the basket. An aerial ballet followed. The probe and basket danced and pirouetted, cavorted and teased. They touched and kissed. The audience held its breath. They willed a union. They wanted to shout encouragement, to get out and hold things steady, and their muscles ached in the helplessness of inactivity. When the union came it was not the sweet reunion of lovers; it was more the savage handshake after the quarrel. Reluctant and giving little quarter, but an ending nonetheless.

'Fuel flows.' For the first time the faceless voice within the tanker held a note of humanity. No congratulations, no 'well done', not even a sigh, but the words were music to the ears of all who watched. Cookson made a note that he would fly with Hunch, and sort it out once and for all. Guy made a note that he would sort it.

Chapter Twenty-One

The bounce stayed with the formation. Cookson wanted four aircraft on this target run. He wanted no extra reasons for Kelsall to find fault, and had asked them to fill the empty slot. MacKensie, being the professional he was, had a copy of each of the runs. They followed the tanker to the western edge of its racetrack, and as the great aircraft, which had been the centre of their world for fifteen minutes, turned away, they all felt a sense of loss. The sky became a void, and it took moments to readjust to the new horizon.

They dropped to low-level, picked up the route to the south of Montrose, and widened into the standard battle formation. The initial point came quickly. Cookson held a straight line, while a thousand yards to his left he saw Stamper make a slight turn away. He followed the points on the ground, his thumb expertly following the line on the map. The map between his legs shifted slightly. Frost had just made the first update on his radar, and he watched the cross in his head-up display hunt for the next point. Cookson realised that he was just a back-up, but more than once he had talked Frost into a correct update when the expected points had not materialised.

'Fifteen seconds, Tom,' Frost grunted monotonously.

Cookson looked to his left. He could see his wingman, back in his eight o'clock, almost nose-on to him. He would pass behind, but the distance looked less than he had expected. He told himself that it was all right and that he was just used to seeing a greater separation. Over his right shoulder, he could just make out Hunch in the far distance, yet to turn in.

'Ten seconds.'

'Visual, Jack, the line up looks good.'

He could see clearly the old, cracked and broken runway of the disused airfield. The wind was from the right and, as the sight corrected for it, the aircraft appeared to be sliding down the side of the strip. Cookson held the line and waited until the bombsight reverted to normal to indicate that the run was complete. It seemed to have taken a lifetime to get rid of the simulated load of bombs and minelets. 'God, I wouldn't like to sit through that for real,' he gasped between clenched teeth as he hauled the aircraft through a tight turn and strained to look over his shoulder for the next one through. 'It was all I could do to keep the wings level as it was. If someone down there were shooting at me it would be near impossible.'

'You're not kidding. I had exactly the same thoughts. How are the others doing?' Frost grunted, as he in turn strained to peer over his shoulder.

'I can see the number two, he looks in the right place and yes, there's number three coming up behind him. The spacing looks pretty good, although I can't see the Boss.' Speaking against the pressure of the G the words seemed to be coming out of his nose.

Cookson jinked the aircraft sharply one way and then reversed the turn to get a better look behind. As he did so, the fourth aircraft passed over the far end of the runway. The whole thing had been compressed into less than forty-five seconds and, as Cookson straightened to continue on track, he was able to look directly across and see Stamper and MacKensie in perfect battle formation.

'Well, so far so good, Tom. All we need now is the Boss to approve, and we might be able to make some headway working out the tactics for this bloody thing, because whatever we say, it looks like it's here to stay.'

★

Guy Kelsall and Robin Granger were bringing up the rear of the attack. This was the slot that would be most vulnerable in an airfield attack. The guns would now be fully manned and their crews alert. If the attack were solely oriented to the runway direction, it would not take a man with much intellect to predict in which direction the next aircraft would be coming. Had the first three aircraft been lucky enough to survive, number four would have had to be extremely lucky. The atmosphere in the cockpit had been nothing short of icy since the airmiss, and no matter what Granger did, it was wrong. He was fast losing confidence, which was only making things worse. By the time they reached their initial point, it was all he could do to keep the navigation equipment up to date. He knew Kelsall blamed him for the airmiss, but the more he thought about it the more unjust it seemed. He was no longer being asked for information, but had the feeling that his pilot had reverted more and more to single-seat methods of operating. He was being cut out of the loop. If it had been any other pilot in the front seat, he would have folded his arms and said, 'Okay, if you're so bloody clever, you get on with it,' knowing full well that a JP233 attack could not be carried out from the front seat.

Guy was now in no doubt that Granger was to blame for the airmiss, and his performance since had hardened that opinion. The man seemed like a total incompetent. He was so flustered that even simple checks were beyond him. Guy had already made his mind up that this would be the last time they would fly together and the sooner Granger was off his squadron the better.

Guy was now working very hard, but in his element. This was how it had been in the early days, just him and the machine. He was not too worried about the navigation. He had been able to watch the other aircraft, and could see from his moving map display that Granger had kept the inertial platform reasonably up to date. The target was close, and he increased his vigilance. In the clear Scottish air he could see the number two swing out to his left, and he put all his effort into finding the IP. In his opinion, it was the worst of all the IPs that Granger had chosen. It was a small wood and, although unique, it was on the down side of a hill. It would be a late show.

Guy glanced across and saw his wingman turn away, starting his run. The IP could only be a mile away; less than eight seconds and he had yet to make contact. Not for the first time that day, he cursed his navigator silently, and wished he had taken the trouble to do his own planning. Then he saw it. It was almost abeam him, and he was unable to overfly it. No matter. He started the stopwatch instinctively and corrected hard to his left. The suddenness of the movement surprised and alarmed Granger, but he kept his mouth shut. His head was buried in the cockpit furiously trying to find his radar fix, and sudden turns were not helping his cause.

Guy had the aircraft back on track. This he could do. He had done it a thousand times. It had been his forte. He was the best. What he had failed to take account of was the nature of this attack. This was a back-seat attack. Only Granger could generate the correct symbology in his head-up display. He could overfly the target as accurately as possible and still it would be futile.

Granger got his fix position. It was the sharp corner of wood, and it showed up on his radar like a dream. He moved his mark, changed the gearing and finely tuned it. As he inserted it into the kit, the map slewed to the correct position, and he went through the weapons selection checks. He was ready. He moved his cursor mark forward down the run and searched the scope for his next feature. This one was only a small building and a bonus if he found it, but now, today of all days, he wanted it. His heart leapt with joy. There it was; not much of it, but it was sharp and well focused. He moved the cursor and inserted. The response was almost negligible, but it was the difference between a good mark on the target and a great mark. He knew the mark was great. 'Ten seconds to go,' Granger muttered.

Guy almost resented the intrusion on his run. He was on the line; he was in total control – who did Granger think he was? He had done nothing right all day, and now he was stating the obvious. He had even had time to watch the other aircraft through the target. They had been close to each other but the attacks had all come from different directions and so the separation had not mattered. It appeared to work.

'Commit.' Granger sounded urgent.

'What?' Guy was slightly startled.

'Commit or the weapon will not come off. It's your release button that's active.' Granger wanted to add 'You fucking moron', but he left it unsaid.

'Of course.' Guy tried to sound as though it were all under control, but in reality the thought had not occurred to him. He just managed to raise the guard and hit the bomb-release button as the bomb-release cursor hit the first mark in the head-up display. The two lines indicating the start and end of the weapon's release straddled the runway perfectly. It was a good attack, and it dawned on Guy for the first time that no matter how good his map-reading had been the real work of setting up the attack had been done in the back cockpit. He said nothing. As far as he was concerned, Granger was history on his squadron.

*

The Grampians loomed ahead of them, bathed in full summer sunshine. The small amounts of cloud they had encountered further south had completely dispersed. These were the Highlands at their perfect best. The edges of the mountains cut into the sky like a photograph in perfect focus. The early bloom of the heather had passed its best, but the hills retained the sheen of purple. Stamper wanted to stop and admire the view, but the mountains demanded attention of a different kind. This was hard, physical graft. It was sweated, manual labour and contrasted sharply with popular public image of the fighter pilot. They crossed the valley floors and the G-gauge registered four as they pulled to avoid the sides. The pressure relaxed for a moment, and then seconds before the ridge line, the aircraft was almost on its back as Stamper rolled and pulled down the other side of the ridge. Then for a breath-stopping moment, it was like diving inverted into a blue hole before the machine was righted, and they skimmed down the other side. For long periods the other aircraft were out of sight as they followed their own tracks, only momentarily appearing on ridges, before quickly disappearing. The effect when viewed from afar was like dolphins jumping in the wake of a boat.

They passed through Glen Coe and the Three Sisters glowered down, the noise disturbing their regal slumber. Halfway between valley floor and summit, a small group of walkers stopped to watch their progress. Whether they cursed the intrusion or admired the sight, MacKensie could only wonder. He could see one of them raise a hand; then they were gone.

This was the nearest that Great Britain had to a wilderness, and yet the marks of man were everywhere. A reservoir, a small single-tracked railway fighting its way through the barriers of the ground, as though still looking for the best route to take, and man-made forests on every hillside. The moorland, scarred by the fires of the gamekeepers, looked like giant Paisley-patterned ties. Yet the dignity and majesty of the place was untouched.

The Great Glen appeared in breathtaking suddenness. The fabled home of the Loch Ness monster lay quiet and mysterious between the mountains guarding it on either side. To the south, the waters danced and glinted in the afternoon sun, but to the north, they appeared dark and brooding. A small craft chugged its way defiantly down the centre, leaving ripples in its wake which lazily stretched to both banks, its smallness emphasising the greatness of its surroundings. The formation hugged the sides, looking for protection from the great banks surrounding them. Two aircraft on each side, they flew towards Inverness and the Tain range.

'Fucking brilliant.' MacKensie's words broke the spell.

'Is that the son of Robbie Burns speaking, or did you come up with that poetic soliloquy on your own, because it does seem to measure the moment perfectly.' Stamper grinned to himself.

'No.' MacKensie sounded serious. 'That was entirely my own work. Such poetry, as we Scots have, is drawn from the surroundings that we have. If your chap Shakespeare had been given this sort of inspiration, think what dizzy heights he might have reached.'

'You have a point there. We could have had Juliet wearing a kilt, and Romeo, standing below the balcony, giving her a few reels from the bagpipes. It does have a certain ring to it.'

'Might not have ended in tragedy though,' MacKensie reasoned. 'They could all have got together at the end and had a couple of whiskies.'

'And I suppose in the end, she would have got her trollies off and they could have had a rare old romp in the hay,' Stamper added.

'Now, you're talking my kind of play.'

They skirted to the west of Inverness, and turned towards the mouth of the Firth of Cromity. Cookson changed frequency and checked them in.

'Tain, this is Trent formation. Four aircraft for lay-down target three.'

'Trent, from Tain. You're clear to attack, call me thirty seconds out.'

They heard the controller order his other traffic up to two thousand feet and both wingmen turned behind their section leaders, until they were in long line astern.

'Okay, we've got a package; the left pylon is selected and it's armed; confirm that it's my bomb.' MacKensie was businesslike again.

This time real lumps of metal were going to fall from the aircraft, and although they were practically inert, giving only a small flash and some smoke, there was no room for error.

'That's confirmed,' Stamper replied. 'Your bomb unless it looks horrendous.'

Stamper could not resist the proviso. Squadron averages were all.

They rolled onto the attack track behind Cookson, and the aircraft bucked slightly as it caught the slipstream of the leading aircraft. Stamper watched MacKensie work through his head-up display. He could see the marker move almost to the periphery of his screen and flash. He was looking for a small lighthouse. The marker stopped to the side of the building, then moved over it and stopped flashing. MacKensie had found his point. The head-up display jumped to follow the insert, and Stamper looked down the line of his own sight for any sign of the target. He knew from experience that it would be a late show, which is why he did not mind MacKensie running the attack. The split target line which marked the position of the target was slightly to his right, and he moved the aircraft so that the bomb-fall line ran down the middle of the split.

The coast looked almost yellow from the combined effects of sun and wind. For a time it appeared still, and then suddenly rushed towards them.

'You've got the target marked?' Stamper could feel the slight increase in his adrenaline levels.

'It's... just... coming... in. Got it,' MacKensie enthused.

The mark moved again, and came to rest right in the middle of the target area at the same time as Stamper saw it.

'Good mark, Ian.' Stamper was hard pressed to keep the admiration from his voice.

'I'll just refine it a little.'

Before Stamper could shout, 'No', the mark shot about thirty yards to the left of the circle. He could not stand seeing a good run wasted. In the remaining three seconds before the release, he moved three switches, drove his own marker back to the target, and hit the bomb-release switch. He banked the aircraft hard, looked into his rear-view mirror, and silently prayed that the score would be good enough to justify him taking over.

'Trent two, ten feet at two o'clock.' The range controller showed no emotion.

'What the hell were you playing at? I thought it was my bomb.' MacKensie sounded annoyed.

'When I say "good mark", it means precisely that.' Stamper's precise English accent for once grated on MacKensie's ears. 'What it doesn't mean is, go and have a play with it because you might improve on perfection. You moved it to at least forty feet away from a direct hit. I just couldn't let you be ranked with the also-rans.'

'Trent four sixty feet at twelve o'clock.' The controller interrupted them at just the right moment.

'Like the Boss, for instance,' Stamper added.

They both laughed. 'Nevertheless, you owe me a pint for gross interference,' MacKensie snarled.

'Done. In fact, I'll buy you two, if you promise not to tell anyone I interfered with you.'

Chapter Twenty-Two

The peace and quiet of altitude returned as they cruised back to Norfolk at twenty-five thousand feet. The responsibility of lookout had been given over to the radar unit. It was the perfect place to be, and except for the temperature gauge which registered minus forty-two degrees and the wind reading of ninety-six knots, it looked as though one could step outside and enjoy the scenery. Above them the sky was a deep navy blue. The old Lightning pilot's domain of 'where the blue turns to black' was now the playground of astronauts. Stamper was worried about his fuel. He had used more than the others as the bounce, and had lingered longer than he had wanted, waiting for Hunch to take on his fuel. He had done the calculation several times, and MacKensie had assured him that there was sufficient to get home. Nevertheless, the uncomfortable feeling remained, and he had mentally listed all the bolt holes he could make on the way back to base. He had disciplined himself to leave the throttles alone, and in consequence was slowly dropping behind the other three.

The sun was now well out over the Irish Sea. The Lake District, North Wales, and the Isle of Man stood out dark against the golden shimmer of the sea. Beneath them, the dark greens and browns of Scotland and Northern England were slowly changing to the yellowing cornfields of the South. The crews, after the best part of three hours of intense concentration, allowed their minds to wander. They looked down on familiar places, and remembered boyhood holidays in Blackpool or hiking trips to the Lakes. The pilots glanced across at the familiar landscape of Wales, and remembered days of training on the Gnat.

Guy shut it from his mind, and turned away. Cookson and Stamper saw it as a place of happy memories. A place of exciting flying, and alliances that come all too infrequently in life and fade too soon.

Hunch had different recollections. He had arrived early for his course, intent on savouring the last few autumn days by the sea before the arrival of winter. It had rained. When it stopped raining it blew, and more often than not, it did the two together. The arrival of winter went unnoticed in a blur of fast-moving rain squalls. Walks on the beach were synonymous with crashing waves, screeching gulls, watering eyes and obscured views of the distant mountains through clouds of spray. For the first time in his life, he felt far away from home, stranded behind a mountain range which could only be breached by an interminable road journey or an even longer rail trip. The line seemed to hug the coast for ever, as though afraid of getting lost, with the train insisting on calling at every small station along the way, seeking reassurance that it was still going in the right direction. Each station looked exactly the same, possessed an unpronounceable name and allowed one passenger to get off and one to get on at each stop.

Also, he had struggled with the flying. The Jet Provost had been more suited to his coarse flying technique, and the robust little aircraft had been forgiving of his big hands and feet. The Hawk, with hydraulically operated controls, had been less understanding and forgiving. Gradually, from a start when even the instructor, used to the rough touch of students taking control for the first time, had been drawn to mutter, 'Fucking hell, I have control', he had settled down. It had not been easy. A combination of willingness to work and a likeable nature got everyone on his side, and as long as the progress graph went from bottom left towards top right, excepting the odd downward blip, they were reasonably happy. The happiest moment came when he climbed out of the aircraft following his final handling test to be told he had passed. The grin did not leave his face for a week.

He continued his progress at the Weapons Conversion Unit, so much so that he won the prize for the most improved student. It was not specified whether the trophy was awarded for improving from poor to average, or from there to something better. Hunch was content to take it at face value and he would have simply settled for the posting to Tornado.

Guy Kelsall kept his eyes firmly away from the place. The injustice he felt at his treatment all those years ago still rankled. As the weeks passed at the Weapons Conversion Unit and he heard no mention of what had happened, he began to breathe more easily. He had been even more taciturn and introverted than usual during those weeks. He visited the bar less frequently, and found any excuse not to attend parties. Once more, he gave his all to his flying. He lived with the constant fear that the past would catch up with him and with it the end of his dreams, but as the days turned into weeks and then months passed, he began to be more positive. His flying was as good as ever, and when his posting to Harriers was confirmed, he was almost in tears.

'Something wrong, Guy?' the interviewing officer had asked with a note of anxiety in his voice. Guy had sniffed hard and assured him that it was just the start of a cold.

'There is just one thing, Guy,' the man had continued. 'If you're going to make your mark in this Air Force, and you have the potential to do so, then you will have to show a little more assertiveness than you have shown to date. Get yourself in the bar a bit more. Mix with the others, and remember that life is not all work and no play.'

He had wished him luck for the future, and Guy had struggled to find the words to reply. The fact that he was talking about a career alone, never mind the possibility of a good one, had been music to his ears. Time had done much to make the memory of that incident lessen, but it had never left him.

*

'Time to descend, sir.' Granger's voice cut through his thoughts.

'What?' he asked.

'Time to start down. We've been cleared to descend; the others are already on their way.'

Guy could see the rest of the formation at least five hundred feet below him, and wondered what he would have to do to get this chap working with him rather than against, as he seemed to be doing. He slammed the throttles shut and pushed the nose of the aircraft down. Granger felt himself pushed upwards against his straps as the negative G came on. He hated the sensation and as the pressure eased he could see little black dots floating before his eyes.

'Trent, arrow go.' Cookson's command crackled through the headsets.

He needed to manoeuvre the formation to avoid small piles of cumulus cloud which had built up during their absence. The four aircraft eased towards each other. Stamper tried to keep his throttle movements to a minimum and was loath to get too close as it would take more of his precious fuel to stay there. He would be all right as long as they could get on the ground first time and if Air Traffic did not mess them about. If they did, he would have something to say to that little blonde controller he was seeing for the first time in a few hours. His mood lightened slightly at the prospect. That was, if he got on the ground. He snapped his mind back to the job, and closed to fifty yards on Cookson's starboard side. Jennings and then the Boss appeared on the opposite side, but more swept-back. The formation could now cope with any manoeuvring without sacrificing too much lookout.

Hunch loved this. He could not get enough of it. As a student pilot, he dreamed about becoming a member of the Red Arrows, and although he still had the dream, he had thought himself too rough on the controls. Someone had recently told him that to be a good formation pilot was not a question of being smooth, but a question of being there. Since then he had allowed himself the full vigour of his technique. Bertie was not a fan, but he had to admit that Hunch held position as well as the next man. Pity he could not do it when there was just a basket there.

Looking across the formation, Bertie could see the airfield in the distance. He stretched his neck, and realised how stiff it was. It had been a long sortie, and he was gasping for a drink and something to eat. He would be glad to get out of this machine. Another burst of negative G hit him quickly, followed by a more prolonged dose of positive. He groaned. 'God, this is great, isn't it, Bertie?' Hunch was panting from the effort.

Bertie watched the two aircraft to his right silhouetted against the ground. If he could have stopped his teeth from chattering in the buffeting, he might have agreed.

The lead rolled level and again the control surfaces worked overtime as Hunch followed. Bertie looked over his left shoulder and watched the boss for some moments. He was probably working hard trying to follow his pilot but, although nothing rested when Hunch was at the controls, the aircraft was not wallowing about the sky as it did when some of the others were flying. The wings dipped again and they turned onto a long finals.

'Trent thirty seconds.' Cookson's call brought a sensation of relief to the four navigators.

'Trent, clear for the run and break. Circuit clear.' The female voice in the tower sounded upbeat.

Stamper breathed a sigh of relief to echo those of Granger and Grice, but for completely different reasons. The ground moved more quickly as Cookson descended from two thousand to five hundred feet. Hunch was hanging on grimly; this was not a time to lose concentration. He saw the runway lights and the airfield boundary pass in his peripheral vision. Suddenly, Cookson seemed to lurch upwards and across his nose. He was expecting it, but it still left him breathless as thirty tonnes of metal passed a few feet in front of him. He fixed his eyes on Stamper and counted, 'One banana, two banana.' The second aircraft leapt across, following the first, and he was left looking into a void before he adjusted to the new horizon. 'One banana, two banana,' he repeated, and heaved the controls to the left.

Both their stomachs were left behind in an instant, as Hunch craned his neck to see the others. 'Airbrakes, wings forward, keep them on the horizon,' he muttered to himself.

He knew that someone, somewhere on the ground would be watching, and if the line of the aircraft and the spacing were not perfect, he would hear about it.

'Speed, yes, gear down, flaps, airbrakes in, power on, don't leave the turn too late, come on, come *on*, get it right. Three greens.'

'Trent three finals.' Hunch transmitted his call.

'Trent three, clear to land.'

Hunch could see the smoke as Stamper's wheels hit the runway. He would be well out of the way by the time he came to the touchdown point. He checked his gear again, put full flap down, and checked for the umpteenth time the angle of attack indicator in his head-up display and made a correction for the wind.

'Okay, just fly it down.' The ground rushed up to meet them. Hunch gave a last-second correction. The two met and Bertie groaned again. The penguin was back on the rocks.

Chapter Twenty-Three

Squadron Leader Tom Cookson manoeuvred the aircraft in a tight circle in front of the shelter. The doors had been left closed, indicating that he could shut down the aircraft outside without having to be dragged into the shelter. He was pleased – all he wanted was to get out of the thing. He had been cooped up long enough.

He applied the parking brake, put the refuelling probe out and shut the engines down. The silence was like the sudden end of a toothache. He flicked his mask from his face, carefully inserted the safety pins in the seat, and pulled the canopy lever. The great single piece of perspex swung upwards and warm gusts of air replaced the cool artificial atmosphere of the cockpit. Quickly taking off his helmet, he stood up on the seat. His hair was flattened to his head and curious grooves criss-crossed it where the webbing had dug in. Dark marks left by the mask ran from the bridge of his nose, across his cheeks and below his mouth. It gave him an unwashed look. He blew out his cheeks and gazed across the distant farmlands, heavy with ripening corn. He wanted to be walking among them with his dog, enjoying the afternoon warmth. In fact, he wanted to go anywhere but to the debrief.

Debriefs could be a bloody business at the best of times, but today's would be worse. He would undoubtedly have to face-down the Boss. It gave him no pleasure, but it had to be done. It was no use berating the junior crews for their mistakes if the hierarchy were allowed to get away scot-free. He took another gulp of air and watched the crewman place the steps against the side of the aircraft.

'Any snags, sir?' The airman shouted up to Cookson.

'No,' he shouted in reply. 'I think for once she performed as advertised, thanks. You got any snags, Jack?' He looked down at his navigator, who was busily stuffing maps which had been spread all over the cockpit into a home-made satchel. Frost shook his head and Cookson could see from the set of his jaw that similar thoughts to his own were going through his mind. Frost took off his helmet, refastened the strap and slipped it over his arm like a shopping basket. He stood and faced Cookson.

'I'll bet he tries to wangle his way out of coming.' Frost sounded grim and a little angry.

Cookson had no need to ask who he was talking about. 'I wouldn't bet with you,' he replied, 'but he'll be there, I'll see to it.'

He carefully climbed down the ladder. Once on the ground, he felt a little wobbly. The feeling would quickly pass, but he could sympathise with sailors stepping ashore after weeks at sea. They walked silently together to the squadron and hung up their helmets and life preservers before going through to the operations room. As Cookson signed in the aircraft, the Ops Sergeant stuck his head through the hatch and handed him a note. 'Good trip, sir? The bombing scores from Tain, some of 'em aren't bad.' He sounded low-key as he nodded at the piece of paper.

'So, so,' Cookson replied. His tone suggested that any conversation could wait. The sergeant returned to his chair knowing something was up. Ord and Langstaff had returned early with ashen faces and thunderous looks. Then the rest of the formation had appeared, the junior crews talking ten to the dozen and the more senior silent and sullen, particularly the Boss and Tom Cookson. He was dying to know what had happened, but knew better than to ask.

'Right, you lot,' Cookson shouted in the direction of the planning room. 'Get a quick cup of coffee and bring it with you. We'll get on with the debrief while it's still fresh in your minds. Anyone who is not here, get them here fast. The Boss has a meeting and he's in a hurry.' Cookson looked directly at the wing commander as he spoke, almost daring him to find an excuse for not attending. It had occurred to Guy to do just that, but any thoughts that he might get away with it were dispelled after one look at Cookson's face.

The crews shuffled into the briefing room in dribs and drabs, coffees in one hand, maps and notes in the other. The room again resounded to the general clatter of people taking their seats.

Jennings almost tipped his coffee down the back of the Boss's neck, and reacted like a silly school boy, clamping his hand over his mouth and bulging his eyes in mock alarm. Bertie Grice gave him a playful cuff round the head and pointed to the place where he was to sit.

Ord and Langstaff were already sitting at the rear of the room. They had the faces of undertakers waiting to be paid. Ord's cheeks quivered in righteous indignation. Langstaff was immobile apart from giving a wad of chewing gum a vigorous workout. His eyes stared, unfocused, ahead of him.

Cookson stood at the front and waited for them to settle. As the room went quiet, he nodded at Ord. 'You got back okay then, Ian?'

'I wouldn't say okay, but we got back, thanks, Tom,' he answered.

'Any lasting damage?' Cookson asked, and Guy swiftly glanced to the rear of the room, afraid that a damaged aircraft might provoke unwanted questions from the other side of the station,

'Not to the aircraft, apart from it needing a stress check and a few electrical snags. '*It*,' Ord emphasised the word, 'blew the inertial system to kingdom come and some of the stabs and trims wouldn't reset, but as you see, we got back.'

'I'm not sure I'll ever be the same though,' Langstaff added in funereal tones.

'Well, if you don't mind, we'll come back to that later. I want to go through the trip in some kind of order first. The briefing?' Cookson addressed the room as a whole. 'Did everybody understand it?'

He was greeted by sundry nods and the odd muttered 'yeah'.

'Okay, the start-up seemed to go quite well, with the exception of number four. What was the matter with you, Boss?'

'Flight data recorder not working,' Guy replied. 'No option but to go for the spare.'

'Why didn't you let Ops know you were going for the spare?' He rattled the question at Kelsall with a hint of reproach in his voice.

'Well,' Guy muttered, 'we were strapped for time, and I was trying to get on with it as quickly as possible.'

'Okay,' Cookson growled, 'but in saving yourself time, you cost us some trying to find out what had happened to you. Call Ops in future if you go for the spare.' The remark was addressed to the room but Guy knew he was being singled out and he felt a wave of irritation.

'Let's go through the route.' Cookson closed the discussion before it could begin. 'Jack, you take it from here.' Frost stood up and gave the creased map a final smoothing before turning. 'Any points about the route? Most of you were there during the planning phase, and you should have made your inputs then.' He glanced at Guy as he spoke; the inference was not lost on him.

'I've got a couple of points, Jack.' Ord's voice was still a little crackly despite drinking three coffees since landing. 'The two legs across the Grampians starting at Montrose.' Frost found the position on the map and pointed to it. 'Yes, those two.' Ord continued. 'Tactically a bad bit of planning. You had us going straight across all the high parts and, apart from the obvious problems with the weather on high ground, we would have spent an awful long time being skylined. What do you think, Jim?' He looked for his allies before Frost could reply, knowing he would get an argument.

'I agree with that,' Stamper was quick with his support. 'We had it marked down on the route as one of our attack points. My Scottish friend was already polishing his dirk before we had left the changing room.' A ripple of laughter followed the remark.

'I'll take your point and you *are* right,' Frost reluctantly conceded. 'But it's hardly representative of any terrain that we are going to find in Eastern Europe, is it?' Like Jennings, he was keen on having the last word, and the set of his jaw defied any further discussion on the subject. He dealt with a couple more minor points, but the room, including Frost, was getting restless for the main event.

Cookson, however, was not going to be rushed. He resumed his place at the front. 'Target runs. Any points?' he asked almost too casually.

Guy wanted to say how much he had liked the simulated JP233 attack on the airfield, but he was in no mood to throw compliments around, particularly to Cookson. Instead he merely nodded and said, 'I thought the airfield attack went okay. Needs a bit more thinking about, but the plan has some potential.'

'I don't like that bloody weapon.' The Glaswegian accent was unmistakable. 'Bloody good way to get your arse shot off, if you ask me. Someone ought to get an air marshal to trial it, with real people shooting real missiles and real bullets. Might be a good way to reduce the defence budget.'

Jennings and Grice started to laugh, but quickly stopped as the wing commander's head swung round in front of them. 'That's quite enough of that sort of talk.' His voice was raised and his cheeks flushed in anger. 'Whether you like it or not, MacKensie, the thing is here to stay, so get used to the idea. Keep remarks like that to yourself or you'll quickly find yourself somewhere where they've never even heard of JP233.'

The threat was left hanging. At the rear of the room several pairs of eyebrows were raised in surprise. No one had ever heard the Boss so angry before. The main event was looking more interesting by the minute.

'Okay,' Cookson took the initiative again. 'Jim, come up here and talk about the bounces from your point of view.'

Stamper picked his way to the front. He was clutching several small pieces of paper which had drawings on them resembling large Chinese letters. 'The first bounce,' he said. He faced the board, his back to the room, and transposed one of the drawings onto it. Three small aircraft in a triangular shape were shown in green. 'You lot,' he muttered. He drew a red aircraft in the four o'clock position of the right-hand aircraft. 'Me,' he added. Then with a series of quick lines, he drew the track he had flown and the countering tracks of the formation with surprising recall and accuracy.

'At this point you were looking good.' He stabbed a finger at the board and almost obliterated one of the aircraft. 'You had kept the formation together well, and we had not been given anything like a clear shot. I was having one more go and had crossed to the other side of number three.' He paused and looked sheepishly towards the back of the room. 'Then all hell seemed to break loose. Squadron Leader Ord called, "Knock it off." I'm not sure what happened then.'

He looked across at Cookson, and several voices started to talk at once. 'Right, hold on a minute.' Cookson was again on his feet. 'Sit down, Jim. I'll take it from here.' He faced the room. 'I think we're all clear that the Boss and Ian Ord had an airmiss. From what I can gather, it was pretty close. Now, without getting all hot under the collar, let's see if we can get to the bottom of what happened, not necessarily to apportion blame,' he looked hard at Kelsall, 'but to see if we can avoid the thing happening again. Boss, would you like to start?'

Guy Kelsall cleared his throat and shuffled uneasily in his seat. 'Well, Granger here calculated that if we took a direct route at five thousand feet, we could cut out part of the route and catch up with you somewhere in the Whitby area. We made the transit with Linton and let down just to the north of there. By Granger's reckoning, we should have been five miles behind you at the time of the incident and catching. He seems to have patently got his sums wrong, as we pitched up right in the middle of the thing.'

He gave Robin Granger a withering glance as he finished the sentence. Granger was staring hard at the floor, his fists clenched. Two small spots of red heightened the colour on his cheeks, otherwise his face was pale. He had no doubts that he was being hung out to dry, but was unsure of how to defend himself. The last thing he wanted in his life at the moment was turbulence. He had been on the squadron only a year. In that time he had married and bought a house in the local area. It had taken the best part of the year to settle his bride down and she was just beginning to like the place. On top of all that, she had just announced that she was pregnant. If it meant a quiet life, he could take some of the blame. He just wished he did not have to take all of it.

A short silence followed.

'Why didn't you make a call? You must have heard the calls to counter? It seems to me that if we had not been engaged in a prolonged bounce, we would have been five miles further down route and Robin's calculations would not have been far out.' Cookson was gazing steadily at Guy's face and the implications were rattling about his head.

Guy glared again at Granger, and then back at Cookson. He sighed. Implicit in the sigh was the statement, 'I didn't want to tell you this, but you are forcing it out of me'.

'Because,' he sounded weary, 'Robin had forgotten to change the radio frequency from Linton approach.'

It was a statement to end the discussion and Granger's mouth flew open to say something, but Cookson was having none of it. 'Why didn't you prompt him? You've more than enough experience to realise that it was terribly quiet on the airwaves for a three-ship and a bounce.'

Guy Kelsall's look changed from defensiveness to one of pure hatred. For a moment Cookson was stunned by it. This was just another debrief. It was not personal. The fact that the boss was coming in for a little more flack than normal should have made absolutely no difference. Kelsall's voice changed again to a murderous calm. 'It's the navigator's responsibility to look after the radio. It's his responsibility to change the frequency. If he had done what he was bloody well supposed to have done, we would have heard the calls and the airmiss would not have happened.'

Kelsall's look was now unwavering and he held Cookson's eyes like a rabbit in the headlights. Cookson wanted to let it go but something inside him would not. This was not a witchhunt, and he was not trying to humiliate his boss, despite what he thought, but if the issue was not straightened out now, the whole manner of operating the Tornado would be thrown into doubt. Cookson could not see what the Boss was trying to achieve. It was in his own interests that a crew-operated aircraft relied on crew co-operation, and if that went then there was nothing. He cleared his throat. 'So you don't accept that you were in any way responsible for the incident?'

The two men were effectively alone in the room. Bertie's coffee cup was poised in front of his mouth, his lips pursed to drink. Frank Langstaff had stopped chewing. His eyes, and all the other pairs of eyes in the room, were firmly fixed on Guy Kelsall. Time seemed suspended. Guy was the first to break eye-contact. He looked down to his hands, which were writhing about between his knees, showing his inner turmoil. His voice, when it came, was on the edge of control. 'No, I do not. I've given you the sequence of events and explained the background. I do not have to account to you, and I will not be spoken to in this way. I will speak to you later. I must go now and talk to the station commander at a very important meeting.'

He stood quickly and knocked over his chair, which Jennings managed to grab before it hit the floor. He pushed past his navigator, hurried through the door and slammed it behind him. An astonished silence followed, and it was some moments before Cookson calmly broke the spell. 'Right, Jim. If you would come up here again and go through the rest of the bounces please.' The main bout was over, and though the supporting cast did its best to breathe some life into it, the contest was over. 'Just one final thing before you go: the tanker.' Cookson sounded tired.

Hunch buried his head as far as he could between his shoulders. 'Hunch, if you performed sex with the same technique you displayed out there today, you would either be in and out before she noticed, or she would be bruised from navel to kneecap.' The tension in the room evaporated into a burst of loud cheering. Even Hunch found himself joining in. A face briefly appeared at the door to see what all the noise was about. 'But all is not lost,' Cookson continued, 'because I am going to make it my personal crusade that nothing, not even a basket, should have to go through that again. We will go up to the tanker on a dedicated sortie and we will not leave until the tanker has run out of gas or we get it right. By the time we've finished, they'll name a technique after you.'

'Oh they've already done that, sir. It's called the Hunch crunch.' Bertie grinned at his pilot.

Cookson quickly left the room and headed out of the building. He suddenly felt tired. Jack Frost caught him by the main entrance and clapped him on the shoulder, before looking round to make sure that they were alone. 'Nice one, Tom. You stuck your neck out in there, but it had to be done. I can't believe the cheek of the man, trying to pin it all on Robin Granger. He might not be the smartest of operators, but he's by no means the worst by a long shot. If I were you though, I would start looking for a new job. He's not going to forget this in a hurry.'

'Well, I don't feel as though it was a nice one. If only the silly man had accepted some of the responsibility, nothing more needed to be said. I don't know, but every time we meet these days, we seem to be at daggers-drawn.'

Cookson suddenly stopped talking and pointed towards the corridor. 'Listen to that,' he whispered. A grin spread across his face. Jennings's voice clearly preceded him down the length of the changing room.

'Bertie, my dear chap, I am going to buy you a pint.' He was making no attempt to keep the volume down. 'No, in fact, Bert. I'm going to buy you two pints, not because you're an average navigator who is constantly rude to his pilot, but because I wish to embed in your tiny brain the magnitude of what you have just witnessed. That was a belter. A veritable humdinger. Indeed a cup final of a debrief. More than that, a Man U-playing-Liverpool job.'

'Keep your voice down, Hunch,' Bertie hissed.

'No, lad. It must be lauded. Sung from the rooftops. You'll tell your grandkids of this one. They'll stare at you opened mouthed... Oh, hello, sir.' Jennings suddenly found himself face to face with Jack Frost as he turned the corner. 'I was just telling young Grice here that I was going to go down to the betting shop to get an early bet on Manchester United playing Liverpool in next year's FA Cup Final, sir. I know it's a very early bet, but the odds will be so much better.' He looked at his watch, then back at Frost's glowering features.

'Would you like me to get you a piece of the action, sir?' he asked.

'Shut up, Hunch.' Frost spoke through clenched teeth.

'Right, sir, perhaps you would like some time to think it over?'

'Hunch, just shut the fuck up.' Frost sounded unconvinced.

Chapter Twenty-Four

Guy Kelsall drove his service Mini round the perimeter track like a man possessed. Not only had the group captain been kept waiting through that damned debrief, but he needed to burn off his anger and frustration. He would have his revenge. Granger would certainly go, but what to do about Cookson was the main question.

'The station commander is waiting for you, sir.' The PA indicated the door with a nod. 'Go straight through.' Guy tapped on the door and opened it at the same time as he heard a voice say 'Come in.'

'Sorry to have kept you waiting, sir. The debrief seemed to go on for ever, but we had something fairly important to discuss, so I thought I'd better stay.'

'Hello, Guy. Come in and take a chair. We haven't started, so you haven't missed anything.' The group captain sat behind a large G-plan desk which had been cleared of everything except a blotter and a couple of family photographs. Across from him, three chairs were lined up, two already occupied. Guy gave each of the occupants a cursory nod and sat down. 'Like a coffee or tea before we start, Guy?' the group captain asked.

'No thanks, sir. I had one during the debrief.'

The man across the desk never failed to impress Guy. He was scarcely a year or so older than him, but had seemed destined from very early in his career to achieve great things in the RAF. It was rumoured that a 'golden book' existed which contained the names of those officers whose life should be closely monitored and guided. If it were true, then Tom Gorton's name would surely be near the top of the first page.

Tom Gorton had joined the RAF straight from school with three A levels. After three years at Cranwell, he had graduated not only with his wings, but also with the sword of honour, presented by Her Majesty, the Queen. His career in the intervening years had shown no signs of stuttering. A promotion had occurred like clockwork every four years, and his postings had been varied and challenging, including an exchange tour in the United States where he had found a wife. His appearance was always impeccable. His short, cropped hair was smoothed tight to his scalp, his complexion fresh and his features regular. He gave the impression, even when climbing out of an aeroplane, that he had just taken a shower. He was liked, respected and just a little feared, but it was doubtful whether outside his immediate family, he was really close to anyone. If he did not burn out with the punishing routine he inflicted on himself, then he would reach retirement a friendless old man and wonder what it had all been about.

'Well, you haven't missed anything,' Gorton smiled at Guy, 'apart from one of Jeremy's jokes, which I'm sure he'll tell you later, if you express even the slightest interest.' He made it sound as though he liked the joke, but did not really understand it. Jeremy Smith leaned forward and gave Guy a wink. He was a minefield of jokes, only some of which were worth repeating. He got some sort of perverse pleasure telling them to the station commander because the reaction was always the same – 'Ah yes, Jeremy. Very amusing', followed by a dutiful laugh. Smith was Guy's counterpart, and commanded the sister squadron on the station, 627 Squadron. They were rivals and friends, but neither passed up a chance to put one over on the other.

'This one's a corker, Guy. You'll love it.' Smith grinned at him. Guy nodded. He probably would.

'Right.' The group captain spoke softly. He was a very still man. As he looked in turn at the three men, only his eyes moved. His hands lay motionless on the desk, the fingertips of one hand resting lightly on the other. 'I'll get straight to the reason why I've called this meeting. Whitehall are getting a bit hot under the collar about this chap in the Middle East, Saddam Hussein. I'm sure you've all read about him in the papers, so you probably know as much about him as I do. Anyway, what it boils down to is this. He is assembling quite a sizeable military force on the southern border of Iraq, and making noises about taking over Kuwait, which he claims to be his rightful property. The kind of practise manoeuvres he's carrying out would certainly indicate that he planning some sort of offensive against that country.'

He paused, and again looked at each man in turn. His fingers moved slightly, otherwise he remained in the same position. 'At this stage,' he continued, 'the planners and the Intel people are not inclined to think it will amount to much and that all the posturing is to take the minds of his people away from the country's internal problems and shortages after the recent war with Iran. But', for the first time he showed some animation by pointing one finger at the desk, 'Whitehall do not want us to be caught with our pants down. So, while on the one hand they do not want us going around indicating to one and all, the press particularly, that we are doing anything other than our normal training, they do want us to start looking at plans for getting some aircraft and back-up out there and working on some tactics for that part of the world.'

'Have they given any indication of the numbers they might be needing, sir?'

The man, OC Operations Wing, sitting between the two squadron commanders, spoke for the first time. He was a tall angular man, with pointed features and a high forehead; his ears protruded severely from the side of his head almost at right angles and had earned him the name of Wingnut. The name suited him in more ways than the obvious because diplomacy was not his strong suit. He was given to rushing in when wiser men would think twice.

'Well as I've said, Richard,' Gorton replied, 'It's early days yet, but I did hear the number was up to six aircraft from each squadron.'

Jeremy Smith whistled quietly through his teeth. 'That leaves us tightly stretched on all the other commitments, sir,' he said, scratching his head.

'Now, Jeremy. Before you go and blow a gasket, they've already suspended all exercises and we'll not be given a taceval in the foreseeable future. Does that answer your point?' Gorton came close to smiling.

'Thanks, sir. Sorry to interrupt.'

'The plot, as I understand it, is that a task force comprising mainly of Americans, ourselves, the French and the Italians will be assembled – no jokes please, Jeremy.' The hands came off the table, palms towards them in a sudden show of body language and the three men smiled. 'For our part, as I've just said, up to twelve aircraft, sundry manpower and equipment as yet to be decided. Having said all that,' he continued, 'the main thing I want to discuss is JP233. I understand, Jeremy, from talking to some of your chaps in the bar, that they are not too keen on the thing.'

He looked directly at Smith and the tall man cleared his throat and shifted uncomfortably in his chair. He did not like his crews talking to the 'old man' in the bar, particularly when the subject came back to haunt him. Guy was more than pleased that the remark had not been addressed to him, and took some pleasure at the predicament of his counterpart.

'It's not that they don't like it, sir.' Smith looked at the wall behind Gorton's head, searching for inspiration. 'If it works as advertised, it will be a cracking piece of kit. Should be able to close down an airfield for a considerable period after just one attack.' He tried to sound upbeat. 'I think what is bothering them a little is that four or more aircraft, following each other down a runway at twenty-second intervals, and having to hold straight and level for thirty seconds makes them feel... well, a little vulnerable. That's all,' he added weakly.

'So they think the weapon is a good idea, but the delivery a bad one?' Gorton nodded imperceptibly. He was not going to let Smith get away lightly. In contrast to the stillness of the one man, the other was all movement. Smith wriggled in his chair, crossed and uncrossed his legs and constantly chewed his bottom lip. Guy was jubilant. A matter of hours ago, if he had been put in the same position, he would not have faired any better, but now he felt confident and certainly in a position to score some brownie points off his rival.

'Not necessarily a bad one, sir,' Smith was furiously trying to dig himself out of a hole, 'but we do need to do some work on refining the tactics.' He made a mental note to warn his aircrew not to share doubts with the station commander, but to stick rigidly to chat about the weather.

'What have you come up with so far?' Gorton was not going to let go.

'Not much I'm afraid, sir. We keep coming back to the same problem. How to decrease the spread of aircraft.'

It was Guy's turn to wriggle about in his chair. He felt like a kid at school burning to answer the question. Wanting to shoot his hand in the air and shout, 'Me, Miss, me, Miss'. 'Mmmm.' The group captain looked down at his fingertips for a moment. 'And what are your thoughts on the matter, Guy? Having the same problem?'

'We were, sir.' He allowed a frown to crease his brow, and put slight emphasis on the word 'were'. 'But I did some serious thinking about the thing and, although I am not saying we've found a solution, we've made some progress.' He paused to let the point sink in. From the corner of his eye, he could see Smith staring hard at him.

'Are you going to let us in on the secret then, Guy?' Gorton asked gently after a few moments.

Guy was enjoying himself.

'Sorry, sir, of course. As I just said, it's early days. In fact, we only put the theory to the test for the first time today, that's why I was a bit late arriving. I wanted to get feedback from the rest of the formation on how they thought the attack had gone.'

'And how was that?' There was a note of irritation in Smith's voice that cheered Guy greatly.

'Oh, I think it went quite well for a first effort.' He tried to keep his voice from sounding too smug.

'You still haven't told us what the plan is, Guy.' The group captain showed no sign of impatience.

'No, I'm sorry, sir. I was coming to that. Well...' he cleared his throat. 'As Jeremy said, I too was getting feedback from the aircrew about the vulnerability of the delivery method, and I could see their point. The first two or even three aircraft to cross the target might get away with it, but those coming after would probably not. It would take more than three aircraft to close down an airfield, the size they are today. Then it occurred to me, it was not just hitting the runway that was important, it was *where* on the runway. If attacks were made at angles across the runway, and at different points along its length, then it would achieve the same object. But...' he let the word hang in the air, 'from our perspective, the aircraft could almost attack simultaneously.'

'You could straddle the runway with bombs that way,' Smith smirked.

He was quick to see the weakness, but Guy was ready for him.

'True, Jeremy,' he allowed his tone to become slightly patronising, 'but the angle at which you attack is the critical thing.' He was aware that only three or four hours previously he had been voicing exactly the same doubts, but he was not going to let that interfere with his moment of glory. 'Attack at ninety degrees and you're correct. Bring the angle down to forty-five degrees or less and you get three or four or even more hits, and,' he held his hand up to stem an objection before it came, 'you stand a much better chance of hitting the target and not flying down one side of it. As I'm sure you would agree, flying down the length of the runway, particularly at night and with somebody shooting at you, is not the easiest thing in the world. So what we did today was to vary the theme. The lead flew down the length of the runway and the others cut it at angles, one from the left and the other two from the right. I haven't seen the film yet, but I'm fairly confident that it will show a good attack.'

A short silence followed. Smith crossed and uncrossed his legs and made small sucking noises in his teeth. Gorton remained motionless. 'Sounds good to me.' OC Ops Wing spoke for only the second time, breaking the spell.

Gorton nodded imperceptibly. 'Yes it does to me also. You say you've only flown this once?'

'Yes, sir. Today.'

'And how much time in total was spent over the target?'

'I would say about a minute, sir. No more, and we could probably get that down to even less. We were back in good battle formation within two minutes,' Guy added almost proudly.

'Well, I would say that was pretty good also, wouldn't you, Jeremy?' Gorton looked at OC627, almost defying him to object. 'It must go some way to alleviating your chap's fears.'

He waited for Smith to reply, but all he got was a reluctant nod. It warmed Guy's heart that he could not come up with an objection. He had been the one that Guy had feared would blow the scheme away. That he had not been able to do so had further enforced Guy's view that the attack was feasible.

'Yes.' Gorton was so quiet that he was almost talking to himself 'It seems to have all the ingredients – surprise, weight of numbers and the bomblets and the mines still get spread around, causing the maximum damage and annoyance. Right, gentlemen, thank you for coming. One last thing, if the balloon goes up, I see us not only in the role of airfield attackers, because we're the only ones with the weapon, but I see it happening mostly at night. I know it's going to be unpopular, but I want more night work. Get your night terrain-following work up to scratch, night-tanking sharpened up and fly with four ships or even more if you can. What I don't want are any statistics, if you take my drift, through over-enthusiasm or tiredness. Work hard, but do it as safely as the task allows. Guy, get on to the manufacturers and make sure they agree with your figures.'

'Already done it, sir, and they bear them out.' Although Guy had passed the whole thing off as his brainchild, he did not feel the slightest prick of conscience. After recent happenings, he felt that Cookson owed him.

Gorton smiled and patted him on the back as they walked towards the office door. 'Good. You've done some good work there, Guy. Thank you very much, I'm grateful. See you in the bar later for a beer?'

'I'll try and get there, sir, but I've got a few loose ends to tie up.' He knew damn well he would be there. He would not have missed it for the world; not today. 'You going to the bar later, Jeremy?' he asked, a smile of triumph creasing his face.

Chapter Twenty-Five

The meeting had made all the difference to Guy's day. Instead of ending on a low note, as it looked like doing, it had been quite the reverse. Now, he had put most of the recent upsets behind him. After all, it did not matter a jot what his squadron thought of him. The only man he needed to impress was the group captain and he seemed to have done just that. He returned to his office, made one or two phone calls to the postings department at MOD and shuffled some papers around for a few minutes. He made sure the Adj had enough work to keep him busy past his normal knocking-off time and left for the bar.

He arrived home a few minutes after six. It was by no means an unusual time for him to get in, but he knew that once his wife smelled beer on his breath her attitude would change. It was one thing to work late, it was another to spend time in the bar at the expense of his young family. The sound of the children playing upstairs floated down to him as he closed the front door. They were making so much noise that his shout of, 'Hi kids, Daddy's home,' went totally unnoticed. He hung his coat in the cloakroom and slowly examined the mail which had been left on the stairs.

'Bills, bills and more bills,' he sighed and threw them back onto the step.

No matter how far he progressed in the RAF or how much money he earned, there always seemed to be more days left in the month than money in the bank. Nothing he said or did seemed to change that.

He wandered slowly through to the kitchen. His wife had her back to him, stirring something on the cooker. He admired her shape. Despite three children, she had still kept her figure. He was tempted to snuggle up behind her and cup her breasts in his hands but resisted, knowing full well that such an advance would be unwelcome.

'Hi.' She half-turned towards him with a small smile on her face. 'Busy day?'

'So so,' he answered, 'a few problems here and there, but nothing that couldn't be sorted out.' The fact that he had nearly had a mid-air collision, a bust-up with his flight commander and scored a major coup with the station commander would not interest her. 'You?' he asked, knowing that he really did not want the answer.

'Horrendous!' She spat the word out. 'The kids have been little devils all day. In fact, you're going to have to have a word with Tommy; he's been nothing but a pain in the neck. He has irritated and teased the girls all day, and he just doesn't listen to a word I say. I told him you would see to him when you got home.' Guy hated that. He loved his children and got on quite well with them, but to be set up as some sort of ogre in his absence was not the way he thought it should be done. Was he supposed to come home riding on a chariot of fire and set about them? More often than not, his having a word with them turned into a joke at the expense of his wife and that made her more angry. What did she expect? She should be capable of disciplining them herself.

'Okay, I'll see to it,' he muttered. 'What's for dinner? I'm a bit peckish.'

'Nothing much, I'm afraid,' she answered. 'I've been far too busy running round after them all day to think about it.' She nodded towards the ceiling and half-turned towards him. She gave a small sniff and a look of disappointment crossed her face. 'You've been to the bar.' It was not a question, it was an accusation.

'Yes, just a quick one. Tom Gorton invited me. I could hardly refuse, could I?'

'Tom Gorton's children are older than yours, and Elizabeth has a maid to help her.' He raised his eyes to heaven, looking for some kind of divine guidance. It was the same old line. She was trying to make him feel guilty and, despite himself, was succeeding, which somehow added to his annoyance. Well, to hell with you, he thought, turned and left the room. He was thinking to hell with her rather a lot these days. She seemed to have lost her sparkle over the years they had been married. The only time she seemed to come alive was at parties or functions, where she made a special effort. Then, when he saw her laughing and looking her best, he remembered what had attracted him to her in the first place. But this evening was gradually becoming more typical, with her becoming more engrossed in her own cares and problems.

★

Mary had been a close friend of one of his sisters. He had known her most of his life, although she had just been another girl in an overcrowded houseful of girls. They were just there to taunt and tease, much as his son seemed to be doing now, until they ganged up on him and forced him to run to his mother for protection. She had flitted in and out of his life. When he had been in flying training, she had been away at university and their paths had crossed infrequently. Then he had returned home for some leave, having almost finished his first tour on Harriers. He had not recognised her at first; she had changed so much from the skinny, tomboy figure with a couple of plaits. Now what he saw was slim but well rounded; in fact, her breasts were possibly a little too well rounded for her shape. She would later confess that she thought them too big. But from his perspective, then and later, they were ideal.

When he had finally dragged his eyes away from them, he had noted that the rest was not bad either. Short brown hair, a slim face with slightly pointed features. Her full mouth was pulled upwards at the corners as she watched him. 'You don't remember me, do you?' Her gaze was steady and confident.

'Of course I do,' he lied. But from all the girls his sisters had brought back to the house over the years, it was hard to put a time and a place to her, never mind a name.

'Who am I then?' she asked, the large hazel eyes not wavering from his face.

He had not expected such a direct challenge and was a little flustered. 'You're Louise's friend, of course.' He tried to bluff his way out of it, but she was having none of it.

'We all know that,' she sounded a little patronising. 'It would be easiest if you just admitted that you can't remember which one.'

'Okay, you win.' He was in no mood for games, having just been on the road for several hours. It was not the kind of start from which great relationships emerge, but throughout the fortnight he was home she kept popping up, and each time with a new taunt. It was as though she was getting her own back for all the times he had taunted them as children. Although irritated at first, he slowly came to realise that there was nothing malicious about her. She was only having fun and not really at his expense. She was light and jolly and a smile was never far from her lips. As the days passed, he found himself increasingly looking forward to her head appearing round the door. He was still not inclined to take the relationship any further. It was too close to home for comfort and he was still unsure about women.

They had always seemed to fill his life, often in greater numbers than he would have wished. They were people who did things for him. Tied his shoelaces when they came undone, protected him from being bullied. They cooked and cleaned, fed him, clothed him and in return wanted nothing from him. Then there had been the two incidents with girls. One had shown him the moon and the stars while the other had appeared to offer them, but at the last minute had taken them away, leaving him looking like a monster.

Mary was different. For the first time in his life, he wanted to do things for someone other than himself. He wanted to make her laugh. He wanted to make her turn her head in a certain way and look at him, knowing it was a special look just for him. He wanted to touch her, not in a sexual way, but just to make some sort of contact with her. He was happy when she was around him, but somehow the sparkle went out of his life when she went out of the room, even for a few minutes. She was easy to talk to and made no demands on him.

He was not used to love, did not know what it was, but if this was it then he liked the feeling. When she was not there he spent time thinking about things to tell her at their next meeting. He wanted to give her a gift, but was put off knowing that it would only bring derision from his family.

The days of his leave rushed by, and for the first time since joining the RAF, he found himself not wanting to go back. He counted the days and the hours to his return, desperately trying to think of some way to communicate his feelings to Mary. Every time he got close, something or someone would get in the way and the moment would be lost. Then, as so often happened in his life as far as women were concerned, she solved the problem for him. 'Aren't you ever going to ask me out, or don't you like older women?' She had the same expression on her face as when they had met a few days earlier.

'Older women?' He had asked to cover his surprise. 'Who are you kidding? You must be all of a year older than me.'

'Sixteen months to be exact,' she had knowingly answered, 'but don't evade the question. Are you going to take me out or not?'

'Okay,' he said, secretly overjoyed that one of them had got round to making some headway, but more importantly knowing that she had some kind of feelings towards him. 'I'll take you out, where do you want to go?'

'That,' she pointed a delicate finger at him, looking demur, 'is for the gentleman to decide.'

The relationship staggered on. He wanted it and yet he didn't. They wrote to each other on a regular basis. Long chatty letters which said nothing. He visited his parents more times in the ensuing months than he had done in the previous four years and each time they were overjoyed to see each other. But to Mary's frustration the thing was not going anywhere. They kissed, cuddled and flirted with each other, but despite her best efforts, he would not go any further. She was beginning to wonder if he had any particular hang-ups, especially where women were concerned. But all the evidence, when they were having a cuddle, pointed the other way. For a reason she could not fathom, he was holding himself back.

She racked her brain for a solution. The only thing that seemed to make sense was that he was not on his own territory. If she was going to progress, she would have to get him away from home ground. Eventually, she came up with a plan. They had been to the cinema and were sitting in her parents' front room. It was late April and the long nights of winter were at last giving way to springtime. They had been seeing each other for several months and both sets of parents were in favour of the match, but her mother in particular was positively enthusiastic. So much so that whenever Guy arrived at the house she would go to great lengths to give them as much time alone as possible, often shuffling Mary's long-suffering father out of the way into less comfortable surroundings.

'Don't you have summer balls or something like that in the RAF?' she asked in her best matter-of-fact voice.

'Well, as it happens, we do. We tend to have them in the summer.' His sarcastic tone earned him a sharp prod in the ribs. In response, he made a grab at her and they wrestled around. They were both well aware of the arousal this caused, particularly Guy. Those large, well rounded breasts seemed to be everywhere, but just as the wrestling was turning into something else he stopped himself, much to her disappointment, and suddenly asked, 'Would you like to go to one?'

'A ball?' she asked, suddenly forgetting the last few minutes.

'No, Cinderella, I was thinking of a football match.'

The remark earned him another poke in the ribs but this time she evaded his lunge and became all business-like. 'I would need a gown. When is it? Where would I stay? How would I get there?' The questions rattled off one after the other. They both quietly congratulated themselves. He for apparently making her happy, she for getting what she wanted – Guy on his own turf.

Chapter Twenty-Six

The weeks leading up to the ball passed quickly for Guy. The squadron went on its annual detachment to Sardinia for intensive weapons training, and to his satisfaction he came out of it as top gun. His boss had written good things about him in his annual report, and was even making references to promotion if he kept up his present standards. His star was in the ascendancy again. The horrors of being thrown off the station were now a distant memory. He found himself thinking more and more about Mary.

He had attended two of his friends' weddings that year and was constantly hearing of others he had known in training taking the plunge. Perhaps it was time for him to start thinking about it. After all, if he were to get promoted, a wife who could conduct herself well in company, would not be a bad thing. Was he in love with her? He was not sure, but if missing her was love then it was probable, because he was certainly looking forward to seeing her again. He liked her company and her humour. She brought out the less serious side to his nature, but a proposal of marriage was a big step. He would think about it.

He booked her into a local hotel, which although not the Ritz, was neat, comfortable and well within his price range. Buses would be laid on to get her there, so there was no problem with drinking and driving.

By mid-July, a large high-pressure system had settled itself over the United Kingdom and, while flying at low level was an absolute misery in the thick haze layer, it was ideal for the ball. The mess was transformed. Rooms were given a theme and, between the artists and the grafters, scenes from Parisian boulevards replaced the everyday decorations of a working building. Guy never failed to be surprised at the talents and the ingenuity of his fellow officers. There appeared to be nothing that they could collectively not achieve.

Mary insisted on driving her little Mini up to the camp. The journey was not difficult and she said it would save him having to meet the train. In fact, she wanted to be alone when she saw an RAF station for the first time and not have to register her disappointment in front of Guy. He arranged a pass at the guardroom that would allow her on to the station and told her to ask for directions to the officers' mess. He would meet her there.

She was not sure what to expect as she drove through the gates, but the reality came as a surprise. Perhaps she had thought that men who deliver death and destruction for a living would surround themselves with austerity and drabness. The widely spaced red-brick buildings, interspersed with green lawns, well-tended flower beds and avenues lined with cherry trees, was really very attractive and looked and felt like a public park. The place was like a sleepy hollow. The sun beat down through a hazy sky and people in shirt sleeves sauntered about. Then the air was split with the sound of a jet engine at full power and between the trees she caught a glimpse of a small green aircraft as it disappeared into the distance, slowly dragging its noise with it.

She was excited. This was a whole new world to her, and although Guy had spoken about his work, it had been in muted terms which went no way towards describing these surroundings.

The corporal at the Guardroom had been more than helpful and she had been thrilled when he had called her 'ma'am'. Her first impressions had been favourable, but they were only endorsed by the officers' mess. The two-storey red-brick building had an elegance all of its own. Built in the days between the wars, it hinted at the grandeur of a country house while retaining the purpose for which it was designed. The main entrance had large, arched openings which housed a grand double door at the centre and lattice windows on each side which extended to the tops of the arches. The building then spread itself on each side, first housing the social areas and then the bedrooms and living quarters of the bachelor officers. Ivy had been allowed to grow along its length. The front of the building looked out onto well tended lawns and flower gardens. The whole place had an air of calm and tranquillity. From the moment she saw it she loved it.

She parked her car to one side in the slots marked 'visitors' and walked a little hesitantly towards the main doors. She had a feeling that she was intruding, of almost stepping back into the past. The main doors were painted black and held great brass fittings. They were open and she was pleased. She suspected that she would not have had the courage to try them otherwise, they looked so daunting. Slowly she stepped into the foyer.

Again, she liked what she saw. It was not a big room, but it had grandeur. The ceiling was high and vaulted. Light from the high windows streamed into the room. The furnishings were Spartan; a few chairs set against the walls, and pictures of men in old-fashioned flying suits hung on the side walls. On the far wall, two photographs, one of the Queen and the other of Prince Phillip, hung either side of a narrow table. The centre of the room was taken up by a large mahogany table, perhaps ten feet in diameter, which was so highly polished she could clearly see her reflection in it. On top of the table was one of the biggest arrays of flowers she had ever seen. Again she had to shake her head slightly to remember that this was a place from which wars were fought.

Two corridors led off from either side and she wondered which to take. For a moment she felt like Alice in the story and would not have been surprised if a large white rabbit had suddenly appeared from one of them crying, 'I'm late, I'm late'. Instead Guy appeared. It took a moment for her to recognise him. He was wearing a flying suit which was covered in badges, and around his neck was a small chequered scarf. Still bronzed from his trip to Sardinia, she could not help thinking how handsome he looked. He stopped in front of her and took her hand a little shyly and smiled as though wondering what to do next. He gave her a peck on the cheek. 'Lovely to see you, how are you? Good journey? Take you long, did it? Come on, I'll try and find you a cup of tea if you would like one.' She laughed a little at the barrage.

'I'm well. Yes. Not too long and I would love a cup of tea,' she replied, smiling.

It was his turn to laugh and it seemed to relax him. He placed an arm around her shoulder gave her a little squeeze and steered her into one of the corridors. 'Sorry the place is in a bit of a mess, but as you can see everyone is trying desperately to get the decorating finished before tonight. I'll give you a quick tour, but it doesn't resemble normality in the least.' He led her quickly from one room to another muttering 'dining room', 'anteroom', and 'ladies' room', but under the welter of painted paper it was a wasted exercise. People seemed to be all over the place, up ladders, carrying, shifting and painting things onto great brown sheets of paper that hung from the ceilings. She would be amazed if the place could be made to look anything but a tip before the evening, but Guy assured her that it would be all right.

He seemed a little different from the Guy that she was used to. He was more confident, more assertive and she found herself warming to the new, slightly improved model. They went from a Parisian bistro, to a street scene, to a grand vista of the Eiffel Tower. She was fascinated, and marvelled at the talent of the people who had created the effect. 'Have you hired people in to come and do the paintings?' she inquired.

'No, they're just people from the squadrons and some of their wives. Quite good, aren't they?'

She was amazed that Guy, with a perfunctory wave of the hand, could dismiss it all so easily. He seemed to know just about everybody and waved and smiled at them as they went past. Some of them shouted things at him and generally inquired why he did not get on with something useful instead of just swanning around. 'Right,' he said, taking her by the hand again, 'this room is being decorated by my squadron, so don't mind what they say, they're just trying to wind me up, that's all.' He led her almost shyly into the room. In the background a radio was blaring away and people were shouting to make themselves heard above the din. The place was lit by artificial light, most of the windows having been covered up. Paris was again the theme; that much she recognised because she could see the Eiffel Tower dominating the skyline, but the rest looked like all the other rooms – chaos. People, pots of paint and ladders were all over the place and with the ball a matter of hours away, she again wondered how they could be ready in time. Her reverie was interrupted by a great booming voice.

'Kelsall, you idle young bugger, where have you been? Skiving off as usual, I suppose.' The owner was as big as the voice, not tall, but with a great barrel chest and massive forearms. He was clinging precariously to a ladder, a paintbrush in his free hand.

'Mary, I would like you to meet Squadron Leader Ty Retief. He's from South Africa,' he added, as though by way of an explanation. 'Sir, this is Mary, my girlfriend.' She thrilled at being described as his girlfriend. It was the closest he had ever come to making any declaration of affection.

'Mary, I'm more than pleased to meet you.' The demeanour of the great gruff man changed immediately. He swung down from the ladder, held out his hand and gently took hers into his huge fist, looking directly into her eyes. 'My dear, what an absolute pleasure it is to meet you. Guy has told us absolutely nothing about you and, looking at you, I'm not surprised he's kept you to himself.'

She blushed a little under his direct gaze and wondered if he was being sarcastic, but everything about his tone seemed genuine. 'Kelsall, you get back to work and I will introduce Mary to the others. We might even find her something to do, after all, she's already been here two minutes and should feel thoroughly at home.' The booming voice returned. Guy gave her a little smile before she was led away.

She was introduced to everyone in the room, told who and what they were. Her head was spinning with all the information, but they all seemed friendly and before she knew it an hour or so had passed. Each time she glanced towards Guy he seemed to sense it and gave her a little wave and a smile from his vantage point up a ladder. Mary was more than pleased that she had come.

The miracle when it came was instantaneous. One moment the room was a disaster, the next it was cleared of everything and in its place a street in the heart of Paris appeared. No wonder Guy had been missed – he seemed to be the artistic director and either from his brush or his direction most of the artwork had been achieved.

'I didn't know you were such a talent with a paintbrush,' she commented.

'Oh, it's just something I picked up along the way,' he answered modestly.

'Good thing he picked something up along the way,' the voice boomed between them, 'because he has precious little talent elsewhere.' A large hand slapped Guy on the back and he staggered a couple of strides forward.

'Thank you, sir. It's most kind of you to say so.' Guy touched his forelock in mock servitude.

'Is he always like that?' Mary whispered to Guy.

'He has a heart of gold but tries hard not to show it. He likes to be the hard man, but never quite succeeds. Follow him anywhere, particularly in the air,' Guy said, looking at the great bull of a man. 'Right, let's get you to your lodgings. I've booked you into a nice little hotel that's not too far away.'

Chapter Twenty-Seven

He dropped her off and promised to pick her up at seven on the dot. The hotel was clean and comfortable. Mary had no difficulty filling in the next couple of hours. She bathed, did her hair and slipped into her new dress. She had spent considerably more than she wanted buying it, but, as she did her best to study the effect in the small mirror, was quite pleased with the result. She found herself desperately hoping that Guy would like it as much.

At seven he appeared. She watched him drive to the front of the building and timed it so that she would make her entrance just as he was coming into the small foyer. The staircase did not exactly lend itself to a grand entrance, but she did her best to stage-manage the last few steps of the stairs, carefully holding the dress to her knees and trying to be as demure as possible. From Guy's perspective, it was all that she could have wished for. As she came down the stairs, his initial view was her shoes and ankles. Then with each step more of her came into his field of vision. He did not rush forward to help her, but simply stood and enjoyed it. The long, black dress accentuated her slim figure. He watched almost spellbound. With four steps to go, she was complete. It was a masterpiece of simplicity, yet the effect was stunning. The dress hung from a single strap tied around the back of her neck, her shoulders and arms bare. It followed the contours of her body, and a single split up one side allowed her to move. She had not changed her hair except to part it down the middle and the only jewellery she wore were small gold earrings and a very fine gold necklace. As she stood before him, he remembered to close his mouth and not stare, but it was some moments before he found his powers of speech. 'You look lovely,' was all he could manage.

'So do you,' she replied, looking at his mess uniform. He self-consciously brushed the palms of his hands down the sides of his trousers.

'No, I really mean it, you do look lovely.' The words refused to come out in the order he intended. He held his hand towards her and she took it.

'I had no idea you dressed in this sort of thing,' she said. 'I thought you would wear a dinner jacket or something, but this is much nicer.' She stroked the sleeve of the short, cashmere jacket. 'And little tiny wings too.' She pointed at his left lapel. He blushed and muttered that it was an inheritance from the Army.

'Come on, we've been invited to pre-ball drinks at the Boss's house, seven thirty sharp. He's a bit of a stickler for timekeeping.'

'Is that the house of Squadron Thingy Retief?' she asked.

He laughed at her ignorance and gave her hand a little squeeze. 'That was Squadron Leader Retief, and no he is not the boss, just one of the flight commanders, and,' he added just to make sure she had the picture, 'there are two of those per squadron and one wing commander in charge. He's the one whose house we are going to.'

'It all sounds a bit formal to me.'

He sensed the doubt in her voice.

'No, not at all. You'll knock 'em dead. Just be yourself, that's all. They're all just like you and me. No difference, honest, you'll like them and anyway, you met most of them this afternoon.'

When they reached his tiny sports car, which he had parked round the side of the hotel, he saw the look on her face. For once he wished that he had bought something a little more sensible. As he reached to open the door, she looked down at the seat, then at her dress and then at Guy and with a graceful wiggle hitched her skirt above her knees, sat down and swung her legs into the footwell. He was treated to a glance of gleaming white thigh and patted the car affectionately as he went round to the driver's side.

They were greeted at the door by a smiling, pretty woman in her mid-thirties. She nodded at Guy and before he could introduce Mary, she turned to her. 'Hello, I'm Jane, you must be Mary. You look gorgeous and I do like your necklace.'

For the second time since her arrival, Mary had a fleeting thought that the greeting might not be genuine, but the warmth of the woman was undeniable. Guy was left wondering how she had come up with Mary's name as he did not recollect telling her. They followed Jane into a large room that was already nearly full of people. Mary was introduced to some of them and a drink was placed in her hand. She glanced nervously around the room and soon realised that most of the people there were barely older than she was. She began to relax and enjoy the chatter. Before she knew it, Guy was telling her it was time to leave.

'What did you think of Jane, then?' he asked once they were back in the car.

'Which one was she?' Mary's mind was awash with faces and names.

'The one who met us at the door.'

'Oh yes,' she remembered. 'I liked her.'

'She's the Boss's wife.'

'She didn't look old enough to be the wife of a boss and, anyway, which one was the Boss, as you call him?'

'Oh, he was just the chap you spent the best part of half an hour talking to. You know, the chap with three gold rings on his arm.' He turned the car into the front of the mess and an immaculately dressed RAF policeman bent to open Mary's door.

'Him? Oh yes, I remember him. He was rather dishy. Are all bosses as nice as he is?'

Guy had no time to answer before the corporal boomed, 'Good evening, ma'am.'

Guy felt a pang of jealousy but the look on Mary's face told him that she was just having him on. 'Come on, Miss, I'll give you a hand.' Before she had time to feel embarrassed she had swung her legs over the side and had been hauled to her feet. 'These pilots are all the same, miss; unless it's small and makes a lot of noise they're not interested. Tell 'im to buy something a bit more comfortable next time.'

'I might just do that,' she said, out of Guy's hearing. 'Thank you.'

Inside all was noise, light and colour. The evening passed in a whirl of dancing, eating and drinking. Mary could not remember when she had enjoyed herself so much. Guy was more than attentive, aware that she was in strange surroundings, and was never far from her side, but she lost count of the number of nice-looking young men who asked her onto the dance floor. Everyone seemed so friendly. Any doubts she might have had about coming were long since dispelled. In fact, she was beginning to feel that she did not want to go home.

'Right that's enough of dancing with all those other blokes. I'm the one who invited you, so I get to dance with you from now on.' Guy took her by the hand and led her to the dancing area.

'Aren't we the little masterful one then?' she teased, but was secretly pleased that he was beginning to view her as belonging to him.

By the early hours of the morning, the music got slower and the numbers on the dance floor thinned out. Guy and Mary danced slowly, their arms entwined about each other. Suddenly Guy started and looked at his watch.

'Geez, I'm sorry, it's four o'clock and the taxi will be waiting outside. The time seems to have gone so quickly,' he added, as though trying to find an excuse. He could see from the look on her face that she was disappointed. 'I'm sorry,' he said again. 'I thought this thing would be almost dead by now.'

'It's not that.' Her mouth puckered into a slight pout. 'I just wanted to stay with you.'

'Oh, that's no problem, I'll pick you up in the morning and we'll spend the day together.' He smiled at her.

'No, not spend the day with you,' she said with some emphasis. 'Spend the night with you.' She flicked her finger through his hair behind his ear and the penny dropped. He was caught by surprise.

'Well, yes… I see…' His mouth went dry and his brain into a whirl. 'What I mean is are you sure… no, no, not are you sure, but do you…? Do you think it's a…'

She had her hands clasped around the back of his neck and leaned back from the waist and gently rubbed herself against him. If that were not enough, the look in her eyes dispelled any remaining doubts that he might have had.

'I'll go and pay the taxi then.' He broke away from her quickly before he suffered any further loss of self-control which would leave him unable to walk across the dance floor without embarrassment. Although the rules were not nearly as strict about entertaining members of the opposite sex in mess rooms, he was pleased that the corridors which led to his room were deserted. They wandered along slowly, Guy wanting to hurry, but Mary happy just to saunter, almost enjoying making him wait and asking all sorts of questions about the people she had met. His mind went racing back to a similar situation some years ago. He simply could not go through the same thing again. He had asked himself a thousand times since cancelling the taxi whether he was doing the right thing or not. Surely the signals were unmistakable this time, but he had thought the same then and look where that had got him – almost thrown out on his ear.

They reached his room and Guy unlocked the door and stood back to let Mary enter first. She walked in slowly, as though expecting someone to be hiding behind the door, and carefully looked around. He was pleased he had not left the place in a mess. 'Um,' she nodded approvingly, 'not bad for a bachelor. At least you made your bed.'

'Not really,' he muttered. 'The cleaning ladies make the bed when they come round in the mornings.'

'A cleaning lady?' She tossed her head. 'That'll change when we're married.' She stopped and put her finger to her lips and looked at the floor. A moment of embarrassed silence followed before she slowly brought her eyes up to his, a small smile on her face. 'Er, that wasn't supposed to come out like that. Sorry, it must be the drink talking.'

He gaped at her for a few moments and she turned away, pretending to take a deep interest in a painting of a Harrier that was kicking up lots of dust whilst taking off from a small clearing. 'Was that a proposal?' he asked.

'Certainly not. That's not my job.' She had regained some of her composure.

'Well then…' he paused for a moment, looked at his shoes and then back at the slim figure who was tracing lines in the dust on top of his chest of drawers.

'Doesn't do much of a job, your cleaning lady. This thing is covered in dust.' She held her index finger towards him.

'Will you do a better job when we're married?' he asked quietly. It was her turn to stop and stare.

'Is that a proposal?' she asked after a time.
'It might be,' he answered.
'What do you mean, it might be?' She sounded a little haughty.
'Well, it depends on how good you are at dusting.' He grinned at her, half-expecting a loose object to come sailing through the air. She looked around the room as though searching for something, before turning to face him. Slowly, without taking her eyes from his, she reached up behind her neck, undid the fasteners to her dress and lowered it to the floor until she was able to step out of it. Then for a moment she stood facing him dressed only in a pair of brief, black panties. She stooped down and picked up the dress and gently ran it along the top of the chest of drawers.
'How's that?' she asked.
'Will you marry me?' he croaked.

Chapter Twenty-Eight

Events moved very quickly in Guy's life over the next year. Two months after the ball, Mary announced that she was pregnant. Three months later, with everything frantically arranged, they married, and three months after that he was told that he would be promoted on the next list and could expect a posting to Jaguars with all the attendant upheaval of training courses and moving house.

The marriage very quickly settled into a routine that neither of them, given a choice, would have wanted. They had had insufficient time to get to know each other properly, and although certain that they were in love, had little time to relax and enjoy their new relationship.

A second, and then a third baby, followed in as many years. Guy pursued his career in earnest. Having made the great leap forward into the ranks of the senior officer, he was not going to let any opportunity to further advance himself go astray. Mary was as supportive of him as she could be with three small children to look after, but the strains of running a family and trying to be the loyal, supportive wife were difficult acts to balance. She worked hard at it and to all intents and purposes appeared a good wife.

Mary enjoyed service life, as she had thought she would. She was surrounded by like-minded people and there was no shortage of support when she needed it, but as the years went by she found that Guy was more and more preoccupied with his job.

The more time he gave to that, the less time he gave to her and the children. Now, as the wife of the squadron boss, she often remembered the lady who had greeted her at the pre-ball drinks and wondered whether amid the non-stop, near-chaos of her life she presented a similar picture to the world. She suspected not, but tried her best.

Guy, for his part, often wondered what he had got himself into. He loved Mary and enjoyed her company, but things had never been quite as he imagined they should be. One great event seemed to clatter on top of another; a birth, a promotion or a posting, and before he could fully adjust to one another came crashing down on him. He loved his children, and had readily agreed when Mary had suggested that having started with babies they might as well continue and get them out of the way in a short spell of time without stretching it out over several years. As she had set her heart on having three, and he was not averse to the idea, within as many years the house seemed to be brimming with small, demanding objects and all their accessories. He saw himself as nothing but a provider and little else in his own house. Mary looked after him quite well; his meals were invariably on the table when he arrived home and his clothes were washed and ironed. In the bedroom she went from willing accomplice to a dutiful wife and the periods between and the enthusiasm with which they attended to their sex life became greater on one hand and less on the other. Guy found himself craving for something more. He was used to being the centre of attention, especially where the women in his life were concerned.

It was three years after the wedding that he was first unfaithful to Mary. It was nothing serious, but a tawdry one-night stand with a nurse when he had been away on a detachment in Cyprus. It had given him short-term relief, but, weighed down with a sense of guilt, it had not achieved the desired effect. Still, having strayed once, he found it easier the next time and, while not for a minute wishing to jeopardise his marriage, he continued to look for opportunities to relieve his sexual frustrations. It had not always been easy. Not being at his most natural with women, he had found, as he had often in the past, it difficult to read the signs as to when he should make a move or not. This on occasion had led to some embarrassing incidents, although nothing as serious as what had occurred in the snooker room years previously.

He had, however, unknown to either himself or Mary, developed something of a reputation among the squadron wives as a toucher. During dances he would allow his hand to wander lower than might be considered appropriate, or brush against girls in an intimate way in the hope that these moves might elicit a favourable response. Far from the reaction he wanted, it merely achieved the reverse. He was considered a dirty old man by the younger ones and something of a fool among the older ones. It was rare that such talk reached the ears of the husbands, for fear that a reaction might jeopardise a career. Guy was not popular with the wives, while Mary, well liked, was viewed with sympathy as a long-suffering wife.

Chapter Twenty-Nine

Two days after the airmiss, Robin Granger replaced the receiver carefully on its cradle and stared ashen-faced at the far crewroom wall. 'What's up, Rob? You look like you've seen a ghost or Hunch's underwear.' Bertie Grice put down the magazine and looked at his fellow navigator with some concern.

'It's no laughing matter, Bert.' Granger looked close to tears.

'No, I'm sorry, Robin. I didn't mean to be flippant but then Hunch's underwear is no laughing matter either. No, no,' he quickly held up his hands, 'I'll try and be serious. What's the matter?'

'I've been bloody posted. I've hardly been here a year and the bastards have posted me back to Nav School as one of the instructors. I don't believe it. I just don't bloody believe it. I don't know what I'm going to tell Wendy. She's three months from popping and we've only had the house a few months and now I'm supposed to up sticks and move to deepest, darkest, bloody Lincolnshire at the drop of a bloody hat. Wendy'll have a bloody fit, I know she will.' He paused for breath and wiped the back of his hand across his mouth. Then his frustration gave way to anger and two small areas of pink appeared on his cheeks. 'Fuck 'em, just bloody well fuck them.' His voice was shaking and a fist came hard down on the arm of the chair to add emphasis. 'More importantly, fuck him,' he added, motioning with his head towards the squadron offices.

'Go and see the Boss, he'll sort it out for you,' Bertie urged. 'That's what I would do. There must be some mistake or something, go on, go and see him. What have you got to lose?'

'You must be joking,' Granger hissed. 'I'll bet a pound to a pinch of shit that he was the one who set it all up in the first place.'

'What did the poster say on the phone?' Bertie asked. He sounded hesitant. The thought that the Boss might have had something to do with the posting had shocked him a little.

'Oh, he just made the right noises, said that he was sorry and said someone had dropped out at the last minute and they needed a replacement in an hurry and my name was the next to come out of the hat.' He waved his hand airily round the room and then allowed it to flop onto the chair; all of his energy seemed suddenly spent. 'I told you the Boss blamed me for the airmiss, didn't I? Well, this is his revenge. He might be all sweetness and light on the surface but underneath he's just a self-centred bastard like the rest of them, with only thoughts for his own arse.'

'Keep your voice down, Robin, someone might hear you.' Bertie glanced anxiously towards the door.

'You mean they might give me a shitty posting with a week's notice for mouthing disloyalties?' Granger's lip curled in a sarcastic leer.

'Why don't you go and see Tom Cookson, then? He might be able to help you.' A deep frown furrowed Bertie's brow. He was finding it difficult to come to terms with the accusation, although sure that the Boss was blaming Granger. Suddenly, Granger grasped the arms of the chair and propelled himself across the room.

'Where are you going?' Bertie was afraid that he was rushing off to confront the wing commander, and in his present frame of mind that could only get him into more trouble,

'You're right, I'll go and see Tom Cookson; at least I'll get some straight talking from him and he might be able to sort something out. The worst of it is, I don't really mind the thought of going back to Nav School for its own sake, but a week's notice of a posting is just ridiculous. It's just so bloody unfair, but at least when I'm there I'll be miles away from that bastard.' Again he nodded towards the Boss's office, stuffed his hands deep in his flying suit pockets and slumped dejectedly towards the door.

Tom Cookson was spending one of his rare afternoons at his desk. He hated paperwork and the thought of spending most of the rest of his RAF career locked up in a dim office somewhere in the bowels of the MOD was making him think seriously of quitting when his contract finished on his thirty-eighth birthday. He was not overly enamoured with the prospect of flying airliners, but it might well be the lesser of two evils. He put the thought from his mind and tried to concentrate on the report he was writing. The tap on the door came as a welcome break. 'Come in,' he yelled. He had been so deep in concentration that the knock had made him jump and the pen had left a nasty little mark on the page. The funereal features of Robin Granger appeared around the door.

'What can I do for you, Robin? I'm afraid Squadron Leader Seagrove's not in. He went out over an hour ago and I haven't seen him since.' The two shared an office, but Seagrove was Granger's flight commander.

'No, sir, it's you I'd like to see, if that's okay.' In fact, Granger had made quite sure that Seagrove would not be present, well aware that he would not have been given a sympathetic hearing and probably just told to get on with it and stop making a fuss. Cookson eased back in his chair and clasped his hands behind his head.

'Have a seat, Robin.' He nodded at the chair in front of the desk. 'What can I do for you?' he repeated.

'I've been posted, sir. Barnham have just been on the phone, and they've given me one week before I have to report to Nav School as an instructor.' Cookson let the chair tip forward onto its two front legs and they hit the carpet with a slight thump.

'That's a bit sudden, isn't it?' He sounded surprised. 'You've only been here half a dog's watch. What's the story? What did the chap from Barnham say exactly?'

'Just said it was one of those things, sir. They needed someone in a hurry and it happened to be me, tough luck.'

Cookson ran his forefinger across his lower lip as he considered the matter; the chair was again tilted backwards. He had his own suspicions about what was going on, but kept them to himself.

'Right,' he said after some moments, 'leave it with me. I've got a mate down there. I'll give him a ring and see if I can find out what is going on. I'll get back to you, okay?'

He tried to smile at the dejected face in front of him. He was in no doubt that if the Boss was involved in the deed there would be very little he could do about it. He watched the hunched figure leave the office and, as the door closed, picked up the phone and dialled. Ten minutes later he had explained the full circumstances to his friend, including the airmiss. He would make some discreet inquiries. Cookson doubted that he could influence the course of events, but at least he might be able to fill in the background. Even the most bizarre postings that he had known to come out of Barnham usually allowed more than a week's notice, and if they had to hurry one through then it was with the consent of both parties with some sort of sweetener involved. He pondered the possibilities for several minutes and made some attempts to get back to his report, with poor results. The more he thought about it the more he could see the involvement of Guy Kelsall. When the phone rang he was on to it immediately.

'Tom?' The voice at the other end sounded slightly puzzled. 'I've found out what I could, which I'm afraid is not much. This all happened further up the line and they are keeping it pretty close to their chests, but this I can tell you – the initiative for this one did not come from this end.' He paused and let the weight of what he was saying sink in. Cookson made no comment and the voice continued, 'It seems as though the request for the posting came from your end. It was put through yesterday morning and, although I can't get anyone to tell me who it was, from the winks and nods I'm getting I would put big money to short odds that whoever it was has an office very close to yours.'

There was another long pause as both men allowed the information to be digested. At last Cookson broke the silence. 'This doesn't surprise me in the least. You don't think there is any way we could get the thing changed, do you?'

'Not a cat in hell's chance, Tom. This deal, however it came down, has got some pretty heavy fingerprints on it. Whoever your man's pal is, and I have my suspicions, he sits in a fairly high place and is not given to changing his mind.'

'Okay, John.' Cookson sounded dejected. He hated the old boy's net and this was clearly an example of it working at its worst. 'Thanks for all your efforts. I appreciate it. How's the family by the way?' The two men chatted for several minutes about the more mundane parts of their lives before Cookson carefully replaced the receiver. 'Well, you bastard. You sneaky, self-serving, underhand little bastard, you,' he muttered. 'Pick on little boys and pregnant wives would you? You sneaky, cowardly, bastard.'

A new image of his commanding officer was beginning to form in his mind. This was a new animal. One to be watched. One who could be dangerous and use what weapons he had in a devious, underhand way. Cookson shook his head sadly and moved to the door. The paperwork could look after itself for the day.

Cookson found Granger in an empty crewroom. Granger half-rose from his chair as the more senior man walked into the room, but Cookson waved him to sit down and slumped into the next chair. 'I've been on to my contact at Barnham, and he has been doing some snooping around.' Cookson kept his voice low, although there was no one within earshot. 'It seems pretty much as they told you; they needed someone in a hurry and you picked the short straw.' He paused to let the younger man absorb what he had just said.

'But next week, sir. I can't get it all together by then,' Granger pleaded.

'I know,' Cookson murmured gently.

In the couple of hours since he had learned of the posting, Granger had adjusted to the idea of a tour at Nav School. He would be one of the first Tornado navigators to return to the staff and it would give him a certain amount of credibility, but the trauma of organising his personal life still remained.

'I was coming to that, Rob. I've arranged for you to have two weeks' leave, only one of which need come out of your entitlement.' Cookson was now playing it off the cuff, knowing he would have to do some very fast talking with the admin section to fix it up, but was confident he could arrange it. The offer seemed to mollify Granger.

'Okay,' he sighed, 'thanks for your, help, sir. I appreciate it. I must say that I thought there was more to it than that. It occurred to me that possibly the wing commander had…' he paused, searching for the right word, 'might have tried to get rid of me after the airmiss.'

'Good Lord, no, Robin.' Cookson gave him a friendly pat on the shoulder. He hated lying, but telling him what he knew would not help the situation at all. It was better that he started his new job feeling wanted, and it was highly unlikely that whoever had fixed it up would go about bragging. It was wise not to show Wing Commander Kelsall that one of his flight commanders had a different perspective of him. Mister Nice Guy, like so many reptiles, had teeth that only showed when he was riled. Tom Cookson made another mental note to watch his own six o'clock.

Chapter Thirty

The rumours began to intensify. Training was being concentrated more and more on airfield attacks. The ground crew were working overtime, practising loading JP233 and, to many people's disgust, night flying was becoming the norm. In the middle of a British summer that meant very late nights. The papers were full of it – troop movements, the build up of arms, political posturing.

'Just who is this chap Saddam Hussein anyway?' Hunch sprawled in one of the crewroom chairs, a cup of coffee in one hand and a day-old newspaper in the other. 'I mean, just who the hell does he think he is, trying to tell the world that our good and loyal forefathers, who colonised the entire world practically, could have made a mistake when they drew a line in the sand and said, "You lot stay that side and you lot stay on the other"? It just doesn't make sense to me.'

'I don't know why you're getting so hot under the collar; when that was going on your lot were probably swinging from a tree somewhere being told exactly the same thing.' Bertie was on thin ice and knew it.

'I'll have you know that our lot, as you so rashly refer to us, were of royal descent and lords of all they surveyed.' Hunch waved his hand in a grand sweep that encompassed the room.

'So you want us to go around bowing and scraping and referring to you as Your Royal Highness or something?' Bertie grinned.

'I've got to say that a little courtesy and respect would not go amiss, but anyway, to get back to the question, just who the hell does this bloke think he is? I'm up half the night practising dropping a weapon that I think should be kept under lock and key until someone comes up with a little motor to propel it. The ground crew are working their butts off loading and unloading the damn thing, and every time I pick up a newspaper all I get to read about is some politician attempting to talk sense into these people and now, to cap it all, he's gone and put hostages in all the likely target areas. Well, it's just not bloody cricket, that's all I can say.

'Are you having difficulty finding the comic section of the paper?' John Sommerton looked up from his magazine with an embarrassed grin on his face. He was fairly new on the squadron and was still an unknown quantity.

'Did you hear something then, Bert? Maybe not. I just thought for a minute that someone said something.' Hunch made an extravagant search of the room.

'He's got a point, Hunch. Unless it's brightly coloured or has two global things practically hanging out of a dress then it doesn't usually get your attention.' Bertie poured himself a coffee and smiled at Sommerton. Anyone who took the mickey out of Hunch was all right with him.

'These are troubled times, Bert.' Hunch tapped the paper on his knee to add emphasis. 'Serious political happenings are afoot, and they require serious attention. As they say, all things in season and a season for all things. It's beginning to look like this may well be the season when some faceless politician is going to ask me to put my arse on the line, and when that happens I want to have some inkling of why I'm doing it. Blasting Russians, now I've been reared on *that* notion. It's been plain for centuries that they, for whatever reason, were the enemy. Now, I'm told to forget all that. They are now the good guys and we now have to turn our attention to this lot in the Middle East. Work all night in the middle of an English summer trying to find enough darkness to cover the bit between take-off and landing. Practise with JP233. Try and get through as many fighter CAPs as you can, and for what, I ask?'

'Protection of a small country's sovereignty.' Sommerton spoke again.

'Did you hear that, Bert? I swear I heard that noise again. Oh, it was you, John. I'm sorry, I didn't see you sitting there. Did you say something?' Hunch peered closely a the small, fair-haired young man on his right.

'Kuwait's sovereignty, that's what it's about,' Sommerton repeated.

'Well, that's it then, Bert. John here seems to have put his finger right on it. We all go to the desert and get our butts shot off to protect the right of some unheard-of sheikh to continue to get rich. Makes perfect sense.' Hunch slapped his newspaper down on the adjacent chair and looked away in disgust.

'Hunch, give it a rest, will you?' Bertie sounded careworn. 'It's the role of the powerful to protect the weak and the vulnerable against unfair aggression.'

'You don't think the fact that a fair proportion of the world's oil supplies come from that region has anything to do with it, do you?' Hunch was not about to be fobbed off.

'It might have a very small bearing on the matter.' Sommerton was becoming quite animated. 'But the bottom line has to be freedom, and that is surely worth fighting for.'

'John,' Hunch leaned towards him, 'I've only known you a very short time and I notice that you have a particularly serious side to your nature. Would you mind if I asked a particularly personal question?' He paused as though trying to frame the question in his mind. 'Have you ever been laid?'

A flush of colour came to Sommerton's cheeks and he looked quickly down at the magazine resting on his knees. 'I don't see that it is any of your business and I certainly don't see what it has got to do with this conversation.' He sounded angry.

'As I thought, Bert. Now there's a boy who needs something worth dying for.'

'Give it a rest will you, Hunch.' Bertie sat down heavily and slopped some of his coffee onto the arm of the chair, which he disdainfully brushed away. 'You don't half go on at times. Pay him no heed, John. It's one of his well-known tactics when he's losing an argument – change the subject. He just likes the sound of his own voice.'

'Jennings,' Tom Cookson's voice could be heard coming from the corridor. Hunch groaned and muttered, 'What now?' and slumped even further into his seat.

'Jennings,' the voice was getting closer. Cookson appeared round the door. 'Get your arse into gear. I've got a tanker booked in just over an hour and a half. Just you and me and no one else in sight.' He sounded as though he were relishing the thought.

'Love to come, sir, but I'm just in the middle of a very important philosophical discussion about the developing situation in the Middle East. Oh, and John Sommerton's suspected *virgo intacta*, so tanking is completely out of the question at least for the morning.'

'Jennings, if you are not changed and at the outbrief in ten minutes precisely then I will personally see to it that no *virgo*, *intacta* or otherwise, has the pleasure or otherwise of your attentions again.' Cookson could not help but grin at the look on Jennings's face.

'Well, if you're that keen on me giving you a few tips on tanking then far be it from me to hang around here putting this lot right. Sorry, fellas, you'll have to sort it out on your own, this thing we were talking about.' The tall man struggled to his feet and the three others simultaneously raised their eyes to the ceiling.

'See you, Hunch; remember to try and hit the hole in the middle of the basket and not the open spaces round the outside.' Bertie grinned at his pilot who aimed a kick at his foot.

'Get stuffed, Grice.'

'Ah, the merry banter of men who fly aeroplanes.' Sommerton quietly had the last word.

Cookson was in the middle of a difficult morning, the only bright spot being the prospect of a few hours in the air, although his plans did not include sitting watching Hunch ravage a refuelling hose. The three squadron executives had been trying to draw up a list of those who would go on the detachment to the Gulf, should the need arise. Hunch had been on Cookson's list. He saw him as a good, reliable sort who would stand up well to the strains of combat if it came to that. The Boss had taken another view, arguing that his tanking abilities were poor and that his constant chatter occasionally got on his nerves. To settle the dispute, Cookson had said that he would sort the tanking problem and report back. They had left it at that and Cookson had been obliged to make the arrangements straight away.

Chapter Thirty-One

Within two hours of the meeting breaking up they were at twenty thousand feet off the coast of Flamborough Head. Cookson left all the flying and radio to Jennings in the front seat. He did not get much pleasure from flying in the back. He had done too much instructing in his time, and considered sitting in the rear seat akin to being in an open dustbin, but he saw Hunch's problems as something of a challenge. Half-listening to the conversation on the radio, he gathered that the tanker was at eighty miles at a height of twenty-two thousand feet. He idly flicked on the radar and watched the gentle sweep of the head. Usually the sole preserve of the navigators, he found the movement quite therapeutic. He lowered the angle of the head until the scope was full of ground returns and then slowly raised it until nothing was illuminated. 'A black art,' he muttered under his breath. The navs made such a big deal of it. He set the range rings at sixty miles and waited. Frost could sometimes pick the thing up at that range, but he was good. He tweaked the tilt and watched for a couple of sweeps and then he saw the dot. He dismissed it at first, but in two more sweeps it had moved a fraction down the screen.

'Got it,' he muttered, trying to hide the excitement in his voice.

'Got what?' Hunch asked.

'The tanker, clear as a bell at fifty miles, just slightly right of the nose and it looks like it's on track to cross our nose at about thirty miles.' Cookson sounded matter-of-fact.

'I think you're seeing things, sir. Even the navs aren't that good. Go back to sleep and I'll give you a shout when we've got some petrol on board.'

'Tanker forty-six miles, very slightly right of your nose.' The fighter controller who had been quiet for some time broke into the conversation.

'I rest my case,' Cookson allowed his voice a note of triumph.

'Can you make toast as well?' Hunch asked.

'Only the crispiest kind.' Cookson replied.

'My hero,' Hunch breathed and both men smiled.

'Yep, it's still there and at about twenty miles. With your eyesight you won't be able to see it for another two minutes, so I'll keep talking.'

Hunch knew that in two minutes, with a closing speed in excess of eight hundred miles an hour, the thing would be past them. He squinted into the distance, constantly refocusing his eyes on distant clouds to avoid myopia in the vastness of the upper air.

'Got it.' It was Hunch's turn to sound triumphant.

'Not bad,' replied Cookson. 'Eight miles, not bad at all.'

Hunch tried to find a note of sarcasm in the voice, but there was none. Cookson took his eyes away from the tube and blinked hard, adjusting to the brilliance of the outside world. It was several moments before they focused on the small, black dot.

'Visual with the tanker.' Hunch relayed the message to the ground.

'Clear to make contact with the tanker.' The slightly bored voice of the controller clicked off as he completed his part in the join.

Hunch was in no way intimidated by the senior man in the back. He made no reference to him, going about his business as though he were not there. Cookson liked that. He had lost count of the number of times he had come across men on check rides, some of them quite experienced, who had not been able to operate without asking what he wanted to do next, when all he wanted to see was how they operated the machine.

Hunch misjudged the turn by going too early and was in danger of being in front of the tanker as he rolled out, but he kept his nerve, not breaking the golden rule of climbing towards the Victor. Instead, he allowed the Tornado to slide to the other side and, as the gap between them widened, pulled into the six o'clock position, before climbing the necessary thousand feet into the correct place on the port side. It was not pretty, but it was safe and achieved the object. Cookson mentally applauded the move. The tanker captain peered at them from the Victor's cockpit before clearing them to join on the starboard basket.

With the checks completed and the probe out, Cookson could see the extra inputs that Hunch was putting into the control column as it danced between his legs. The tension was mounting. The aircraft slid backwards and downwards relative to the tanker, stabilised and then slowly moved across below the tanker's jet wake. The manoeuvre behind the basket was copybook, the only give-aways that Hunch was working hard were occasional bursts of breath which activated his microphone, and the feeling that they were travelling over cobblestones. With his first movement forwards, the basket twitched as it felt the Tornado's bow wave. Now, the stick between Cookson's legs was a blur as it moved around in tight, little jerks mirroring what was happening in the front cockpit. Much as he wanted to, there was very little he could do to help.

The lights on top of the pod changed from red to green, inviting the contact. Again the aircraft shook a little as Hunch realised that this was the moment of truth. He moved forward at a steady pace and the basket responded by moving outwards on the bow wave and then upwards to meet the probe. It looked for all the world like it would be the perfect contact and Cookson momentarily worried that he would not be able to prescribe a cure if he could not see the fault. Hunch did not let him down. With three feet to go the control inputs increased and the basket and probe started their familiar dance. Cookson suddenly felt a small movement on the rudder. The aircraft yawed almost imperceptibly, but the probe, several feet away from the aircraft's axis swung through several feet. The basket passed by it on the outside and, as the yaw reversed, came back to meet the aircraft and gave it a solid cuff just behind the rear cockpit. Cookson instinctively ducked and the hose snagged under the arm of the probe. Hunch, to his credit, resisted the urge to panic. He had been here before, although the more experienced man was breaking new ground.

'Just got to ease her up a little, then ease forward... there.' The basket whipped away as the hold on it slackened and cavorted like a newly released colt in a springtime meadow. 'Ah, sorry about that. I thought I almost had it that time.'

'You almost had me.' Cookson could not resist the comment, despite a lifetime vow never to ridicule the student. 'I'm not surprised Bertie is rude to you most of the time if that is how you treat him.'

'Yes, now you mention it, he is occasionally rude. I'm glad I'm not the only one who's noticed. Perhaps you'd like to have a word with him, sir. Just joking,' he quickly added.

'You've got big feet, Hunch.' They were behind the basket again.

'That's a very personal thing to bring up at a time like this, sir.' Hunch sounded a bit hurt.

'You're an ass, Jennings.' Cookson tried to sound annoyed to make the point, although he found it difficult to be upset by the man. He seemed indomitable. 'Keep your great feet off the rudder pedals and stop trying to correct with yaw.'

'Right you are.' The basket hovered invitingly, waiting for the next onslaught.

'Just let go of the stick, Hunch.' Cookson's voice was quiet and measured.

'Well no, sir. I'd rather not, if you don't mind.'

'Just let go, Hunch.' The voice was slightly threatening, but Cookson's hands were very close to the controls.

'I don't want to, sir.'

'Why not?' The question had bite.

'We might roll and hit the tanker.' Hunch sounded nervous.

'Why is that?'

'Because I might not be quite in trim.'

'Then trim the fucker.' It was almost a shout and Hunch jumped. Cookson could almost feel the aircraft relax in the airflow as Hunch worked the trim switches.

'How's that?' Cookson asked after several seconds. 'You in trim?'

'I think so.' Hunch sounded less than positive.

'I have control.' Cookson took hold of the control column and gingerly relaxed his hand. The aircraft held its line. 'Okay, not bad. You have control again, now just do it like the book says.

Ignore the basket, watch the lines.' It was a long speech for Cookson.

The gap between basket and probe closed. Twitch, steady, forward and then repeated. The two men held their breath. Achingly slowly, the probe entered within the rim of the basket, seemed to sniff to see if it liked where it was and then rammed home.

'Fuel flows.' Hunch exhaled so loudly that his microphone was activated.

They took a small amount of fuel and then broke contact.

'Right, just do it several more times and we'll go and enjoy ourselves.'

Hunch was rather hoping that once would be enough. He scraped in a couple of times and then made two perfect contacts.

'That's enough. I couldn't bear the boasting in the crewroom if you got any better.' Cookson tried to sound low-key but was quite proud of the day's work.

On breaking away and moving to the starboard, Hunch noticed for the first time that two other Tornados were waiting their turn.

'How long have they been there?' Hunch asked in surprise.

'Just the last couple of efforts.' It was out before Cookson realised what he had said.

'Showed them how it should be done, eh, sir?' Hunch snorted down his nose. 'Do you think they know about trimming? Think I ought to mention it, sir?'

'You're just full of shit, Jennings. Just take me home before I get covered in it.' Both men smiled again.

Chapter Thirty-Two

The pattern of squadron life had changed gradually over recent weeks. More and more work was finding its way onto the desks of the two flight commanders. The Boss was absent for longer periods, ostensibly to attend various meetings around the station. In reality, Guy Kelsall had decided that no career was worth dying for and, no matter what the pressures, he was not going to become a statistic, as the station commander was fond of calling it. Neither was he going to throw away his valuable career. There was a vast amount of difference between working to death and appearing to be working to death, as he was well aware. There were plenty of people around who could adequately do the work. He merely saw it as his job to delegate, which in no way barred him from taking the credit for any successes. After all, if he were to get any of the brickbats going, he should also be the recipient of any glory.

An additional problem were the extra visitors who seemed to accompany the deepening crisis in the Gulf. Senior officers, politicians and their hangers-on arrived daily, each demanding time, effort and endless explanations of the arrangements that were in hand for any deployment. It all added to the work. It would have been acceptable if they could have taken the place at face value. But, even if they had wanted to, the station commander would not have been happy. Even a simple visit lasting for only a few minutes involved taking an aircraft away from flying and having crews standing by to answer endless questions. Suddenly the world wanted to know about JP233.

Cookson had been back and forth to the manufacturers with his ideas. Even they had been a little surprised at his more flexible usage. Numbers had been crunched and distances between the cratering devices calculated in order that the best angles to cut across the runway could be ascertained. After all his hard work, it was a bit galling to hear the Boss spouting knowledgeably to visiting dignitaries about the weapon, as though all of it was his idea.

Relations between the two men, which had never been better than cordial, deteriorated. Not only was Kelsall ducking out of his share of the work by off-loading jobs, but he was also adding to the pressure by demanding that the work be completed within shorter timescales because pressure was brought to bear on him from further up the line. The adjutant and his small staff had never worked so hard in their lives. Demands for them to produce operation orders seemed to come from every direction at once. It was just the adj's luck that when the opportunity arose go somewhere nice and hot, there would probably be a bloody war going on.

Kelsall and Cookson skirted round each other like boxers in the opening seconds of a fight, neither wishing to tangle with the other. Kelsall, now openly admitting to himself his hatred for his flight commander, realised that he needed the man and his expertise, especially where JP233 was concerned, more than ever. This was certainly not the time to get rid of him. But that day would come, Kelsall was sure. In the meanwhile, Cookson's undoubted expertise was invaluable, especially as the likelihood that the weapon might be used in anger increased with each passing day.

Cookson, for his part, was not inclined to pick a fight with his superior just for the sake of it. While his view of his future was by no means clear-cut, it was not his way to close doors unnecessarily. When the bust-up came it was, like many such incidents, born of a trivial thing.

The endless discussion about who should go to the Gulf and who should stay behind was still continuing. The plan was to deploy six Tornados and twice that number of crews. It had been agreed, much to Seagrove's disgust, that he would remain and run the rest of the squadron. No matter what the crisis, commitments to the European theatre still existed. The three executives had started like school boys picking the playtime football team. 'I'll have him', 'No, you can't have him, you already have one weapons instructor and I need one'. The meeting had progressed quite well with no major disagreements, and Guy finding himself more a spectator, interfered very little.

'Hunch Jennings,' he heard Cookson say. 'I think he should go. He's quite good under pressure. If the balloon goes up, he'll be an asset to the moral of the others.'

'I'll go with that.' Seagrove readily agreed and was adding his name to the list when Guy spoke.

'No, we can't possibly send him, he's useless at tanking. He'll just be a liability.'

'He used to be, that's true,' replied Cookson, a slow smile spreading on his face, 'but I took him up on the tanker a couple of weeks back, pointed out a few flaws in his technique, and since then he's been fine.'

'How many times have you watched him since then?' Guy snapped.

'Well, personally only a couple of times, but…'

'Not enough,' Guy butted in. 'He doesn't go.'

'I was about to say, sir,' Cookson tried to sound patient, 'that I've asked several people who have been up with him since, particularly young Bertie, and they can't believe the change. Word on the street is that he is like a young god on the tanker. In first every time. As smooth as a cat pissing on velvet was how it was described to me.'

'I still don't like it,' Guy said. 'He doesn't go.' The room was quiet for a moment.

'Look, sir.' Tom Cookson broke the silence. 'I don't want to argue with you, but Jennings and Grice are one of the best crews we have, particularly under pressure. You saw what they did in the inter-squadron competition, nearly swept the board, and there were some good crews in that event. It would be foolish not to include them.'

'I agree with Tom, sir,' added Seagrove. 'Much as I would like them to stay, I think they should go.'

'I didn't say anything about Grice not going.' The wing commander spoke in quiet measured tones. 'In fact, he is going, as my navigator. I would like that to come into force as soon as you can arrange it.' The two flight commanders looked at each other in some surprise.

'Well, I would congratulate you on your choice, sir. That's not a bad idea. Give young Grice some responsibility, which won't go amiss.' Cookson sounded upbeat. 'It also solves another problem of who to crew with young Sommerton.'

'Who?' the tone of Kelsall's voice indicated that he knew what was coming.

'Hunch,' Cookson made it sound as though there was no other solution. 'Once he has got over the shock of no longer flying with Bertie, they'll get on well together.' Cookson added quickly, 'Yes, the more I think about it, the better that sounds. They go to the Gulf as a crew.'

Guy drew his breath in sharply, staring hard at his hands, which were poised in front of his face like a church steeple. A tight little smile spread across his lips, but the eyes were hard and unblinking. His face reddened and he spoke slowly, softly and deliberately. 'I do not want that black bastard to go.'

The stillness which fell on the room was deafening. Seagrove froze with his pipe inches from his mouth and his lips slightly open to receive it. He stared at his boss dumb with shock and horror. Cookson was more animated. He clenched and unclenched his fists, shifted in his seat and alternatively looked between floor and ceiling as though trying to get some divine inspiration before finally looking at the man who had spoken.

'What exactly do you mean by that remark?' The tone was measured and challenging; it held no hint of compromise.

Guy Kelsall shook his head as though waking from a dream. 'No, no,' he smiled. 'I didn't mean it like that. What I meant was that if he got shot down and captured, his colour might count against him. I've no problem with it myself,' he added weakly. He opened his hands and held them upwards and outwards in a gesture which suggested that there could be no possible misunderstanding. 'What I'm trying to say is that it might go harder with him, that's all,' he continued, looking at each of the men in turn as though craving their agreement.

'For Christ's sake, Boss,' Cookson spat the words. 'He's Afro-Caribbean, not Egyptian. There is no reason why he should be treated differently to anyone else. Anyway, one of the reasons I want him to go is that with his skills and aptitude he is less likely to be shot down than some of the others we're talking about, and he might actually hit the fucking target as well.' His voice rose to a near shout and he clapped the palm of his hand against his forehead in frustration.

'Do not take that tone with me, Cookson.' It was Kelsall's turn to be angry. 'You might think you're the ace of the base around here, but I still call the shots and I won't be spoken to in that manner by you or anyone else.'

Silence again returned. Seagrove starred unblinkingly at Kelsall. Over the last few weeks he had made a drastic reassessment of the man. He had joined the squadron about a year after Guy Kelsall and had been in awe of his flying skills and the way he apparently ran his squadron. But things had slowly changed. Firstly, his wife had told him that all was not as it should be between Kelsall and the rest of the wives. He had chosen to hold his counsel on the subject, believing that they were all old enough to look after their own affairs. Then he had watched as the Boss had shirked important decisions and off-loaded problems onto others who, in theory, were less qualified to deal with them. But mostly he had been disgusted at the way Granger had been treated after the airmiss, having been made to shoulder all the responsibility. He had felt guilty about his own inactivity, excusing himself by pretending that he could not change things without making matters even worse. Now this. In one sentence Kelsall had shown himself to be a racist to add to his other shortcomings. Seagrove was boiling.

'Sir,' his tone was measured, cold, and menacing, 'you will put Jennings on your list to go to the Gulf or,' he held up his hand to stop the wing commander speaking, 'I will expose you as the cowardly, racist, womanising son of a bitch that you really are. I know that what I'm saying will mean the end of my career, and for that I have some regrets, but I can no longer stand by and allow what you have said here today go unchallenged. Now if you will excuse me I have other work to do.'

Seagrove stood up rather stiffly, turned and slowly walked to the door. His gait was that of a man much older, but his head was held high. The astonished gaze of the others followed him until the door softly clicked into place behind him. Cookson turned to face the senior officer. He had never seen or heard of anything like that in his life and suspected, with some delight when he saw the look on Kelsall's face, that he had not either.

Guy stared unblinking at the door for several seconds. Only his cheek muscles moved. Slowly his eyes came back into focus and he turned to Cookson. The look of hatred and malevolence that Cookson had seen at the briefing was there. 'Put Jennings's name on the list.' It was a voice from beyond the grave and cold shivers ran up Cookson's spine. 'But, if you ever breathe a word of what was just said in here today you're history.' A pointed finger was thrust in Cookson's direction. 'As for Seagrove,' the corner of Kelsall's mouth was drawn in a sneer. 'He was right about one thing for sure – he's on the beach.'

Part Two

Chapter One

Wing Commander Kelsall raised the lever and felt the slight thump beneath him as the wheels settled in the wells. The aircraft was clean and away. He was pleased to be leaving the damp, drizzly October day behind. He was angry, the departure had not been what he wanted. He had asked the crews, as discreetly as he could, to say goodbye to their loved ones and families at home but as usual no one had listened to him. Wives, girlfriends and children had been all over the place; mixing tears with brave little smiles and clinging like grim death to each other, while their offspring had been allowed to run amok. Even Mary and his own kids had defied him and turned up and, far from setting an example, she had allowed herself to cry when he had started to leave. It had been most unsettling.

The last couple of weeks had been bad enough as it was. Politicians made decisions one minute and changed them the next. Military chiefs responded by calling instant-readiness states only to cancel them just as quickly. The work had been intense. A new enemy to learn about. They had progressed from nothing, not even having a map of the region, to a comprehensive knowledge of the area and its military potential. Early prognostications that it would be a jaunt to 'kick ass' were hurriedly reassessed as the size and scale of Saddam's airforce and army became clear. If the man chose not to be moved by political force, it could prove difficult to move him by military might. The task had been taken very seriously: heads had been buried in books and a whole new war scenario learned.

Guy had watched his crews change over the weeks. They had driven themselves hard, flying their backsides off. He had seen the young ones, some with only a year or so's experience, return in the early hours of the morning, eyes bloodshot from peering into 'E' scopes while blackness surrounded them and the ground rushed past unseen two hundred feet below the belly of their aircraft. Daily routine had been one thing; the war that probably would not happen. Now they were preparing for a war which, as the days went by, seemed more and more likely, as one diplomatic effort after another failed. Death in their environment was not unfamiliar. Anyone who had flown military aircraft for any time had lost a friend or an acquaintance. It was part of the job. 'So-and-so has bought the farm'. 'Oh, shit, really, he was a good mate of mine in training. How did it happen?' Each would quietly contemplate for a few moments who would be the next one, inwardly shed a tear, shrug, whisper 'tough luck' and get on with their lives.

This war would be different; it would not be a rational war. Not a war fought between sworn enemies, who had frothed and sneered at each other down the years; enemies who gloried in different ideologies and were prepared to fight for them; enemies who had grown up together so that they knew each other, if not like brothers, then as enemies. This was not like that. This was a stranger in the street who was going to knock you down for no reason whatsoever. Could you beat him? You didn't know. Could he beat you? You didn't know. All you could do was prepare or run, and running was not an option.

Kelsall had not had to browbeat the young men into the air. They had gone willingly, knowing that skill was life, knowledge was safety. They had honed their skills. Night-tanking became just a routine, not a test of flying proficiency, but a means to getting more fuel and more range. Navigators learned to keep their radars switched off, relying on precision timing to avoid the other aircraft in the formation which were unseen a few hundred yards away. What lighting a cigarette had been to a sniper in the trenches, a radar beam was to modern equipment. Information came in a few seconds or something more permanent replaced it – death.

To Guy, even the shape of faces had changed. Jaws had become firmer; eyes held a look of steel. History had told him that the British were a warrior nation, born out of countless conflicts, created from a melding of bloods from staunch defenders and ruthless attackers. Now he could see it in the faces around him. They would make a terrible enemy because they would see it through, it was as simple as that.

'Tanker in about fifty miles, sir.' Bertie Grice interrupted his thoughts. Guy had decided that if war was a possibility, he was going to have the best navigator. Although Bertie was not the most experienced, he was certainly proving to be one of the best. The change had not been popular. Grice and Jennings had been made pairs leaders, and it was only a matter of time before they would become four-ship leaders. Now, while Grice would have it all, Jennings would have to wait while his new nav caught him up. He knew of their friendship and compatibility in the air, but that did not matter to Guy. All that mattered was his own survival and Bertie was just another step towards it.

To his right, a couple of hundred yards away, Guy could see the other Tornado. Its sandy brown colour took a bit of getting used to after the dark green that had been such a part of his life. He had briefed the crew to stay closer to him than normal, knowing that the civilian controllers in the busy London control area would not want them spread all over the sky. Later, as they crossed into France and the airways became less congested, they would spread out and conserve fuel. It seemed slightly incongruous to Guy that they should be going to war in an airway.

'Less than ten miles, sir,' Bertie intoned. Now far ahead Guy could see the black dot that was the tanker. Bertie had called it correctly. There was no need to hurry, they were catching up, closing the gap at a rate of a mile a minute and the bracket was planned for north of the island of Elba.

The plan was to make Akrotiri, on Cyprus, the first day, have a night stop and then continue to Muharraq on Bahrain Island in the Persian Gulf the following day. Apart from the bracket at Elba, there would be a second one south of Sicily and then the tanker would turn and land at Palermo.

Guy, despite his concerns, suddenly felt relaxed. Over the past few weeks he had pondered the idea of dying, but more especially the thought of being captured and tortured by an enemy who might not be as gentle and forgiving as the Geneva Convention required. It had certainly worried him, as it had the others, but he had done what he could to prepare and now he felt ready. He felt a surge of excitement at what lay ahead. He had been further buoyed by the words of the station commander as they shook hands in front of the HAS sight: 'Good job, Guy. You and your squadron have done well. I'm pleased and proud of you, particularly the work you did with JP233. I know you'll do a good job in the Gulf.' To gain the spoils he had to come back alive, and that, one way or another, he intended to do.

Chapter Two

In the second pair, Cookson and Frost were leading Jennings and his new navigator, Sommerton. Hunch had taken the split with Bertie very hard. He had begged Tom Cookson to intervene, but had been told that it would probably be for the best in the long term. Cookson had insisted that his experience needed to be spread around and that new navigators needed some guidance from the older hands. He had taken comfort from that, but it was still a bitter pill to swallow not flying with his old mate. He had made one last effort to sway the Boss, but had been told in no uncertain terms that if he did not like it, a posting could quickly be arranged. After what had happened to Granger, he was in no doubt that the threat was valid. He had quickly and quietly beaten a retreat, terrified of not going to the Gulf. Not because he wanted to fight, but because he was more afraid of missing out and of the others thinking that he had ducked the issue.

John Sommerton had the face and innocence of a cherub. Although twenty-six, he still looked like a teenager. A graduate of Cambridge with an honours degree in English Literature, it was a mystery, even to him, how he had found his way into the back seat of a Tornado. Three years at university had not increased his worldliness and the relatively short time he had spent in the RAF had been something of a culture shock. Bookish discussions had done little to prepare him for life in the real world, and it had suddenly dawned on him that life was hurrying by without even giving him a nod. A sudden, almost inexplicable, curiosity about the RAF had led him to try his hand at being a pilot. Only a few trips in a Bulldog had been sufficient to persuade all concerned that it was not for him. He was assured that if he wished to stay in uniform then being a navigator was his best bet. He grew quite used to the idea of a life in uniform, the orderliness of it, knowing where he stood, and, rather than go back to the uncertainty of looking for a job, especially when he hadn't the faintest idea what he wanted to do, he took the option. If anybody had predicted that he would be going to war in such a short time, he might have thought again. The long arguments over the waste and immorality of war, which had filled his days at Cambridge, seemed so far away. He idly wondered, as he looked at the Channel below, what his former friends would think if they could see him now.

The academic feel of Nav School appealed to him. His brain adapted well to plotting and astronavigation, and he had graduated second in the class with a full choice of what he wanted to fly. He had chosen the Tornado, not only because it was the newest and one of the fastest in the RAF's inventory, but because his mother had been dead set against it. It was dangerous. She had not forgiven him for joining the RAF. If he was intent on playing soldiers, why could he not join a nice Guards regiment as a prelude to getting on with a proper career in the law, like his father and elder brother had done?

Arriving on 58 Squadron, he had still been in awe of his own situation. Everything had seemed larger than life, and any lingering doubts about his previous decisions had been instantly dispelled. Everyone had been so kind and made him feel welcome, particularly Hunch and Bertie, who had taken him under their wing. They had advised him about all sorts of things that seemed commonplace to them, but which to him were wondrous. Some of the advice had been good, some had turned out less so, particularly the bit about the Boss whom, he was assured, in deference to his Australian background, was not adverse to being called 'Sport' in the bar or other off-duty occasions. Also, despite what they had told him, MacKensie had got into quite a lather when he had suggested that all navigators were chopped pilots like himself. On both occasions, he had gone away surprised to get a flea in his ear, but he had failed to spot the giggling pair in the corner.

He could not help but look up to them. They had a reputation of getting the job done and, although their sense of humour sometimes passed him by, he liked them. Then suddenly they were split up and he found himself flying with Hunch. Replacing Grice had both surprised and alarmed him; they had seemed such big boots to fill. The first few sorties, if Hunch's attitude was anything to go by, had not been a success. Any attempts he had made to be helpful had been met with disdain, and the relaxed friendliness that the more experienced man showed him on the ground was not replicated in the air.

Hunch hated the change. All the old routines, which he had taken for granted, had to be taught to the new man. But the more they flew together, the more Hunch began to realise that Sommerton was a very professional and capable operator. What finally swung Hunch's opinion came on a very difficult night exercise. They were flying number four in a simulated attack on an airfield in Devon. Low cloud and drizzle masked most of the countryside. In normal circumstances the flight would not have gone ahead, but these were not normal times. The aircraft and their crews were being taken to their limit. Because of the weather, the crews were unable to keep a visual watch on each other. There were long periods when they were unable to see anything at all. It was imperative that each aircraft kept its station in time and space perfectly, particularly over the target, where the separation had been reduced to less than twenty seconds.

Hunch had neither the time nor the capacity to keep an eye on their position, monitoring the 'E' scope was more than enough. The thin wavy line on the small screen was his whole world. If the line was penetrated by a ground return, he would have little enough time to react. Dark moorland, unseen two hundred feet below the belly of the aircraft, was sufficiently absorbing for one mind. Throughout the sortie, Sommerton had remained calm and collected, and a steady précis of information had been fed to Hunch without overloading him or adding to his problems. The radar had been used in such short bursts that Hunch wondered how he had been able to get anything useful from it, but following a couple of sweeps, he had reassured Hunch that all was well and each aircraft was where it should be. His announcements were so monotonous that Hunch was reminded of a Victorian lamplighter. On later analysis, the radar film, what little there was of it, had shown their attack to be easily the best of the night. Hunch had preened himself in the reflected glory, assuring Sommerton that if he stuck with him, he would someday be a navigator of whom his mother would be proud.

As bachelors, unencumbered with heavy farewells, neither had any qualms about going to the Gulf. They were even looking foreword to it in a strange way. Hunch had no doubts that Saddam would back down, although he had told a different story to a few of his girlfriends and their final farewells had reflected their concern, much to Hunch's delight. No one in his right mind, Hunch reasoned, was going to take on the might of NATO. Nevertheless, each in their own way had addressed the possibility of death. Hunch had given a whole minute's serious thought about who should inherit his beloved golf clubs, coming to no firm conclusion, but reflecting that someone or other would probably have the decency to give them a good Christian burial. Preferably in the middle of the eighteenth hole, where each golfer could pause for a moment's mellow remembrance in his passing.

Sommerton had sort of said goodbye to his family the week before. He had been going out of the door before plucking up sufficient courage to mutter, 'I might not see you for a few weeks.'

'Why?' His mother barked the question. 'You haven't found a woman or something, have you?' She added, her tone accusing, 'I trust she comes from a good family?'

'No, mother, nothing like that.' How much she exasperated him. He knew she meant well, but his twenty-six years, a good number of which had been spent away from home, had done nothing to change his standing in her eyes. It never ceased to amaze him how his father coped.

'We're going on rather a long detachment, that's all,' he said.

'And where, might I ask, is this detachment going, or is it some major military secret?' Her posture indicated instant disapproval.

'The Gulf.' He said it under his breath, hoping that she would not catch the significance of it. He hoped in vain.

'You're not going there, and that is final.' Her face was quite florid and her mouth a tight little line. He remembered a conversation she'd had with one of his schoolteachers. The poor man did not know what had hit him.

'It's not a question of whether I want to go or not, it's a question of having to go. I'm not, for the next few years at least, able to pick and choose where I go and even if I did,' he tried to sound defiant, 'I would still go.'

'I shall write to your commanding officer.' It was as though he had not spoken. 'I'll tell him you're not experienced enough to go gallivanting around war zones. That's what I shall do.'

'Mother,' he was trying to stop getting angry, 'if you do such a thing, I shall never visit this house again.'

Her face suddenly changed. Gone was the firm mouth in an instant and her face melted before his eyes. A tear welled in the corner of her eye and slowly trickled down her cheek. She aged as he watched. This was a face he had never seen.

'Mother,' his tone was now confused, 'what's the matter?'

She covered her face and for the first time since he had been a child, he put his arms about her, half-expecting her to brush them aside. Instead, she buried her head in his shoulders and sobbed. It took several minutes before she regained her composure.

'It's all right, thank you, John. I'm all right now. Of course you must go and do your duty. I'm just being silly, that's all. You're all I've got, that's all.'

She turned and walked slowly down the hallway. He watched her go; in all his life he could not remember her showing such affection. He had an urge to follow her, to tell her it would be all right, that he would return. Instead he shook his head sadly and let himself out into the road. Women were a complete mystery to him.

Jennings had no such problem; sometimes he wished he did. His parents were on some grand tour of the United States. He had dutifully written to tell them, but so far had received no reply. It had occurred to him that they might not notice if he failed to return. The thought saddened him for about ten seconds. Packing had been his main problem. What to take and what to leave behind had always been a major issue in his life. He had lived so much of his life from a suitcase, that if he left something behind, he was never sure when he would get to see it again. The RAF had been the first real settled home he could remember, and suddenly that didn't seem so settled.

His first inclination was to take very little. A quick war suggested a few changes of underwear, his flying clothing and a good book. Then he had heard rumours that their billeting arrangements might be somewhat out of the ordinary for a war scenario; no less than an hotel in Bahrain. That had changed everything. Now, he attempted to get the entire contents of his drawers and wardrobe into a suitcase. DJ or mess kit or both? He decided neither, then had second thoughts. He had one in each hand, held at arm's length when Bertie burst through the door. 'Can't make a decision, Bert. Which do you reckon?' Bertie looked at his friend with a wry smile on his face. He had been here before.

'If I were you, Hunch, I should take them both. You'll need the DJ for the pre-hostilities drinks in Baghdad, and the mess kit will come in handy when we have the post-hostilities ball in the middle of the bloody desert.'

'You're taking the piss out of me, aren't you?' Hunch looked hurt.

'Me? Take the piss out of you? You who have circumnavigated the world several times, a modern traveller, a man for all seasons?' Bertie's face was a masterpiece of wrinkled concentration.

'You are, you're taking the piss out of me. You don't think I should take either, do you?'

'Not exactly, Hunch. And if you're thinking of taking your golf clubs,' he pointed at the bag which was lying under a pile of clothing, 'I have to tell you, that apart from a bloody great bunker, there is not much by way of golf courses in the district.'

'You disappoint me, Grice. You really do. I try to bring you up to be an officer and a gentleman, to tune you in to the finer things in life, and all I get is the downside of things. The negative angle. No golf course, no drinks parties, no balls, just a sodding war. Well, I'll listen to you this time, but if it turns out to be anything other than you've described and I don't have a bow tie with me, you'll never hear the fucking last of it.'

Chapter Three

Jennings, Sommerton and Grice had walked slowly to their aircraft. Bertie had left his new pilot in the thick of saying goodbye to his family and various other well-wishers. The three had found it all slightly embarrassing. They had decided to keep the thing low-key in their minds. Treat it as a detachment. If it came to war, then they would deal with it as and when it happened. Weighed down with extras, such as chemical biological suits, gas masks, pistols and maps, it was difficult to stay cool even on this dismal day.

'It was very kind of the mess to make us a packed lunch, don't you think, Hunch?' Sommerton was trying to peer into a nondescript white, cardboard box. Hunch looked at his navigator as though he had two heads.

'They didn't do it out of the kindness of their hearts, John. It's part of their job. We live there. We pay them money to live there, and in return they feed us. Not too well most the time, I grant you, but they do put a meal on the table.'

'I know that, Hunch, but well, they seem to have gone to a bit of trouble, that's all.' Sommerton was dying to look into the box to see what had been provided. It reminded him of the one picnic they had had as a family when he was a child. It had been such a nice day, a rare family outing. He smiled at the memory. Hunch always had a way of reducing things to a base level. It would get to him if he didn't watch it.

'While we're at it,' Hunch flicked the box with his finger, 'if you take my advice, you'll not get them out before we're abeam Ponza at least. It'll be a long trip if you use up all the good things too early.' Hunch sounded like his dad and it heightened the feeling of the picnic. He just wished he knew where Ponza was; he didn't like to ask. In this company he had learned that silence had its compensations. The lesson in the bar had been well learned.

They followed Cookson into the air an hour later. Cookson seemed to have adopted them as his wingmen for reasons that they neither knew nor cared to ask about. It was enough for them that it was the way of things. The flight commander was a good operator and an approachable figure. They were pleased to be under his wing both literally and metaphorically. They climbed to their cruising level of twenty-eight thousand feet using the afterburner, partly to assist London air traffic control and partly for the thrill of it. 'Greased weasel shit,' he heard Hunch mutter, and gasped as they were spat out of the clouds, passing ten thousand feet, seemingly in a vertical attitude. With the first tanker bracket little more than an hour away fuel economy was not a factor.

In the calm void of high altitude, the magnitude of what they were about to do and of where they were going hit them. Sommerton could not particularise a point of no return, he just instinctively knew that it was behind. The questions started to come. How would they perform? How would they react under the pressure? Each man in his own way prayed that they would not let themselves or their side down. It was a moment for quiet contemplation.

It was Sommerton who broke the silence. 'Hunch, could I ask you a favour?'

'Sure, Sport, almost anything, but I will not now, or at any time in the future, have anything to do with that horrible cousin of yours.'

'What do you mean, you bastard? She's not so bad; anyway, you only met her once, and then she was not at her best, having just ploughed through her exams.'

'Sport,' Sommerton had been landed with the name as a further legacy of his *faux pas* in the bar. 'If she were the last girl left on earth, and I had not had it away for a decade, your cousin would only come second on the list of candidates for my attentions.'

'Shut up, will you?' Sommerton sounded exasperated. 'It's not about that at all. What I was going to ask you, if you can keep your big mouth shut for just a nanosecond, was far more serious.'

'All right, I'm all ears.' Jennings lifted his visor and swung his head round as far as he could and stared at his navigator with wide unblinking eyes. 'Shoot.'

'No, I don't want a favour now.' He sounded sulky. 'It's far too serious for a prat like you to be entrusted with. I'll find someone else to do it for me.'

'Aw, stop being an idiot, Sport. Of course I'll do you a favour. Just pull yourself together and ask me. I'm serious again.' He pulled his visor down and faced the front.

Sommerton was quiet for a moment. 'Look, this is fairly confidential, and I'm relying on you to be discreet, something that's not readily apparent in your nature,' he quickly added.

'Yeah, yeah,' Hunch interrupted.

'Just be quiet for once and listen, will you?' Sommerton was exasperated now; even Hunch could pick up the intonation. 'Look,' he repeated, 'I've never really been close to my parents. I know they love me in their way, and have always tried their best for me, but with one thing and another, careers and whatnot, we've never had much time for one another. I was thinking that if anything happened to me, I would, just for once, want them to know how I've felt these last few years. I've written a letter. Not to send, particularly if nothing happens, because then I should feel a bit of a fool, but if something does happen, and I don't make it, would you see that they get the letter?'

'You melodramatic bastard, Sport,' Jennings snorted. 'Does it not occur to your tiny, little, Oxbridge brain that if you "don't make it" as you so eloquently phrase it, I would have preceded you to the hereinafter by one of your nanoseconds, and as such would be well into a conversation with St Pete at the Pearlies about what an absolute berk was coming up the celestial stairs in my wake?' Hunch exhaled an exaggerated sigh.

'I *know*,' Sommerton practically shouted, 'but if you make it and I don't, would you send the bleeding letter? That's all I'm asking.'

'All right, I'll do it, now let's change the subject. You're getting me all morose, and I've just realised that I've forgotten to pack my favourite teddy bear.'

'Fuck off, Jennings.'

Hunch smiled to himself. He could not recall his new navigator even swearing mildly before, never mind using language like that. He was obviously settling in.

The mood in the cockpit lightened, and they droned south through the clear skies, now with the tanker for company. By Lyon, they got the first view of the Alps, newly encrusted with the first snow of the coming winter. To pass the time, they played mountain-spotting. Mont Blanc was easy, its great bulk dominating the skyline. They argued over the Matterhorn, agreed on the Massif Centrale, which was easy, and ended the game with Hunch sulking because he had never even heard of Mont Venteau. Fuel was taken on as they coasted out over Nice, and in the blue of the Mediterranean the hazy outline of Corsica could be seen in the distance.

Sommerton's stomach was beginning to grumble, and he wished that Ponza had never been mentioned. They left Elba in their wake, passed abeam Rome, and the green of northern Europe had long since given way to the ochre and sienna of the south. The air was less clear, and great banks of cumulonimbus, were scattered about triggered by the heat and the distant mountains.

'Ponza,' Hunch boomed from the front seat. 'If you haven't already dipped your sticky little fingers into the delights prepared for our palates, then now is the time to begin.' The silence which followed was broken only by the odd curse as each man laboured with the massed layers of cling film in which the kindly chef had enclosed his offerings. Hunch stared malevolently at the spread before him. Four great wedges of bread, hacked from the loaf, encased slices of corned beef which had been bedded for eternity into sleepy lettuce leaves and margarine. The world had yet to see a mouth that could easily encompass such an obstacle, particularly since every bite required the removal and then the replacement of the oxygen mask. The number of times the kitchen staff had been urged to present the sandwiches in small, bite-sized format had been lost to history.

'God, it's simply amazing what they can get to pack between two slabs of bread these days, isn't it?' Hunch casually remarked.

'What's so amazing about a piece of corned beef and a lettuce leaf whose mother must have been shagged by a cabbage before she gave birth to this?' Sommerton sounded disappointed; he disdainfully held up the offending leaf and examined it, before placing it to one side, careful not to cover the radio.

'Corned beef? *Corned beef?*' Hunch sounded incredulous, 'Is that what you've got?' Sommerton grunted. 'You seemed to have dipped out, old boy.' Hunch oozed enthusiasm. 'Oh no, this is much more interesting than that. In one lot I've got prawn mayonnaise with some pungent spice of the Orient.' He gave a pronounced sniff. Sommerton frantically searched the box to see if he were missing something. It failed to register with him that sniffing through an oxygen mask was a pretty mean trick. 'In the other, let me see…' He made a great performance of lifting the edge of the bread to peer underneath. 'Oh yes,' he enthused, 'in the other, I've got finely cut roast beef layered with what looks like mustard. I'm going to enjoy this.' He made smacking sounds with his lips.

'How the bloody hell did you get that in your sandwiches and I get corned beef and an out of work lettuce leaf? It's some sort of bloody conspiracy.' He sounded agitated. Hunch noted that his rate of swearing was increasing markedly by the minute.

'How often must I tell you, Sport,' the voice was that of a tired schoolmaster about to inflict corporal punishment, 'this will hurt me more than it will hurt you? It's not what you know in life that counts, it's who you know. My cousin's sister just happens to be shagging the brother-in-law's brother of the chef's wife. It's really that simple.' A long pause followed.

'You're a bastard, Jennings. Without doubt you'll end up with a very hot arse after you're dead for telling such porkers.' A piece of lettuce leaf flopped on the side of Hunch's helmet and draped itself over the corner of his visor. In the laughter a crew was born.

Chapter Four

Cookson left Easeham with a heavy heart. He had a sense of foreboding that had been with him for some time. He had no explanation for it, but he knew that the trouble brewing in the Gulf was not going to go away. Since the early days of the standbys and false starts, he had not for a moment pretended to himself that the squadron would not deploy to the Gulf or that a war would not be fought. As a consequence, he had mercilessly drilled the people who would be going. No stone had been left unturned in the training of both aircrew and groundcrew and no excuses for shortcomings had been accepted. If things had not gone right the first time then the exercise was repeated, over and over, until they had.

He felt he had been given minimal support by the wing commander. After the Seagrove outburst, the two men had come together for a short time through sharing a common purpose, but that had not lasted. More and more work had landed on Cookson's desk, and to get the job done he had assumed more of the responsibility, often taking decisions without referring to the more senior man. This had rankled with the Boss, causing the relationship to deteriorate until it was worse than it had ever been. It had been Cookson's initiative to invite the families to see the aircraft off. He knew Kelsall had not wanted it, but he also knew that the families had made sacrifices in the last few weeks, while absent daddies and husbands had worked all hours preparing for war. They deserved some recognition.

Another bone of contention had been a party which Cookson had arranged. Convinced that the squadron would not be around for Christmas, he had directed a couple of the junior officers to organise something for the children. The Boss had found out about it only a few days before the event was due; he had immediately thrown a wobbly and demanded its cancellation. Only some fast talking by Ord, of all people, had convinced

Kelsall that it should go ahead. When Cookson saw the expressions on the faces of the younger children as Father Christmas had stepped down from the back seat of a Tornado, he knew the confrontation had been worthwhile. Nevertheless, it was a further widening of the rift between the two men.

Guy Kelsall had again considered leaving Cookson behind, but as Seagrove communicated with him only in monosyllabic grunts, he was in no position to disregard his experience. Guy contented himself that Cookson, in a time of crisis, would be solid and reliable; but apart from meetings and discussions which were necessary for the smooth running of the squadron, they kept their distance from each other.

★

Hunch and John Sommerton made their meal last from Ponza to Sicily. Hunch had the added problem that the autopilot was playing up, and was having to balance the badly made cardboard box on his lap while wrestling with the controls. Twice, he had dropped part of his sandwich on the floor, and each time, as he had tried to retrieve it, the aircraft had banked to an alarming angle, causing Sommerton to yell out. Now he was thirsty. He had been careful to avoid tea and coffee before the flight. The thought of having to use the 'P' tube had never appealed to him and today of all days, with no autopilot, it would have been impossible. Now that they were over halfway along the route, he could risk having a drink. He reached for the box of orange juice and hurriedly tore at the seal. The liquid was warm but satisfying and he had to tell himself not to overdo it. Clamping his mask back on his face, he surveyed the pomp and majesty of Mount Etna with the air of a satisfied man. A small wisp of smoke streamed from the dark hole just below the summit. 'Biggest active volcano in Europe, that is, Sport,' Hunch proudly announced.

'So, they did teach you something in the red bricks then?' Sommerton seemed to be getting the hang of the conversations.

'You cheeky shit,' said Hunch, the best he could manage by way of a witty reply. They were drifting back on the leader. He gave the throttles a nudge before realising that he still had the better part of a litre of orange juice in his hand, and cursed softly as some of it spilt onto the throttle quadrant. He scanned around the place for somewhere to put the carton, tried to jam the thing between window and combing, almost spilling the lot behind the instrument panel.

'Hold this for me, would you, Sport?' He proffered it back towards Sommerton.

'Not a chance, mate. I've got the same orange juice holder as you.' The boy was catching on. Flat surfaces were at a premium. In fact, as he quickly discovered, the manufacturers had made no provision whatsoever for little picnics at twenty-five thousand feet. By now the next bracket was less than fifteen minutes away. The choice seemed simple. Spill the bloody stuff all over the electrical panels or drink it. He chose the latter, belched loudly, muttered 'pardon' and crumpled the box between the side of the seat and the fuel panel. Again, he surveyed the world with a degree of satisfaction. He was actually looking forward to the next bracket; it would relieve a little of the boredom which was setting in.

The tanker came and went. The lazy afternoon droned on. All around them was sea and sky and a sun-washed layer of golden haze to the south. 'Where the hell is Crete? You promised it hours ago.' Hunch was beginning to sound like a kid on a long car ride who had eaten his chocolates before leaving the street. 'You haven't got us lost, have you?'

'Just go back to sleep, Hunch. I'll give you a nudge when it's time for one of those crashes you try to pass off as landings.'

'Sleep? I'm working like a one-armed paperhanger to keep you from becoming a statistic. It's graft without an autopilot.'

Crete came into view. A long, thin, blue-grey monster rising from the sea. It bathed itself in the late afternoon glow. Hunch heaved a sigh of relief. His back was beginning to ache and he was dying to stretch his legs. He had wound the rudder pedals forward as far as they would go to stretch his legs, but gained little comfort. The litre of orange juice was beginning to filter through to his bladder. He cursed the person who had so thoughtlessly packed the thing and cursed the person who had designed the cockpit with nowhere to put a simple thing like a drink. The island seemed to stretch into eternity. On other days, he might have enjoyed the view.

'Minator.' He nodded to his right as though it were sufficient explanation.

'Gordion Knot,' Sommerton replied.

'That's in my arse.' Hunch wriggled in his seat and Crete finally slipped into their six o'clock. He heaved a great sigh of relief. He had looked at the 'P' tube and contemplated using it, but it all looked too difficult, especially as he had a wayward Tornado in one hand. He could hold out.

'How long is it now, Sport? Must be nearly there.' The child spoke again.

'Not long now, Hunch,' the parent replied. 'Only about an hour.'

'An hour? Sixty bloody minutes.' Anguish.

'Yep, that's right, Hunch. You seem to have got the hang of that one, a twenty-fourth of a day.'

'You're lying, aren't you? Just tell me you're trying to get your own back for all the nasty things I've done to you.'

'Ah, so you admit that you've done nasty things to me in the past?'

'Well, only small, nasty things, but I was young, immature and influenced by that Grice person. If you come clean and tell me it's less than an hour I shall wipe the slate clean and treat you in the future like a god.'

'Well, in that case, Hunch, I can tell you that it's now only fifty-eight minutes. So try and keep your pecker up. Or down,' he mused almost to himself, 'whichever is appropriate.'

'Shut up, Sport.' It was delivered through clenched teeth. 'Who ever said that this job was glamorous?'

'Not my mother.'

★

The engineer marshalled the Tornado onto a stand in the middle of the massive concrete apron. Bleached almost white by the sun, the heat shimmered from it even in the late afternoon. The

Tornado was going rather quickly for his liking and he tried to slow it down by slowing his arm movement. The driver was in some hurry, and the marshaller leapt to one side as it rocked violently when the brakes were aggressively applied. The canopy was on its way up instantly, the pilot standing and gesticulating before he had the steps in place. The man appeared in pain, bent almost double, holding his lower stomach with one hand and beckoning with the other. The steps in place, they met in the middle, the engineer going up to check the pins, the pilot coming down. The engineer had the sense to jump before being knocked off. He watched the madman rush towards the nearest building. Then it dawned on him. 'Welcome to Cyprus, sir. Mind you don't piss on your fingers, and wash your hands afterwards.'

Chapter Five

The ground glistened below them. The aircraft on the aprons at Muharraq were so densely packed that the sun glared off the upper wings and canopies, causing Guy to look away. They had left the tanker an hour before; Cookson and Jennings had gradually caught up; now they hung loosely behind him in arrow formation. The earth had changed again. The relatively fertile areas of the Mediterranean had been replaced by endless tracts of desert. The aircraft which had looked out of place in the green of England had come home.

The prompt clearance for a run-and-break had come as a relief. Kelsall had half-expected the long drawn-out approach favoured by the Americans. After two days strapped into a cockpit, he would be glad to get out and stretch, not to mention having a long, cool drink and a hot bath. The rest of the formation tightened about him. At five hundred feet, he had brief moments to marvel at the amount of hardware already in situ. Row after row of F15s, F16s, AWACs, Hercules and Starlifters seemed to fill every available space. He wondered if Saddam really knew what he was up against; this was only a part of the force ranged against him. The sudden burst of adrenaline, knowing that he was part of it, eased his tiredness.

Oven-hot air rushed into the conditioned cockpit the instant the canopies moved upwards. The change was breath-taking. Guy did not like it. Out of his environment, he almost longed to feel the cold rain of an English autumn on his face, to be running with the kids through leaf-littered woods – anywhere but here. This was not his place or his fight; he suddenly wanted out. He whipped off his helmet and his tiredness returned. A hand appeared over the side of the aircraft clutching a can of beer, dripping with condensation, and pressed it towards him. He took it in gratitude, but made a mental note that the practice could not continue. He put the can of cold lager to his lips, drank thirstily and smiled at the grinning face that had followed the hand.

'Welcome to the land that everyone else forgot, sir. Good to see you. After all these American kites, it's good to see something that's British. It's bloody hot though.' The face didn't wait for an answer but hurriedly stuck the safety pin into the ejection seat before scurrying down the ladder. Guy took another long drink and slowly followed. His limbs felt heavy and, although he tried to stretch the feeling away, it stayed with him.

Their accommodation was spacious, modern and well equipped and, judging by the number of planning tables, maps and charts around the place the advance party had not been idle. A crewroom had been arranged with comfortable chairs and a fridge well stacked with soft drinks and snacks. If they were to fight a war, then there were worse places to do it from.

Guy listened attentively as Ian Ord, who had been in charge of the advance party, briefed him on the situation.

'Good job, Ian. Well done. You've obviously been very busy.'

Ord's cheeks quivered in satisfaction at the praise, knowing it was only rarely given. 'The best is yet to come, sir. Wait until you see the living accommodation.'

'You've got us a few tents in the local wadi or something?' Guy gave one of his rare smiles. He tried to appear in good spirits and as if he was pleased to be there, but he was just putting on an act.

'Not so, sir, no less than the Hilton downtown. No accommodation on base, so it was the second best.' It was Ord's turn to give a rare smile.

'Right, you lot.' Guy turned to the rest of the crews. He could see from their tired faces and bloodshot eyes that trying to achieve anything more that evening would be like flogging a dead horse. 'Put your flying kit away and we'll go to the hotel. We'll be back here in twelve hours; six local and I can promise you nothing but flying, flying and more flying, so go easy on the local brews this evening.'

'That a promise, Boss?' It was Jennings as usual with his puerile humour. He chose to ignore it. He hated the bastard.

They drove off the base and marvelled at the piles of equipment that seemed to be haphazardly scattered around as though there were not enough places to put it all. Thousand pounders lay alongside JP233 and next to them spare drop tanks. The threat was being taken seriously; it was sobering to the crews.

The base behind them, they drove across the causeway to Manamah city. Here the other face of Bahrain showed itself. A long palm-tree-lined road led towards a line of skyscrapers. Mercedes cars, mingled with expensive off-road vehicles, hurried past in both directions. This was not a place of war, it was a holiday centre. Bertie Grice softly whistled between his teeth as the bus stopped in front of the hotel. No one moved. This could not possibly be the right place. The RAF simply did not go in for marble edifices.

'Come on, you lot, this is home for the duration.' Langstaff jumped to his feet, grinning. The heat hit them again as the doors of the air-conditioned bus opened.

'I could bloody well get used to this,' Bertie muttered.

'So could I. Here, leave that alone.' Hunch was chasing after a uniformed doorman who had taken hold of his suitcase.

'Leave it, Hunch. It's what he does.'

'They expect me to get up in the morning, wash, shit and shave in a place like this and then go out and die. Unreal, man.' Hunch was incredulous.

'Well, if you do as you say, you'll at least die clean, and that way your mother won't be ashamed of you.'

They wandered inside ready for someone to rush over and tell them there had been some terrible mistake and their accommodation was out back in a tent. They were given rooms, the only drawback was that they had to share. Hunch glared at Sommerton. 'You'd better not snore, or fart for that matter.'

'Listen who's talking. King of the heap himself. It's you who should worry on that score, Sport. I should go to sleep in your gas mask, if I were you.' Bertie was enjoying himself, as the Boss's navigator, he had a room to himself. It was the first positive perk to come his way.

'Right, you lot, the three S's and back in the bar in fifteen minutes,' Hunch ordered.

'What sort of code is that, Bertie? The three S's?' Sommerton asked.

'It's Hunch speak for a shit, shower and shave, but he'll probably skip round the second one, so if you want to come with us you'd better get your skates on.'

The bar was packed. Every ex-pat in the place seemed to have heard of the newcomers in town and had gathered to herald their arrival, taking the opportunity to break with routine. They came offering friendship, help, encouragement and more gin and tonics than would be wise, given that an early start had been called. 'If this is war then I shall die fighting,' someone had grinningly proclaimed after several drinks. By five o'clock in the morning, they were not so sure. Hunch clutched his head and felt for the alarm clock. The light in the room was already on and he could hear someone moving around. It took him a few seconds to orientate himself before he remembered where he was.

'That you, Sport?' he croaked. His throat was parched and he tried to swallow to get some moisture to it. Sommerton emerged from the shower, a towel wrapped around him. He looked fresh and wide awake, as though he had been up for hours. 'Tell me, Sport. Have you been sent by some higher authority to haunt me with your brightness and goodness? Would it not be possible for you to have a human hangover like the rest of us? The aura about you is hurting my eyes.'

'Bus leaves in ten minutes, Hunch. War might break out while you're lying there scratching whatever it is you're scratching.' Hunch sat on the edge of the bed and groaned.

'Tell me, Sport, was I dreaming last night, or did someone really tell me that there are four hundred hosties in town working for Gulf Air?'

'No, Hunch, for once your memory serves you well.'

'Mmm... suddenly this hangover doesn't feel so bad.'

'It will if you miss the bus.'

Chapter Six

Flying in the desert presented its own problems. Flat, featureless terrain, no vertical references such as trees and hills, and glare gave very little help to navigators or pilots. Height perception was difficult and there was nowhere to hide. Night would be the only cover they could expect, apart from the might of American electronic counter-measures, and it was early days to be relying on them. By taking it easy, the techniques were quickly learned and soon all the pilots were able to fly safely and with confidence at fifty feet above the ground.

The days to Christmas hurried by. Training was interspersed with swimming and socialising, while the world held its breath and wagered on the possibilities of war. Politicians postured, huffed and puffed, held meetings and gave opinions, but no agreements were reached and the date of 16 January set by the Allies for the withdrawal was creeping closer.

*

Guy had noticed her several times, either using the pool or just quietly sitting alone watching the world go by. She was older than most of the girls who had crowded to the place, attracted by the flying suits, and did not join in the boisterous bar-room sessions when the crews were stood down. Not beautiful, the features a little too sharp for prettiness, she had something about her which attracted him; neat and trim, exuding an aura of self-confidence. Calmness and with just a little mystery. Guy guessed they were of a similar age. He had at first assumed that she was an ex-pat, or, if from the school, perhaps one of the instructors, but she didn't seem to know any of the others.

She was sitting alone at the end of the bar when he came in from his shift. It had been another hard day, with pressures from all sides crowding in on him. The world's press, which had gathered in almost the same numbers as the military, all needed an angle; that special little story, different from the others, which would set them apart. Despite daily briefings, they wanted more. It was a relief to get in the air and escape from it all. Tension was growing among his men. Small things, which would normally not have been noticed, were causing flare-ups and even crews who were normally the best of friends were occasionally at each other's throats. He needed a break.

The bar was almost empty as he slowly wandered in. She was sitting on a high bar stool; it was almost impossible for them to ignore each other. Smiling, he gave her a slight nod and was encouraged when she returned the smile. He waited for the barman, ordered a drink and almost as an afterthought turned to her. 'Can I get you a drink?' he tried to sound matter-of-fact. She smiled, tossed her golden hair back with one hand and studied her half-finished drink for a moment.

'Why not?' Again the flick of the hair, and the faint glimmer of amusement that he should have offered. 'That's very kind, I'll have a Martini, please.' Guy placed the order and sauntered across the few yards separating them.

'I'm Guy Kelsall.' He held his hand out toward her. She took it and he noticed that her grip was surprisingly firm for such a slight frame. Her eyes never left his.

'I know, I'm Sam Waterson.'

'You know who I am?' He was surprised. 'How do you know who I am?'

'There aren't really that many British flying suits around the place, and even fewer with wing commander braid on the shoulder. It wasn't that difficult to learn who you were.' He found the ordinary explanation a small disappointment, having hoped that she might have gone to some trouble to find out. He studied her for a long moment; there was something familiar about her now that he had seen her close up.

'Don't I know you from somewhere?' Again the slight toss of the head, the hand raking the hair back, and the small, infectious chuckle.

'Not much of a chat-up line, is it?'

He reddened beneath his tan.

'No, no, it's not a chat-up line, honestly. I really feel I know you from somewhere. Are you sure we haven't met before? Do you have anything to do with the military?'

She shook her head. 'No, not until now, that is.' She studied Guy's face and shook her head. 'No, we haven't met. I would have remembered.'

Again he was unsure how to interpret the remark. Did she mean he was unforgettable? Her expression was void of any clue.

'What are you doing here, then?' he asked. 'That's if it's not too secret to tell.' He gave a chuckle as though he had made a joke.

'No.' Her smile unsettled him. 'I'm a doctor. They asked for volunteers, so I came. I don't know why really; I thought the experience would do me good. Certainly staying in a place like this is doing me good, but all I've done so far is to stick needles into people's arms.'

'Let's hope it stays like that.'

'I would say that, but I thought all you gung-ho airmen couldn't wait to have a crack at the enemy, with all your fancy, expensive toys.' Was she taunting him? There was a hint of mockery in her voice but her expression stayed the same.

'Well,' he hesitated, 'in a way, yes, and in another very real way, no. It would be nice to see if the training and the expensive toys, as you put it, work, but on the other hand the need to have people like you here to stop the bleeding tells its own story.'

She looked down at her foot which was gently moving up and down. It was her turn to colour slightly. 'You're right. I'm sorry, I didn't mean to give offence.'

'None taken. Here, let me buy you another drink.'

'Now you're trying to get me drunk,' she laughed.

'Who knows?' he replied, content that the ice was broken.

Chapter Seven

Over the coming days and weeks, Guy and Sam spent a great deal of time in each other's company. When their busy schedules permitted, they swam, played tennis or just sat quietly talking over a meal or in the bar. The more Guy saw of her, the more he was impressed by her. Not only was she intelligent and good company, but in a bathing suit her small, well-proportioned body stirred strong feelings in him that were something of a mystery. He was in no doubt that he wanted her in a physical sense, but there was something else. Was he in love? He was not sure. The very thought of love surprised him. He'd had affairs of course, told women he loved them, but apart from to his wife, in the early days at least, had not meant it. Now he was feeling some rather strange emotions. Was it the almost surreal circumstances in which he found himself? The closeness of war, the loneliness? He knew that he and Mary were not as close as they might be, but at least she had always been there to listen to him. Now, he was very aware that he did not have that and missed her for it. The one person who could have filled the role was Cookson, but they had virtually ceased to communicate on anything but business. Was it the closeness of death? The fact that tomorrow or the next day, he might be asked to strap himself into a Tornado and set off into the unknown? To test himself and his courage when, in his heart of hearts, he had never expected the day to come?

He began to need the woman, to miss her when they were apart. He found himself dreaming about her like some spotty teenager; thinking of things to ask her about. Sometimes, even at fifty feet above the desert and travelling at five hundred knots, he found her in his thoughts and had to shake himself out of it and concentrate on what he was doing, or the score would be one-nil to Saddam without a single shot being fired in anger.

Sam Waterson, on the other hand, did not appear to be so like-minded. She seemed to enjoy his company and was content to pass her leisure time with him, but that was all. There were no physical exchanges between them. She did not keep him at arm's length, but he was not allowed inside the emotional barrier that surrounded her. He tried all the angles he knew, from subtle suggestions, to light coercion, to outright pleading that their relationship should be allowed to bloom in a more physical sense, but she would have none of it. In fact, the moment he mentioned the subject, she would give him a knowing smile, suddenly remembering work which needed catching up on, or the early night she had promised herself. He was in limbo, torn between making his feelings known or losing her company. He was a frustrated man.

He took his frustrations to work. He was snappy, irritable and given to outbursts of temper at the smallest things. People avoided him and put his mood swings down to the pressures of the job. Others who had been more observant just wished that the lady would screw him so they could all get some peace and quiet.

*

Jennings and Grice were not suffering from the same problem. They had died and gone to heaven. The flying was unbelievable and the social life was out of this world. They had flown up-country to Tobruk, the other base. Here, everything they were beginning to take for granted was missing. Men were huddled together in makeshift accommodation and tents were everywhere. It was more like a scene from World War One. 'If we were down on that piece of sand, I might very quickly forget what we're fighting for. I think we would just have to pack up and go home,' Hunch was quick to point out to Sport as they got airborne.

'We're fighting for the freedom and independence of Kuwait,' Sommerton reminded him, 'not just a piece of sand, as you so eloquently put it, or a good bonk, as you're coming to believe.'

'Talking of bonks, as you so eloquently put it, Sport, I don't notice you making the kind of progress I would have hoped for among our fair friends from the hostie population. Is there anything I can do to help matters along? I have some quite good contacts in that neck of the woods, or should I say, sands of the desert. A little introduction, say?' They were flying back to Bahrain, down at low-level, skimming above the desert having just left the tanker. The height was becoming second nature to Hunch. Sommerton, with no control over the matter, had other thoughts.

'You keep an eye on the way ahead, and keep yourself well clear of my personal life.' Sommerton sounded annoyed.

A large outcrop of red rock whizzed down the side of the aircraft, rather closer that he felt comfortable with. They were coming to an area where the monotony of the endless dunes was broken by a cluster of hills and wadis which had been exposed to the winds and weather over centuries. A conversation with Hunch about his sex life was not his idea of a good chat at any time; now, particularly, it was better left alone.

'Only trying to help.' Hunch had not taken the hint. 'That's all, no need to get all shirty. You know me – a friend you can rely on.'

Another outcrop shaved the canopy, and the aircraft rolled violently, swooping downwards as Hunch followed the contours of the earth. 'I'm relying on you now to get me home in one piece.' Sommerton's voice held an edge of quiet concern, a David Attenborough voice while lying five feet from a great silverback gorilla and chatting with the camera as though he were ordering the weekly papers.

'Not a problem, Sport.' The aircraft reversed the bank and the G meter registered four as they bottomed out along the valley floor. Great boulders were strewn along the path of a dry river bed, witness to the power of the floods which visited the area infrequently. 'Though I would just like to add, that if there are any introductions you need, then I'm ready to help, that's all.'

Sommerton could see the end of the valley rushing towards them with no obvious way around from where he was sitting. Co-operation with his pilot was the lesser of the two evils.

'Hunch, if you get me out of here and promise to keep your mouth shut for the rest of the trip, I'll attempt to shag the whole population of Bahrain if it will keep you happy; you can probably throw in a few goats as well.' It was a long speech in the circumstances and the end of the valley loomed over them.

'No need to go that far, Spor...' The end of the word was lost in the G pressure. Sommerton's world reeled as the aircraft was thrown to the right and a small valley opened up before them. Jagged rocks stretched clawing fingers towards the top of the canopy and a silent whimper squeezed through his constricted throat. They were in and out of it in a blink and, as the aircraft lurched level, endless miles of sand stretched before them. It was several moments before he caught his breath and a few moments more before he found his voice.

'One day, Hunch, you'll go too far. I'll lose it and they'll find you with a meat cleaver sticking out from between your eyes.' Sommerton gulped for air. 'You knew all along about that valley, didn't you, you bastard? You were just trying to wind me up.'

''Fraid so, old Sport, came down here last week with Frank Langstaff, thought you'd like it. Now, about this introduction?'

'Hunch, if you so much as come close to trying to fix me up with one of your slappers, I'll... well, I'll swing for you.'

'That's not what you were saying moments ago, Sport. One of the problems I have with you navigator chappies is that you just can't make up your minds.'

Chapter Eight

'Karen, we need your help.' They were sitting in the bar of the hotel. Hunch leaned towards the girl with a plaintive look on his face.

'The answer is definitely no.' Karen, from Harlow in Essex, had a very worldly view of most things, particularly Hunch. She rummaged in her handbag, the conversation at an end.

'I haven't even asked you the question yet.' Hunch sounded hurt.

'You don't need to. I remember the last time I did you a favour, and look how it turned out. The sprain has just begun to mend.'

'That was an accident and you know it.' Hunch's face registered a rare look of embarrassment .

Bertie showed an immediate interest. 'Tell me more. I'm always interested in other people's sprains, especially when Hunch is involved.'

'You mind your own business.' Hunch was quick to slap him down. 'Look, love, it's nothing like that, honest, we need your help with Sport.' Both girls smiled and their expressions softened at the mention of Sommerton's name.

'Oh, he's sweet.' Bertie's girlfriend had a dreamy look on her face. He glared at her.

'Mmm, he is,' Karen agreed. 'He's a real gentleman, unlike some I can mention.' She gave Hunch a prod on the arm. He feigned hurt, dramatically rubbing the spot.

'Now that's unfair. I'm known for my modesty and self-effacement. I'm kind to children, animals and old ladies. I even went home last year to visit the folks, and wrote them two letters, neither of which were answered,' he added forlornly. 'Now, what more can a chap do?'

'Sure.' Karen remained unmoved. 'What favour do you want anyway?' Her curiosity was roused. 'If it's for that nice boy, I might be persuaded to help, but don't bank on it,' she added quickly.

'Well,' Hunch shuffled about in his chair, making a great thing of studying the backs of his hands. 'It's a little delicate really, and we're not absolutely sure of our ground.' He glanced at Bertie, who nodded in agreement. 'But we think that Sport still retains the flower of his youth.' Both girls looked at him with mystified expressions and waited for him to continue. 'You know.' He waved his hand about expressively, but the miens remained fixed. In frustration, Hunch blurted out, 'He hasn't lost his cherry; he remains as pure as the driven snow, he's a blinking virgin.'

The penny dropped. 'You want me to...' She pointed at her chest and her cheeks reddened.

'No, no, not you personally, I don't.' Hunch looked aggrieved.

'Oh.' For a moment she sounded a little disappointed, but then quickly added, 'I should think not as well. I'm not that kind of girl. What do you want me to do then?'

'Find someone... er... suitable.' He looked quickly away, expecting trouble.

The girls looked at each other and spoke together. 'Daisy!'

'Daisy?' Hunch and Bertie replied in unison.

'She doesn't sound quite like the kind of girl we had in mind,' Bertie added.

'Ah, Daisy by name, tigerlily by nature,' Bertie's girl assured him. 'But if it's a volunteer you need... er... I wouldn't mind...' She let the sentence drift away.

'What's with this guy that has you girls mooning about all over the place?' Bertie sounded irritated.

'Oh, I don't know. He's just so nice, polite and innocent; you just want to give him a great big cuddle.' The dreamy looks had reappeared.

'Well, you can't and that's all there is to it.' It was Bertie's turn to sound annoyed. He was beginning to wonder what Hunch had got him into. Like all his ideas it had sounded good at the start, but, again, like most of them, it quickly failed after the planning stage.

'Bertie, you're so masterful when you're jealous.' Karen stroked his arm, and he brushed her hand away.

'We're getting off the point. This Daisy person, is she the right sort? You know, presentable. I'm sure he would run a mile if she were any old… well, you know what I mean. If he even whiffs that I've had a hand in this, he'll be off and we'll never get close to him again.'

'She's perfect,' Karen assured him. 'Pretty, about the right height and not too long since she left some kind of finishing school.'

'I wouldn't mind meeting her myself.' Bertie was almost thinking aloud and earned himself a slap on the arm.

'Ouch, that hurt.' He feigned injury.

'It's nothing to what you'll get if you don't watch it.'

'Is that a promise?' He gave a playful push and rolled his eyes.

'Look, you two,' Hunch interrupted, 'just pay attention. This is an important matter. No man should have to go out into the field of battle unless he's fully prepared, and Sport, in my opinion, is not yet in the right condition, so we need to help him, even if he doesn't think we do. So, how are we going to go about it? As I said, if I'm anywhere around he'll suspect we're involved.'

'Look, it's simple,' said Karen, warming to the idea. 'You just get him into the bar. We'll sort out the rest.'

Chapter Nine

John Sommerton and Daisy Grey glanced suspiciously at one another across the table. The other two girls chatted to each other as though nothing in the world was amiss. Hunch and Bertie's absence added to his suspicions. The whole thing had a whiff of set-up about it. After all, these were their girlfriends; they should have been present. 'See you in the bar,' Hunch had said. 'Just a few beers, nothing more. We'll meet you there.' It had all sounded a little too contrived and he had fallen for it. The arranged time had long since passed and, although Karen kept looking at her watch and muttering veiled threats about their absence, he was not convinced. Instead, he was surrounded by girls and suspected he knew why.

Still, she looked quite pretty, had a firm handshake and her voice was nice. He liked that in a girl. By comparison, Karen's nasal tones in the background were beginning to grate on his nerves. She gave him a little smile. Her face lit up when she smiled, forcing a response; nevertheless he glanced quickly away at the others. They paid them no attention; his doubts lessened. If this were a set-up then they would have gone in for someone a little more tarty than this girl.

'Do you—' They spoke at exactly the same time.

'Sorry, you were going to say—' Again they overlapped and she chuckled. It was a nice throaty laugh; he liked it. They paused, each waiting for the other.

'I was just going to ask if you liked Bahrain?' he said.

'Oh yes, I love it here.'

Sommerton had a sudden urge to be somewhere else, and was about to go. Despite all his suspicions, he felt some small regret at leaving the girl behind. He would have liked a few minutes' conversation with her. Suddenly, she got up from her seat and came round and sat next to him.

'I'm sorry, I could barely hear what you were saying from over there.' Her manner was open and honest, further confusing his doubts about the situation. The two girls stopped their conversation for a few moments, exchanging looks. Daisy in action.

Sommerton barely noticed Hunch and Bertie join the group, and was deep in conversation when Bertie stifled a yawn, took his girlfriend's hand, muttering something about getting an early night, and left. Moments later, Hunch's protestations that he needed some fresh air went largely unnoticed. He had never had a conversation like this with a girl. She was so interesting, so knowledgeable and they seemed to have so much in common. After weeks of being on a diet of aeroplanes and weapon profiles, it was such a relief to talk about art and music with someone who didn't think that Mozart was some kind of Roman flooring, or that Puccini was an Italian striker currently playing in the English Premier League. The time flew by. When he looked at his watch, it was way past the time he should have been in bed. 'I'm sorry,' he blurted, 'but I've got an early start in the morning, I must get to bed. Can I get you a taxi?'

She gave him a long demure look, as though she were going to say something, then changed her mind. 'That would be kind.' she said.

They shook hands as the taxi drew up opposite the door. She was just about to get in, when he found the courage to ask if he could see her again. The smile which accompanied the acceptance warmed his heart. As the taxi drove away, he watched it into the distance; he had a strange feeling that he was in love.

*

'My dear Sport, how are you this fine morning?'

Hunch's forced jollity had an odd ring to it. He rarely surfaced mentally much before ten in the morning. At five o'clock on a cold desert dawn, it was positively unheard of. They were standing in front of the hotel waiting for the bus. Clouds of condensation escaped with every breath.

'Never better, thank you, Hunch, never better, and yourself?'

'Thank you for asking, Sport, but likewise I must admit to never having felt better.'

Sport pulled his flying jacket tightly about him. It felt colder than a January day in England and the bus, which was well geared for air conditioning, seemed incapable of providing any heat. 'So, you had a pleasant evening then?'

'A lovely evening, thank you, Hunch.'

'And Daisy? How was she?' Hunch shook his hands together to warm them before adding. 'That is to say, how is she?'

'She's fine, thank you, Hunch. A lovely girl. You'll be pleased to know we got along splendidly.'

'Splendidly eh? That's... um... splendid.' He paused for a long moment and played with the straps of his flight bag. He looked for all the world like a man with a major burden on him. 'Anything you would like to tell me? Anything you would like to get off your chest to good old uncle Hunch? That is to say, you didn't get something off your chest last night in a manner of speaking?'

'I don't think so, Hunch.' Sommerton sounded hesitant and made a big thing of studying his fingernails in the gloom. 'I'll give the matter some thought. If I come up with something, you'll be the first to know, of course, but as it stands at the moment I'm fairly sure that I have nothing to tell. Now, is that clear enough?'

'Oh perfectly, old chap, clear as the proverbial. If you don't want to tell me anything then that's all right with me.' He tried to sound indifferent.

The bus rumbled across the causeway and the waves crashed angrily against the rocks. The sky was leaden and rain threatened. It was promising to turn into one of the drabbest winters the region had seen for years, and they all longed for a return to the warmth that had greeted them on their arrival. But in another sense, if they had to go to war, then this weather would be to their advantage. Fighters at low level, in rain and low-scudding cloud, were not happy.

'So you enjoyed having the room to yourself last night, did you, Sport?' Hunch tried to sound uninterested, his face turned towards the weak streak of light creeping over the distant horizon.

Before going out for the evening, he had made it abundantly clear that he would not be returning.

'Hunch, it's always a pleasure to be free of your farmyard noises and more particularly your farmyard smells.'

'Smell? I don't smell. I shower twice a day and use the most expensive deodorants. My local chemist loves me. I enable him, his wife and a multitude of little chemists to holiday at least twice a year.' He was beginning to sound angry. 'I admit that might not be up to much coming from the rural glades of Norfolk, but I am not aware that he markets any called Cow's Arse or Pig's Bollocks, or even Sheep-Shagger's Delight, so I take great exception to that remark.' It was Sommerton's turn to be on the defensive.

'I don't mean that *you* smell. It's what comes out of you that smells.'

'Well, that's all right then.' Hunch sounded relieved. 'That's just a natural function. Sign of a healthy diet. Plenty of fruit and high-fibre. Mark of a good digestive system, and anyway, just because all the kids in your school were anally retentive doesn't mean that kids in all schools are like that. If God had not meant men and women to fart, he would not have allowed Mr bloody Heinz to make his bloody baked beans.'

Sommerton ignored the outburst and peered through the window. It was beginning to mist up, and he idly drew a small circle in it.

'Anyway, speaking of women, Sport, and last night in particular, are you absolutely sure that there is nothing you want to tell me?'

'I've already told you that there is nothing to tell.' He finished the sentence and turned slowly towards his pilot, a look of malice on his face. The penny was just beginning to drop. 'Are you implying what I think you're implying? Are you for a moment suggesting that I made untoward advances to that sweet innocent girl whom I met for only the first time last evening. You are, aren't you?'

Hunch began to bluster his innocence, pretending to be rather taken aback by the suggestion. Sommerton took a deep breath, as though trying to control himself. 'Sometimes, Hunch, you're the bloody limit, you really are.' He turned and glared out of the window.

'Sport, old chap, you do me completely wrong, you really do. All I wanted to know is whether you had a nice time, that's all. I wouldn't dream of suggesting that Daisy was anything but the sweetest of girls.'

'Right, well let's have no more on the subject, okay?' Sommerton smiled to himself.

The bus reached the squadron and, for the first time since their arrival in the Gulf, Hunch was the first to get off.

★

'Karen, you assured me that Daisy was the hottest thing since the Indians came up with the idea of walking on red-hot cinders as a social pastime. Now all I get from Sommerton is what a sweet and innocent young thing she is, and how much he respects her. As far as I can tell, he's still in the wholesome state that he was born into, only now with a silly moonstruck look upon his face.'

'Honest, Hunch, I swear she's entertained more men than Dartmoor Prison. Pure man-eater. I saw her this morning and all she could talk about was what a nice gentleman he was, and how unlike the others she has known. He walked her to the door, called for a taxi, gave her a peck on the cheek, and she thought it was wonderful. I just don't know what to say.'

'God, Sommerton in love. I don't think I can cope with it. He's already forgotten several vital checks this morning, and if I hadn't been on the ball, the Boss might have got a missile up his chuff. I've heard of the inadvisability of going to war with a wanker on your wing, if you'll pardon the expression, but going to war with a lovelorn loon in the back must be nearly as bad.'

Chapter Ten

Both Guy Kelsall and John Sommerton remained celibate in the days running up to Christmas. One through choice and the other anything but choice. Sommerton was happy and bright and, to look at him, one would never have thought that a war was becoming more of a possibility by the day. Guy, on the other hand, was quite the opposite. The prospect of war disturbed and depressed him, and Sam Waterson, instead of helping him forget his troubles, was only adding to them by keeping him at arm's length. As Christmas approached his mood deepened. He tried to bury himself in his work, but it only partially solved the problem.

The squadron, much against Guy Kelsall's better judgement, had been stood down by the group captain for the two days over the holiday. Guy had opted to continue working, but had been overridden in his decision. Anything to take his mind off what would be going on at home. He missed the kids more than he thought possible – their grinning faces and mischievous antics, particularly Tommy. The prospect of mooning about at the hotel alone, or sharing a Christmas dinner with the group captain, was not to his liking. Sam was working.

Hunch, Bertie and their respective girlfriends were mystified by the relationship between Sommerton and Daisy. She not only seemed happy to go along with Sommerton's old-fashioned style of courtship, but positively revelled in it, brimming over with love and affection for the little man. Her friends were quite sick and tired of 'John says this' or 'John thinks that'.

The hotel had done its best to make the place look festive. Most people had been invited to the homes of the ex-pats, who had gone to a great deal of trouble trying to make them feel at ease during the difficult time.

The three bachelors and their girlfriends sat down to a full Christmas dinner in the late afternoon. Bahrain had never ceased to amaze them. Where the chef found the turkey, never mind the crackers, was anybody's guess. The party had gone well. Too much was eaten and drunk, but in all the noise and gaiety, no one noticed that Sport and Daisy had gone very quiet and were gazing rapturously at each other. Sommerton suddenly jumped to his feet.

'You'll have to excuse us,' he croaked, grabbing Daisy by the hand and quickly leading her from the room.

'What was all that about?' asked Bertie. His paper hat, torn and hanging precariously over one eye, gave him the appearance of a rakish eighteenth-century land owner. He shrugged and blew hard on the balloon he was attempting to inflate.

'Dunno,' replied Hunch, 'nothing is normal as far as that pair is concerned. They lost me some time ago.' He raised his glass. 'To the course of true love. They'll be back soon.'

The door to the room was locked when Hunch tried it some hours later. 'You'll have to come back later.' The voice was muffled, accompanied by a soft giggle. Hunch grinned widely and punched the air, uttering a whispered triumphant, 'Yes!' before wandering back towards the bar for a celebratory drink. When he tried the door a couple of hours later and got the same response, he was less pleased.

'Bloody glutton, that boy,' he muttered. 'First you can't get him on the nest and the next minute you can't get the sod off it. Still, it might clear his head.'

★

The weather turned even colder and wetter after Christmas. It was far more reminiscent of a January in the United Kingdom than the Middle East. It made the training all the more difficult, and as the deadline of the fifteenth approached all the crews were becoming tireder and more edgy. The politicians seemed to be playing a waiting game, the only option left open to them. The talking had long since finished, and they had all gone home with reports of intransigence. Only one man now held the key – Saddam; the world waited with bated breath for his move. The condition was simple: leave Kuwait and everyone could go home in peace. Stay, and the full might of the western powers would be brought into action.

The crews of 58 Squadron were in no doubt about the outcome of the current stalemate. They had seen the massed ranks of aircraft, the ships bristling with aircraft and missiles lying just off the coast, and the tanks and guns assembled in the desert ready for use when the Iraqi airforce had been softened up. The squadron had flown attacks against the warships, only to find their radar's illuminators coming to life before they got within twenty miles, knowing that behind the radar sweeps, missiles were being turned in their direction and primed for firing. Alongside, the guns were sniffing the air in case the missiles failed to do their job. They seemed invincible.

Night after night, they silently flew to the tankers in ever-increasing numbers, relying on only the occasional sweep of the navigators' radar and precision timing to separate the aircraft from each other. They had perfected their technique for laying the contents of JP233 across an airfield and, although the crews were no fonder of the thing than they had been several months previously, they had come to tolerate it. They were ready.

Chapter Eleven

The sergeant left the dais and walked with quiet dignity to the back of the briefing room. The crews ignored him, keeping up the level of chatter that masked his heavy footfalls on the concrete floor. Unnoticed, he locked the door, carefully put the key, as though it were the most precious thing he had ever owned, in his pocket, before making his way back towards the front. Starting from the back the talking ceased. The silence followed the sergeant as though he were magically switching it off when passing each row. His low grunt, as he mounted the wooden platform, could clearly be heard at the back of the room.

Hunch could feel his heart pounding. He wanted to place his hands across his chest to stop the noise being heard outside his body, the din was so loud in his ears. He stared directly ahead, not daring to show emotion, not wanting to see emotion in others. Apart from his heartbeat, time seemed suspended, held in an unknown mighty grasp along with all their beings. This was it. This was the moment. The condemned man asked to walk this way. The soldier told that when the flare went up he would have to climb over the edge of the trench and go into the void. A child in a dark room fumbling for the light switch.

Slowly, he started to breathe again. He swallowed and focused on the board at the front. A large blank piece of paper covering a map. He'd seen it all before, he told himself. Seen it a thousand times. He tried to grab on to what he knew. He had been here before. Nothing had changed. His shoulders had locked and, slowly, he tried to release them without anyone noticing. He wanted to stand and stretch; he stifled a yawn although feeling not the least bit tired. Quite the opposite, he wanted to run; he had energy to spare, wanted the briefing over, wanted to be in the aircraft, wanted the aircraft to be in the air and on its way. Christ, what if it didn't bloody work? Not an engine, that was easy. Engines either started or they didn't; he could explain that. But the kit? Could he carry it, or would he climb out, mumbling that it would not have been worth going? How would he explain it away? Nightmare. It was almost worse than being shot down. It had to work; he would make it work. Shit, he would worry about that when he got to it. Concentrate. Listen to the briefing. Take it all in, because it was a matter of life and death. A matter of *his* life and death.

Wing Commander Guy Kelsall stood and slowly walked to the front. He had the look of an old man about him. A small stoop of the shoulders that had not been there before was apparent. His breathing was shallow and a little laboured, and he stood for a moment as though trying to catch enough air to say something; a smoker climbing a hill. He had searched his mind for weeks for his opening words. Small steps for mankind, fight them on the beaches, fill the breeches with... the words had not come.

'Okay, tonight the practising is over. Tonight we are going in for real.' He paused to catch another breath and let the words sink in. 'We've all seen the targets, we know the plan and we've flown the profile almost to ad nauseam, so we are ready. The SQINTO will give an updated situation brief, and then Tom will go through the plan again. You're ready, you can do it, so go and have a good one.'

A good one: he was talking about going to war, not a shag in the back seat of a car. Hunch wanted something more. A rebel rousing. Something to raise his anger or at least get him out of the chair, a manoeuvre he felt would be a little difficult when the moment came. A few German marching songs might not have gone amiss.

Guy sat down quickly. He had purposefully not wished them good luck; it seemed a little melodramatic and, besides, it was no longer a matter of luck. Behind him, he could hear the tension break in a series of coughs and shuffling feet. 'Fuck Saddam,' he heard from somewhere and suspected he heard the tones of MacKensie. What do you expect when the recruiting standards are lowered, he thought. Suddenly and for no apparent reason, he found himself thinking about Mary. He had hardly thought about her at all recently, except for the duty letters and the odd phone call. She would be putting the kids to bed now. They would be arguing, telling her it wasn't time, begging for just a few more minutes. She would breathe deeply, hold her head to one side, hands on hips, little red patches appearing on her cheeks and they would know it was time. How many times had she threatened them with his absent authority? He wondered if she was now substituting the words, 'When Daddy comes home', with 'If Daddy comes home'. He shook his head slightly as if to clear the thought and looked sideways towards Tom Cookson.

Cookson and Frost would be leading the first wave. How Guy hated the bastards. When he had told the pair of them that tonight it would be for real, neither had shown the slightest reaction. For that he had hated them both with an intensity which stuck in his throat; he had been cheated of his moment. He had wanted to see a little crack, a small signal of fear, if not to match his own, at least enough for him to feel that he was not alone. But there had been nothing.

'Okay, Boss, we'll see to it.' A stroll in the park; a ride to the supermarket. Now Cookson was quietly going through his target runs and waiting his turn at the briefing as though waiting for a bus.

It had not come as a surprise to Cookson. He had known in his bones that it would happen. He had prepared himself for it, quietly putting his affairs in order, and, although not a religious man, had prayed that when the time came he would behave with dignity. Now, as he heard the breaking of the tension, he wanted to shout and scream and do three laps of the car park. Instead he limited himself to a small cough, recrossed his legs and waited his turn. He, also, had searched his mind for the magic phrase, the pre-battle incentive of the great leaders. It wasn't there. Just give another briefing. Another day, another sortie. If he didn't mention that someone would be shooting real guns with real ammunition then perhaps they wouldn't, and they would all come back safely. He thought of his small daughter who, when in her bed, was absolutely certain that she was safe from everything. He needed the bed psychology now. Perhaps if the cockpit were warm nothing could harm them. He smiled at the thought and brought his mind back to the briefing.

The SQINTO was on his feet. A small, round flight lieutenant with a thick pair of spectacles that refused to stay on the bridge of his nose. They gave him an owl-like appearance. He tried to sound clipped and business-like, although the slight tremor of his jowls and the ruddy glow to his cheeks told of the gravity of the information he was imparting. Even in the cool of the building, he was in danger of breaking out into a sweat. He had never seen such intensity on the faces of an audience. A magician in front of toddlers, they hung on his every word as though their lives depended on it. It was a matter of life or death.

He spoke slowly. Time was not an issue. The attack was several hours away; the small hours of the morning when even the most vigilant of guards is lowered, if only a small amount. Perhaps too much time had been allowed. Too much time to worry and dwell on what was in store. Some would show the strain, others not, but they would all feel it in the hours ahead. For once in his life, he was glad his vision had caused him to fail the medical.

He went carefully over the timings of the push. Where they would fit in the overall picture. The American F111s would go first. Pick out the radars, suppress them, or put them out of action. Fighters would follow and then the bombers. They were in the middle. They were at low level. They would be alone at low level. That bloody weapon. It was nothing new. They had heard it a thousand times before. Been over it a thousand times, and yet they listened like they were hearing it for the first time. Enraptured, unblinking, a matter of life or death.

He covered the threats. There was plenty of information: satellites, reconnaissance planes and people up-country on the ground. They knew what the threats were, where they were located and what to do to counter them. This was not the problem. They had chaff to counter the radars, they had flares to repress the missiles, and anyway, at the levels they were flying not many guided missiles could touch them. It was what he couldn't give them that troubled him. The man on the ground with the gun who that night might win the lottery, and, with a lucky shot, down one of the world's most expensive and sophisticated aeroplanes. Or the handheld missile, listen, wait, point and fire and hope that the thing sniffs the enemy. Feels its heat and is attracted to it. That was what he couldn't give them, and they knew it. He could see from their faces. He could read it in their posture. Stiff, alert, silent.

He sat down. Great patches of dark stain grew from his armpits, and another formed between his shoulder blades. In other times, it would have drawn a comment but now no one noticed. In other times he would have stayed cool; now it was a matter of life and death.

Cookson got to his feet. He felt heavy, but checked himself by becoming more animated. He grinned at them, forcing himself to relax and could see one or two of the faces in front of him lose some tension. 'Life,' he began, 'is like a pubic hair on a toilet rim. You're bound to get pissed off sooner or later.' He had not meant to say it; it just came out and the moment he said it, he wished he hadn't, knowing it was a weak effort. He had read it somewhere on a toilet wall. The response amazed him, far outweighing the quality of the joke. It broke the dam. Men released in laughter what they might otherwise release in tears. This was not a time for those. They might come later, but this was not the time. He got into the briefing. Simple, ordinary, everyday stuff. Things they had gone over time and time again. No changes, no surprises, just the normal everyday things that they were used to. He covered the take-off, the transit to the tanker and the order in which they would take their fuel. Frost went over the route and the target runs. He told the navs what they could expect to see on their radar screens. He nursed them through it as though they were hearing it for the first time, knowing they had heard it a thousand times before. It was a matter of life or death.

Check time. Check ID tags, check maps, check safety equipment, check pistols, check you are carrying nothing which could be useful to the enemy if you are captured, check, check, check, check and check again. It was a matter of life or death.

Chapter Twelve

They shuffled out to the aircraft laden with extras. Extra water, extra maps, bullets, pistols, clothing and small personal things; a bag of sweets, some sticking plasters, a saint's medal and a strange mixture of fear, apprehension, doubt and excitement: it was a heady concoction. The ground crew waited at the aircraft. Spots of rain splattered through the night air and the stars were hidden behind low-scudding clouds. No bomber's moon tonight, none wanted. The cover of cloud would be like a blanket; they would wrap themselves in it and the aircraft equipment would do the rest. 'Give me your name and address and I will bomb your house at midnight.' On another night, in another place, they would have felt the cold, but not here, although Sommerton was having some difficulty stopping his jaw from quivering.

The ground crew avoided eye contact, not knowing where to pitch their remarks and conversation. These were condemned men. Would they want to walk in silence to their fates? Would they want to be jollied along? A chat about the weather seemed inappropriate. They waited for the aircrew to set the scene.

'You've put the bombs on the right way round, have you, Chief?' or 'Evening, Chief, is the thing serviceable?' They replied in kind: 'Same way as the aircraft is pointing. If you can manage to point the right way, they'll go the right way,' a little laugh, or 'It's fine, sir,' with the mind screaming, 'I'm here to share your moment, cut me in'.

Checks, checks, checks. Slow, painstaking, thorough. No mistakes – not me. Each one lost in his own world, his own tasks, his own thoughts. One by one the canopies closed. The worlds divided. Outside the questions: 'Did I take the pin out? Did I screw that box in tight? Did I? Did I?' Inside the doubts: 'Can I go through with it? Can I find the target? Can I get on the tanker? Will it work? For God's sake, let the bloody thing start'.

The clock ticked slowly. It knew their pain. It taunted them. They were the condemned men. They wanted to get to the chamber, get it over with, but part of them wanted a stay of execution. Even now Saddam could pull out. But then they would be cheated of the experience. Thoughts rambled on, confused and argumentative. But the clock held its pace and they waited.

The clock gave in and the quiet of the night was broken by the roar of engines. They all started, and both worlds sighed in collective relief. Chocks removed, the great, dark masses rolled into the gloom. The ground crews watched them, not wanting to break contact, a lover's look from the departing train, searching for the memory that would endure and carry through until the reunion. Quickly, only the noise remained. But still they waited. Then great blowtorches lit the night, the thunder roared and they counted. Another sigh of relief; they were all up. The sound slowly died and the night regained its composure. Now the real waiting started.

The darkness welcomed them like a friend, but on its own it was not enough. The enemy had eyes to see through the darkness. They came out of the clouds at nine thousand feet and felt relief. The waiting for them was over. Now they could apply themselves to their jobs. The earlier thoughts of dying, of losing a friend, were filed to the backs of their minds. Now it was time for work.

The sky seemed extra bright. Guy looked across the great void at the stars, and vowed for the umpteenth time that he would learn something about them, their names and how they moved. The moon far to his right was just above the horizon. It was new, the smallest crescent he had ever seen. He would study that as well. If he lived. The thought that he had put from his mind was suddenly with him again, and he strove to banish it. Of course he would live. He had too much to live for. He had his career and the kids and Mary and Sam. He couldn't have them all. He would have to choose. On the ground, it had been simple, he had made his mind up. It would be Sam; but then would she have him?

'Tanker in ten minutes.' Bertie's voice brought him back to the present. He liked flying with Bertie. He didn't say too much and when he spoke it was usually good sense. Yes, they would come through it, and then he would think about the other things.

Hunch knew that about eighty aircraft were assembling into his formation alone. How many other formations were involved he could only guess, but he was still dumbfounded by the logistics of it all. Behind him, out of harm's way, the great AWAC aircraft, complete with their own protection, were sweeping the sky, the disembodied voice announcing in monotone that the sky was clear. He knew that ahead the F111s and Wild Weasels were already making their way across the border, waiting, almost hoping, for some brave soul to switch on a radar and give them some business, while around him were the fighters, F16s and Eagles, giving comfort. He had never been on such a high in his life. He felt so alive that every nerve in his body seemed to be singing. He was on and off the tanker before he knew it. What a difference a few weeks could make. Then they were descending. He could hear the silence. It made its own noise. Heartbeat, rushing blood, screaming nerves and nothing. The silence and the darkness were allies. They went together. They enclosed, wrapped themselves around their victim and wanted to choke him. Hunch's mouth was suddenly dry and he swallowed so hard that he operated his microphone.

'You spoke, Hunch?'

'Just clearing the old throat, Sport.'

'I must say, Hunch, that I didn't think it would take a war to keep you so quiet. For once, I hardly knew you were there.'

'Well, if I were you I would savour every moment. I've got a peculiar feeling that this war is going to take a whole lot of talking about.'

They dropped into low level and for a few seconds the canopies misted up. All was now concentration. The ground, moving at five hundred miles an hour and two hundred feet below, was not friendly ground. It was an enemy in its own right and claimed respect. Pilots dealt with the ground and navigators dealt with their position in time and space. No time for idle thoughts; no time for chatter.

★

'Five minutes to the target.' Frost spoke for the first time in many minutes.

'Arm it,' Cookson replied. Not a time to worry about inadvertently dropping something down the wrong chimney, as they would have done back home. Get the checks done early. Keep the flow smooth. No rush, just get it right. Each man went through the switches routine. It was too quiet, there should have been some enemy fighters; instead all they got was the monotonous voice from the AWAC pronouncing the all-clear like some medieval night-watchman.

'I've got a package.' Frost again.

'Fine.'

The correct symbology in the head-up display confirmed it. Frost switched on his radar. They were too close now to worry about being spotted. It was more important to do what they had come for, and to do it right. Soon the whole world would know where they where, or at least where they had been.

'Four-forty, four-sixty, four-eighty.' The speed increased as Cookson said the words.

'Okay, looking for offset one.' Frost was now buried in his radar scope, slowly winding the contrast knob, hoping to find the tell-tale shadow to update the kit. 'No good, going for the second.' Frost sounded calm but Cookson felt his tension matching his own with each passing second. He almost held his breath. 'Slight shadow, inserting.' Cookson breathed again and saw the bomb fall-line in his head-up display shift slightly. The aircraft followed the line. 'Two minutes.' Cookson went through his switches again, cursing the designer whose thoughts had been concentrated only on stopping inadvertent releases. 'Offset three.' Frost was lost in his own world, His voice was overly calm. 'Great, just the cat's bloody whiskers.' The relief in the voice came flooding through. The mark moved again and the aircraft dutifully followed. 'Forty-five seconds.' A blip appeared on the E scope. The airfield, they knew, was surrounded by a high wire fence. Would the aircraft react to it and pitch up? Cookson held his hand close to the control column and watched the mark move across the tube. It touched the non-penetration line and the aircraft kicked a little but held. Then it seemed to change its mind, wanting to climb. If allowed, the aircraft would not only clear the fence, it would go into a four-G pull-up and they would be meat and drink to anyone with a gun.

'Shit, going manual.' A note of panic entered Cookson's voice for the first time.

He clicked out the autopilot and alarms sounded for a few seconds before he could find the cancel switch. Cookson would now have to fly the aircraft. It was an extra burden he could have done without. The alarm appeared to wake the airfield. The world lit up; Bonfire Night, the Blackpool Illuminations and a night at the opera all rolled into one. All that seemed to be missing was Handel's fireworks music. Great, lazy arcs of light, like someone waving a hosepipe around in the sunlight, lit the sky, each arc interwoven with the other. It was fascinating, hypnotic, almost compulsive viewing. Cookson no longer had any problem avoiding the ground; he had walked into a dark room and someone had kindly turned on the light. There was no way round and no way through.

'Twenty seconds.' The sound of Frost's voice drew Cookson away from the lights. The rabbit released from the headlights.

'Commit,' he muttered to himself and pressed the switch as hard as he could. His thumb was already in place and he idly wondered how long it had been there.

The arcs of light were random, but one was creeping ominously in their direction. They heard the shells explode close on their right side and the aircraft rocked gently in the blast, then the arc moved away.

'Ten seconds.' The clock had taken on a new beat. Each one was a lifetime, and each a lifetime lived to the full. A perimeter track disappeared under the belly. They were close. 'Five, four, three, two, one.' Frost could not count fast enough.

The aircraft developed a kind of indigestion. It groaned and retched in small convulsions as it disgorged its load. Around their heads the lights flashed and threatened. One by one the gunners sensed their position and weaved their deadly hosepipes towards them. The bullets hissed above and below them and it was all Cookson could do to keep the aircraft on an even keel. The clock had again turned into an enemy. Cookson watched the mark in his head-up display move towards the end of the run, laughing and mocking him, dancing round him like a dog knowing it was time to go back on the lead but not wanting to. He silently cursed the mark and held the line. He was hot, and sweat was beading on his forehead, but he held the line.

'Bombs gone.' Frost broke the spell.

Cookson now had freedom to manoeuvre, desperately wanted to manoeuvre, but which way? So far they had failed to hit him; if he turned now he might just as easily turn into one of the deadly arcs of fire and do the job for them. Just as he was making up his mind, they were through. The blessed, coal black night of Dylan Thomas lovingly took them to her bosom. A soft, smooth, welcoming darkness; water to a thirsty man; comfort to a lover; solace from a mother to an injured child. They were out and running and breathing and living. They had done it.

They both cheered together, Frost pumping the air as best he could in the confines of the cockpit.

'Right, settle down, settle down.' Cookson was talking to them both. He quickly went through the switch sequence to re-engage the autopilot and with the final switch the aircraft climbed fifty feet to the operating height. They had been closer to the ground than they should have been. Only one enemy was behind them. He suddenly remembered the others and craned his neck to look behind. The bonfire was still blazing. He waited and held his breath again. How could time pass so slowly at five hundred knots.

'Two off.' – eternity.

'Three off.' – another eternity.

'Four off.'

'Trent check in.' He said it with pride.

'Two, three, four.'

'Right, let's go home.'

Chapter Thirteen

Cookson opened the canopy and leaned back against the headrest. He closed his eyes tightly as though in pain, before gazing towards the dawn light appearing in the eastern sky. He took a long, slow breath. The air tasted sweet, sweeter than he ever remembered, and clear. The last of the stars, now peering through broken cloud, appeared brighter than previously. He would see another day. He would absorb it, use it, and be grateful for it. It was not his divine fight.

The face above the edge of the cockpit woke him from his reverie. 'You nodded off or what, sir? You've got half the world's press out here waiting to see how you got on.' The man paused. There was something else. He started to climb down and then reappeared. 'How did it go, sir?' His tone was almost apologetic.

Cookson grinned at him. 'It went well, Chief. We all seemed to do well.' He waved his arm about in an expansive gesture as though including everyone, men and machines alike.

The man's face broke into a broad grin and he nodded his gratitude. 'Thanks, sir, fucking good.'

'It was like nothing you've ever seen.' Cookson was warming to his subject. The man had a right to share, he too had had a long night. The flight sergeant had kept them busy, but still the time had passed slowly. 'There were more lights in the sky than I can describe, but we did it.'

'The kit, sir. Did it work okay?' Again a note of anxiety.

'Perfect, just bloody perfect.' Cookson allowed the words to engulf him. A feeling of pride swept through him.

The corporal grinned again and moved down the steps to allow the crew to get out. By the time Cookson reached the ground, Frost was already there. He turned to his pilot, grinned and held his hand out. Cookson took it and slapped the shorter man on the shoulder. Immediately several flashbulbs exploded around them and a microphone was thrust between them.

'Any comments? How was it? Can you give us any details of the attack?'

The questions rained down and an arc light was suddenly switched on in front of them. Behind the lights, Cookson could see several cameras at work. This was going to be a very public war.

'It went according to plan.' Cookson was trying to sound low-key. 'We hit the target at 0430 local time and, as far as I know, it was successful, although I'll have to go through the debriefing before I can tell you more.' He started to walk away.

'What about you, have you any comments?' They turned to Frost.

'I've got plenty of comments but they're not fit for your audience.' He grinned and walked after Cookson. The reporter, not satisfied, followed after them.

'Can you elaborate? What were the conditions like over the target?'

'No problems. The Iraqi airforce appeared to stay in bed and, apart from a few gunners and searchlight operators, it was just like any other war.' He puffed out his cheeks, slowly exhaled, grinned and walked after Cookson. The reporter gave up and the arc light went out. Frost walked another few yards then turned and shouted to the ground crew, 'Put some more petrol in, Chief, and load her up again; we can make another eighteen holes before breakfast.' The reporter cursed; he had switched off his equipment, and it was just the sort of remark he was looking for.

Jennings, true to his word, was in full chatter mode. He had started talking seconds after leaving the target area, kept it up all through the tanking and the recovery to base. Sommerton had long since stopped listening. He was glad to give him to the ground crew, who received an earbashing, before Sport could drag him away. He managed to keep him clear of any of the reporters, who could easily have filled their copybooks with the thoughts of Jennings, and was greatly relieved to hand him over to the day crews who, getting ready for their own operation, were hungry for news and impressions. In a way, he had been glad of the chatter. He had never packed so much tension and emotion into his entire life as he had into the last few hours. One emotion had quickly followed on the other. Anticipation had turned into excitement which had given way to fear and then elation and joy and then just plain relief. Now he was just tired, a tiredness the like of which he had never experienced.

They had fully debriefed the mission both among themselves and with the intelligence people. Sommerton found a quiet armchair in the corner of the crew room and flopped down. So much seemed to have happened to him in the last few months that it was overpowering; rookie navigator to war veteran, boy to man and with it had come love. He could admit that to himself now; it all seemed so clear. Daisy. He wanted her with him now to share his joy and despair, to spend the rest of his life with her. Suddenly, that might not be much. A little voice in his head kept telling him that he would have to go out and do it all again, that night and then the following night. The thought kept coming back, taunting him. He was so tired that he was not sure he would have the energy to go back. He lifted an arm from the chair and then released the tension. It smacked down on the leather under its own dead-weight. He did it again with the other arm and giggled. The giggle turned into laughter and before he knew it, the tears of mirth were rolling down his cheeks.

'What's so funny, you small hero?' Hunch stood above him, gazing down with a puzzled expression on his face. 'Have you finally cracked?'

'Hunch, I was just sitting here thinking what a great windbag you are. You haven't stopped wittering on for hours and most of it was pure horseshit.' Sommerton spluttered through the words between great gusts of laughter.

'I say,' Hunch assumed a hurt look, 'Is that any way to talk to the chap who has brought you through the most intensive ground-to-air barrage seen in the modern era?'

'You're forgetting that you were the idiot who drove us into it in the first place.' Sommerton wiped the tears from his eyes with the backs of his hands and tried to breathe. He was beginning to feel much better. The tiredness has left him.

'True, but then I was acting under orders. To get you out, I was using some of my legendary initiative. So if you feel that you must grumble, and I must warn you it is a woeful failing in you navigators, then you should do it to someone who gives a shit. That said, I am about to go to what those in authority laughingly refer to as a restaurant, to eat the buggers out of house and home, and then I shall sleep for a week. If you would care to join me, I should be humbly grateful.'

Sommerton watched him thread his way across the room among the scattered chairs. He smiled and wearily dragged himself to his feet. There were worse people to die with.

Chapter Fourteen

Guy Kelsall knew only fear. From the moment he saw the lights and the tracers it consumed him. It was all he could do to concentrate sufficiently to get the weapon off and resist putting the burners in and getting the hell out of there more quickly. He was almost indifferent to where the bombs landed, wanting them off the aircraft so badly that it took a shout from Bertie Grice for him to keep the thing straight, level and in the right place. He had held his breath for so long before the blackness engulfed them again that he needed great gulps of air to redress the balance. The leader's request to check in needed a prompt from Bertie before he replied, and he had to go through the switch procedure twice before getting the terrain-following radar to come on line. He was trembling from head to toe and had to rip the oxygen mask from his face before he was able to obtain the quantity of air that his body demanded.

'You all right, Boss?' Bertie asked after some moments.

Guy replaced the mask. 'Sure, sure.' He sounded breathless, as though he had been running. 'I had a problem with the mask. I had to take it off and give it a bang. It seems okay now.'

Slowly, as the distance between them and that place of horror widened, his senses began to return. He could hear Bertie talking, but it was as though he were in another room, and he was only picking up snatches of the sentences: '...fucking great... never seen anything like it... I think we hit, didn't we?'

'Yes, I think we did.' Guy sounded unsure. Already, it was as though it had happened on another day, in a different life even. It might even have happened to someone else. Slowly the fear subsided and he was able to bring himself back to the job in hand. The aircraft was skimming along over the ground without being monitored and if something went wrong they would hit it. Wanting to burst into tears for some reason, he had to grit his teeth to stop himself sobbing aloud. Through chattering teeth he tried to banish all thoughts of the future. Surely Saddam would now see the folly of his position and the seriousness of the Allies. He could not win. He must know that he could not win. Why, even his airforce had not been in evidence. All he had heard from the AWAC were the words 'all clear' droning out over the air waves. Where were the enemy fighters? How much worse would it have been if they had been around? He groaned to himself, and his stomach ached with tension.

Somehow, he got the aircraft on the ground, and by the time he had taxied into the bay, he was feeling better. He felt drained, but somehow managed to grin at the ground crew and look as though he had meant business out there. As his foot touched the ground, the group captain stepped forward to meet him and held out his hand.

'Congratulations, Guy. That looked like just the start we needed. They all seem to have come back in one piece and the weapons all behaved as advertised. I'm afraid I've got a bit of a welcoming party waiting for you.' He gestured to the rear with his head, and Guy could see a group of people bustling about in the semi-darkness. 'The world's press.' As he said it the place lit up, and Guy was reminded of the place they had just come from. He blinked hard and an American voice shouted, 'Colonel, if we could just have a few words, Dan Singleton, CNN News.'

'Shit,' Guy muttered under his breath and his throat felt incredibly dry.

'Sorry,' the group captain said again, stepping back into the shadows.

Guy looked around, suddenly aware that apart from the media, he was alone. Even Bertie had disappeared. Then it occurred to him that this was his moment. The world would be watching his performance. Medals would not be given on where his bomb landed, but on how good he was in the next few minutes. He drew himself up to his full height and wiped the back of his hand across his mouth, swallowing hard and trying to lubricate his throat. He wanted to spit, but didn't think it would create too good an impression with any air marshal who might be watching. He smiled in the direction of the voice.

'How did it go, Colonel?'

'Wing Commander, if you don't mind.' He tried to sound the archetypal Englishman, wanting to give his full name as well, but feeling in the circumstances that it might not be a good thing; not if he were captured. Bugger it, if he were captured he would probably tell them everything. 'Wing Commander Kelsall,' he added.

'I'm sorry, Wing Commander,' The voice sounded anything but sorry, more irritated. 'Can you answer the question?' Implicit in the tone was the word 'fucking'.

'It went well, thank you.' Guy smiled in the direction of the camera. 'We all came off the target as planned, and we all got back here okay. I strongly suspect that we all hit the target; I'm reasonably sure that I did, but we'll have to wait for confirmation of that once we see the film.'

No '*us*', no '*We* hit the target', Bertie thought, waiting in the shadows. He winced, wanting to stick his head into the spotlight and adding, 'Thanks to me'.

'I'll have to hurry off now, if you'll excuse me. I have a fairly important debrief to attend to.' Guy nodded and smiled again at the camera as though his understatement was a good joke and stepped into the shadows. He made sure that he loudly thanked the ground crew, knowing that the tape was still running, and then took Bertie by the arm and strode out towards the operations building, leaving the group captain to field any further questions. Overall he felt he had done rather well.

They reached the building and his legs began to feel heavy again. The bustle of activity around the aircraft had reminded him that it would be on its way again in a short time with a different crew, but before too long it would be his turn and he wondered if he could get himself ready in time. All he wanted to do was find Sam Waterson and bury his head in her bosom and not come out until it was all over. From the show of intransigence by both the woman and Saddam Hussein it was difficult to know which would surrender first.

Guy grasped the door handle, steadied himself and took several deep breaths before entering. The guard on the door held his sub-machine gun across his chest and muttered a 'well done' as they walked by. The room was alive with people. It had the atmosphere of a happy hour in the mess on a Friday evening. People were grinning and shouting and clapping each other on the back, as though they were seeing each other for the first time in years. Suddenly, there was an air marshal in front of him holding out his hand and grinning from ear to ear.

'Well done, Guy, a good show. I'm sure we taught that so-and-so a lesson.'

'I'm sure we did, sir.' He was again beginning to enjoy the moment, allowing the euphoria to wash over him, and was quickly giving encouragement and bits of advice to those who were planning the second wave. He was the man again. He had been there. He had survived. He felt sorry for them. They would have no cover from the night and if Saddam's airforce were going to leave the ground they would do it now.

He watched the second wave get off the ground. It was confirmed that the night attack had been a complete success. There had been no losses and heavy damage had been inflicted on the enemy's airfields. The world heard about it as they munched toast and cereals for breakfast. In the midst of war, children were being packed off to school and mothers, desperate to pick up every item on their screens, were trying to shield their young from watching in case some disaster were reported. Guy idly wondered if Mary would be watching and then instinctively knew that she would. All her letters and their telephone conversations had been full of concern for him and the squadron. He had been a little surprised at the depth of feeling she had shown and had felt momentary pangs of guilt that he was not able to return those feelings. He decided he would call her before he went to sleep.

*

Cookson's mind was full of thoughts of home. He tried to shut them out, to concentrate on the job in hand, get it over with and get back as quickly as possible, and pick up where they had left off. But now, in a world of instant communication, it was not possible. People had started to ring home from the moment they had arrived in the Gulf. It would have been better to have relied on the old-fashioned letter and let the passage of time fill in any of the blanks, but now the wives had come to expect the calls. No contact was a signal that something was amiss. He would ring to say that he was safe, but she would probably know that by now anyhow. The 'count them out and count them in' brigade would have seen to that.

More than that, though, he had the urge to put his real thoughts down on paper. Not just 'I'm okay, how are you?' but the real deep thoughts that only he knew and he hoped his wife had guessed. It was almost as though he wished to leave something as part of his inheritance which he could bequeath if something went wrong. He was not by nature an open person. His heart had never even reached as far as his inside pocket, never mind to his sleeve. Where he came from people were not like that. Although times and living conditions had softened greatly, too many hard-working, tight-lipped people, who would share their last crust but not their innermost feelings, had poured their blood down the ages into his.

He sat down at the hotel writing table and stared at the blank piece of paper in front of him. So many feelings welled up inside of him and demanded to be set down on the page. 'Go on, tell her,' they shouted. 'Tell her how much you really love her. Tell her how much you have needed her in the past, how you have come to rely on her and, God willing, will need her in the future. How she has been your strength and your solace, your comfort and your refuge. Tell her that everything you have achieved or will achieve is because of her or for her. So that you could tell her about it, share it with her. Tell her that life would be meaningless without her. Tell her that every time you looked across a room at her, watching her laughing and smiling, the feelings had welled up inside you, and that they still do. The surprise and joy that she could in some way feel the same and want to share your home and your life. Go on, tell her that you love her more than life itself.'

The words fluttered around in his head and his hand, clutching the pen, moved towards the paper. It stayed for a few seconds and then moved away. He pushed it back towards the page but still the words did not spill onto it. It was too much to burden her with. Too much weight to carry if he lived, and even more if he died. He could not do it. A diet of chip butties and stiff upper lips had left their mark. He pressed his fingers against his temples and rubbed them in small circles. It had been a hell of a night. He knew that he had not been to hell, but he could still, in his mind's eye, see the flames and smell the brimstone. He picked up the pen again and instantly started to write: *'My dear Janet, I hope you are well and that Lisa is over her cold...'*

Chapter Fifteen

Guy woke from a deep, dreamless sleep. It was already dark outside and raindrops splattered on the window. For a moment he was unsure where he was. It was always the same after pill-induced sleep and he wondered if he would ever be able to get by without them when he returned home. *If* he returned home. The realisation of where he was and what he was doing there, came rushing back and with it the cold fear. He had tonight to get through and the night after and, if that lunatic in Baghdad did not see sense, the night after that. He put his hand to his brow and felt the cold clamminess of his skin. Perhaps he was ill. The thought cheered him for a second until he realised that he would not get away with it. He would have to go and do it. It was his turn to lead.

He put his feet over the side of the bed, feeling the cold touch of the tiles and groaned. This place was built for temperatures of forty degrees or so, and here they were in the equivalent of an English winter. He padded to the bathroom and was shocked at his reflection in the mirror. Great dark blue rings surrounded his eyes; he looked sallow and drawn and the eyes were bloodshot, the eyes of a man who had not slept; the eyes of a man who was staring his destiny in the face and did not like what he saw – a drowning man. He turned away quickly, trying to occupy his mind with dressing and shaving, attempting to concentrate on the method of the attack and not the reality of what was waiting for them. However much he tried, the vision of those lazy orange snakes, sweeping the sky looking for him with their deadly tongues of lead, kept returning. It froze his guts and then, just as quickly, melted them. He rushed to the toilet.

The bus was waiting, the engine already running. His problem had made him late, and the crews were all inside. A silence greeted him as he climbed in, muttering an embarrassed, 'Good morning', before remembering that it was the evening. The faces looked as pale as his own and each held an expression of expectation, hoping for news that the thing had all been called off. 'What I really mean is, good evening.' He tried to smile at his own mistake.

'Evening, Boss.' The reply was general, muttered and low-key. He sat at the front of the bus and glared at the darkened image of himself in the windscreen. He saw Tom Cookson stand up some rows behind him and make his way slowly towards him.

'Good evening, sir,' he sounded a little formal and was looking at Guy in an inquiring way as though expecting some kind of response.

'Evening, Tom, sleep okay?'

'You haven't heard have you, sir?'

'Heard what, Tom?' Guy's spirits rose inside him. The man in Baghdad had seen sense after all. Then as quickly as they had soared, they plummeted. Cookson was not wearing the expression of a man who was bearing good news. 'Heard what, Tom?' he repeated and tried to keep his voice on an even keel while his insides did a somersault.

'One went in today.' He let the statement hang in the air. 'Not one of ours. One of the other squadrons'.'

'Are they…?' Guy's hands started to tremble and he stuffed them into his pockets out of the way. 'Are they okay?' He wanted to say dead, but tried to sound positive.

'We don't know, sir. We just heard it on the grapevine from someone coming off duty. I expect we'll find out when we get there.'

'You don't know what happened?'

'No, sir, just heard that they were flying as number three and they didn't check in after the attack. Number four thought he saw a flash, but with all the other things going on he couldn't be sure.'

A burst of laughter came from the back of the bus and both men turned. Guy wanted to ask what could be so funny at a time like this, but thought it would sound schoolmasterish. He bit his lip and turned to the front again. 'Let's just hope they got away with it, then. Even if they are alive…' He let the sentence hang. The prospect of facing the rigours of an Iraqi prison did not bear thinking about either.

The bus lurched to a stop in front of the ops building. Cookson was halfway to the door before he noticed that Guy had not moved. 'You coming, sir?'

'Oh yes, Tom.' He seemed to wake from a dream.

'Does anyone know if the Iraqi airforce got airborne today?' The voice sounded like Jennings's.

'No,' Cookson replied, 'we don't think so.' Guy wondered how his flight commander knew so much about what was going on and he didn't, but kept the question to himself.

'Veeree strainge.' The voice was heavily accented to mimic a Frenchman and again a ripple of laughter followed.

'Are you leading tonight, Boss?' MacKensie looked down at him as he rose to get out of his seat. He felt a pang of dislike towards the man for putting him on the spot. He was considering ways of trying to get out of it. It was almost as though the Scotsman was reading his mind.

'Yes, Bertie and I will be leading tonight.' It came out more stiffly than he had intended. Guy thought he could discern a look of satisfaction on the younger man's face. It seemed to say, 'Get out of that one if you can'. Guy hurried past him into the building.

★

The briefing room was cathedral-quiet. The lone figure on the dais was closely studying his watch with one finger pointing at the ceiling.

'Now.' He brought the finger down as though starting a horse race. 'Exactly 2030 local time.' A few coughs broke the silence. He turned to look at the large map behind him. 'Same target as last night.'

'Boring,' someone said and a ripple of laughter followed.

'Bored, you will not be. I have Saddam's personal guarantee here.' He waved a piece of paper in the air and smiled maliciously in the direction of the voice.

'Get on with it, I've got a hot date later.'

'You've got a hot date over the target before that.' The room appreciated the quick response and there were a few 'oohs' and 'aahs' before Cookson called for some quiet. He was surprised at how quickly they had adapted to the situation. He knew that deep down they were all as frightened as he was, but at least they were trying to keep up their spirits. He glanced across at the Boss, who was sitting staring towards the front as if he had not heard a word. He was a little worried about him.

'You've probably heard the news that we lost one earlier. Well, that's the bad news. The good news is that they both got out and we heard from the Red Cross in Baghdad that they have been captured, although we don't know what state they're in. It might give you a little incentive for this evening's work,'

The briefing was long and painstaking. Despite the fact that they had all studied the plans, nothing was left out. The intelligence officer went through his usual routine of wrestling with his spectacles and getting redder and redder until it looked like he might explode. When it was Guy's turn, he tried to sound casual and matter-of-fact, but frequently pointed at the wrong piece of the map, and when he held his hand up it visibly shook. Bertie, in contrast, was more business-like, and left no one in doubt that he was competent to lead such an operation, despite his relative inexperience. Hunch was proud of him and reached forward to give him a pat on the back as he sat down. Guy rose to his feet again, desperately trying to think of something positive to say before they all went to do their own personal things, but nothing came to him. The best he could do was, 'Have a good one'. It sounded lame.

The sergeant from the intelligence cell followed with a couple of small updates, addressing his audience with rounded Welsh vowels, in a graveyard tone and with an expression to match. Nobody would have been surprised if he had finished with a hymn, but he just stood silently for a moment staring mournfully down his long nose, sniffed and left. The crews shuffled out behind him.

'Miserable shit, I was feeling particularly jolly until he came and put the damper on it.' Hunch nodded in the direction of the departing sergeant.

'What have you got to feel so jolly about?' Sommerton asked, more out of habit than curiosity, busily gathering his maps together.

'I've got my health, I've got my reason and most of all, Sport, my dear chap, I've got you.' Hunch made a lunge at the smaller man trying to put an arm round his shoulder, but Sommerton dodged out of reach. 'Sport, since you have been seeing that girl Daisy, you don't seem to love me anymore. Was it something I said, or have your affections strayed in another direction?'

'Jennings, can't you take anything seriously? We're supposed to be fighting a war here, and all you do is fool about.'

'A war, you call this two-bit little scenario a war? Why, I can tell you, lad, when I were a lad we 'ad the war to end all wars. In fact we were so good at it that we 'ad two of 'em. One fer practice like, and t'other were fer real. We 'ad t'whole world teking part and no one knew who were fighting who. Now that's what I call a war.'

Hunch had his thumbs stuck under his armpits and was sticking his chest out. Behind him, Sommerton could see that Jack Frost was carefully listening to the monologue and moving closer. Hunch was still deeply absorbed, expounding on the merits of trench warfare as Frost gently whispered in his ear.

'You wouldn't be taking the piss out of all good Yorkshiremen, would you, Jennings?'

'Absolutely not, sir.' Hunch, instantly recognising the voice, spun to face the shorter man. He found himself an inch from Frost's face with a chair blocking his retreat. 'That was just my own feeble attempt at taking the piss out of Lancastrians, sir. I have, as you well know, the greatest respect for Yorkshiremen.' Hunch smiled weakly at the glowering features in front of him.

'Tom, did you hear that? Hunch was just taking the piss out of Lancastrians.' Frost gave Sommerton the smallest of winks and turned to watch Cookson stroll across the room.

'You're taking the piss out of Lancastrians are you, Hunch?'

'Absolutely not, sir.' A look of concern crossed his face as Frost stuck his face very close to Jennings's cheek.

'Are you calling me a liar, Jennings?' Frost's tone was threatening, his chin stuck out so far that his lips had almost disappeared. Sommerton was beginning to enjoy this. The biter was bitten.

'A liar, sir? I wouldn't dream of calling you a liar. I have the greatest respect for you. In fact, I was telling young Sommerton here what a great navigator you were and that he could do worse than to model himself on you. Wasn't I, Sport?' He looked imploringly for help from his navigator, but saw there was little to be had in that direction.

'Well, you can't have it both ways, Jennings. Either you were taking the piss out of Lancastrians or you're calling me a liar.'

Cookson had taken station on the other side of Jennings and was glaring at his other cheek. Hunch glanced nervously from one to the other and then round the room. For once in his life he was struggling for an out.

'It wasn't that I was taking the piss out of Lancastrians,' he began very hesitantly, 'I was in fact trying to demonstrate to Sommerton the difference between the rounded "O" of the Lancastrian, particularly of someone who comes from the… eh… Burnley region, and the very pronounced "O" of the Welsh, which was so ably demonstrated by the good intelligence sergeant in the briefing not a few moments ago.' In warming to his subject he had run short of breath and panted slightly, while checking the expressions of the two squadron leaders, hoping that his explanation had been plausible. Frost looked across at Cookson and gave that small wink that Sommerton had seen a few moments before.

'I told you, Tom, didn't I?' Frost said.

'You did, Jack.' Cookson replied equally deadpan. 'I take my hat off to you. I'll pay you back at the hotel.'

They both simultaneously walked away, leaving Hunch with a bemused expression on his face. It was almost more than he could bear, not being in on the secret. He watched them cross to the other side of the room.

'Sirs,' he called after them. 'Would it be possible to let me in on your little secret? What's this about a payment?'

'Oh, nothing to concern you, Hunch, It's just that the good squadron leader here,' Frost patted Cookson on the back, 'was foolish enough to wager that you weren't totally full of shit, while

I said that you were. Now you've just proved it, so I win the bet, okay?'

'Well, thank you, sir.' Hunch looked pleased for a moment, as though he had been paid a compliment until the realisation of what had been said began to dawn on him. 'Actually, wait a minute, sir. That's not exactly a nice thing to be saying about a chap who, in a couple of hours, will be in the thick of battle and may have to meet his maker, or one of Saddam's henchmen.'

'Hunch, if tonight you have the misfortune of meeting either St Pete at the pearlies or Saddam himself, just start talking and they'll probably let you go in seconds. You have nothing to fear.' Frost patted Hunch on the shoulder and a peal of laughter swept around the room.

Guy heard the laughter, but he was far too engrossed in his own thoughts to pay it any attention. He was bent over the planning table apparently studying his maps, but his thoughts were fully occupied in trying to get out of leading. If he were not in the lead, it would be easier to duck out of going all together. A technical problem, possibly. He felt the tap on his shoulder and turned to see the group captain standing behind him. 'A word if I might, Guy.'

'Yes, sir, what can I do for you?'

'Not here, Guy. In my office if you don't mind.'

Guy followed him to the door, then asked, 'Is it going to take long? We should be walking out in a few minutes.'

'No, it won't take long.'

Guy saw his chance. 'I'll just nip over and tell Tom Cookson where I am in case he misses me. I'll catch you up.' The group captain nodded and continued on his way.

'Tom,' he caught Cookson by the elbow, a look of near panic on his face. 'I've just been called in to see the group captain, he says it shouldn't take too long, but it's important, and if I should be more than a few minutes, then you'd better walk without me. In fact,' he added almost as an afterthought, 'you had better take the lead and then there will be no cock-ups.'

Cookson stared at his boss open-mouthed in disbelief for several seconds before he found his voice. What could be more important than actually going on an operation? He shrugged slightly in bewilderment.

'Okay, give me your maps. I'll get Jack to swap with Bertie and you can fly at number four.' He sounded disdainful and looked at his superior for a reaction to the rebuff but saw none.

'Fine, I'll see you in a few minutes.' Cookson thought he saw a look of relief on Kelsall's face and turned away to disguise his disgust.

The meeting amounted to nothing that could not have waited until his return, but Guy found himself dragging it out by asking as many questions as he could think of to try and emphasise the importance of what was being discussed. In fact, he almost overdid it and a quick glance at his watch told him that the final out-briefing was just about to start.

'Shit,' he muttered quietly, 'must rush, I've got a war to fight.' He laughed a little at his own joke and hoped the effect was one of bravado.

'You're right, Guy. I'm sorry to have kept you. Best of luck.'

You can stuff your luck, Guy thought as he hurried towards the door, You wouldn't be so full of sanctimonious crap if our positions were reversed. He turned into the corridor and hurried towards the briefing room.

'Sir, sir.' The voice sounded urgent, and he turned to see the intelligence sergeant rushing towards him.

'I can't stop now, Sergeant,' he sounded angry. 'I've got to be at the briefing in a minute. I can't talk to you now. See me when I get back.' He half-turned, but the sergeant grabbed him by the sleeve. He looked down at the hand and his face reddened. 'Get your hand off my sleeve.' The voice was low and threatening.

'Sir, it's vital. Thank God I found you in time. You must listen.' It was a plea and the deep resonant tone of the valleys was raised to a near squeak.

'Quickly, Sergeant.' The tone suggested a last remark before sentence was passed.

'It's a convoy movement. Heavily armed, we think, and it's just popped up on your route. My guess is that it's pretty close to one of your target runs. Here's the co-ordinates.' He thrust a piece of paper towards Guy and waited for him to take it. It held just a group of numbers which were meaningless unless transposed to a map. Guy looked at the man. His expression was intense, almost imploring the senior man to take the paper. Guy noticed that his eyebrows almost met on the bridge of his nose. It repulsed him, making him almost feel sorry for the man, the sympathy of someone for a wounded animal. He took the paper and gave it a cursory glance as though he had the power to decipher its contents without the need for a map.

'All right, Sergeant, I'll look into it.'

'Must avoid it, sir. You'll have to go round it.' The last desperate plea for some acknowledgement. Guy merely nodded and walked away, leaving the man standing.

When he entered the briefing room all the crews were assembled by the door waiting for the last briefing. He hurried towards them before realising that he had yet to collect his helmet and Mae West.

'Sorry,' he shouted across the room, 'I'll just get my things. I'll be with you in a moment.' He crashed through the door and almost knocked over the ops clerk, but hurried on without apology. He grabbed his G-pants, flung them over his shoulder, unconsciously stuffed the piece of paper into his pocket and took his helmet from the shelf. As he re-entered the ops room he caught Cookson's eye; he was staring at him with a mixture of disbelief and hatred on his face.

'Sorry,' he muttered again, 'how are we for time?'

'Pushed,' said Cookson, 'get on with the brief, Pete.'

The flight lieutenant held the board in front of him and mechanically went down the list of dos and don'ts. Cookson tapped his finger on the edge of the table.

'Got your pistols? Got a magazine of bullets?' he monotonously intoned. 'Got the survival map? Got a water bottle? Dog tags? Nothing to give the enemy a clue about identity? Like a letter from mummy?' He glanced at Sommerton.

'Piss off.'

'Ooo.'

'Shut up with the innuendo, and get on with the brief.' Cookson was angry. The rest of the briefing was given without interruption, and they walked in silence to their aircraft.

Chapter Sixteen

The young man sat on top of the turret. He was more a child than a man. His face had not felt the touch of a razor, and he had yet to hold a woman in his arms, although he dreamed of the day. They called him a gunner, and he liked to tell his friends at home that he was one; it impressed them. But he was not really a gunner, more a dogsbody. He fetched and carried. He humped the great shells into the tank and cleared up after everyone. They all wanted to give him orders. 'Do this', 'fetch that', 'go here', 'don't go there'. He did as he was told. Too many times he had been knocked to the ground for a sneer or a wrong word that he had learned the hard way. Learned to keep his thoughts locked up inside and be the big man at home, where no one knew any better.

Now, he had been told to sit on top of the turret and listen. What for, or why he had to listen, he was not sure; after all, he had been told that the gun on which he sat had eyes that could see in the dark. He just hoped he would know when the time came. The sergeant who had given him some instruction on the thing had pointed to a small round screen and grinned. 'Shoot anything, day or night, doesn't matter. When the enemy appear on that screen, we've got them.' He had spat in the sand to emphasise the point, simulating gun barrels with his fingers and firing into the air, making noises with his mouth and allowing each finger to recoil as the imaginary bullet had gone. The young man had nodded knowingly, not really understanding.

Now, the sergeant and the others were in the trucks keeping warm, while he sat on top of the turret listening. At least the rain had stopped, but the wind whipped through the thin material of his jacket and he was very cold. He cursed, as he had learned to do in the last few weeks, turning his back to the wind and blowing into his cupped hands. He had become good at cursing since he had been ordered from the farm and into the army. They had all told him that it was a great honour to be going and he had been feted by the people of the village before leaving, proud to be the one selected, but now, after only a few weeks, he was no longer so sure.

They had been taken to camps and had marched up and down in the heat of the day. They worked until they were exhausted, but he had seen things which he had never dreamed existed, good and bad. Once, he had seen one of the recruits shot in the head when he had refused to get up out of the sand. No one had said a word as they dragged the limp and bleeding body away, but everyone had found a little more strength to carry on. In the end, he had marched as proudly as the others.

They had been told that this was one of the greatest armies the world had ever seen. He had no reason to doubt it. Everywhere he had gone, the places seemed to teem with soldiers, tanks and guns. Even the convoy he was part of had more than a hundred vehicles. They were taking more equipment to join the main army in the south, and together they were going to liberate the people of a country that rightfully belonged to Iraq.

It was his job, with the others, to protect this convoy from the aggression of the foreigners, particularly the Americans, who were greedy for oil and power. His lip curled at the thought of the Americans. They had attacked the night before, dropping bombs on schools and hospitals, killing innocent people, but soon it would be the turn of his people to take their revenge. Soon the mother of all battles would be fought and he would be part of it. A great victory would be theirs. How many times had he been told that by the great leader of the nation? They would chase the aggressors from their lands and give them a lesson from which the world would learn. Then he would return to the farm a hero and there would be much to celebrate – but for now he was cold.

He cursed under his breath again and spat with the wind, wishing it would all happen soon, so he could go back to the farm and his family. He had been away for long enough.

The turret of the gun moved unexpectedly as the operator inside played with the controls, causing the young soldier to nearly lose his balance. He shouted his annoyance at his comrade but was only greeted with laughter. The four great barrels behind him moved upwards and across, appearing to sniff the empty sky for prey. Each of the barrels, he knew, could fire twelve hundred rounds in one minute, filling the sky with lead so that nothing could escape. It was indeed a formidable weapon. He patted the cold steel with his hand, glad that the weapon belonged to them and not the enemy.

A great blast of wind moved across the desert, bringing with it grains of sand and a few drops of rain, further misery for the soldier. He closed his eyes tightly and whispered a short prayer to Allah that he might soon be spared from his torment and be allowed inside into the warm. Then he heard it.

At first he thought it was the wind and huddled further into his meagre jacket, silently complaining that the greatest army in the world should have thicker coats. The sound came again, not like the wind, but deeper, angrier. He was alert now, his discomfort forgotten. This was what he had been told to listen for. Every instinct in his body told him. The sound was increasing in volume and intensity and he wanted to shout, but a small voice inside told him to be sure before wakening the others. He had felt the boot of the sergeant too recently to want another. Now he was sure. It was different from the wind, and he had heard the sound many times before as the great jets of the Iraqi airforce had flown low over the farm.

'They're coming,' he shouted. 'They're coming from the south. Do you hear me? They're coming.' A terror filled him that he would not be heard in time, allowing the Americans to drop their bombs before anyone reacted, and he would get the blame. Then he would not go home a hero, but would be shot like a dog and dumped at the side of the road for the birds to devour. The sound seemed to fill his ears, and he stood on the turret and shouted again with all his might. The cry was echoed down the line before he realised that he had not been the only one who had been out listening. He took some small comfort from it. The turret beneath him moved again, the barrels now moving quickly in the direction he had given, although giving no indication that they were looking, or sniffing, or whatever they did for the unseen enemy.

For the briefest of moments, he felt sorry for the enemy and then quickly remembered all the thousands who had died last night. He jumped to the ground; all around men with guns in their hands were running to the side of the road and away from the trucks. For a moment he hesitated, wanting to be inside the truck, to wallow in its protection, however small, but then he followed the others and flopped down into the mud. The wet shocked him and he was starting to get up when a rough hand grabbed him, pulling him back to the earth. He looked back at the guns. In the dim starlight, he could make out that their movement had lessened into little circular jerks, as though they had seen what they were looking for. They were angled low to the ground, almost parallel with it, possessing the tension of a dog who has picked up the scent of its quarry.

The guns moved again. A final, small jerk and the world lost all meaning for the soldier. He wanted to curl up into a small ball and roll in the protection of the mud which moments before he had found so offensive. The noise did not just enter his body through his ears, it seemed to go in through every pore in his being. It consumed him. Through tightly closed eyes, the night lost its meaning in the brightness of the flashes. Then, as quickly as the mayhem had started, it stopped. Opening his eyes and readjusting to the dark, he could see the barrels of the guns glowing a dull red. He turned in the direction they were pointing. In the distance, he could see a small flame. A man lighting a cigarette at the end of the street. A piece of paper carelessly lit and then allowed to blow away on the wind; its flame slowly dying as it fluttered to the ground. His ears were still ringing from the noise of the guns, but, through his hands and knees, he felt a slight tremor as the scrap of light extinguished and then appeared to flare in one last defiant gesture before the blackness returned.

Chapter Seventeen

'Trent, check in.' Cookson's voice cut through the silence.
'Two.'
A long pause. 'Four.'
Cookson waited, his throat restricted by lack of moisture and fear. 'Trent, check in.' He tried to keep the concern out of his voice.
'Trent two.' Another pause and the tension increased.
'Four.'
'Trent three, check in. If you hear me squawk emergency,' he added as a desperate afterthought, before flipping the switch on the IFF box to pick up the distress tones. Silence.
'I saw a flash over to my left a couple of minutes from the target, when we came through that spat of fire, but I couldn't be sure exactly where.' The voice trailed away.
'Identify yourself.' Cookson allowed his fear to vent itself in irritation at the poor RT.
'Trent Two,' Hunch replied almost apologetically.
The crumpled piece of paper in Guy's pocket seemed to take on a life of its own, the corners digging into his leg. He remembered the concerned look on the face of the sergeant and the urgency in his voice – 'Glad I caught you... must go round' – the words echoed in his brain like a voice coming down a long tunnel.
'Jesus,' he whispered to himself, but loudly enough to operate the microphone.
'Doesn't look good does it, sir?' Bertie asked from the back. 'Did you see anything?'
'No, I had my head stuck in the cockpit.'
'Trent two to lead.'
'Go ahead, two.'

'Trent two, the nav says he saw a flash and put a marker into the kit where it happened so, if that was three going in, we've a good position report.'

Guy groaned loudly. Bertie, mistaking it for a groan of concern for the crew, added, 'Well, that's something isn't it, sir.'

The last thing Guy wanted was an exact position of where the aircraft had gone down. If it tied in with the position of the convoy, he would have some trouble explaining why he had kept the co-ordinates to himself. If the crew were alive the Iraqis would soon find them and if they were dead it didn't matter, but without the position it could take some hours to spot the wreckage, particularly if the solid cloud cover continued. By then he might be able to separate the two events, but now that was not possible.

The flight home took for ever. For once, Guy did not mind. He needed the time to think and the longer the better. Obviously, he could not allow anyone to think he had forgotten to pass the co-ordinates to Cookson; it would be the end of him – but how could he swing the blame? He was ice cool. The early flush of misery had left him. Now it was either Cookson or himself who was going to take the rap, and he had no intention of taking the blame. The options whirred in his brain. Bluff it out. Check the route again and then confront Cookson about why he had not reacted to the convoy. Cookson, of course, would deny any knowledge but, in the circumstances, that is what Guy would expect to hear and he would say so. He had the added advantage of knowing all the facts. If he confronted Cookson in the right way and in front of the right people, then it would come down to one word against the other. Better still, if he could get the sergeant's copy of the co-ordinates onto Cookson's person, he would hold all the right cards; but that was a tricky one and he would have to tread carefully. Just in case the opportunity arose, he hastily scribbled the numbers onto a scrap of paper he found in his kneepad before carefully smoothing the original and folding it into four.

He would be believed, he had to be believed and, when that happened, Cookson would be out of the way – for good. If Cookson brought up the past, Guy could just laugh it off as the act of a desperate man. The more he thought about the scenario the more it appeared to be some kind of blessing in disguise. He was sorry of course for Ord and Langstaff and their families, and desperately hoped that they were alive, but if through this he could gain something for his own career then all was not lost.

★

The gap in the line after they taxied in told its own story. The ground crew made no attempt to be cheerful. 'Did they get out, sir?' One of them asked.

'Don't know.' Guy sounded curt, then added quickly, softening his tone, 'I don't think so. We didn't hear anything. We'll just have to wait and see.'

The corporal carried his helmet to the bottom of the steps and handed it back to him without a word. Guy took it and once more the glare of the camera lights took him slightly by surprise. He shook his head as the microphone was thrust in his face and wordlessly side-stepped the reporter. The world would have to wait. He marched into the crew room, pleased to be first in ahead of Cookson. It was important to be in a position to confront, rather than the reverse. The group captain met him just inside the door. He looked a little paler than normal.

'What happened, Guy?'

'I don't know yet, sir. We think number three went down. Sommerton thought he saw a flash and took a fix on it, but I want to check a few things first before I talk to you.' He found the master copy of the route and smoothed it onto the table. Boldly, in front of the group captain, he took the crumpled paper from his pocket and made a show of checking the number and then applying them to the map. 'Eastings first.' He muttered in a stage whisper, aware that both Bertie and his superior officer were watching his every move. He traced his finger from the left side of the map until he got to where he wanted. 'Then northings.' Again the finger moved from the top of the sheet and stopped when it got to the mark he had just made. 'Right,' he sounded funereal as he turned to Bertie. 'What would be your estimate of where the aircraft went down, Grice?'

'I'm not sure, sir.' Bertie sounded confused and scratched his head. 'I can only give you a rough position from what was said in the air.'

'Give it your best guess, then. There is number three's route and we were flying in this direction. Four minutes or so out from the target and that takes us to here.' The pointed finger again stopped at the new mark on the map. 'Would you agree, Bertie, that this is the rough area where three was last seen?' Bertie did his own mental calculations and slowly nodded his head.

'I would say it was about right, sir.' He glanced towards the group captain, who stood motionless, apart from chewing his bottom lip.

'Right.' Guy could not resist a note of triumph creeping in to his voice. He had timed it perfectly. He could hear the others begin to filter into the room.

'What's this about, Guy?' Gorton asked. 'I don't follow.'

'I'll explain, sir. Just as you called me into your office before tonight's trip the Intel sergeant came to me with the position of a large, well-armed convoy that was sighted in this position.' He jabbed at the map to add emphasis. 'As I was rushing about like a blue-arsed fly, worried that I might miss something, I handed the lead over to Tom Cookson, told him to plot the co-ordinates and to re-route anyone who came close to it. I must admit some responsibility in that I didn't check specifically that this had been done, but with a man of his experience and rank, that should not always be necessary. But, sir,' he paused to add drama and looked at his feet as though wishing there was some way round what he was going to say, 'I must tell you that I don't think the information was acted upon.' Again he paused, letting the tension build. 'As a result, we seem to have needlessly lost a jet.'

It was perfect. He could not have timed it better in a million years. The group captain was eating out of his hand, looking even paler than he had been a few moments previously. Guy was tempted to say that he thought Cookson would probably deny the whole thing, but that might implicate him just a little. No, he had said just enough. One man's word against another, but he had made the first impression and, looking at his CO, he had made a good start.

Guy looked towards the door as Cookson entered. At least the press were good for something in this war; they had given him time to set up his alibi. Tom Gorton walked towards Cookson. Guy went with him. 'A word, Tom, in my office.' Gorton gave the slightest of head movements to indicate the direction.

'After the debrief, sir?' Cookson asked. The slight shake of the group captain's head and the serious expression defied argument. Cookson looked at Guy for some kind of clue, but the face was impassive.

'You as well, Guy.' Gorton beckoned with his finger, grabbing the map as he went past it. The two men fell in behind him, Guy in the rear. Cookson had his G-pants over one shoulder and his maps, carelessly stuffed into a home-made canvas bag, were hanging over the other. As they left the room and stepped into the corridor the bag seemed to yawn invitingly in front of Guy. Taking his chance, he dropped the first copy of the co-ordinates between the maps. Getting Cookson to fish it out was another problem, but he would come to that all in good time. For now he could not believe how well it was going.

The group captain stood to one side and allowed the two to file past him into the office before quietly closing the door. He indicated chairs for both men and then sat at the desk. It was several seconds before he spoke. He looked at his hands, which were motionless on top of the desk, appearing to be in communion with them. Guy had a sudden panic that he was not going to be believed, and for a moment had to stop himself from shouting the accusation at Cookson. He calmed himself. A guilty man would protest. An innocent man would have nothing to fear.

'Tom,' the CO spoke in a quiet, controlled voice. 'There is a serious matter here. The convoy? Did you take any action to avoid the convoy?' Cookson looked stunned and Guy seized upon the moment before the inevitable denial.

'You know, the convoy I told you about before I handed you the lead of the formation.' Cookson turned slowly towards Guy, a look of incredulity crossed his face, his cheeks flushed red. 'The position of the convoy which I have marked here on the map would seem to tie up with the point at which the aircraft was shot down, and I told you about it.' Guy allowed his voice to rise in anger.

'Okay, Guy, I'll deal with this,' Gorton interrupted.

'Sorry,' he muttered, but again had made his point, pleased at his timing.

'Sir, I knew nothing of a convoy. I was told nothing about a convoy.' Cookson sounded weak, a little unsure of himself. Guy knew enough to keep the pressure on.

'Of course you knew. I told you myself and because you didn't act two men are missing and an aeroplane is lost.' Guy spat the words.

'Thank you, Guy.' Gorton sounded a little impatient and Guy warned himself to hold his tongue. Everything was in place; all he had to do was allow it to come out.

'Tom, the wing commander says he gave you the co-ordinates of a convoy, asked you to plot them and take any action you thought fit to avoid it.' Gorton's eyes were burning into Cookson's and he shook his head slowly in bewilderment.

'I gave him the note the sergeant gave to me with the co-ordinates on it,' Guy quickly interjected. He wanted to scream 'look in the fucking bag,' but he bit his tongue.

Then Cookson buried himself. 'If he gave me the note then I would have it with me, wouldn't I?' He stood and tipped the contents onto the desk. Guy simply couldn't believe his luck. The man was so self-confident it was laughable.

'That's the route map,' he pointed at the crumpled piece of paper, 'that's the target run, that's a list of frequencies and that's it. I took everything else that could have been useful to the enemy out.' Cookson stood with his hands on his hips and glared at the two men.

Guy was beside himself. Where had the bloody thing gone? Surely Cookson was not going to get away with the paper not being found. Gorton idly pulled the target map across the desk. It had been folded in two to make it easier to carry. He flipped it open and out dropped the piece of paper.

'There.' To Guy's own ears it seemed like a scream, but he knew he had sounded reasonably calm. 'That looks like it.'

Gorton slowly unfolded the sheet, turned it the right way round and then slid it across the table for both men to read. 'That it, Guy?' Gorton quietly asked.

Guy merely nodded. He acted like it was a painful moment for him. A fellow officer had not only lied, but his carelessness or dereliction of duty had led to the probable death of two men. His face showed that he took no pleasure in it. Inside, his very soul screeched out in triumph. He had won the day. Cookson was out of his hair for ever. He was home and running. Now only this damned war stood between him and a golden future. Dimly, as though from another room, he could hear Gorton saying what a serious matter this was. Cookson had better stay on the ground until the thing could be sorted, but at this stage a court martial could not be ruled out.

Cookson looked a broken man. His face had lost all its colour and his mouth moved as if he wanted to speak, but the words would not come. The men before him looked rational and reasonable, but the world had lost its senses. An hour or so before he had witnessed the probable death of his friends, and now he was being blamed for the whole matter. Pieces of paper were in his bag that he had never seen in his life before, and grown men were talking about a convoy that he had never heard of. The whole scene was so bizarre that his first inclination was to laugh, but he could see from the expressions on the faces in front of him that this was no laughing matter. The group captain was still muttering on about the pressure of the situation and extenuating circumstances, but he was not really listening. Any moment now he would waken up and it would all be a dream. A bloody bad one, but that's how it would turn out.

What to do? He had no more idea than the man in the moon. He was over a barrel, and every other metaphor that he could think of. He rose slowly to his feet. 'If you don't mind, sir, I've got a debrief to sort out and a bit of thinking to do. I'm sure we'll talk some more about this.'

Gorton merely nodded. He could not remember when he had last felt so sorry for anyone. Cookson seemed to have aged before his eyes.

Chapter Eighteen

They found the crash site the next day. The sky cleared sufficiently for the satellites and the spy planes to do their work and the results were rushed back for analysis. The interpreters were looking at the convoy when they found it. At first it looked like a piece of camouflage netting strung across one of the dreaded Scud missiles, a mobile site which wandered the desert, indiscriminately launching its deadly wares into Saudi Arabia and Israel, hoping to split the alliance and draw Israel into the conflict.

The negative had provoked excitement, but a closer look at the large positive print revealed the fin of a Tornado lying close by, and brought a different reaction. The Red Cross had not reported the capture of any airmen, and the conclusion was that they had almost certainly perished in the wreckage. It cast a gloom over the squadron and, coupled with the mysterious grounding of Cookson, created a sombre atmosphere.

The hideous humdrum of war set in. Exaltation on landing, having completed a successful mission, was gradually replaced by the realisation that it was all to be done again. Wanting to fight and create as much havoc as possible, but wanting to get the hell out of there. Wanting to get the hell out of there with their backsides in one piece. Night after night they took their weapons to Saddam's airfields and endured the terrible flak that was poured into the sky by the defenders. Saddam's airforce either refused to come out and fight, or had been ordered not to do so, but either way, the futility of bombing airfields which were not going to be used was not lost on the crews. The RAF was taking casualties, while the Americans, who were operating at medium altitudes out of reach of most of the ground fire, were getting away clean.

The crews were dealing with the problem in their own ways. A glass or two of the hard stuff, comfort in the homes of the expats, where they could unload their worries onto sympathetic ears, or in the case of John Sommerton, solace in the arms of

Daisy, which, much to Hunch's chagrin, barred him from their room. He, in turn, started eating more, only to feel guilt and to exercise furiously as soon as he spotted the extra pounds being put on. Others spent time on the phone home and ran up enormous bills.

Cookson simply did not know what had hit him or, more frustratingly, what he could do about it. Guy Kelsall seemed to have stitched him up so completely that he had no idea how to get out of it. He had talked to the Intel sergeant, only to be assured that the numbers on the piece of paper found in his bag were written by him. How Kelsall had got it into his bag, he had no idea. Why Kelsall should have done it also eluded him, but he was prepared to give it a good guess. He tried to busy himself by giving the crews as much support as he could, but the combination of guilt, of not being able to go with them and an inability to do anything about his position was beginning to get to him. He had appealed to Kelsall to allow him, at least, to continue flying, but the Boss had resolutely refused it.

Then suddenly Kelsall reversed his decision. Cookson was relieved beyond anything he could have imagined. To be pleased to be going back into the jaws of hell would have seemed illogical earlier, but now he wanted it more than anything; to regain his self-respect and the respect of others. Although judging from the reaction he was getting from most people, he was still well respected. Frost, particularly, needed restraining from physically confronting Kelsall.

Guy Kelsall barely lived with his fear. He took more and more pills to create the oblivion of sleep, only to wake with a feeling of dread that was unshakeable, no matter what he tried. Sam Waterson listened to his problems and gave him a sympathetic shoulder to cry on, but it was not enough. She would not cross the boundary between friend and lover and he had never wanted anything so much in his life.

His feeling of triumph over Cookson had been short-lived. He had felt some guilt, but not nearly enough for him to change his position. The grounding of Cookson had given him other problems. With Ord out of the way, probably dead, he had not realised how much he had come to rely on the man and, having grounded him, the majority of the leading was coming his way. He had to do something about it and reasoned that even if Cookson were allowed to fly again, it would not change the position of things. The blame for not avoiding the convoy would still be seen to rest squarely on his shoulders. It also crossed Guy's mind that Cookson might get killed, and although he did not necessarily want it, a few loose ends would be nicely tied up. No messy court martial, no giving evidence and the matter would be forgotten, with no fall-out coming his way. In fact, the more he thought about it, the more that scenario appealed to him.

The group captain was reluctant at first. Guy argued, given the situation, that Cookson's expertise was invaluable. He tried to sound benevolent and forgiving. Surely a man of Cookson's character would continue to act in the best way possible? He might even redeem himself; after all, anyone could make a mistake. Tom Gorton had relented, and although Guy had tried to push Cookson into the lead for that evening, the group captain had insisted that Guy fly it himself.

There was talk of changing the tactics. Mutterings were coming down from on high that the Tornados where picking up too many casualties. Gorton had made representation that if the Iraqis where not going to launch their planes then it was no use bombing their airfields. The powers were reluctant to change. JP233 was keeping the Iraqis on the ground and if they let up on the attacks then their opponents would fly.

The dreadful routine. Get up and face the dark. Eat when you are not hungry. Ride in silence. Brief, trying like hell to hold your concentration. Keep your thoughts on the job. Let the thoughts of family, comfort and home stay away. Dress. Plan. Check. Walk. Keep cheerful for the ground crew. Climb into a cold, dark cockpit. Check. Wait. Live alone with your thoughts. Try not to think who might get it tonight. Try not to think that it might be you. Take off into the night. Tank. Let down into the black hole of the desert. A darkness the like of which you had never known. Count the absences: horizon, vision, warmth, friendship, love, family. Get back to the job. Watch the instruments like there is no tomorrow, because if you don't then there will be no tomorrow. Listen. 'All clear.' And pray. Pray like you have never done before.

Pray that your nerve will hold. Pray that you won't let the side down. Pray that the aircraft would not let you down. Pray that you will see your family again. But don't think of them – it hurts too much.

Chapter Nineteen

'Five minutes to the target, Boss.' They were the last words that Bertie spoke on this earth. The Roland missile ripped through the belly of the aircraft. It cleanly removed both his legs and half his pelvis and his life force dropped from him in an instant. The upper part of his body hung in the seat straps as if nothing had happened. A missile, made in France and delivered in Iraq, had torn a great hole in the part of the aircraft which had been made in Germany and had sent an Englishman to eternity. Through the miracle of modern communications, the world would know of it in hours. War was truly an international event.

The impact of the missile jarred Guy so violently that he bit off the end of his tongue. The noise and the dust filled the cockpit and seemed to cloud his thoughts. 'You okay, Bertie?' The question failed to reach his own ears and Guy wondered if he had even said the words or whether they were just drowned out in the noise. He could not believe the noise. A thousand hosepipes trained on an empty drum. The loudest wind imaginable whistling through a girder bridge. It numbed his thoughts and his senses, banned reason and rational thought, negated training. His only reaction was to leave, to pull the seat handle and get the hell out of there. The thought of the cold and the dark stayed his hand. In what seemed a lifetime, but which in reality had been little more than the time taken to swallow the first mouthful of blood, he adjusted to the situation. His subconscious told him the aircraft was flying. The engines were still working, or as far as he could tell, at least one of them was. Outside there was emptiness, and whoever had done this to them was not far away. A missile first, a boot in the head later, followed by another. He had seen the television pictures of what they were doing to downed aircrew. A wing commander would be a fine prize. 'Here you are, lads. This is the big one, see how long you can play football with him before he deflates.' No matter how cold it was in the cockpit, it was colder out there.

The dust cleared and with it his thoughts. Turn away. Turn back the way you have come. Which way was that? The bloody instruments were all over the place. The moon. The moon had been behind and that was the way out of here. To safety and freedom.

Slowly, painstakingly, he inched the aircraft away from the ground and it began to turn in response to his inputs. It was very heavy. He guessed that the fly-by-wire system had failed and that the back-up mechanical linkage was all that was working, a triple, totally independent fly-by-wire system for the controls that could not fail, unless the loom which carried all the wires were hit.

He fought on. He found the moon and put it in the front window. It had grown since he had seen it on that first evening, a lifetime ago. He could not remember whether it was still in the same cycle or not. It didn't matter. All that mattered was that it was there, and he prayed that cloud would not obscure it. Time seemed to stand still. He was still in space and the earth slowly moved past him. It occurred to him that he was a sitting target for anyone to take a pot-shot at and prayed that his identification equipment was still working. The last thing he wanted was a gung-ho American sticking another missile up him. The thought seemed so bizarre that he almost smiled – almost.

The seconds turned into hours and the minutes turned into weeks and still he managed to keep the thing in the air. The aircraft refused to fly a straight line, wallowing and pitching like a cork in a stormy sea. The main instrument panel was black and, in the glare of the emergency lights, he tried to use the stand-by instruments, which he had rarely seen, let alone used. The speed was reducing, dropping below three hundred knots; he was now sure that one of the engines was out and the other one was damaged. He tried to make a call, but in the noise he couldn't even hear himself. *Squawk emergency*, he suddenly thought and reached down to find the switch. Unable to feel it, he realised how cold his hands were, so cold he couldn't feel them at all. He bashed his right hand against the side of the aircraft. The pain in his shoulder caused him to scream in agony. He fought the white light behind his eyes and grabbed once more onto consciousness. Then he realised that while most of him was freezing, his right side and lower back were warm. He wrenched his glove off with his teeth and stuck his left hand as far as he could reach down his right side. He felt a warm stickiness and when he withdrew his hand he could see that it was red in the dim light.

The aircraft shuddered and yawed violently to the left. Instinctively, Guy pressed forward with his right foot to correct. Nothing happened. His knee travelled further than it should have done. He was aware of a great numbness in his foot; when he looked down his foot was not there. The pain hit him with the knowledge. He felt faint and had to fight to stop himself from blacking out. Now he had no choice. If he didn't go now, he never would. He grabbed the handle between his legs, suddenly remembering Bertie. He would have to take his chances. Their seats were linked together, if he were still alive he would go on his command. He pulled upwards with all his might, heard a muffled bang as something hit him in the base of his spine and knew no more.

Chapter Twenty

The man third from the back on the right-hand side of the twin rows of consuls heard it, or thought he did. The night was again quiet. The Iraqi airforce had given them no trade at all. The great AWAC aircraft, with its mushroom obtrusion, droned round its racetrack well inside the safety of its cordon of fighters, and the men at their stations did their best to concentrate. Anything to take his mind away from Illinois, where his wife was about to make him a father for the first time. Just one or two fighters would have been fine. Something to get the adrenaline going. Something to get their teeth into. They had watched the bombers go in. The fighter cover was high, their squawks painted on his screen, numbers that danced a ballet on the darkened background. He felt sorry for the RAF. Night after night they were going in where it hurt and were taking the losses. He watched as the little groups of four split and wended their own ways towards their targets. It was like watching small spots of rain slowly dribble down a window. A little movement and then stop. The blink of an eye and they moved again. Then one seemed to stop moving with the other, slowly diverging and dropping back into a large turnabout, before heading the way it had come.

'Lost his kit, or something.' The thick, lazy drawl of the southern States went unnoticed by those working alongside.

He watched fascinated, barely remembering to monitor the progress of the rest of the formation, and then he heard it. It sounded like a man standing under a railway bridge and shouting while a train was going over the top. He thought he heard the word, 'Mayday!' but that was all. Almost immediately, the radar point disappeared.

'I think one's gone down, Charlie.' He leaned towards his colleague in the next seat and pointed to the spot on his screen. They both looked at the screen and waited. The three points of the main formation continued on their way. 'There was four of 'em for sure.' The rate at which he spoke belied his urgency. 'Get someone to get the chopper alerted; I'll keep looking and plot the position. He's in a good spot at least; not far from the border – good chance our guys'll get there first.'

Chapter Twenty-One

The formation check-in after leaving the target came late. Hunch, not sure where anyone was, waited for the Boss to make the call. Something had not been right about this attack. Instead of flying into a wall of fire it had been relatively peaceful, as though he had surprised the gunners. The lazy tracers only came when he was well into his run. The Boss and Bertie should have roused them. He wondered if the Iraqis had had enough and packed it in. But that had changed when he had started the run and the sky had lit up with the usual intensity. They had returned to the blanket of darkness before Sommerton spoke. 'I think we were first through the target, Hunch.'

'I'd have to say you were right, Sport, but it's not like Bertie to get lost.'

'More serious than that, Hunch.' Sommerton's tone was gentle and he sounded close to tears. 'Make the call.'

'You mean do the check-in?'

'No, order three rounds of fish and chips.'

'Sarky.' Hunch had not grasped what Sommerton was saying. 'Trent, check.'

'Trent three.'

'Four.' Crisp replies.

Hunch waited a few seconds. 'Trent lead, check in?' He made it sound like a question but got no reply. 'Trent lead, check in.' He tried again with more urgency and with a real fear creeping into his mind.

'Trent two, just take us home.' The voice sounded dog-tired.

'Do you think we ought to renumber, Sport?' Hunch sounded confused.

'I don't think so, Hunch.'

'Shit, Sport, what about that? Not yet twenty-five and four-ship leaders in a war. Well, three-ship leaders really. Wait till I tell the old parent, he will be proud.'

'Don't be such a bloody arsehole, Hunch. We're not just talking about the Boss; there's Bertie as well, and all you can do is babble on about being four-ship bloody leaders.'

'Yes, but they'll get out, won't they? They'll be okay, won't they? Bollocks, I never thought of that. If the bastard has done anything to Bertie I'll…' The words died in the sob.

Chapter Twenty-Two

'Trent, to Ops.'

'Trent, this is Ops, go ahead.' Cookson hurriedly swung his feet from the desk and grabbed the transmit switch on the radio.

'Ops, we're about twenty minutes out. ETA 0425.'

'That's copied, Trent. Is everything okay?' He knew he should not ask the question on an insecure line, but couldn't help himself. It was Hunch's voice; all was not well.

'Ops, from Trent... er... not exactly. We're one short. Not sure where he went down.'

'Trent, roger.' Cookson left it at that. It was no use telling the enemy more than they needed to know, and even that might be too much. The press would probably be tuned in also, and half a story in their hands could be damaging.

'Sarge, man the lines. I'll go and tell the old man and get in touch with the rescue services. They might know something. One thing at least, the Americans are good at rescuing people. With any luck they've got the thing underway already.'

Cookson got up quickly, his chair falling backwards to the floor. Ignoring the crash, he hurried towards the door.

'Fuck, damn and blast,' he muttered to himself, 'Fuck the man.'

'What was that, sir?'

'Nothing, Sarge. Just get on as I asked.' Cookson felt embarrassed at his outburst, but this was the last straw. If Kelsall had gone in and wasn't coming back it left him in limbo. There was no way he could clear his name. With the main witness for the prosecution out of the picture then there would be no court martial. He was going to find it difficult to clear his name anyway, but now it would be impossible and the stigma of the accusation would stay with him the rest of his life. At least in a court of law he would have had the chance to face down his accuser and call him a liar.

His mind was a turmoil. Perhaps he was all right. He should feel sorry for him, but he didn't. He felt sympathy for Kelsall's family and for Bertie, but at the moment he was feeling more sorry for himself. The thought of Bertie brought him back to reality, remembering that Hunch was leading on the way back. He had better get out to meet them. He found the group captain and between them they made the inquiries. Yes, an aircraft had been seen to go down. Yes, there was a helicopter trying to find them. No, they had no further news. They would let them know. At least that was something.

Cookson looked at his watch. They would be on short finals. He grabbed his tin hat and NBC kit and hurried outside. The early morning chill sent a shiver through him. To the east the sky was turning from the black of night to a silver streak across the horizon. For once the forecast for the day was good; they all might get a little heat in their bones. He gave a thought to the armies who were massing for the attack. The combined airforces had failed to elicit any response from Saddam, except for the scuds, and rumour was rife that a ground strike was a matter of days, if not hours, away. He wondered what sort of weather they would like. Perhaps hot would not suit them. He shrugged his shoulders. It was all becoming too difficult.

He watched the aircraft taxi onto their parking slots. The ground crew were on them like ants the minute the wheels stopped. Cookson absently wondered how they didn't get in each other's way. The canopy split from the fuselage and juddered its way to the vertical. Hunch uncoiled from the front cockpit and stood on the seat. He held his arms out horizontal to the ground, a Christ-like image against the breaking dawn. They must all be getting tired now, Cookson thought. They could use a break, like he had just had, but it had seemed to him more wearing than when he was flying: the waiting, the worrying and the feeling of total ineffectiveness.

Hunch slowly put his pin in the safety mechanism and began to climb down the steps. His body language suggested a man of twice his years. Cookson met him at the bottom of the steps. As he removed his helmet, Cookson could see the wet tracks of the tears down his dark cheeks.

'The bastards got Bertie. If the Boss had left him with me he would still be alive. I hate that bastard as well.' Cookson had never heard Hunch talk in such a way. His eyes were narrow slits and the whites showed red through a combination of sorrow and anger.

'I know how you feel, Hunch.' He put his arm around the shoulder of the taller man and steered him out of earshot of the ground crew. 'We don't know if he's dead, do we?' He offered a small glimmer of hope. 'He might have got out. You didn't see it happen, did you?' Hunch shook his head and starred blankly into the night. Cookson could see the press waiting by the security fence, hungry for news and a drama. This was right down their street. A pilot in tears over a lost comrade was meat and drink to them. They waited for Sommerton, and Cookson steered them towards the operations building.

'Stay calm and don't say anything you might regret,' he whispered as they approached the wire. 'You never know, it might turn out okay.' Hunch nodded and wiped his sleeve across his face.

'Okay, it's okay now. Just a bit of a shock that's all.' His mood brightened. 'Got the others back though, didn't we, Sport? Did a bit of leading there, sir. I hope you noticed and remember it when you want a couple of good chaps to be promoted to pairs leaders. In fact,' he was back in the old Hunch mode, 'as it was a three-ship and in a wartime scenario, you might want to think about skipping the pairs leading bit and put us straight on to four-ship leading?'

Cookson's face broke into a grin and he looked across at Sommerton who raised his eyes wistfully to the heavens. 'Hunch, just shut the fuck up.'

No one wanted to go back to the hotel. Sleep, in any case, would not have been an option. The conversations were quiet and subdued. Small groups scattered around the planning room. The oncoming shift waiting for their targets and the night crews just waiting. Time moved slowly. The strain of the last weeks and days were etched on the faces. Young men turned old before their time. Cookson leant on the corner of the communication consul and watched them. They never ceased to amaze him. They were ordinary people, drawn from all walks of life, each with a myriad of different reasons for wanting to do this job. None of them, in their wildest dreams, would have seriously thought that they would have been involved in a war, yet day after day they had trained for it. None had known how he would react, and somehow each in their own ways had found the inner strength to go about their business. Some were tight-lipped and silent, some talked too much, some hid behind a facade of humour and, he knew, some had taken to praying.

The phone rang, a raucous sound in a holy place. Cookson grabbed it from its holder before the second ring ended. Every conversation stopped, every eye in the room was focused on him. 'Right,' he said and replaced the receiver.

'The chopper was on the scene of the crash within minutes. It seems some bright spark on the AWAC had a grandstand view. They've picked up the Boss. He's in a bad way, lost a lot of blood. They didn't want to hang about the site in case whoever fired the missile was still about, but from what they said it doesn't look too good.' Cookson watched Hunch's face and almost whispered, 'There's no sign of Bertie.'

The mask crumpled. Hunch muttered, 'I'm going for a kip,' and turned away. He was growing by the day. He would grieve alone.

Cookson's moods were on a helter-skelter ride to hell. Firstly down, when he heard there had been a loss and who it was. Then it had soared when he heard they had found Kelsall, only to plummet again when he realised the precarious condition he was in.

'Please don't let him die.' He hadn't prayed since he was a child. He had forgotten how. Then, he had done it through bribery. 'You do this for me, God, I'll do that for you.' It had worked as well as anything, perhaps that was why he had stopped. 'I'll tell you what, God. If you let him live I'll give you three conkers and that picture of Jimmy Greaves that you always wanted.' He smiled to himself, hoping that if the Boss survived, he could put his hands on that picture.

Chapter Twenty-Three

The Almighty seemed to take kindly to Cookson's offer. Guy Kelsall opened his eyes and quickly shut them again. The light seemed blinding.

'Too bright for you? I'll close the blinds.' The figure moved from his bedside towards the window and he heard the rustle of the blinds being lowered. 'It's really a nice day for a change.' The voice carried the sounds and smells of a green, English summer's day. Guy made a further attempt to open his eyes, picking out the shape of the woman standing silhouetted against the light. The light surrounding her hair gave her a halo effect.

'Have I died and gone to heaven?' he croaked.

'Nothing so grand. You're in Muharraq, but you very nearly made the trip to the other side. If the "good ole boys" in their little helicopter had not got to you as quickly as they did, then I might have been an angel. You're a very lucky man in more ways than one.'

'Okay, Doctor Waterson.' He recognised her as she moved to the other side of the bed. 'This sounds like a good news, bad news kind of conversation. Let me see.' He tried to look around him and winced at the pain in his shoulder. 'Shit.'

'Hurt a bit, does it?'

'Do you know that is the most fatuous question anyone can ask a person lying injured on a hospital bed.'

She smiled. 'Good bedside manner, that's all.'

He glanced around the bed. Plastic bottles hung at each side of him and when he put his good hand to his mouth it seemed to be terminus for tubes. Looking towards the end of the bed, he could see the covers raised in a mound.

'Good news, I'm alive. Bad news, break a leg, did I? Your turn.' He tried to sound casual. She looked away and he could see from her expression that something was not right. 'Bad news, a bit more serious,' he added.

'Little bit more, I'm afraid.' She smoothed the covers of the bed, glancing away, before turning to look him fully in the eyes.

'The really bad news bit, eh?' he asked.

'"Fraid so.'

'Well, get on with it, let's get it over with.' The tough-guy voice had gone, to be replaced by an irritated tone.

'It's your foot.' She paused, absently moving one of the tubes. 'Whatever hit you took off the end of your foot. To save your leg, we had to cut the rest of it off at the ankle. I'm sorry.' She looked quickly away, not wanting to see the expression upon his face, and heard him take a deep breath. She sat quietly while he became adjusted to what she had just told him.

'This is where I do the brave thing, is it? The stiff upper lip thing. Crack a smile and ask for a cup of tea. Ask if you can still love a one-footed man.' He flung his face towards the window as a tear trickled down his cheek. 'Well, you can fuck off,' he whispered.

'People react in different ways,' she said, pretending not to have heard.

'I suppose some run around the room screaming?'

'They do, but I'm afraid that is not one of your options. If you're bent on screaming it will have to be the prone variation.'

He smiled. 'Bertie?'

'I'm afraid not. He must have died instantly.' She didn't want to go into any more details and hoped he wouldn't ask. He knew enough about aircraft crashes not to do so. He looked at the ceiling for a long time and Sam sat quietly, letting him come to terms with his loss.

His mind was a whirl. He was alive, he had made it. Sure, it was bad news about his foot, but he had made it. No more going to bloody war. No more fear. It all came flooding back to him. He was home and running – well, not exactly running – he supposed he might get to some sort of fast hobble with a bit of practise. Cookson was off his back, he was out of the war and would go back some sort of wounded hero. He might even pick up a medal or something. A group captain with a bit of a limp didn't sound too bad a deal. Just one more thing would make his life complete.

'We never got around to the good news,' he asked.

'As I said at the beginning, you really are very lucky to be alive. You nearly bled to death.'

'With a foot missing, how come I didn't?'

'The Americans for one. They got to you very quickly, but there is a bit of a miracle as well.'

'You're going to tell me about guardian angels and such like. I can see it from the look on your face. Save it.' He almost sneered.

'I wasn't actually going to mention one of those.' She ignored his sarcasm. 'But if you have the slightest belief in a higher power then you might like to count yourself among the chosen.' She held her hand up to stop him interrupting. 'Because you landed heavily in the sand, it clogged up the blood and formed a very effective bandage. It was almost a shame to scrape it off. So someone up there appears to like you.'

'How about down here?' He reached across towards her and held out his hand. She took it; her touch was warm and soft. He smiled across at her. 'Is it possible to love a man with one foot?'

'It's possible, but I don't think it's going to happen. Your wife has been on the phone every day, sometimes twice a day. Obviously worrying about you. She might even be coming out to lay claim to you.'

'What do you mean every day?' He searched the room for some sign of the date.

'Oh, you've been a sleepy little lad,' she chided. 'You really shouldn't stay up so late dropping bombs all over the place. Let's see now.' She counted on her fingers. 'The best part of three days now. Quite a sleepy chap, eh?'

'Is she coming? Mary, I mean.'

'I don't know. I understood from the nurses that she might if she can get the clearances.'

'I'm not sure that I want her to.' He looked at Sam, but she turned her head and avoided his eyes. 'I think I'm falling in love with you.'

She looked directly at him and a colder look came into her eye.

'No, you're not. You only think you are. You're a wounded little hero and I'm a pseudo-guardian angel in white.' She smoothed her white coat as she spoke. 'One minute after getting out of here, you'll rush back to your beloved aeroplanes and out of my life.'

'I don't think so and, anyway, aeroplanes, or at least flying in them, are a thing of my past. The best I can hope for now is a desk – a mahogany bomber.' He gave a wan little smile, but inside felt the relief he had experienced a few minutes before. 'We could have a good life together,' he added.

'Are you proposing to me?' She was beginning to think that they sounded like a pair of star-crossed lovers from an old black and white movie – 'Will you marry me, Daphne?' 'No, I can't, George. John needs me, especially now he is wounded, but I will always love you'.

'I might be.' He interrupted her thoughts.

'Don't be so daft. We hardly know each other and this place is hardly reality, is it?'

'Well, my reality is knowing that I don't want to go back to where I was before. Mary and I got on okay, but it was not that great.' He licked his lips. 'Can I have a drink of water, please?'

'Of course.' She got the glass and leaned across him, gently placed a hand behind his head and raised him from the pillow. His entire body felt stiff and painful, but the water tasted nice and her scent filled his senses.

'You don't love me then?' he asked.

'No,' she answered quickly.

'That's a bit brutal for a man who has recently had his application to pass through the Pearly Gates turned down, isn't it?' He tried to make light of it.

'I'm sorry, I didn't mean to sound like that, but it's better to be honest. I'm not given to telling lies. If I were you, I would just concentrate on what I had in reality and not what I thought was on offer in dreamland. You've got a nice wife and children, who all love and worry about you, you've said so yourself. So why don't you just accept it. It's something most people strive to achieve all their lives.' Her face was a little flushed from her outburst.

'Quite the preaching philosopher suddenly, aren't we?' he sneered.

'I'm sorry. I'd better go. I shouldn't speak to you like that.'

'No, no, I'm sorry, just sit down for a little longer. I've got a lot on my mind at the moment. You might be right in the long term.'

'You seemed to be having some very serious conversations with yourself while you were out for the count.' She blushed and looked away as if having said something she had not intended.

'Serious conversations, what do you mean?'

'Nothing,' she said quickly. 'Forget I spoke.'

'No.' He looked hard at her, trying to read her thoughts. 'I'd like to know what you meant.'

'Well, it's nothing really, it's just that you talk a lot in your sleep, shall we say.'

He looked away from her towards the window and tried to sound indifferent. 'Oh really, anything I should know about?' There was a long pause while she tried to find the right words.

'Let me just say that it was something weighing heavily on your mind. Something that seems to bother you. Something that you might like to get off your chest.' She glanced at him expectantly. 'Perhaps you would like to tell me, get it out in the open. Something only you seem to know and, from what I could gather, others would like to know also, but you don't want them to.'

He shook his head as if to clear it. 'You've lost me there with all your "knows" and "don't knows". You're beginning to sound like a character in an Agatha Christie thriller. Could you be a bit more specific?' He needed to find out what she knew, even though he didn't want to. The events of the last few days came rushing back to him. She could be dangerous.

'You know what I mean.' She almost sounded silly and girlish.

He smirked. 'There you go again, talking in riddles. I don't know, that's why I'm asking.'

'I'll just give you a few clues.' The corners of her mouth were tight with the tension. 'The words "Cookson" and "co-ordinates" and "my fault really" were very popular, while phrases like "mustn't find out", "ruined career" and "just keep to the story" were in close second place. Do I need to elaborate further?' There was more than a hint of sarcasm and disgust in her tone.

'You know the whole story?' He had the look of a naughty boy in need of forgiveness.

'Not the whole story, only you know that, but I know enough to be able to put two and two together. Cookson, for some reason, is under a cloud that no one will talk about and you're muttering away ten to the dozen. I know you've not been totally honest and that Cookson is about to collect the fall-out.'

He paused for a long time, weighing the consequences of her knowing. Now, instead of being out of the woods, he was well and truly back in them. 'What are you going to do about it?' he asked at last.

'Me? Nothing. I leave that to you and your conscience.' She turned and walked out off the room. He gazed at the door for some moments, a smirk playing on his lips. *What does she know?* he thought. She wouldn't tell anyone. She might not love him, but she was too bound up with duty and honesty. He would spin her a line. He was still in the clear. Suddenly, he felt extremely tired.

When he awoke it was dark. He could hear the raindrops pattering on the window. The break in the weather had been short-lived. He wondered how the war was going. In all the chat earlier, the fighting had not been mentioned. He was well out of it and a little tremor went through him. 'Are you all right?' He turned to see Sam sitting by the bed.

'Hi, how long have you been there? Come to listen to a few secrets?' Her look registered her hurt.

'You have needed a bit of care as well, you know,' she answered.

'I'm sorry, a low blow. You're looking particularly lovely tonight.' He waved his arm expansively and grimaced at the pain.

'You really will have to work on your chat-up lines,' she laughed.

'I know, I've never been too good at it.'

'Perhaps a little bit of sincerity thrown in might help.'

'Ouch!' He pretended to clutch his abdomen. 'My turn for a low one.'

'Now I'm sorry, perhaps we should start again. How are you feeling, anyway?'

'Well, apart from this woman who keeps coming in and tormenting me, I'm not feeling too bad for a man with one foot.'

'Did you think about what I said?'

'About what?' He could see from her expression what she was referring to.

'Seeing the group captain, clearing the air, doing the honourable thing.'

'Look, Sam,' he half-rolled towards her and his features hardened. 'I know you mean well, but this has nothing to do with you. You're out of line and way out of your depth. I would be obliged if you would forget about what you thought you heard and mind your own business. I'm tired now, so if you don't mind…'

He closed his eyes and turned away from her. Slowly, she rose from the chair and crossed the room. As she reached the door she turned and looked at the form on the bed. A small look of triumph was etched on her face.

Chapter Twenty-Four

Tom Gorton listened carefully, his hands pressed together like a church steeple, occasionally touching his lips, but otherwise making no comment or interruption. She found it a little disconcerting, wondering if he were taking what she was saying seriously or just patronising her. When she finished he merely said, 'So, you got all this from an unconscious man in a state of delirium?'

'No, not exactly. We've had a couple of conversations since he regained consciousness and he was very furtive. Although he never actually confessed, he was quite forceful in telling me to mind my own business. More importantly, he never denied any of it.'

'But he doesn't have to deny anything; he's not being accused of anything.' The group captain allowed the question to hang in the air for a moment.

'No, sir.' Sam's voice was low, showing no sign of her inner turmoil. 'He's not being accused of anything, but someone else is. This would point to the innocence of that person. As I understand it,' she continued, 'it's one man's word against another and one of those men has the benefit of rank to back him up. What I am telling you is not evidence which would lead to a conviction in a court of law, but it is sufficiently strong to point to the fact that Guy Kelsall is not being truthful. Perhaps the whole truth will never be told, but it seems clear to me that Tom Cookson, for whatever reason, is being held to blame for something he didn't do.' A note of desperation had crept into her voice.

A long moment of silence passed. Gorton did not take his eyes from her face, but they were unfocused as his mind raced.

'I agree with you,' he suddenly said and Sam started at the forcefulness of his words. 'Yes,' he continued more quietly. 'I'm afraid I have to agree with you, but what to do about it?' He was almost talking to himself. 'What would you do about it, doctor?'

The question surprised her and for a moment she was lost for a reply.

'I wouldn't do anything about it.' Gorton raised his eyebrows in surprise at her answer. He had expected more. 'It's not my problem,' she continued. 'It's a problem for the military, and even they must retain some sort of common code and decency which does not condone this kind of behaviour. At the very least, Tom Cookson must be shown to be free of any kind of guilt. Having said that, some of the guilt, or at least a question mark, should hang over Guy Kelsall's head. How you get round that is your business. I'm sure you'll find some way of sweeping it under the carpet.' She was flushed at the strength of her outburst.

'You don't like the military, as you put it, do you, doctor?' The question was so quietly put that she almost missed it.

'I neither like nor dislike them,' she sounded hesitant, guarded. 'After all, who are "they"? Individually there are some very fine people for whom I have the greatest regard, but it does seem to me that you tend to look after your own and cover your tracks.'

'Possibly that is so, Doctor Waterson.' He was careful not to drop the formality, which in other times he would have been more than happy to do with the handsome woman who sat before him. 'You think we'd do that now? Sweep it under the carpet and pretend nothing has happened?' He looked at her with a gentle, inquiring smile. She could see the strength of the man in his eyes and in the line of his jaw. She was glad she had come to see him.

'Possibly.' She gave a defiant little toss of her head. 'It wouldn't surprise me.'

'No, doctor.' The flat of his hand hit the desk and she was again startled by the intensity of his face. 'This will not be swept under the carpet. Not only will justice be done, it will be seen to have been done.' His manner calmed as quickly as it had flared. He stood and held his hand towards her. 'Thank you for taking the time to come and see me, I'm most grateful.' The grip was strong and reassuring. 'Thank you,' he said again.

★

'Tom.'

'Yes, sir?'

'A quiet word, please.' Cookson had the feeling that he had been here before as he followed the group captain to a corner of the planning room. That time the outcome of the conversation had left him reeling. 'With immediate effect, you are to assume command of 58 Squadron as the acting commander.' Gorton allowed the words to sink in before continuing. 'You will answer directly to me, no one else. As to the future? Well, we'll see how this goes first. Get this war out of the way, but I would just like to add my apologies for any, should we say, upset that has been caused.'

Cookson found himself lost for words. He had almost resigned himself to the possibility of facing a court martial, and now, out of the blue, he was being told that all that was behind him and he was the boss.

'What's happened?' he blurted out. 'What's changed your mind?'

'Let's just say, in the words of the constabulary, that acting on information received, I went to see Guy Kelsall and confronted him with what I knew. He stuck to his story at first but, when I pressed him, he admitted that he had not passed the information about the convoy to you, but was just trying to cover his own error.'

'But the paper with the co-ordinates on? How did it get in my bag?' Cookson was having trouble closing his mouth and his breath was coming in short bursts.

'He just slipped it in there when you weren't watching and relied on the fact that you were so sure of your own innocence that you would open it up. And that's precisely what you did, with no prompting from him, making it all the more convincing to me that you had failed to take account of the information. The really stupid thing is that he genuinely forgot about the co-ordinates in the rush to get to the aircraft. If he had been more upfront and honest, we could probably have found some way round it but now…' His voice trailed away.

'What now?' Cookson asked.

'Well, it's not altogether clear, but I've had a word with the powers that be back home and the possibility of a court martial was mentioned. I really don't think it will come to that, although it probably should, but the evidence, if presented in a court of law is a bit woolly and a smart lawyer would make mincemeat of it. But rest assured, either way, the RAF career of Guy Kelsall is well and truly over. There is no room for cheats and liars.'

'Sad, that.' Cookson could not help feeling some sympathy for the man, despite all he had been through in the last few days. He knew only too well how much Kelsall's career meant to him. Suddenly, Cookson wanted to punch the air and at least do a lap of the planning room, but restricted himself to a simple, 'Still, I'm much relieved it's all sorted out.'

'By the way, if you see that attractive, blonde doctor in the bar, buy her a drink.' Cookson nodded, failing to understand. 'And enjoy the rest of the war.' The irony was not lost on him.

Chapter Twenty-Five

'You must really hate me.' Guy swung in his chair to face her. His face was contorted with a mixture of anger and hurt. He had thought that she cared for him, even if she did not love him. They had at least shared a friendship. He had come to rely on her, and had not even dreamed she would run to the group captain with the story. She had betrayed him and robbed him of the most precious thing in his life – his career. He had thought long and hard in the hours since Gorton's visit, and was no nearer resolving it. How could she do this to him? Why would she want to? The thoughts had swirled in his brain, had taken his strength until he could think no more. She had not been near him for hours. He was beginning to think that she had gone and he would not see her again. The pain of losing her had mingled with the pain of his betrayal. 'You must hate me,' he repeated sadly.

'No, I don't hate you.' She sounded tired. 'I did once, but I don't any more. I even feel a little sorry for you.'

'What do you mean? You hated me once?'

She let the moment hang. 'You don't remember me, do you?'

'Of course I don't remember you.' He sounded as though they were playing some silly game that he didn't understand. 'Why should I remember you? We only met a few weeks ago.'

A sad, half-smile played on her lips as she thought back to distant days. 'I thought you'd recognised me when we met in the bar, you know, when you used that silly line, "Haven't I met you somewhere before?" but that's all it was, just a line.'

'You're saying we've met before?' He sounded incredulous, his mind searching through the faces of his sister's friends. 'And you hated me then? Is that what you're saying?' She nodded. 'When? Where did we meet? What on earth could I have done to you that was deserving of this… this betrayal?' He spat the word.

'It was a long time ago.' She was speaking slowly, her mind in some distant place. 'A party in the mess. We were chatting and dancing and you invited me to your room. I wouldn't go, so you suggested that we go for a walk around the place. We ended up in the snooker room...' She watched him and saw the slow dawning of recognition in his eyes. 'We had enjoyed ourselves and started kissing... it was all right and then you tried to take it too far...' She stopped and a tear welled up in her eye. She could see his understanding; his eyes narrowed to slits and his lip curled almost imperceptibly. She had the feeling that he might rise from the chair and strike her if he could. He was in that room again, living the moment with her; the years had not dimmed his memory, and she wondered if he had his time again whether it would be different.

'You wanted it.' The anger contorted the face until she hardly recognised him and she had an overwhelming urge to run. 'You wanted it as badly as I did.' He spat the words.

She shook her head and a tear rolled down her cheek. 'I didn't.' She said it so softly that he almost missed it. 'I said no.' She knew that she had to stay. She had run once, it was not going to happen again; even if he got out of the chair, he was not going to win again.

'You got me in the shit then, and now you're back to reap more revenge. I almost got the chop then, because of you. I've had to live with that little incident coming back to haunt me all my life, now you've come and done it. Between you and Cookson...'

'What has Cookson got to do with it?' She was animated again, angry.

Kelsall raised his head and looked at her with a loathing which she had never seen. 'He was there. He was the orderly officer, the one who came into the room.'

She shook her head slowly. 'No, he wasn't.'

'How do you know?' he asked, and then answered the question himself. 'You became friends and plotted my downfall. All these years, and you waited until I had most to lose and was at my most vulnerable. Then you struck.'

Again she shook her head. 'We became friends, the orderly officer and me. We almost married, but it didn't work out. He was not Cookson.'

Kelsall looked confused; for the first time a doubt came into his mind. He started to speak, but she ignored him.

'It wasn't like that at all.' Her face was flushed red and she grabbed a handful of hair and thrust it away from her eyes. 'I'd almost forgotten about you. It was gone, history, then we met by accident. I tried to forget. I tried to let the past lie; you can't live on hatred, it just grows and consumes. I thought you'd changed; I gave you the benefit of the doubt, maybe some of it was my fault... I don't know.' Her voice trailed away. 'And then, when you asked if I loved you, I had to think about it... hard, because the truth is that I could have loved you, but you would never have loved me.'

'But I did. I still do.' There was a note of pleading in his voice.

'No, you don't,' she said with an edge of contempt. 'You don't love anyone but yourself. You never have and you never will.' She sniffed hard and rummaged in her coat pocket for a tissue and gave her nose a blow.

'And all this, because of a little misunderstanding when we were little more than kids?' He shook his head in bewilderment.

'No, it's more than a little misunderstanding. It's much more than that.' A hardness had returned. 'The reason I was at that party was because my sister lived in the mess. She was an officer on the station. Like you, she loved the RAF. It was her life. It was all she had ever wanted to do. To be around aeroplanes and the people who flew them. She wanted to be a pilot, but she knew that she couldn't in a man's world, so she settled for the next best thing. Then you came along.' She held up a hand to stop him interrupting. 'Oh, I know you never met her, and what was she to you? But because of you she gave up the RAF. Because they did nothing about what you had tried to do to me, she lost faith in them. She left. The RAF represented such goodness and truth, a knight in shining armour if you like, that when she saw the warts and all, it was too much for her. I know you'll say that she was naïve and should have known better, and probably you would be right, but that is the way that some people are made. It was the way she was made.' The tears were now freely flowing down her cheeks.

'What has this got to do with me?'

'Six months after leaving the RAF, she killed herself.'
'But…'
'You still don't get it, do you?' Her anger was at boiling point. She made no attempt to hide the tears, an unseen blanket of hair hiding half her face, but she was not finished. 'You destroy people. Your stupid ambitions and your single-mindedness. It hurts others. When you drop a bomb, you don't mean to kill innocent bystanders, but you do. You all shake your heads and say sorry – price of war and all that – but it doesn't stop you dropping the thing. You even have a name for it – collateral damage – as though that makes it somehow more acceptable. You're like that bomb, Guy. You want things and you go after them, and if someone or something is in the way they become a statistic – a little bit of collateral damage. My sister was collateral damage and you didn't even know her. Cookson would have been some more and who knows how many other there have been?'

A limpness seemed to take her, her arms dropping to her side unable to carry the load. She stood for a moment looking at him, forming a memory she could take with her, the shattered remains of a bomb case. Her head shook slowly and then she walked slowly to the door, closing it quietly behind her. He stared at it for a long moment. 'Stupid bitch,' he muttered, and turned his chair towards the window.